Three

A story of betrayal

Beth Cameron

Dedication

To Duncan, my rock

Prologue

Late Summer 1976 – A Drought Year

Craig is sick today so Ellie and I are heading out on our own.

Mummy hands me an empty ice cream tub for the blackberries. Ellie's already taken hers. We'll only squabble if we have to share.

We tear out the back door and sprint up the lane towards the woods. It's unfair that Craig can't come, but Ellie has already forgotten him. She's keen as mustard to reach the woods before me. I run faster to try to keep up but she races ahead.

'Wait for me!'

'Hurry up, slow coach! Second place is first loser.' It's like sports day all over again. Her ponytail mocks me as it bounces behind her. I'm fast but can't keep up the pace, just as I couldn't pass the baton when it mattered and we lost the relay.

The path is dusty and cracked because of the drought. I speed up but trip over a tree root and hit the ground skinning my knee. Bright red blood almost sends me home in tears, but I can hear the teenage boys coming out of number 20, so there's no way I'm going back.

Those big boys scare me. Whenever I see them my tummy goes funny and I have to make myself invisible.

Unseen. The best way to hide is to look down at the pavement and hold your breath until you think you might burst. At Easter I saw two of them sniffing glue over by the smelly, stagnant stream. I shouldn't have told Daddy what they were up to because he marched to the bottom of the garden and yelled his head off at them. You'd think they'd be embarrassed, but they actually threw stones in his direction. Daddy shouted at them and called them yobs. I hate to think about it. Unhappy memories make me squirm and that's why I steer well clear of all boys apart from Craig, but he's my brother so doesn't really count.

At last I find Ellie. She's pulling blackberries from the prickly bushes that grow over the path. They're laden with fruit even though we've had no rain. I prefer raspberries but only blackberries grow here amongst the stinging nettles. Ellie's shoving fruit straight into her mouth. Her ice cream tub lies on the ground, upside down.

'You haven't saved any blackberries.'

'So what?'

A poison ivy frown creeps across her forehead. She stares at my bleeding knee and looks pleased at the sight. Her mouth is jam-packed with fruit and her hands are stained.

'Ellie, they haven't been washed. We shouldn't eat them until we've washed them. That's what Mummy says.'

Ellie shrugs. She doesn't give a fig about following rules. Not even at school. She sticks out a deep purple tongue and starts licking her palms. Her teeth are dark with juice.

'That's revolting. You look like a vampire.'

'Well you're a boring, goody-goody two shoes.'

We glare at each other. I look away first. Sometimes I think I hate her even though Mummy says it's wrong to hate people. We're told how to behave by our parents and we hear it all over again at Sunday school. 'Treat others the way you want to be treated'. Ellie must want people to be beastly to her the way she carries on.

Unluckily for me she smells weakness a mile off and thrives on attack. She knows how much I hate getting into trouble and how wretched that makes me feel. A rotten day is when adults shake their heads and say, 'I'm surprised at you.' I wouldn't dare laugh like Ellie does. Grown-ups can be very fierce. I'd love to be able to run around without a care in the world but I'm too frightened.

Our relatives make comments about the differences between Ellie and me every time there's a family get together. All the aunts and uncles say I am 'the sensible one.' Ellie gets called lots of other things, accompanied by heavy sighing and throwing of hands in the air. We listen in on adult conversations if they take place in the drawing room. Our parents think we can't hear them from our playroom, but if you cup your ear to the wall you can hear almost every word.

'She's no bother, your youngest. It's that Ellie you need to watch.'

'Oh, Ellie is the most obstinate child. She thinks she can make her own rules in life. Honestly, we've no idea where she gets her notions. And Craig, well he isn't much better, but then he is a boy.' Being a boy allows Craig additional wriggle room. It's not fair.

'It tends to be the eldest child who has their head correctly screwed on, not the youngest.'

I didn't understand what this meant until Uncle Mac started pressing whole 50 pence pieces into my hand, with a wink every time, while Ellie and Craig walked away with a frown, costing Uncle Mac a measly 10 pence each. So I learned early on that good behaviour is worth something. 'Divine justice' is what Grandma used to say. But good behaviour comes with added pressure. For instance, I have to hide my piggy bank from my greedy siblings because they know I receive better hand-outs than they do. At Easter they ganged up on me and locked me in the shed, which was horrible and smelly and full of cobwebs. Then they raided my piggy bank to buy themselves enormous bars of nougat and packets of sherbet dib dabs. The stealing would have been Ellie's idea, but Craig likes sweets so much he'd have been easily persuaded to go along with her plan. Mummy and Daddy yelled at both of them. Ellie had to have two fillings at the dentist last month, so she got what she deserved. But Craig was lucky. He got away with it. The dentist even praised him for having lovely teeth and Craig got another grinning crocodile sticker for his collection. I know he felt guilty because the next day I found it stuck on my pencil case.

Ellie is vile but Craig's not a bad brother. He can be a rotten grump when he's in one of his moods but he's funny most of the time and makes me laugh when he clamps his hand in his armpit to make noisy squelching sounds. Mummy says his behaviour is juvenile and that he won't last five minutes in the grammar school if he behaves like that, but he's not worried because all the teachers love him. It helps that he's sporty as well as clever. He can also climb the tallest tree in our garden and when he reaches the highest branches he squawks like a parrot. This confuses the birds.

Craig's no fun to be around today though, after being sick five times before breakfast. I feel sorry for him lying there under his quilt, in a darkened bedroom, curtains shut tight because he said the light made him feel worse. The truth is he ate far too many sweetcorn fritters last night. Craig is a greedy-guts. Mummy thinks he only had twelve but he also snaffled three of mine. Fifteen battered fritters are a lot to stomach, even for Craig. With a bit of luck he'll feel better by tea-time so won't miss out on pudding. I'd better pick some berries or there won't be any pudding.

'Buzz off, pest! This is my patch.' Ellie acts as though she's allergic to me. Why can't she be nice, just for once? I wish she were the one stuck at home in bed throwing up into the old pink potty. I suppose I ought to be used to her sharp tongue by now but I still can't stop my eyes welling up with tears. I look away before she notices because if she sees me crying she'll call me a baby and I hate that more than anything. I am not a baby. Not like Claudine in my class who wet her pants last term. I know this because I saw her crying in the sick room and heard Mrs Thomson tell her not to worry. Claudine looked up and saw me in the corridor but we both pretended it hadn't happened. I kept her secret to myself, but I don't spend so much time with her anymore.

I move up the path as far from Ellie as possible, but make sure I can still see her out of the corner of my eye because Mummy told us to stick together.

The biggest, fattest, juiciest berries hang just above my head. I don't understand why no one else comes here to pick them. Even the birds haven't dived in for their share. I pick one, two, three until I count thirty ripe and scrumptious berries and my mouth is watering like a fountain.

A whiff of smoke catches the back of my throat. Someone's having a bonfire in one of the other gardens that back onto the wood. It's bound to be Mr Denby who likes burning things. Mummy says he has a problem because he lights fires almost every day. I just think he doesn't like us very much. He lies in wait until we've hung out every last bit of washing and then peeks over the fence to check we've gone. Once the coast is clear, he strikes.

I cough and splutter but Ellie doesn't turn her head. She's plonked herself onto a mound of earth and is throwing stones at a broken bottle of pop. I could be kidnapped right now and she wouldn't have a clue. Am I bad for imagining that she's sitting on an enormous ant-hill? It would serve her right to get ants in her pants.

My arms are beginning to ache but there's a great plump blackberry above my head and I'm not going home without it. I stand on my tiptoes. It's still out of reach. I look around for a stick to pull the brambles a bit closer but can't see anything long enough.

In a different part of the bushes something green catches my eye. It looks like a glove. I don't know how I missed it earlier but I suppose we're out here looking for berries, not odd bits of clothing.

We sometimes find things in the woods that don't belong here. At the start of the summer holidays I found a funny type of balloon, half filled with gloopy, white paint. The balloon was drooping from a tree like a spent Christmas decoration. Craig got close enough to pull it off it but said it had a rotten smell so we left it well alone.

The green glove is 20,000 leagues above that stinky old dangler. For a start it's very elegant. Made from leather, it belongs in a posh department store, not in a bramble bush. It's difficult to tell the size, perhaps between an adult and a child. Ellie's gloves are smaller while Mummy's gloves are much bigger. It's far too expensive to belong to a child and no one I know wears green leather gloves. Mummy's are dull, black things and Grannie knits all the children woollen ones. Ellie loses hers every year, accidentally on purpose because she moans all the time that they make her hands itchy.

A leather glove in the woods in the middle of a very hot August makes no sense at all. It's a forlorn thing stuck in a bramble bush, imprisoned by thorns. It reminds me of the Sleeping Beauty, which also happens to be my favourite ballet. Mummy took me to see it at the Festival Theatre last Christmas. I loved it so much I cried. Ellie refused to come because she's a tomboy and hates ballet. It was one of the happiest days of my life.

Maybe the glove belongs to a rich old lady who lost it while out walking a snooty poodle? Perhaps the lady suffers from that disease that makes your fingers go white when you are cold. Perhaps she comes from some far away country near the equator where it is always hot, so she'd feel the cold here even if it is the hottest summer we've ever had. Or maybe she has those ugly liver spots on her hands like Grannie. She'd want to keep those covered. It's fun to make up stories so I start another in my head.

Once upon a time there was an old lady called Madame Mayran who moved to England from North Africa. She was a respected artist who came over to sell her paintings and to live near her sister who'd married an Englishman.

I want to reunite my old lady with her glove, a bit like Cinderella's glass slipper. I shall track her down and deliver her lost glove by hand. Madame will want to thank me for my trouble. A chocolate éclair from the French Patisserie in the village will be just the ticket. Ellie will be so jealous she will turn the same colour of green as the glove. She'll wish she'd found it and won the prize. Chocolate éclairs are her favourite. I'll let Craig have a bite, but only if he's stopped being sick. It's not a good idea to eat cream when you have an upset tummy.

I put down my pot of berries so I can get the glove. I'm not very tall for my age so have to jump several times to make a grab for it. On my first attempt I'm miles away from touching it. I'm a bit closer the second time. But three is my lucky number. The glove comes clean away. The leather is even smoother and softer than I expected and it's comforting to touch. It reminds me of Mummy stroking my cheek after lights out.

Something hard is stuffed inside one of the glove's fingers, its middle finger to be exact. Once I saw Ellie stick her finger up to Craig when she thought Daddy wasn't looking and she got herself into no end of trouble. Daddy marched her to our room and told her not to come out until suppertime. It wasn't much of a punishment because she made me smuggle her an enormous piece of chocolate cake out of the kitchen.

I'm not sure I want to look inside the glove, just in case the thing inside its finger is Not Very Nice. Craig would joke that it's the finger of a dead person. I wouldn't put it past the teenage boys to do something disgusting, like sticking a dead mouse inside for a laugh. Then again, if I don't investigate properly I won't be able to work out who owns this glove. Madame Mayran might only be a made-up person in my head, but I could still be in for a real chocolate éclair if the owner of the glove can be traced.

I take the glove by its fingertips and shake it, but the thing inside refuses to budge. I summon up my courage, take a deep breath and slide my thumb and finger inside.

I catch hold of a piece of fabric. Not a chopped off finger, thank goodness. It's a bit of material. Feels like cotton. I pull, as a magician might, but don't expect to see a white rabbit. A whole handkerchief emerges. An initial A is embroidered into the corner and as the handkerchief unravels a small, hard object drops into my palm.

The contents of the hanky are even more exciting than the glove itself. In the palm of my hand sits a beautiful gold locket and I stare at it, wide-eyed. It's oval shaped, about the size of a penny piece. On the front is a flower though it's a bit worn so I'm not sure what type. Maybe a tulip, or perhaps a rose? From the bottom left of the flower to the top there is a diagonal strip with little heart shapes along the band. The back is engraved with tiny leaves. I don't know much about jewellery but I do know a locket is something special. Great Aunt Ermance kept a lock of hair in hers that belonged to the little baby she lost. It died of meningitis before Mummy was born. We're not supposed to mention it because it makes everyone sad.

I'm more curious than scared about the contents of this locket. It pops open easily to reveal a tiny photograph of a lady's face on the right hand side. Madame Mayran has a face. It's a black and white photograph that someone has coloured in by hand but the colours have faded. Madame looks about the same age as Mummy.

Her face is a bit strict for my liking. She's hardly smiling at the person behind the camera and she has that same serious look of our teachers in assembly. Her hair is dark and wavy and pinned away from her face. Neat. She is wearing a blouse buttoned up to the neck. Old fashioned.

The Madame Mayran of my imagination was much softer than this. I thought she'd be an artist with a love of life but this lady looks fierce as a guard dog. Not the kind of person who would buy a girl like me a chocolate éclair from the French Patisserie. No, she'll opt for a formal thank you letter, crafted with a fountain pen on watermarked paper and a personalised stamp. Nothing here for Ellie to feel jealous about. There will be no chocolate éclair.

I should still do the right thing and try to track this lady down to return her property. The picture will help. I'll show all the evidence to Mummy who will be sure to know what to do.

The lady sits all alone inside her locket. There's no photo on the left hand side. Only three scratches where a second photo should be. Nothing fell out of the locket when I popped it open. I look on the ground anyway to be on the safe side but can't see anything.

'Ha, gotcha!' I jump as Ellie sneaks up on me from behind, the sly cat. Still excited by my treasure I open my mouth to tell her what I've found but stop myself just in time. Better to keep my mouth shut. I clutch the locket tight in my left hand and pick up the ice cream tub of blackberries in my right to hide the glove from her. I've already stuffed the handkerchief into my pocket. But I must look like someone with something to hide and Ellie misses nothing.

'What's that you've got there?'

'Nothing.'

'Rubbish. I've been spying on you. You're a terrible liar. I know you're hiding something. Show me.'

'It's nothing, Ellie. It's just a stupid old glove. I found it. It's nothing special.'

'Come on, give it here. Let me see. I only want a look.' She raises her command to a shout. 'Give it to me!'

Ellie barges into me with such force that I drop the ice cream tub, casting lovely blackberries all over the place. I cry out and scramble to pick them up. She towers over me. Somehow she's managed to steal my glove.

'Hmmm… Worthless rubbish.'

She spins on her toes and hurls the glove into a thick patch of nettles. Memories of sports day flash into my head all over again. Ellie is a champion thrower as well as a champion runner, and she's the only person I know who can skim stones on water. The glove doesn't stand a chance. It's gone from view. Another loss.

My sister looks down at me and cackles through her purple teeth, wicked witch that she is.

'You're such a pathetic creature sometimes. I can't believe you're actually my sister. Are you sure you're not adopted?'

I half expect her to cast a spell to turn me into a frog but she struts off back to the house. There's a word I want to call her but it's a very bad one. I'm too polite to say it out loud but will write it in code in my secret diary later. She deserves it, the rotten egg.

My eyes well up with hot tears and this time I let them

fall. I'm not just upset. I'm raging at her this time. I dig my fingernails into my palm. At least the locket is safe. Making my way home in Ellie's wake, I vow to hide my treasure in a place she will never think to look.

That locket is mine.

PART ONE

THURSDAY

Chapter 1

Kate leaves home - April 2010

Kate has a restless night waking every hour, on the hour, in anticipation of her 4am alarm. When it eventually shrills she silences it in a flash, keen not to awaken Struan, even though he's well known for sleeping through the loudest of noises including Isla's cries when she was only months old. He stirs in his sleep, mutters something unintelligible but shows no sign of wakefulness.

A hot shower is a gentler friend to Kate than the alarm clock's shrill ring in her ear. Beneath soft jets of water she washes away the night and feels more refreshed, like a plant under the stream of a watering can.

With a taxi due in less than 20 minutes most people would panic, but not Kate, a seasoned traveller, adept at speed dressing. She returned to work when her daughter was six months old and now, four years on, she co-ordinates the morning routine with military precision. On a normal day her first port of call would be Cheeky Tiger Cubs, the private nursery which provides the bulk of childcare for Isla. Shiny, fresh-faced staff wearing bright yellow t-shirts meet and greet them on arrival and Isla is duly handed over into their care. More often than not Isla skips in without complaint, whereupon Kate heads straight for the office before commuter traffic clogs the roads. On Thursdays Struan takes Isla to nursery, allowing Kate to catch up with emails at her desk while radio breakfast shows are still in full swing.

Today is different. Since Kate has only herself to organise she's fully dressed with a light touch of make-up and time to spare before her cab is due. This affords her precious seconds to look in on her daughter and to kiss the sleeping beauty's forehead before tucking tiny toes back under the cosy duvet.

In the hallway Kate grabs a pen and scribbles a simple note comprising three short words to husband and daughter, the same script she writes whenever she goes away, even if she is only absent overnight. Maybe not the most original message, but it's heartfelt and she wouldn't dream of leaving home without penning it.

The front door of the house closes behind her with the slightest of clicks. The door is painted pillar-box red, a marked improvement on the austere and peeling black entrance that faced them when they picked up the keys to their home two years ago. They moved in on a Friday and celebrated with a fish supper from the local chippy and a bottle of fizz from the most expensive off licence in neighbouring Morningside. Whether Champagne or Prosecco Kate couldn't recall, but whatever they drank that night tasted delicious. Isla had been packed off to stay with Struan's parents to make the move less stressful. Everything had gone well with only one breakage. No tears shed over a broken vase, the wedding gift from Struan's parents that Kate found odious.

Amidst the many boxes, Struan had somehow managed

to locate two large champagne flutes and he filled these to the brim without spilling a drop. He handed one to Kate, holding it by its long stem.

'Here's to us and our new home.'

'I'll drink to that.' Struan and Kate smiled at each other before sinking full mouthfuls, excitement accelerating consumption. At this rate the bottle wouldn't last long.

'Do you think the house needs a name?'

'A name?' Struan laughed. 'We've only been in for five minutes and you're already rebranding it!'

'Not at all.' Kate pulled a face. 'I just want to make it ours and I'd like guests to feel welcome when they walk up the path.'

'Then the first thing I'll do is give that front door a fresh coat of paint.'

'Good idea. How about a new colour too? Maybe burnt orange?'

Struan looked cynical. 'I don't even know what colour that is. It sounds a bit radical for this part of town. You haven't met the Nosyhood Watch brigade at number one yet. She practically read me a list of what we can and can't do and when we can and can't do it. How about classic racing green?'

Kate thought for a second before shaking her head. 'Still a bit dark for me.'

'Hmm, let's see. Would red be bright enough for the lady?'

'I can work with red.'

Struan replenished their glasses and popped the empty bottle on the granite worktop. 'Your wish is my command.'

By Sunday afternoon, 6 Forthview Park might still have

been nameless but it no longer sported a black front door. A few different shades of red had been applied before they reached one they both agreed on but they'd got there in the end.

Kate is a home bird now and as she turns away from its bright door in the early hours she wishes she were back on the inside. Classic leather Mulberry clipper bag in one hand, she double-checks her inventory: passport, boarding pass, purse and phone. Her heart rate increases and she feels her chest tighten at the thought of missing the flight. That's not something she'd want to have to explain to Daniel.

A taxi rounds the corner into the street just as Kate closes the gate, a throaty diesel engine signalling its arrival just ahead of its headlights. It's still too early to be awake, let alone out and about. The songbirds are only just dusting themselves down in their nests to commence their dawn chorus.

At least the days are getting longer. The sky promises a magnificent morning with the beginnings of a warm, orange glow. Rather lovely until the thought of Daniel pops into her mind. *Red sky in the morning, shepherd's warning.* Kate waves at the taxi-driver to stop and tries to shake intrusive thoughts out of her head. This whole trip has been meticulously planned and good preparation is central to success. What could possibly go wrong?

The driver is a man of few words. Kate welcomes his silence. She isn't in the mood to converse about the failings of the City Council or the latest fiasco regarding trams, Parliament buildings or the shocking state of Edinburgh's roads. Having acknowledged her airport destination with little more than a grunt, the driver releases the hand brake and accelerates away from number six leaving Kate to sit in the back of the cab to contemplate the day ahead.

Edinburgh Airport ranks in Kate's top five, not just by virtue of its proximity to home but also for its size; small enough to navigate with ease yet sufficiently large for decent shops and cafés within Departures. Kate's experience of airports around the world is extensive and Edinburgh has enjoyed high ranking for some time.

Over a decade earlier and fresh from graduation, Kate rented the tiniest of bedsits in Kensington. It had no view. On the cupboard door above the kettle she posted photographs and a large map of the world. Pins of different colours marked out all the destinations she'd visited, destinations she planned to return to and destinations undiscovered. Each pin told a unique story of adventure and revealed Kate's enthusiasm for diverse places and people. Every time she waited for the kettle to boil she'd explore the map with her eyes and imagine she was attached to a piece of elastic that connected her from London to one of her desired destination points.

She hadn't always had an adventurous spirit. This was something that had been sparked after she'd left home and had a chance to spread her wings, free from the expectations of family. She'd been surprised at first to find that travel didn't scare her and with each new step of discovery her confidence grew. After every trip she found she wanted to go further, to stretch the elastic almost to its limit. After travelling around Europe, The Far East and Australia beckoned, urging her to go further still. Foreign lands drew her like iron filings to a magnet. Resistance impossible.

Airports provided a major source of fascination. Here you

had a collection of people assembled in the departure lounges, only to be scattered around the world within the next 24 hours like marbles thrown into the air. The person who's hand you brushed against yesterday may be thousands of miles away today, whether in cold or tropical climates, speaking different languages or deciphering new sets of cultural codes and values. On arrival in a new place, Kate transformed. She gave herself over to her new surroundings and worked hard to blend in and belong. A chameleon of sorts.

The concept of positive displacement might not have changed since the bedsit years, but her relationship with airports has soured like cream on the turn. The raw excitement that used to accompany her walk through security to the other world of departures? Long gone. Acts of terrorism and fears of more to come have muddied the long walk. New rituals have established themselves; a direct consequence of malevolent acts on innocent people. These days the removal of coats, belts and shoes, necessary for the purposes of security, leaves Kate exposed and sucks all joy out of border crossings.

Instead, joy now comes from living in one place and most importantly her happy home life. In particular, Isla's arrival challenged Kate's wanderlust and brought fresh rewards. As a mother she values stability and peace over the adrenaline rush of adventure. The simple stillness of the house at dawn brings deep contentment; the morning call of birds and Isla's waking sounds. The smell of bacon on a Sunday morning. Struan's soft, grey alpaca scarf hanging on a peg by the front door. The first gift she gave him. How his face lit up when he lifted it out of the wrapping paper.

He wears it all the time. In deference to her new settled family life, Kate even cancelled her long-term subscription to Condé Nast, the travel magazine that was at one time the only constant in her life.

Rising through the ranks of employment, Kate played the role of focused, international businesswoman for many years and it was a role she took seriously, spurred on by gold card access to airport lounges around the world and a ferocious work ethic. But now she works part-time as a director in a small, Edinburgh-based market research agency. She has only an occasional remit to travel and her standard issue blue loyalty card with what was once the nation's favourite airline marks the infrequency of these trips. She'll attend meetings in London or Paris, but seldom is she required to travel further afield. Increasingly she delegates overseas trips to members of her young team in whom she recognises an appetite for travel that was once insatiable in her.

Today is different. It's Paris calling for her attention and no one in the team is better qualified to make this trip than her. Daniel expects the most experienced director for this job. And what Daniel wants Daniel gets. She looks forward to speaking French but has no desire to be cooped up in a small room with his overblown ego for hours on end. Besides which, thoughts of Struan and Isla curled up and fast asleep in the house still leave her wanting.

She shakes off her ennui. An inner voice of reason pops up with a pep talk. *Regret for being away from home is a waste of potential energy. Focus on the task in hand. You're being over-sentimental. In the great scheme of things, a night away from home is nothing.*

The airport throbs with movement already. This is one of the busiest times of the day with vast numbers of employees from Edinburgh's financial services and legal communities heading to London and the Square Mile. Corporate travellers are by far the most dominant group; a clutch of suits, hands glued to the latest smartphones and faces wearing duplicate expressions of self-belief. *We are important because we are flying to business meetings. We are important because we are here not for hedonistic pleasure, but cerebral challenge. We have commercial purpose and value. We are the profit growers in the field of commerce. Our careers are safe where others have faced redundancy. Yes, we can afford to be smug.*

But wouldn't we all prefer to be back in our beds? Kate muses as she takes in their tight faces and the dark shadows under their eyes.

Dressed in a simple black dress warmed up with a bright but inexpensive raincoat, Kate cuts a different figure. She is neither lawyer nor financier. Tall and slim with excellent posture that adds height to her five foot seven figure, she walks with grace and purpose.

'Tummies in. Straight back.' Miss Angela used to say. Kate's childhood ballet teacher drummed good habits into all her young dancers and Kate's maintained good habits into adulthood. Jet-black hair cut into a soft bob frames her attractive heart-shaped face. Slight shyness and a tendency to observe rather than participate makes her appear aloof, but when she smiles her face lights up, radiating warmth. People are at ease around her, reading her as an ally and not a threat.

Having endured the exposure of security controls and

passed to the other side Kate collects herself, retying the belt of her raincoat around her waist with care before making her way at pace to Gate 10. No time to buy any beauty products from the Clarins counter in the gleaming duty-free shop today. Her flight is on the brink of being called and a bank of suited men destined for Paris thrusts towards the gate in impatient expectation of the boarding announcement. An early boarding call for passengers travelling with small children produces a single mother. She carries a crying infant in a sling and is pushing a truculent toddler in a buggy that will need to be folded away before anyone else can get near the gate. Kate recognises the buggy for being notoriously difficult to collapse. She owned the same model for about a month but had to upgrade it after a disastrous and abortive attempt to catch the number 23 bus back from Hanover Street. The buggy refused to compress. At the time the bus driver had been kind but unwilling to wait.

'Sorry, hen. I cannae help ye. I'm already behind schedule.' Isla had wailed at the top of her voice and Kate, the temporary social leper hailed a taxi home in preference to more embarrassment and a long wait for the next bus. Later that evening Struan had applied his own magic to the buggy.

'Leave it to me. I'll fix it.' A confident declaration from a man used to mediation and problem solving. Out came an immaculate tool-box and a comprehensive range of shiny new tools. But even Struan had to admit defeat. He walked into the kitchen with a bloody finger and a grim look of despair.

'I give up. I'd rather represent my toughest client in an

employment tribunal. That buggy doesn't have a co-operative bone in its body.'

'Maybe that's because it's not a living thing?' Kate handed him a plaster and a chocolate biscuit. She shrugged. 'I never liked that buggy anyway.'

'Well, it's in bits now. Sorry.' Poor glum Struan, deflated by the sorry sight of twisted handgrips and wheel parts littering the carpet.

The woman is now pushing her buggy towards the gate. What on earth has possessed her to travel with her small children on this of all flights? The red eye flight isn't cheap. Or renowned for carrying the kind of travellers who will tolerate small people. Even Kate, who likes children, is in no mood to sit beside someone else's toddler. She doesn't fancy spending the flight dodging spillages. And judging by the expressions of other departing passengers she's not alone in praying for a reprieve.

Please don't let them sit anywhere near me.

On boarding the plane Kate releases a small sigh of relief to find her window seat is two rows behind the unfortunate family and diagonally opposed. Far enough away to be spared the stains and spoils concomitant with messy feeding, even if she is still in range of the child's high-pitched demands and the mother's sharp responses. Neither baby nor toddler will settle and from her safe seat Kate's sympathy for the mother grows. Maybe she should have shown some solidarity for a fellow mum. The toxic mixture of young children and travel means parental support is often thin on the ground when you need it most.

'I can't stand the noise of brats,' declares the port-faced businessman in the aisle seat to Kate's right. Most people look away or feign sleep, but a few heads incline in support. Preparing for their safety demonstration, members of the cabin crew are too busy to offer help to either mother or complainant. The family sits beyond Kate's line of vision but she pictures the plentiful distribution of toys and sweets by a mother desperate for a quick fix and a moment of peace. One of the strategies seems to have worked. Children fall silent, the joyless man pipes down and the growl of engines is all they can hear.

The plane accelerates and begins to lift. As it climbs higher and higher the baby shrieks at a raised pitch that cuts through all possibility of sleep. Sick bags are distributed and port-face pipes up again, jabbing his finger towards the mother as though she has committed a heinous crime.

'Can't you stop it from crying? I have very important documents to read.'

The woman turns round in her seat to glare back at him. 'No, I can't. Crying is what babies do best. You're lucky pal. You only have to listen to this racket for an hour or two. I'm stuck with it for the rest of my life.'

It's a brittle and unexpected response from a woman at breaking point. Embarrassed silence hangs in the air. Even the baby stops to take note. Old port-face has met his match. He buries himself in paperwork for ten minutes until little snorts sound from his flared nostrils and his hand drops to the vacant middle seat, the aeroplane equivalent of no man's land. Big, pink sausage fingers curl inwards. Gout in his knuckle joints prevents the thick wedding band from escaping the base of his ring finger. Kate glances across at his sleeping features and spares a thought for the wife at home, alone with any fistful of children he's helped to create. She twists her own wedding ring, a platinum band and smiles at the memory of the visit to Hamilton & Inches where Struan and she chose their rings together. A new ring. A fresh start. So different from the last time. The marriage that never was.

The plane reaches altitude. Kate attempts to doze but thoughts of Daniel and his great expectations poke through until she gives up on the idea of sleep. She opts out of the in-flight breakfast despite the steward's cheerful invitation to give the hot option a try. A tray of oily chipolatas, reconstituted egg, plastic tainted orange juice and instant coffee simply cannot compete with its continental breakfast cousin and Kate focuses instead on the espresso and pain au chocolat waiting at Charles de Gaulle.

Being away from home might have lost its shine, but she still marvels at the view from her window 30,000 feet above the ground. The sun is dazzling in the clear, blue sky. White clouds peak like whipped meringues. Kate is reminded to buy eggs, fresh cream and fruit at the Stockbridge farmers' market. It's been a long time since she made pavlova. Her stomach rumbles at the thought.

The plane makes its bumpy descent into Paris to the tune of a baby's wails, while 2,000 kilometres north a volcano bubbles and bursts into life.

Chapter 2

Alice - a doctor calls

The lady Doctor called on me this morning. She is a smart young thing, although I loathe the green Mackintosh coat she insists on wearing. It makes her look so washed out. Even I can see that royal blue would suit her fair colouring so much better and I'm hardly an expert in fashion.

I'm all in favour of lady doctors but I still prefer to be seen by Dr Grant as we go back such a long way. However, he hasn't been making house calls of late. He didn't look too well himself when I last saw him, come to think of it. When was it now? It must be at least a fortnight ago. I daresay that frightful new computer system at the surgery is turning his hair grey. What a shameful waste of money. No wonder the National Health Service is in such an abominable mess.

Gone are the days when one's family Doctor would sit and talk to his patients. Today our General Practitioners are expected to have secretarial skills as well as clinical competence. They have no time to examine patients properly, preoccupied instead with typing up our symptoms on keyboards. As soon as one's allotted ten minute consultation is over the printing machine spits out a prescription based on who knows what? Frankly, it's insulting. So incensed was I at the last appointment that I didn't even bother to make the journey to the dispensing chemist for my drugs. Dr Grant might be an expert in family medicine but I don't trust his computer an inch. Computers are victims of their own viruses if the reports in The Telegraph are to be believed. It is therefore reasonable to conclude that one cannot and ought not entrust one's health to a machine. Besides, I read what he'd prescribed and didn't agree.

Dr Grant's partner in the practice is the blonde Doctor, so it was she who made the house visit this morning. She examined my shoulder in silence. I must say she has put on a bit of weight around her middle. Not quite the skinny thing she used to be.

'How are you feeling, Mrs Emery?'

'My dear!' Tickled pink, I laughed out loud. 'I should surely be asking you that very question myself!' Her hard stare didn't deter me from asking, 'Is it really wise to be working in your condition?'

Nothing by way of response. Perhaps she was affronted.

'Women these days think they can do it all. In my day marriage put an end to our ambition to work and as for having children and continuing to work, well that would have been quite inappropriate. I do applaud independence of course, and the opportunities for young girls of your generation are marvellous in many ways, but do try to remember that opportunity is not without risk. Do make sure you don't spread yourself too thin.'

This earned me a Mona Lisa smile but a steadfast refusal to spar or indulge me with any reply. I felt a little frisson of disappointment. Conversation without controversy is as dull as a tepid cup of weak tea. My tipple of choice is Lapsang Souchong. Properly infused. No milk.

I don't think my silent Doctor has been eating too many cakes. If she isn't in the early stages of pregnancy I'd be surprised. Other people would fail to notice the signs but I've been credited for sharp observational skills all my life. Of course, no one's skills are fool proof as I know to my cost but on this occasion I have tangible evidence. I snuck a peek inside her handbag when it fell open on the coffee table. Clearly visible, a misshapen cardboard box of Pregnurture tablets. Funnily enough, the packaging is very similar to the brand of calcium tablets I take for my chronic osteoarthritis. Once I even ended up with a packet of Pregnurture from the chemist, much to the shop assistant's embarrassment when I pointed out her silly mistake. The whole episode still makes me chuckle today.

Still in mischievous mood, I pretended to watch the birds outside, and pressed for a more satisfactory response.

'I can understand why a teacher might wish to continue working after having children. Teachers benefit from endless holidays when they can be present for their offspring. But my dear, a Doctor? It's an extraordinary proposition. Tell me, would you rather hold surgery or hold your baby? Will you send it to a day nursery to be cooped up like a battery hen?'

A Doctor's case shut with force makes a startling bang. Poor Puddy leapt from his cushion and tore from the room like a shot. I also grimaced, the noise of the bang amplified by my hearing aids, ill-fitting as they are. I daresay my old-fashioned views caused real offence. I overstepped the mark, though I don't suppose my remarks or conduct will leave any lasting damage. Unlike the behaviour of some I could mention.

'Well, that's us just about done, Mrs Emery.'

Professional mask back in place, she pressed a new script into my hand for those pain-relieving pink pills that look alarmingly like sweets. I glazed over when she suggested a referral to a Physiotherapist who will furnish me with gentle exercises to aid my recovery. She also presented me with one of those patronising leaflets that the NHS sees fit to publish for old people. More gubbins about how to stop yourself from tripping over rugs while shuffling about your home in slippered feet. Such literature is on the recommended reading list for decrepit old fools like me. We are suspended in the Antique University of Life. We are warned that trips and falls are a catalyst for terminal decline and even instant death. I would have handed the leaflet straight back but she was too quick for me, so I made a point of shoving it to the furthest end of the coffee table, or at least as far as my wretched shoulder allowed.

I'm not resigned to fail. Quite the opposite. Failures have darkened my life but there is one corner of light I intend to keep safe. I must not fall over again as next month I am due to receive a special telegram from our Monarch, Her Majesty Queen Elizabeth II, for whom I have the utmost respect. Anticipation of her telegram will steady my balance on the kitchen steps next time I reach for the custard powder. Unlike the blah-blah health awareness leaflet, destined for the waste paper bin, just as soon as I have remodelled it into a paper aeroplane. Never let age stand in the way of a little gentle mischief making.

The Doctor retrieved her green Mac from the hat stand

and prepared to leave. That colour is enough to make me ill but I swallowed my disgust in time to wave her off with a shake of my stick and a brittle goodbye. Her effortless walk down the stairs made me envious. I'd be willing to pay good money to renew my creaking bones with an injection of youth.

What a relief to be left in peace again, though I must concede it wasn't the poor girl's fault we haven't managed to forge the best relationship. She left behind a pleasant, floral scent. Her good taste in perfume making up a little for her dubious dress code.

Back in the sitting room, I turned a dial and the wireless sprang to life. This is my link to the wider world and ranks alongside Beryl and Puddy as a most loyal companion. One is never lonely with a wireless. And now that almost all my friends have passed away I value it more than ever. In fact, I'm rendered more upset by failing batteries on my wireless than the Obituary pages in the local rag. In the last two decades I've been to more funerals than parties. Logic and the natural of order of things tell me that mine will be next. But not a day before the Queen's telegram arrives. I hope.

Oh botheration. The news headlines have passed me by again. Another bad mark against the Doctor. Poor timing. Still, the extended news programme will coincide with lunch and I've plenty of time to warm a pot of soup before then. The gardeners' questions programme is being broadcast but I'm sure it's a repeat.

On a positive note I am encouraged to see that the new couple in the garden flat below have taken an interest in their flower-bed. Not like the last pair who spent so little time on the premises their faces were a blur. They were always dashing in and out but never looked like they achieved very much. They let their weeds run wild and I was glad to see the back of them.

The new couple hail from New Zealand and are friendly, if a little informal. They brought me up an orchid by way of introduction, an unnecessary extravagance, but a thoughtful gesture all the same. They introduced themselves as Andy and Chris, with no hint of a surname to join them together. I'm not accustomed to the modern way of introducing oneself by one's Christian name, and I told them as much, but they just grinned inanely at each other. It seems to me that young people these days have dispensed with surnames as easily as they have cast aside hats, gloves and wedding rings.

My wedding ring is old and worn. It's been on my finger since 1930, though I have lived as a widow for longer than I care to remember. My friend Beryl cherishes her wedding ring because it symbolises happy times with Howard, a compassionate man of substance. My ring symbolises the sanctity of marriage but is no symbolic celebration of my late husband.

Marriage demands sacrifice and how I yielded to it. Those like Beryl, the lucky ones, reap emotional rewards but for the rest of us there are no guarantees. By the time he dropped down dead, my husband Douglas had become a complete stranger to me.

We met in 1928, around the time that penicillin was discovered. The importance of Alexander Fleming's discovery may not have been widely known until around the Second World War but I had plenty going on with my own studies before then. One of a mere handful of women,

I was blessed with the opportunity to work towards a pharmaceutical qualification in London and jumped at the chance to leave home.

Mother stood in opposition to my education from the start. Only to be expected, since she and I failed to see eye to eye over anything, from how to correctly lay a table, to our fundamental right as women to vote. I have my progressive Papa to thank for supporting me. He persuaded my stubborn Mother that I should pursue higher education and a degree, and I never took my opportunities for granted. I soon earned a reputation for being the most conscientious student and caught the attention of teaching staff and students, including one man who would make me a proposal and another who would become my husband. Two men. Two very different proposals. I accepted both in a way.

A walking cliché, Douglas had height and good looks but didn't he know it. Vanity oozed from every pore, which diminished his appeal to me, but the constant stream of girls at his heels indicated that I was the odd one out. If Carly Simon had been a contemporary, that song could have been about him. He glowed with good health, skin tanned from time spent at sea while the rest of us were pale, vitamin D deficient products of the previous harsh winter. Rumours circulated that he'd left the country in a hurry. I've never much been one for gossip but one only had to stand still for five minutes to hear what people whispered about his caddish behaviour. I ignored most of it. His affairs were none of my business, besides which I was studying to gain my qualification, not seek the advances of a man.

When the rain fell hard one Wednesday he pulled aside a

chair to sit beside me in the library, despite there being plenty of free seats elsewhere. I chose to ignore both him and the tight sensation in my stomach. Being an only child, I wasn't accustomed to the company of men my own age. It would do no good to become distracted by this young man, or any other man for that matter. As I say, I wanted a profession, not a husband.

In any case a girl with my plain looks stood no hope of displacing Douglas's latest sweetheart, an angelic faced beauty, as smitten by him as he was with her. They made a good match; upright and self-assured, socially well connected. They were in a league of their own. My league was academic rather than aesthetic, based on hard work and perseverance.

My physical shortcomings were only too apparent when I dared linger on my reflection in the mirror. Vanity had no reason to rest at my door. I was neither fair of face nor a hideous gargoyle, but plainly fell in a neutral place between these parameters. At a little over five feet tall I needed help to reach the upper bookshelves. I dressed practically, not provocatively, favouring clothes that didn't draw attention and shunning the more fashionable items worn by my peers. I was therefore under no illusion that when Douglas sought me out in the library he was not looking for anything other than a brain to pick. I was chalk to his cheese. I valued my independence. He craved attention. He was a narcissist.

If only I'd kept my distance.

Chapter 3

Kate in Paris

While near centenarian Alice Emery listens to the one o' clock news in the comfort of her living room, an old man sits at a pavement café and lets his gaze meander up the legs of the young woman walking along Avenue de l'Opéra. He'd invite her to join him for coffee, but her quick pace suggests she hasn't time to stop and she's 20 years too young for him anyway. Still, he can imagine.

Kate smiles at the man as she strides past, her large portfolio bag swinging in time to her walk. She's heading for a briefing meeting with Daniel and the research agency she's commissioned and she can't risk being late. Her bag is full of advertising concepts for a new range of ready-made meals, all to be tested and refined before the product launch in the autumn. Target market mums have been invited from across the city to attend focus group discussions and build on the ideas.

Kate is on excellent terms with all the members of the French research team and has no concerns about the quality of their work. Her anxiety stems from what she considers to be the unrealistic expectations of the new brand manager for 'Bon Appétit!'. Golden Boy Daniel is hungry to make an impression and is a piece of work in himself. Because he has an MBA he seems to think he is superior to everyone.

Kate shrinks at the prospect of being held captive in a darkened room for hours while a beautiful spring day blossoms outside. The air is crisp and Paris buzzes with life. The yearning to stay outside slows her pace, and she inhales the scent of the city to commit it to memory. If only she could spend the day wandering around shops and stopping off in boulevard cafés to watch the world go by. She did manage to sneak into a little boutique in the fifth arrondissement en route from the hotel, her attention caught by the halter-neck dress in the window. It begged to be bought. The minute she saw it Kate wanted it. She could already see it hanging in her wardrobe. It's the perfect outfit for her wedding anniversary and means she can tick off another job from her never-ending To Do list.

The French ooze style and Kate is an avid disciple of their natural elegance. Well accustomed to making an effort with her appearance, she's inclined to go an extra mile whenever she crosses the Channel. She lifts her chin higher, pulls her stomach in a little tighter and even remembers to practice her pelvic floor exercises, so often forgotten when she's back home under layers of woolly jumpers. This country of liberty, equality and brotherhood stimulates all her senses and she soaks up all it has to offer. She works hard to increase her allure in the hopes that France might accept her as one of its own.

Kate spent her third year university studies in Lyon, the gastronomy capital of France. Underwhelmed by her Anglo-Saxon family tree roots, she entertained herself by re-crafting her own history, at least in her head. She pretended she was not descended from a mining community in the north of England after all but rather from the French Huguenots, proxy ancestors, chased out of France in the 17th century following widespread religious persecution.

In pursuit of claiming and legitimizing a French identity, Kate worked round the clock on her command of the French language and gave herself a big bravo the day that locals stopped identifying her as an English girl. She soaked up French cinema and the New Wave, read Proust, Sartre and Camus until she could quote passages from their novels by heart and welcomed invitations to spend weekends with the families of French students she met on her course.

Throughout that year Kate also scrutinized the male students at the faculty, wondering whether a soulmate might be found somewhere amongst them. But whilst she grew very fond of Christophe, a young man with dark curls and spaniel eyes who showed no end of patience as he taught her how to juggle in the great Parc de la Tête d'Or weekend after weekend, her affection for him never deepened into more intense feelings. She had no way of knowing as she sat through lectures on Baudelaire's poetry, that it would be some years before her love affair with France would even be matched, let alone over shadowed by a liaison with a man. That man. The one who stole her heart. And when this human relationship broke down, her love for France endured, pure and untainted.

Paris. A city punctuated by scent. Thanks in part to the perfume liberally sprayed over the pulse points of its people, but also for its culture of three C's: coffee, croissants, cigarettes. Below ground in the network of passages that were home to the Paris Metro, Kate even found something comforting in the warm, reeking smell that suggested

French deodorant was neither long lasting nor especially effective. The hum that heralded the closing of train doors was not just audible.

Back at street level Kate continues to be charmed, almost perversely, by the congested streets of the city. Parked cars packed as tight as sardines bear bumps and bruises from misjudged manoeuvres and prangs from opposing vehicles. She contemplates the inversely proportional relationship between the care taken by Parisians in their attire and their investment in car maintenance. Or perhaps French cars are designed with their own free will; deliberate, energetic and self-destructive.

Spotting a red Citroën, an image of Kate's beloved father takes shape in her mind. His approach to car maintenance was the antithesis of the Parisian way. As was his fashion sense (conspicuous by its absence). He spent hours in the pursuit of bodywork perfection, polishing every car he ever owned until it gleamed whilst paying little heed to the holes in his jumper or the lack of shine on his shoes. When he passed away, his car was a modest and unremarkable family saloon but it was as spotless as any new car rolling off the production line.

Kate's parents drove to France to visit her after she'd been in Lyon for six months. Their visit had been slightly marred by her father's palpable anxiety over driving in conditions that he likened to the most dangerous form of stock car racing. He hated the aggression of the Routes Nationale and found himself having to adopt a far more defensive driving style.

'Dear God, I almost thought we'd arrive in an ambulance,' he explained, hugging Kate so hard on arrival that she thought her ribs might crack.

'Your father is a little shell-shocked.' Kate's mum gave a weak smile. 'I think we'll fly next time.' That night Kate's parents drank a little more than usual, her dad quick to order a whisky before they'd even sat down in the brasserie on the corner. Every now and then he closed his eyes and shuddered as though replaying moments of horror experienced on the roads.

Unlike her father, driving through France on roads large or small, across towns and départements never fazed Kate once she'd got the hang of shifting the gear stick with her right hand. To this day her road awareness remains good and she dodges oncoming vehicles with ease. Behind the wheel she's carefree and confident. No one would guess of the anxieties that plagued her as a child. Or the anxieties that occasionally overwhelm her even in adulthood, typically when she forgets to breathe properly in times of stress.

With no need to drive today Kate's international driving licence is neatly filed away at home. Not in an obvious place like the desk, the first place a thief would look. For security she keeps it in a pouch in the bottom drawer of her bedside cabinet alongside underwear and a little something that Struan bought her for Valentine's Day 'to keep you happy if I'm away.' The sort of item that would leave her absolutely mortified if it were to accidently start vibrating when passing through airport security.

On arrival at Charles de Gaulle earlier, she'd made her way by RER train into the centre of Paris, then hopped on a Metro to her favourite boutique hotel tucked away on the Left Bank behind Boulevard St Germain.

Her hotel is one of a crop of contemporary design hotels springing up across major cities around the world, ringing the changes for both the dinosaur chains and the often complacent, more traditional smaller establishments. Kate loves everything about it. Each of the bedrooms features a unique design. Her bedroom, Room 11, is heavily influenced by art deco with clean lines, rectangular lampshades and geometric shapes. Against this backdrop, luxurious bedding and a mirrored wardrobe usher in a spirit of comfortable frivolity. The bed is designed for two and in Struan's absence Kate wishes she'd packed his pulsing Valentine's gift.

While awaiting the arrival of her bags on the carousel at the airport, Kate made a quick phone call home. Struan wasn't starting work until later that morning. He'd already given in to Isla's demands to watch her favourite DVD, an animation for pre-school children about the adventures in Paris of two anthropomorphic dogs, Gaspard and Lisa. It was a DVD that Kate had brought back from a previous business trip and whenever left to her own devices, Isla watches it over and over again on a loop. Although her parents aren't averse to this, they try to restrict breakfast television watching to the weekend and Sunday morning in particular. They've fallen into the habit of tip-toeing back to bed for precious time alone while their little girl shouts 'triomphe!' at the small screen.

Sunday morning intimacy is almost as brief as Kate's phone call home. Struan was most likely in the kitchen, coffee in one hand, phone in the other. Kate just about managed to squeeze in her hello before Isla rushed to the phone, arms outstretched, eager to snatch the handset from her Dad.

'Bon joo mummy! Hola!' A precocious child, full of chat and incessant questions, Isla is almost as wedded to Dora the Explorer as she is to Gaspard and Lisa and it wasn't unusual for her to throw an odd assortment of French and Spanish into many a conversation.

'Are you in Paris now, Mummy? I'm watching Gaspard and Lisa. They are in Paris. Can you see them? Are you coming home yet? Daddy's only given me some toast and I want porridge. Please may you tell him I want porridge?'

Monologue over, Isla thrust a sticky fingered, upside down phone into Struan's hand, her attention caught once more by the unfolding adventures on the TV. His voice was muffled until he flipped the handset round the right way.

'Sorry, I just asked how your flight was.' Struan loathed flying and predictably put the same question to his wife whenever she called him from an airport's arrivals' hall. On the few occasions they'd flown together he'd sit in silence with a pale face until the plane was airborne, quick to order drinks as soon as the trolley clattered down the aisle.

'The flight? Not too bad thanks, all things considered,' the struggling lone parent with truculent toddler and bawling infant still fresh in Kate's mind. 'All the same, I think I'm getting too old for this.'

A snort escaped from her husband in response, given his eight year seniority over her and his commitment to early morning runs before work.

'You know what I mean, Struan. Business trips have lost their shine. I love Paris but I'd rather be on holiday here with you and Isla.'

'I'm not sure I'd launch Isla on Paris. Can you imagine

her in Galeries Lafayette?'

'I'd rather not.' Kate gulped as a vision of Isla at her most demanding sprang to mind.

'Remember the garden centre incident?'

'Please, don't remind me. Though it really was a bad idea for the store to place snow globes at child height.'

'Maybe you and I can have a weekend away sometime, just the two of us. I'd come to Paris with you, as long as we go by Eurostar. But listen, make the most of the peace and quiet. Get yourself a proper breakfast, take full advantage of using your French and watch out for those Parisian men with their wandering hands. Not that I'd blame them for trying.'

'There's no chance I'd let that happen. Anyway, I'd better let you crack on. You'll need to get Isla ready for nursery, especially if you want to keep your little job.'

Struan laughed. As a partner specialising in employment law at one of the city's smaller firms he is renowned for putting in extremely long hours on regular occasions. Well regarded by clients and colleagues, there was no question mark hanging over his ability to generate income, nor his job security.

'What would you like to do when the baby comes?' he'd asked Kate when she fell pregnant. 'What would make you happy? You know I'm on a decent package. So you don't have to go back to work if you don't want to. What I mean is if you want to be a stay at home Mum. I'm not saying being a Mum isn't hard work obviously,' he added quickly.

The choice was hers. They'd discussed various options at length before agreeing that it made sense for Kate to keep her hand in the job market. She wanted to keep her options open for the future.

But now, with unmanageable clients like Daniel and a headstrong daughter like Isla, Kate often finds herself wondering if she'd be better off focusing her energy where it really matters. At times like this she worries about abandoning Struan, leaving him to cope with both Isla and a heavy workload.

'You will be OK, won't you?'

'Worry not, my little chou-fleur. Everything's fine here. No reason for you to stress. We can even see the golden orb in the sky so I'm going to jog Isla to nursery and then pick up the canal path to the office.'

The voice of Isla demanding porridge cut Struan short.

'I'd better go before she throws a wobbly. I'll call you at bedtime, OK? Bon courage today. I love you.'

'I love you too.'

'Oh, and watch your bag on the Metro and be sure to take a taxi home when you finish work tonight.'

Kate never fails to be touched by his concern for her. She's well within her comfort zone wandering around this city but knows it's still important to keep her wits about her, especially late at night. Struan's protective nature is well-intentioned and as Kate reaches the offices of the research agency in the full beam of the sun, fears for her personal safety could not be further from her mind.

She stops at the main door and presses the entry button. A young couple glides past. Kate does a double take. The girl must be about eighteen; an adult, but barely a woman, with her fresh-faced, youthful complexion and flushed cheeks. She's arm in arm with her male companion who sports a tan leather jacket. He's older, in his mid-twenties; a young man with a hint of stubble and a confident gait. It's his satisfied smile that brings Kate's first love to mind. Again. His body language tells a tale of a night well spent and a late entry into the day. Posh shopping bag on one arm, pretty brunette on the other, he has a lot to be pleased about and his swagger shows it. Kate freezes as they pass and can't tear her eyes off him. For a few seconds she can't breathe. He's practically Marc's double. He could almost be Marc's younger brother. Except that Marc didn't have a brother. Imagine two of them. Kate shivers at the thought.

It crosses her mind that it's rude to stare but she might as well be invisible to the pair of young lovers. Love is blind, as she well knows. The moment of paralysis passes and she exhales.

Kate has to put all her weight behind the imposing, heavy door at the front of the building, ready to give it a good shove when she is buzzed in. It eventually gives way. Rather than taking the lift, she begins the walk up the imposing staircase to the top floor. Each step brings her closer to captivity and a day with Daniel, his big ideas and his sizeable ego. Will the room be big enough? She'll sacrifice the next few hours of her life listening to women discussing the merits of his plan for new generation ready meals. Although she can't second-guess what Parisians will say, Kate remains unconvinced by the whole concept of ready meals in this market, let alone the 'witty' advertising campaign masterminded by Daniel and executed by his ill-advised creative team. Not for the first time she's sorely tempted to leave the local research team to their own devices.

The urge to play truant builds and builds as she pictures

herself in the Louvre gallery exploring works by Raphael and da Vinci. Is it too late to turn around?

The last step on the staircase marks Kate's final opportunity to spin on her heels and run. Temptation beckons like a hot croissant to a hungry child but Kate's sense of responsibility weighs in as predictable as the cycle of the moon. Taking the deepest of breaths, she opens the door and steels herself, 'Bon Appétit!' on the tip of her tongue. She's mentally ready to greet her client.

But Daniel isn't there.

Chapter 4

Alice - by the fire of the lake

I tidy up the lunch things to the sound of the closing news headlines. Today's main feature proves to be of interest. For once it has nothing to do with the General Election campaign that drones on like an irritating mosquito around one's head. Instead, the rumblings are of a deeper kind and stem from a volcanic eruption in Iceland. I shall make a point of watching the six o' clock news on the television later to see the dramatic footage promised by the report.

The volcano in the spotlight has been sitting quietly for decades, like a well-behaved child lulling people into a false impression of a benign geographical feature. But one should never mistake a quiet demeanour for life long inertia. Its sudden eruption has caught the world by surprise and its thunderous presence felt well beyond Iceland's coastline. The name of the volcano evades me, as the newsreader stuttered over its pronunciation, failing in his job to convey accurate details. No matter. The key point is that this volcano is making a proper nuisance of itself to everyone apart from geologists and post-graduate students of seismology who are closely monitoring the latest activity with heady excitement.

Vast plumes of volcanic ash have been ejected several

miles into the atmosphere, causing disruption to flights across the United Kingdom. They say that the high levels of ash density in the air may be intolerable to aircraft. Those who are airborne may need to brace themselves.

Good gracious me, you have to have a jolly good sense of humour! Evidently being unable to fly from London to Belfast is now a matter of grave national concern. Utter nonsense. People take so much for granted, including the right to traverse the world at a moment's notice. Media commentators rabbit on about '24/7' travel and communication, a phenomenon new to me. Every day I encounter sloppily dressed youths lolloping at the bus stop, portable telephones or some such device glued to their ears. They gabble away as though talking to themselves. Quite mad. As a proud advocate of the telegram generation, the very notion of conversing over the telephone while crossing the road using what resembles a calculator is beyond belief to me. My views may seem Victorian to young people but one doubts whether they care much for the opinions of the elderly in any case.

The big corporations are no better at understanding older people's views and needs. Even the British Broadcasting Corporation is guilty. One can no longer begin to watch Songs of Praise without being implored to press a red button or check something called 'Twitter' for further information. Such interaction is not for me. I challenge the way my licence fee is invested in the 21st century. Things are Not What They Were.

Likewise, today's common habit of hopping aboard an aeroplane is a far cry from the slower modes of transport available to my contemporaries. Today one can reach

Sydney in just over 24 hours. Contrast that with 1926. It took Douglas six months to reach Australia then and just over six months to return home the following year. I wonder what my life would have looked like had he stayed in the Antipodes.

'Travel broadens the mind,' he'd tell me, striding about, filling the room, brimming with confidence. He thought himself worldly wise, but in hindsight his perspective was narrow, his focus insular.

'The people one met at the Captain's cocktail parties were so congenial. Did I ever tell you about the time I beat the ship's Rector at deck quoits after he'd sunk one too many?' He'd shake his head and smile, indulging in the memory. And yes, he had told me this story many, many times.

Douglas assumed central character status in all his stories and talked for hours about his voyage, unperturbed by repetition. A garrulous raconteur, you might say. Odd then that he should be so circumspect about life prior to setting sail from Southampton. And he was positively clam-like when questioned over his reasons for leaving Britain in the first place.

'A change of scene, my dear. A change is as good as a rest.'

I agree a change of scene can be refreshing, but change can also be unsettling, especially if forced or uninvited.

As a young woman I had a healthy appetite for exploration. Opportunities to cruise around the world did not fall at my feet but I made the best of other experiences that came my way. Had I been fortunate enough to embark on a significant world voyage I would have insisted on First-

Class travel every time. And in the early days I would have relished a trip across the ocean with my husband, no matter how choppy the waters. Douglas at the Captain's table, suited and booted, now there's a thought.

He had a look that turned heads, a near perfect symmetry in his face and a cheeky dimple in his chin. Film star looks. His smile dazzled the ladies but it was his hands that worked the magic as far as I was concerned. Wide and generous, they danced through the air, with a lightness that contrasted with his masculinity and height. If he'd had a musical bone in his body he might have become a conductor in a concert hall, an orchestra coming alive with the energy sparked from his hands. The first time he wrapped my hands in his I experienced a heat so intense I thought I might self-combust.

'Alice, I do believe you're shaking! Dear girl.' His voice was sympathetic, not mocking. He gave my hands a light squeeze and blood rushed to my cheeks in a flurry of excitement.

Our courtship began in perfect innocence, fitting for the era. Douglas appeared in the library with increasing regularity. He'd sidle up to the long table under the clock, books in hand and stare until I acknowledged him. He'd pin me to my seat with his laser gaze and engage me in conversation under the pretext of an assignment he was struggling to complete.

'Alice, forgive me. Do you have a moment?' I made time for him, just as I would for any of my peers. I have always felt a duty to help others. Only Professor Mason received extra special treatment and that's because he was the Deputy Principal. A wise man.

If I'm honest, in those early weeks I found Douglas's presence irksome and his questions more so. I'd be hard at work, in deep concentration until he showed his film star face. His constant interruption and ill-conceived arguments made me short tempered, while his physical presence unsettled me. And yet as weeks stretched into months I could see he was working hard. I softened my stance. His analytical thinking improved and his hypotheses made more sense. In time our conversations became more enjoyable, more animated and less clunky. I no longer frowned when he pulled up a chair beside me.

'Hello, Alice. You look almost pleased to see me. Are you ready for my question of the day?'

When a fortnight passed without any sign of Douglas I almost missed him. Instead, Professor Mason appeared one wet, Wednesday afternoon with a question of his own. I couldn't help wishing it were Douglas standing there instead.

I thought the Professor was going to ask how my studies were progressing or if Douglas was becoming a distraction. He sat close beside me, lowered his voice to almost a whisper and looked me straight in the eye. At first I couldn't quite understand what he was asking or what he meant. It seemed so surreal, so unexpected, but suddenly it hit me like a bolt of lightning. He was serious. Deadly serious. There was no mistaking it.

He stood up to leave. 'Do be careful around that young man, Alice,' he warned. 'And please, give my proposition careful consideration.'

'Thank you, Professor. I will.' The words were automatic.

As for Douglas, well he remained a distraction. Try as I

might to nudge him out of my mind he refused to budge. Once he'd settled in my head it wasn't long before he worked his way into my heart.

Everything changed for me one clear, Autumn morning. A Sunday. A short walk to Church during which I berated myself for missing him. I switched attention back to Professor Mason's words, his sage advice and proposition. The chance of a promising future. A duty to fulfil in accordance with my desire to serve others and do good in some small way.

I took a deep breath of fresh air and soaked up the sunset colours. Brittle leaves crumpled to the ground and completed nature's cycle. This resonated with me, in my final year of study. Professor Mason was best placed to advise me on my next steps. I should follow his instruction, even though it might be a dangerous path.

Lost in future contemplation I walked, not to the Church but towards the trees over to the right hand side. The tallest oak tree as irresistible as the man who stood beneath it.

He stooped a little, his normally bright aura smothered by a cloud of despair. He didn't acknowledge me immediately, as though steeped in quiet despair, which gave me a moment to think about what to say by way of greeting. I had no idea what he was doing there. He wasn't a member of my Church's congregation and I'd long assumed he was agnostic. Was he in the churchyard to see me or was his appearance merely a coincidence? I wasn't at all sure whether I should say hello or tiptoe away.

Spotting me he straightened up to full height like a late flowering sunflower, easy smile returning as our eyes met. I tried to return his smile and hoped mine was as warm as his despite my awkwardness. Mother brought me up to smile little and infrequently at that.

'Douglas? It is you. I wasn't sure at first.'

A tiny leaf landed on his shoulder. He wiped his eye with a handkerchief as though feeling the tree's loss.

'Alice, it's good to see you. I've missed our chats in the library. I can only apologise for neglecting you these past few weeks.' Blood raced to my face. I looked to the ground for support.

'You look well, Alice.' Simply stated. It sounded nice when he spoke my name.

'Thank you.' Disarmed, I couldn't think of a single word to say and dared not comment on his appearance. Even when ruffled he cut a striking pose. But something in his demeanour had changed. His face was paler than I remembered. He offered no glib remarks. His greeting had a quiet charm, a departure from his normal, brash confidence. Was this a sign of a greater depth to his character? I hoped so.

He stepped towards me, palms open. Then he stopped short, so close. Even had I wished to move away my feet were rooted to the ground. This new vulnerability was at odds with my opinion of Douglas as a man who is pleasing to be around but shallow. I'd concluded previously that he was charming because it suited him, rather than charming by nature. What on earth did he want from me here outside the safe confines of the library?

My cheeks stayed pink but his face was grey, no longer the bronzed traveller. He looked like he'd been stuck in a bunker.

'I hope you are keeping well?' I framed a general question

rather than enquiring specifically about why he looked so ill. To ask too many questions of someone is impertinent and beneath people of our class. He shook his head and gestured towards the gate.

'Would you be so kind as to walk with me?'

'Of course.' It was a relief to find I could walk after all and less intimidating to be side by side rather than face to face. We fell into a comfortable step leaving behind the churchyard and the great oak tree.

'It's my Mother. She took ill with pleurisy a few weeks ago and my sister Elsie sent for me, thinking the worst. Mother suffers from chronic bronchitis and a weak heart.'

'What a worrying time for you all.'

'Yes, and especially for Elsie. They are very close. More like sisters than mother and daughter.' He shot a look in my direction. 'I'm sure you understand.'

I didn't but stopped myself from retorting that not all daughters enjoy happy relations with their mother.

An image of Douglas's mother and sister sprang to mind, their arms linked and faces alight with laughter, until an unwelcome third figure elbowed her way between them. My Mother, rudely barging into the picture, interfering as usual. No one would ever mistake us for sisters. Since no affection existed between us, my own experience rendered me incapable of relating to the loving relationship described by Douglas. But it was futile to envy an ideal, improbable relationship, nor was there anything to be gained in disclosing Mother's shortcomings. This was his story, not mine.

'I do hope she's on the mend?'

'She's out of danger now, thank heavens. But we thought

we might lose her. I couldn't bear that. Not after my Father.'

He had never before spoken to me of his personal affairs. I really had no idea of his circumstances and would not have made enquiries about his family situation. It's not that I wasn't curious but such questioning would have been improper in our day. He knew nothing of my life either, since I always kept family business to myself. So many of our men were lost in the Great War. My own Papa had a lucky escape. Douglas's father evidently hadn't been so fortunate, as Douglas took pains to explain.

'I'm the man of the household now, Alice. My mother and sister are my responsibility.' He screwed up his eyes and clammed up like a shell. Like a flood defence.

People did not indulge in self-pity when we were young. We all had to get on with our lives without making a fuss. Stoicism was the order of the day. I wanted to hear more about his family but knew to be patient.

We crossed the road towards St James's Park and I was all too aware of women casting surreptitious looks at Douglas while directing envy towards me. I wondered if his courtship with the tall, pretty girl had run its course. I'd heard she was now employed as a sales assistant on the perfume counter of a well-regarded department store near Bond Street. Perhaps Douglas had tired of fashion accessories and was ready to commit to a more enduring classic. Perhaps someone like me.

We walked through the park before stopping to rest on a memorial bench overlooking the lake. Warm now, I removed my new leather gloves and placed them neatly inside my bag although I kept my hat. Ducks splashed about in the water and we sat in comfortable silence until Douglas leaned in to whisper in my ear.

'Clever little birds, mallards. They choose their mating partners for life.'

I choked back shock and searched for safe conversational ground, focusing my attention on a pair of swans standing proud at the water's edge. But rouge circles dug into my cheeks as Douglas's eyes bored into me. He leaned back on the bench, at ease and comfortable in his skin as though his mating innuendo had been accidental.

'Able Alice, that's who you are. Competent and composed. Nothing ruffles you. Or does it?' I did not rise to his question. Even with my inexperience I recognised this as open provocation.

'I prefer order over chaos, that's all. I try to prepare for eventualities before they arise.' But this cosy, lake-side scenario was without precedent. He knew darned well how ruffled I was and any idiot would have seen I was struggling to maintain any semblance of calm. 'And your impression of me is complimentary, Douglas, but you should not flatter me.'

'Why on earth not? You're more than worthy of compliment and if you regard this as mere flattery, this confirms everything I need to know about you.'

'Whatever do you mean?'

'Young Alice, you are unlike any girl I've ever known.' He paused, head inclined in scrutiny of my face, seeking to pin down something to lay his finger on. 'Let's see, what is it that makes you so compelling?' I squirmed under his gaze. 'It could be your independent spirit. How is it that you appear not to need anybody?'

'I prefer to be self-sufficient.' My voice tailed off and my gaze returned to the mallard and his hen. Somehow a string of words took shape in my mouth. 'I believe it's important to be able to stand on one's own two feet. This is the 20th century after all.' Douglas roared with laughter.

'Alice, dear Alice, you are a force to be reckoned with. At the risk of offending you, such independence is unusual in ladies of your age.'

'I'm not so young and you only have to look at the suffragettes to see that independent thinking isn't new anymore.' I protested but he merely grinned and edged closer. I sat rigid, eyes focused on the rippling water, trying not to allow his low voice stoke those strange feelings deep in the pit of my stomach.

'You look very pretty when you blush, Alice.'

'Douglas, please don't embarrass me.'

'I should have noticed you before.'

'Before?'

'Months ago. But I was blind then. These days my thoughts linger on you constantly. What good fortune brought you to me?'

His outburst did nothing to alleviate my embarrassment or reduce the growing tension between us. As a pharmacist in training I should have had a better handle on chemistry. I couldn't afford to become another of his conquests.

'Douglas, your words are still too much. What has brought me here?' It seemed prudent to reframe his question in terms of my reasons for being in London rather than any destined path towards him. 'I'm here for the same reason as you: that is to learn and to make good of my life. But unlike you, nothing would persuade me to return home. My mother and I don't see eye to eye.'

He pulled back, eyes wide open, quizzical. His experience of family discord must be limited with a mother and sister who enjoyed inexorably close ties and mutual affection. I needed to explain. 'The opportunity to come to Pharmaceutical College was too good to turn down. Coming here gives me the chance to make a difference to my life and to the world at large.'

His smile returned but confusion was stamped all over his face.

'How broad-minded of you. And ambitious. I don't suppose I've met a lady with ambition before. I'm impressed, really I am. I've seen that you've caught the attention of the Prof. too.'

So he had noticed. I always thought that my conversations with Professor Mason had been discreet and unobserved by others. It seemed I was mistaken.

'I don't know what to make of you Alice. Ambitious and purposeful, not seeking a husband. Not cast in the usual mould. I have a question for you. What do your parents think to all this? Your mother must be proud of your achievements, surely?'

A thin line of concern showed across his forehead. I almost wanted to reach out to trace his face with my fingertips. How to explain to anyone, let alone a man like Douglas that mother and I lived in perpetual conflict? I sighed and tried my best.

'Mother and I share no common ground. She's a cold fish. Even when I was a child she was distant. She lost a baby boy before I was born and I never measured up.'

'Good grief, that's a sorry affair. And what about your

father?'

Beloved Papa. The sun broke through the clouds when I thought of him.

'He's a very good man. He's done his best to bridge the gaps but it's too far. Efforts to reconcile us are futile.'

'Surely you must have some common ground?'

'I am water to her potassium – we're explosive if mixed together.' At least that produced a wry smile from Douglas and helped him understand without my having to relive viscous arguments. He hadn't experienced family conflict, or so he led me to believe.

Ashamed by my failure to be a loving daughter I locked my hands in my lap. Thoughts of Mother increased tension in my shoulders and I had to stop myself from gritting my teeth. Yet, when Douglas placed his left hand on top, covering my hands like a blanket, my grip loosened and my shoulders relaxed.

I did not pull away. For once I had no desire to move. His warmth provided a comfort I'd secretly craved and for the first time in my life I felt I belonged in this special place; a warm room with roaring log fire and a comfy armchair on which to sit and rest one's weary feet. A safe haven. I was on the inside at last, a welcome guest. No longer the exile stuck outside in the cold, staring in through the window.

We sat, no words necessary, his hand enveloping mine, protecting me. The largest of the swans on the lake stretched out its wings and began to paddle along the water's surface at increasing speed preparing for flight.

The swan rose into the sky, lifting with it all the barriers that I'd built to block Douglas from entering my life. Breaking and entering. The heat from his hands surged through me and filled my aching heart.

'Alice, I have another question for you. Will you be my girl?'

Chapter 5

Kate - under the skies of Paris

'This looks like it was designed by a four year old.'

Kate derives no pleasure in being proved right about the fortunes of Bon Appétit!'s new range of 'delicious dishes'. Acidic comments fall unabated from the mouths of cynical Parisian mums and will be sure to turn the collective stomach of the team behind the product and its advertising. Each concept shown is introduced in the most objective way and the moderator does her best to present positives, playing devil's advocate in the face of criticism, but no amount of discussion can halt the barrage.

'My dog could have done a better job.'

'I wouldn't feed that to my dog!'

Kate's scribbled notes become bleaker and increasingly sparse as the session progresses. Even the most constructive comment is damning:

'For me, there is nothing wrong with this idea that a total redesign wouldn't fix.'

She throws down her fountain pen and places both elbows on the table, supporting the weight of her head with her hands. How on earth will she break this news to Daniel? She'd been dreading spending time with him but finds herself wishing he'd turned up after all to hear this first hand.

When he hadn't turned up she tried to call him. By way of response he'd sent a brief text to inform her he'd been invited to an awards dinner at the Dorchester. It was exactly the kind of event that Kate found tiresome, but evidently too good a networking opportunity for someone like Daniel to miss. Of course, he hadn't bothered to say he wouldn't be in Paris after all. He liked to keep everyone waiting and on their toes.

Ambitious Daniel, the self-claimed 'success in a suit' with his infinite self-belief and incessant demands on others. Kate sees the Emperor's new clothes on him, despite his sharp Armani attire. Headhunted from one of the big supermarkets to turn around the fortunes of stagnating Bon Appétit!, young golden boy Daniel has a point to prove and a crowd of followers to impress. Wildly enthusiastic about his own ideas for the strategic direction of the brand, he'll find even the mildest of criticism hard to swallow. Kate has met his type before. Too often. She will be useful to him only for as long as she makes him look good.

She pours another cup of strong, black coffee. The caffeine will keep her awake for hours; time she'll need to craft a carefully worded email; one that spells out failure in a way that doesn't bruise Daniel's ego or provoke an aggressive riposte.

Don't shoot the messenger, she muses as she tidies away her notes and collects the portfolio bag containing the offending feedback from the day.

By the time she steps onto Avenue de l'Opéra it's well after 10 o'clock, so Kate waves down a taxi. She's wound up and wants to get back to the calm of her hotel room. In keeping with the day's frustration the taxi edges forward in fits and starts, hindered by endless red lights and heavy traffic. For some reason all of Paris has descended on this district and even at this late hour the volume of cars is staggering. If only she could hop onto a scooter and zip past the snaking lines of stationary cars with cool wind on her face.

Kate fiddles with the zip on her bag while her agitated taxi driver drums his nicotine-stained fingers on the steering wheel and shakes his head, looking for someone to blame. He curses everyone from the French President, Nicolas Sarkozy to the driver of the blue Renault Twingo who inches ahead. The Twingo driver gestures wildly back and the two hurl insults at each other like boxers throwing punches in the ring.

'Putain! Saloperie de merde! J'ai besoin d'un clop!' Kate sits tight and lets her driver fume. His bad language doesn't bother her and despite his fury his driving stays safe, unlike many a taxi driver she's come across in Italy. She shudders at the vivid memory of her first trip to Rome and the intense ride in a Mercedes from the airport. The speedometer had spun sharply to the right in seconds until the car in front was in touching distance. She'd prayed for her life.

She'll be unlikely to die in a high-speed crash tonight. They haven't made it past 30kmh. Nonetheless Kate still lets out an audible sigh when they arrive at the hotel, able to let go of the breath she's been holding in her mouth. The 20 euro note she hands her driver includes a generous tip, not for exceptional service but because she hasn't the patience to wait for piles of change. A bad habit she picked up from the past. The dark-haired man mumbles something resembling thanks and pulls away in search of his next job.

Kate hurries to Room 11 on the first floor and loses no time in kicking off her shoes and wriggling her toes. She hangs up her coat and stretches her arms towards the ceiling to release the tension gathered around her neck. It's a shame Struan isn't around to give her one of his munificent shoulder rubs.

Earlier on between focus groups she'd snatched a few minutes to phone home, ostensibly to wish Isla good night but also to reassure herself that Struan was coping as a temporary lone parent. Her timing couldn't have been worse. Isla had been mid-tantrum with poor Struan bearing the full brunt of her rage.

For all she is a bright child, Isla is also terrier-like and her 'terrible twos' evolved into the 'thumping threes' before becoming the 'feisty fours'. It's now clear that her hot temper is a permanent character trait rather than the symptom of a passing phase. Kate and Struan call her their little fire-cracker as it doesn't take much to make her fizz.

'I'm dealing with an explosive situation,' Struan explained over high-pitched screams.

'Sounds bad - a category five?'

'Not quite that bad but she's lying in the doorway and won't let me past. Hold on a sec.' In a calm voice Struan called Isla to the phone. 'Listen, Isla. It's Mummy. Come and say hello.'

'NO! Go away.'

'Never work with animals or children. How is it that I can negotiate a contract and yet I'm defeated by a four year old?'

'It's not your fault,' Kate sympathises. When Isla erupts, the most effective course of action is to let her tantrum run its course. Intervention, with either promise of reward or threat for not toeing the line, is met with fierce resistance.

'Isla knows her own mind.' Kate often feels obliged to explain her daughter's behaviour in the face of disapproving glares from strangers or her mother-in-law. 'The sky's purple in her world no matter what we tell her.' It reminds her of all the times she made allowances for her sister.

'I feel so rotten not being home to help you.' Increasingly Kate feels the weight of carrying on with her career while also trying to be a good Mum. She feels guilty for being absent and unable to give her daughter a cuddle.

'I feel bad for wanting it all.'

'You can have it all, just not all at the same time.' Struan patiently reassures her whenever she voices her troubles. His approach to life is far more realistic than hers. He's also a lot less anxious and uptight which helps.

After reading her notes, having a shower and drying her hair, Kate lies outstretched on the bed. She hopes the day has ended on a happier note for Struan and wonders if he's given Isla a bath and cleaned her teeth properly. The phone rings for almost 10 seconds before his sleepy voice answers.

'Sorry, did I wake you?' The cloak of guilt drops over her again but she shakes it off this time. Most evenings it falls to Kate to put Isla to bed so it's not as though she doesn't do her bit. One night of bedtime duty for Struan won't break him. Besides, it's good for Dads to be hands on with childcare. That's what all the parenting books advise and Ellie says the same. *Involvement of both parents is essential.* All the same, Struan doesn't sound too hands on right now.

'I went to sleep in the middle of Top Gear,' he yawns. 'Sorry.'

'It's OK. You don't have to sound so contrite.'

'I know you loathe that programme.'

'Good thing it's proved to be so soporific on this occasion then! How are you? Has calm returned to south Edinburgh?'

'I'm done in. I'm going to make a cup of tea and then get to my bed. I haven't stopped all evening, well apart from dozing off for a bit. Isla was a total madam, refused to eat her tea and then she nearly flooded the bathroom.'

'She did what? How?'

'She was trying to swim in the bath but most of the water ended up on the floor. It's fine now. I mopped up the mess with today's Scotsman and then I read her a chapter of the Faraway Tree. Eventually she nodded off, thank God.'

'Poor you.'

'And then your brother rang.'

'Did he? On a week night? That's unusual.'

'He has good news to share. Do you want to hear it from me or wait for him to tell you?'

Lying on the bed, Kate has been idly twisting her wedding ring around her finger but as she absorbs Struan's words she sits bolt upright.

'I'd like to know. I've a hunch and if you don't tell me I won't sleep. I can always play the daftie when I speak to him. I won't blow your cover.'

'OK then. Are you ready? Are you sitting down?'

'I'm on the bed.'

'Are you? Now that's an image I like. What are you wearing?'

'Stop it! Just tell me Craig's news will you!'

'Well…,' Struan delivers a theatrical pause, the unintended consequence of watching too many game shows on TV.

He continues with a flourish. 'Juliet's pregnant! The baby's due in November.'

Kate hugs her knees to her chest, a broad smile on her face.

'Yes! That's the best news. Hey, you know what this means? We can get our own back on Craig for all those loud musical toys he gave Isla. Do you know anything else? What did the scan show? They wouldn't be going public unless they were past the danger stage, especially after all the problems they've had. Does Ellie know?' She pauses for breath.

Struan chuckles at her onslaught of questions.

'I can tell you've been locked in a room on your own for too long today. Why don't you just give Craig a call now? It's not that late and he'll have to get used to sleep deprivation once the baby arrives. Juliet's been feeling quite sick so I'm sure she'd appreciate some moral support from someone who knows what that feels like.'

Kate nods in agreement. She'd experienced nausea for eight ninths of her pregnancy. Only fizzy drinks kept the sickness at bay, which might explain why her little girl is such a live wire. And why Kate now has two fillings where previously her teeth were perfect.

'I could try Craig on his mobile. I don't want to disturb them on the landline if they're already away to bed. If Juliet feels anything like I did she'll be tucked up and fast asleep by now. But if I know my brother he'll be bumbling about on the internet looking at the latest baby hardware. In fact, I'm surprised that Top Gear hasn't launched its own over the top range of baby kit for all those men out there looking for a power pram. Craig will buy one of those crazy neon Bronti Buggies and have it customised with Shimano gears and a turbo boost.' It's common knowledge that Craig likes fast cars so a fair bet that he'll be looking for a high-performance vehicle for the baby too.

'Oh Struan, I'm delighted. Craig'll be in his element. I can't believe he's going to be a Dad.' Kate pauses for a second to consider this and giggles. 'He's in for an almighty shock, isn't he?'

'Best not tell him that. Let them discover happy chaos for themselves. Anyway, how are you? You were lucky to get to Paris today.'

'What do you mean?'

'What do you mean, what do I mean? Don't tell me you haven't heard?'

'Heard what? I've been stuck inside since lunchtime, cut off from the outside world, remember?' Struan fills her in with headlines about the erupting Icelandic volcano and its ensuing ash cloud.

'All the flights in and out of Edinburgh were cancelled this afternoon. The authorities are assessing the situation again in the morning. You might be stranded in Paris.'

Kate's not prepared for this second piece of news. She listens to Struan's account of the plume of ash disrupting UK airspace.

'You'd better check the status of your flight. Haven't you heard anything from the office?'

No one from Kate's office has been in touch but this

doesn't surprise her. Although she's part of a larger team, she operates autonomously when she's away. Junior members of staff are on hand to organise travel itineraries but Kate prefers to sort out her own arrangements.

'I've been delayed by fog, aircraft complications and plenty of strikes before now but a volcanic eruption is a first. I'll give Craig a quick call and then check the news. Hopefully if there's a problem with flights they'll divert us to London and I'll just hop on a train up to Edinburgh.' Kate's thoughts turn to contingency planning.

'Well, I don't know if anything's flying over UK airspace just now. It depends on wind direction and the density of ash in the air. Do you want me to look into it for you before I go to bed?'

'That's kind of you but no thanks. You're tired and I need to log on to check messages anyway.' Kate checks her watch again and winces at the time.

'It's late. Get yourself to bed. You've an early start tomorrow and if Isla comes through in the night your sleep will be ruined. I expect this will all blow over by tomorrow.'

'Nice pun.'

'Unintended. Why don't we talk again first thing?'

'OK then, sleep tight and happy dreams. I love you.'

'I love you too. The bed's too big without you.' Kate blushes as she whispers these words. They form another of her travel rituals, dropped into conversations when they are apart even if the opportunity to languish in a king sized bed on her own is one of the best aspects of trips away. Ever since Isla moved into a toddler bed and is no longer constrained by the bars of a cot, she'll appear in her parents' room at least twice a week. She climbs into bed alongside them, kicking off all the covers and taking up more space than is justified for such a small person. For one night only, no bed is too big for Kate but it still matters to her that Struan knows she's thinking about him. She's paranoid these days.

A different rush of excitement courses through her as she dials Craig's number. When she hears her brother's voice inviting her to leave a message she's disappointed but does as she's told, ever the dutiful younger sister.

She switches on her laptop but before she's even had the chance to type anything her phone jingles. It reminds Kate that she must change her childish ringtone, devoid of professional credentials and chosen for Isla's amusement.

'Good evening, big brother and how are you?'

'I'm very good, thanks. Listen. Can you hear that?' The unmistakable shake of ice in a tumbler.

'Highland Park?'

'Good guess little sis, but no. It is an island malt, I'll grant you that, but you need to go south a bit and west a bit. Speed bonny boat an' all that.'

'Too easy. Talisker.'

'Bang on! Cheers.' Craig clinks his glass against the phone and takes a generous mouthful of his classic malt. Kate picks up the conversation while he savours his dram.

'Sorry I missed you earlier. I had some work in Paris and it's been another late finish. I've only been back at the hotel for about 20 minutes.'

Craig chuckles. 'Yes, Struan told me you've abandoned him to undertake crucial research. Glad to hear you're doing your bit to keep the economy going, not to mention lining the pockets of our favourite household brands within the grocery universe.'

'You are so cynical! I don't know how Juliet puts up with you.'

Craig treats Kate's job as a great big joke and delights in teasing her about it. From projects that vary from designing new packaging for ready meals to launching new brand extensions for toilet paper, Kate's repertoire at dinner parties is abundant in amusing anecdotes. But her world of consumer investigation is a far cry from Craig's. His profession as a clinical psychologist and his weighty theses make him the undisputed authority on empirical scientific research. His qualifications are impressive. So it's ironic that he's the big joker socially while Kate has a tendency to take life a little too seriously. Most onlookers would label her the academic and he the commercial marketing executive.

Healthy competition has raged between the pair of them ever since their school days in spite or perhaps because of the three years separating them. Craig insists that he's attained a position of moral and cerebral superiority over Kate but his banter is in the spirit of a bumptious big brother and isn't malicious.

Kate could easily have pursued a more academic path. No one ever doubted that she was an accomplished, hard-working student with potential to go all the way to a PhD but she'd expressed no desire to pursue higher academic study once she'd completed her Masters. Kate enjoyed commerce and took full advantage of the healthy post-graduate salary that came with her first proper job. She was keen to get to work and the opportunity to see the world presented a powerful incentive to pursue a career in the commercial sector. Sending postcards home with tales of

caipirinha drinking in Sao Paulo, walks through Sydney's botanical gardens and scuba diving in Barbados, Kate wouldn't have swapped places with her brother for all the letters he was collecting after his name. When the whole family got together for their annual Christmas festivities Kate would arrive tanned, the picture of good health, while for years Craig remained a pasty-faced and impoverished student. To labour the point, Kate brought back interesting and unusual gifts for her family sourced from the different cities she had visited. Craig's gifts were mass-produced, usually from a factory in China and seldom long lasting.

He's made it now though, with his Poggenpohl kitchen and the biggest flat screen high definition television that money can buy.

'So, what's up?' Kate keeps her voice casual.

'What do you mean? I can't believe Struan hasn't told you already.' His voice is animated. 'Juliet's pregnant! We're having a baby at last. We went for the scan this afternoon and it turns out Juliet's 15 weeks pregnant already.'

'So Uncle Craig is going to be a Dad! Oh Craig, congratulations!'

'I know! Me, a Dad! It's a bloody miracle. Everything looks good. We couldn't make head nor tail of the scan. The picture was too hard to decipher but our radiologist was great. Turns out she and Juliet met at Yorkhill years ago when they were both training. Anyway, all the bits are where they should be and even I had a tear in my eye when I heard the heartbeat.'

'I'm so thrilled for you both. How's Juliet feeling? Struan mentioned she's having a bit of a rough time with the morning sickness.'

Craig burst out laughing. 'You're a minx, Kate. Feigning innocence when you knew all the time. I thought it was weird of Struan to keep quiet.'

'I didn't want to steal your thunder. Anyway, tell me more.'

'My stunning wife is at this precise moment fast asleep. And when she is awake she's throwing up morning, noon and night. Can't take her anywhere without a puke bag. She's finding work really hard going. Oh and she's eating nothing but stodge and washing down her folic acid tablets with diet cola. I've never seen a woman scoff so many almond croissants. She'll be as large as a house by the summer. We might have to get the front door widened and not just for the buggy.'

'Craig, you are truly awful. Poor Juliet. Morning sickness is hellish. I should know. Don't underestimate it. You do understand your primary job from now on is to look after her, don't you?'

'What do you mean, 'from now on'? That's always been the deal. I'm the one who puts out the rubbish bins every Thursday for six o'clock in the morning and the Tesco Club card's in my name. Sometimes that place feels like my second home. So don't you go implying that I'm a passenger in this marriage. Anyway, I'm just kidding. Stop being so uptight. Life is great and we're chuffed to bits. I'm just finding the constant retching in the bathroom is putting me off my food. To add insult to injury, Juliet's banned me from bringing in my Friday night curry and Sunday's sacred fry-up is also off limits. It's not easy being an expectant Dad, you know,' he adds mournfully.

'Well, an embargo on fried breakfasts is no bad thing.

You could do with losing a few pounds.'

They both laugh. Craig's appetite is insatiable and he's a big guy. He's lucky to have a high metabolism.

'My arteries have the same self-cleaning features as my high-tech Neff oven. No need to worry about my health, little sister.'

As the effects of the caffeine begin to wear off Kate suppresses a yawn. 'Well, I'll say goodbye now. Please send Juliet my love. Can you tell her I'll give her a call tomorrow at a more respectable hour?'

'You'll have plenty of time on your hands at the airport. Nothing's flown overhead today. It's been bloody marvellous actually.' Craig and Juliet live in a gorgeous Georgian townhouse by the Thames but their house sits directly beneath the flight path for Heathrow and interrupting noise from ascending aircraft means they often have to pause conversations.

'Oh, God. I hope I'm not going to be stranded here.'

'You're in bloody Paris, girl. It's not exactly darkest Peru. What's the matter? Where's intrepid explorer Kate we all know and love? Has she been abducted by a troop of French gendarmes? I'd have thought you'd relish a few nights away from the routine, especially in Paris. Are you feeling ill? Hang on a minute,' Craig's pace slows. 'Are you pregnant too?'

Kate scoffs, even though she and Struan have been a bit slack with contraception over the last few weeks.

'No, Craig. I'm not pregnant, but as you'll find out for yourself soon enough, once you have a baby in the house and a young family to support, the things you value change.'

Craig takes another healthy swig from his tumbler. 'Wow, from intrepid traveller to sanctimonious parent in a matter of a few short years! I bet you have a life plan for little Isla all set out too. No wonder she's had to strike a pre-emptive rebellion.'

Kate bounces back, quick to retaliate and refusing to be out trumped. 'And I bet you're sitting there looking at the Which? website for the best travel system on the market.'

'Perceptive, Kate. You know, you're wasted in market research. You should have read psychology and followed in my footsteps, n'est-ce pas?'

'I'm perceptive and you're impossible. It's been great to chat. Now get back to your Talisker and I'll make a start on drafting my report of doom. Don't forget to tell Juliet I'll call her tomorrow and congratulations again.

'Roger! Have fun, little sister and remember, don't go speaking to any French men. I know you're happily married and that you've switched your allegiance from Gallic to Gaelic but I also know your weakness for Latin men.'

'Ha ha! Always the joker but don't give up the day job. Night, Craig.'

'Nighty night.'

Craig's warning is meant in jest but neither of them can appreciate how prescient he is. As Kate returns to her screen, little does she know that in just over 12 hours she'll find herself staring into the dark eyes of temptation.

Chapter 6

Kate – turning sweet sixteen

The day of the locket discovery, the sisters returned from the woods within minutes of each other. Much as Kate wanted to talk about what she'd found she kept her mouth shut. She was still mad at Ellie, but she didn't even confide in Craig who'd perked up enough by teatime to manage a few mouthfuls of mashed banana and honey without being sick.

While Ellie washed her hands in the cloakroom Kate chased up to the bedroom they shared. She transferred the locket from her sweaty hand into the blue jewellery box which had been a gift from Great Aunt Dorothy. Kate reckoned the locket should be safe in there, at least for the time being.

She ran back down the stairs, two at a time to join the rest of the family at the broad, oak kitchen table. It marked the centre of gravity in the busy kitchen around which family issues were aired and more often than not resolved. Over the years, many a truth was wheedled out of the children over this great hunk of wood.

The family members sat in their usual formation; Kate's father at the far end by the door, her mother near the Raeburn stove and Craig underneath the big window opposite the girls. Kate kept her legs tight against the legs of her chair to escape bruising from Craig's enormous feet as he kicked back and forth. Being poorly hadn't drained his strength, the big lump.

Kate didn't feel like joining in the conversation, still cross with Ellie for her spiteful behaviour. She spent most of the meal quietly examining the marks and grooves in the wood or turning her silver napkin ring to feel the scratches it had sustained over the years. One of the trio always dropped something onto the stone floor.

'Oops, butterfingers,' they'd chorus as the heavy cutlery crashed to the ground. Their mother said it made her head jangle.

'You're quiet, chicken.' Kate's father's eyes honed in and she wriggled in her seat like a trapped animal. She didn't want to hurt his feelings but wished he'd stop calling her that.

'Are you feeling poorly, darling?' Mummy sprang up from her seat to rest her palm on Kate's forehead. 'You do feel a bit clammy.' Kate knew her mother's hands were still warm from cooking in a steamy kitchen, but went along with the idea that she was running a temperature and allowed herself to be whisked away from the table in double quick time.

'Straight to bed with you, young lady. I'd say you're coming down with Craig's tummy bug.' Behind his mother's back, Craig mimed being sick and Ellie burst out laughing before being silenced by her father's wagging finger.

Being sent to bed early turned out to be good news, even if it did mean missing out on Saturday night television. It gave Kate a bit of peace and quiet to work out a better place to hide the locket before her sister came upstairs. There was no way she'd let Ellie see what she'd found. Ellie would snatch the locket away and Kate would never see it again.

Sharing a bedroom with a nosy sister posed a problem. Ellie was no good at sharing her possessions even though she was super quick to take what she wanted from others. She believed in Orwellian Animal Farm principles that some animals are more equal than others and she was assuredly the most equal of them all.

Their house had a guest bedroom that both girls coveted. It had a big wardrobe and views over the garden, but neither Ellie nor Kate had yet managed to persuade the parents to relinquish it from the aunts and uncles who frequently stayed. Forced to share a room at the front of the house the girls devised strict rules over personal and shared space, few of which were respected. Sick to death of their squabbles their parents even resorted to sticking duct tape on the floor to mark out a tangible boundary. This worked for a while until Ellie removed the tape and reapplied it closer to Kate's leaning tower of books to extend her territory. Kate's books, a deliberate barricade came crashing down with such a thud that their Siamese cat Chocco jumped a couple of feet into the air.

Whenever she could Kate would seize the opportunity to return the boundary to its rightful place. Every so often she pushed her luck by inching the boundary further towards Ellie's 'wall of fame', so called because it was plastered with posters of the latest chart bands pulled from Smash Hits magazine.

'This is how world wars start,' Craig ventured, none too

helpfully. Fights broke out daily. Their parents turned a blind eye as long as the sisters only engaged in silent warfare but physical combat landed them both in deep trouble.

Not long after finding the locket Kate worried that Ellie would stumble across it. She needed a better hiding place. Somewhere safer than a blue jewellery box. Ellie had an identical one. Kate suspected it contained something illicit as Ellie had given her a Chinese burn and forced her into a promise that she would never peak inside. Kate kept her promise but Ellie couldn't be trusted to do the same. Even if she had made a pledge not to trespass, a promise from Ellie had a short shelf life and limited credibility.

Kate was right to be on guard. Nothing was off limits to her conniving sister. Possessions, friends, potential boyfriends all became prey even if they weren't to Ellie's taste. If Ellie wanted something she made damned sure she got it and to hell with anyone else. She'd be sure to rifle through Kate's jewellery box if she were bored or suspicious.

Kate lay on her bed racking her brains for an alternative hiding place, somewhere Ellie would never think to look. Surely she'd read enough Famous Five books by now to be able to come up with a reasonable plan. Then up she sprang, startling Chocco from his feline slumber.

Ellie was no book-worm. Magazines appealed to her with their glossy pictures, fashion trends and personality questionnaires but books she shunned. Kate took a hardback book of Common Prayers for Children from the pile and pulled it open at the middle until the spine cracked. Unusually for a book lover she did not flinch, though she did make a silent apology for the damage.

She took a pair of scissors from the sewing basket. They

weren't designed for cutting paper but would have to do. She sat cross-legged on the floor and set about cutting a small rectangle from consecutive pages of the book until a flutter of papers gathered beside her. Cutting pages out of a prayer book was pretty shocking behaviour and Kate felt a prickle of shame until she placed the locket into the makeshift hole and found it to be the perfect hiding place. She'd atone for vandalising the book by saying double prayers for a few weeks.

Her mind buzzed with contradiction. Although she'd initially had every intention of finding the locket's rightful owner the urge to keep it had proved irresistible and secured her silence. Had she been serious about returning the locket she'd have plotted return visits to the woods in search of further clues. She'd have scrutinised the faces of the dog walkers and other passers-by in a quest to recognise a face among them that matched the stern one in the panel of the locket. She'd have told her mother.

She did none of these things. Her good intentions were unrealistic in a busy summer holiday and she wasn't an adventurous child anyway, too fearful of unpleasant consequences to take risks. The bigger boys had also started hanging out in the woods and they'd progressed from throwing stones to smoking 'herbal' cigarettes. They presented a big deterrent to return. Nothing would have persuaded Kate to cross their path. Too many bad stories circulated about them, made worse by the scream of a girl in the woods early one evening and a hush of whispered conversations by the adults.

Summer passed, a new school year began and the locket lay dormant in Kate's prayer book. At first she lay awake in bed thinking about it but once the nights started closing in attention shifted to homework, piano lessons and ballet exams. By Christmas the locket was forgotten.

It wasn't until Kate's 16th birthday that she chanced upon it. By this time Ellie had left home in search of a proper job and real independence in London. She'd found a house share near Clapham Junction with a couple of old school friends. She'd also wangled a position at a commercial radio station as a production assistant in the newsroom. Her parents urged her to go to university, as Craig had done, but no one really expected her to go. Craig was well into his undergraduate degree at Cambridge but Ellie wasn't one to follow a path already trodden by someone else. Arms crossed over chest, she stood defiant in the face of opposition for weeks leading up to her grand departure.

'I'm not going to university and that's final. Why would I want to waste time studying when I can get a job, earn money and live life?'

'I'd have given my eye teeth for the opportunities you lot seem to have. Please, Ellie, at least consider it.' Their mother's voice trickled out of her tears. Ellie's was more assertive and hot spots burned her cheeks. Their father swore, declaring she was the most stubborn child he'd ever met.

'Why would you walk away from higher education?'

'Oh, give me a break, Dad. There's more to life than study.'

The kitchen table saw more than its fair share of rows but they all knew who'd win the battle in the end.

Ellie packed a few bags and moved to London. The

shared bedroom finally became Kate's and she relished having the whole space to herself. At last she had the freedom to read without Ellie's incessant chat and disruptive presence. And she didn't have to climb through the clothes that Ellie routinely dropped on the floor. Her sister couldn't even be bothered to hang them up or pop them into the laundry basket.

Kate missed Ellie now and again, acknowledging that she did make excellent company on a good day. The sisters had been getting on better in recent months. She also missed the denim jacket that Ellie had pilfered from the wardrobe and the Sony Walkman that just so happened to disappear with Ellie's last wave goodbye. On the plus side, Ellie had left behind a great pile of back issues of Just Seventeen and a handful of more risqué Cosmopolitan magazines. These brought welcome respite from the arduous literature and A-level economics books that bowed the shelves of Kate's bookcase.

Reaching 16 meant being grown up. 16 years old. So much more sophisticated than 15. Kate shared her first real kiss with lush Neil Walker in the wings of the stage at the school disco. And her parents finally relented to her demands to have her ears pierced having resolutely refused for years. Kate had become used to being the odd one out, the only girl in her class who didn't have piercings. Even Claudine's ears sported little diamante studs.

Kate had pointed out this unfairness to her parents but her pleas had met with stony silence. No surprise that Ellie hadn't let parental rules stand in her way. She'd taken it upon herself to pierce her own earlobes with a needle during a sleepover at Susie's house. One bloody towel and a late night telephone call had her brought home in disgrace.

Kate suffered for Ellie's actions. Her sister's deviance strengthened their parents' resolve to make Kate wait for what felt like an eternity to get her ears pierced. It was easy for them. They knew their younger daughter would never do anything rash or stupid.

Kate didn't envy Ellie the row she'd earned for rebelling but continued to envy her sister's fearless spirit. No amount of trouble dissuaded her from a determined course. If anything, the scent of trouble spurred her on. The whole family marvelled that she'd made it through school with only one suspension. And emerged with reasonable grades despite her poor attendance record. Craig and Kate returned school reports that made their parents beam with pride. But their poor father had to sit down with a stiff drink before he'd contemplate reading Ellie's.

'Thank God she's bright. That's all I can say.'

Everyone knew Ellie could have gone to university if she'd wanted to. Just as Kate probably could have had her ears done sooner if she'd really pushed for it.

'But you're not a pushy person, are you?' Ellie pointed out. 'You don't mind if I keep this top, do you? I think it's more suited to my colouring than yours.'

Kate loved being able to wear real earrings rather than clip-ons. When she moved her head from side to side in the mirror she saw an adult for the first time. She hoped Neil Walker would appreciate what he saw and kiss her again at the school leavers' party.

For Kate's birthday her parents gave her a pair of gold-plated, cubic zirconia earrings. In the sunlight they were as precious as diamonds to her and she only wore them on special occasions.

The old jewellery box nestled between a couple of books on the top shelf in her bedroom. Kate reached up for it but then lost her footing and it fell, narrowly missing her head. A tinny, broken chord sounded around the room as the box crashed on the floor, spilling contents everywhere.

On her hands and knees Kate reacquainted herself with the contents she hadn't seen for years. At the bottom of the box she pulled out sheets of text that should have been part of her Common Prayers for Children. But what about that book? It didn't take Kate long to find, covered in dust at the back of the book shelf.

The locket was still tucked away inside and Kate pulled it from its hiding place with a thrill, her mind travelling straight back to that day in the woods. She could almost smell the smoky bonfire and feel the soft texture of the green leather glove. She recalled the punch of Ellie's words as the glove had been tossed away so casually.

Kate climbed into bed and explored the locket as though for the first time, opening up the latch to reveal the photo within. In amongst the pile of jewellery lying beside the bed she retrieved a gold chain. With some difficulty she attached the clasp of the chain around her neck and decided to wear the locket. It wasn't much of a fashion statement for a 16 year old but she felt it lent her an air of sophistication.

Kate was no longer worried that she'd shrouded her original discovery in secrecy, nor that the locket was only hers according to the law of 'finders keepers'. Her family could be led to believe it was another trinket found in Great Aunt Dorothy's flat after the funeral at St Mary's. Any awkward questions could be deflected.

The locket rested comfortably against Kate's skin, just as Neil Walker's kiss had felt so natural. She wished he'd ask her out properly and then she could carry his photo in the locket. But Neil had been spotted in the back row of the Empire cinema snogging one of the popular girls, so it looked like Kate had missed her chance. Instead she looked out a picture of the now elderly Chocco. It wasn't quite the same.

Kate looked at the picture of the faded woman on the right hand side and couldn't bring herself to remove her. It seemed so disrespectful. She reckoned it would be acceptable to paste other pictures over the top but wrong to erase the poor woman. This was more than a principle of ownership. Identity mattered.

Kate stared at the woman and the woman stared back.

'Who are you?' they said to each other.

PART TWO

FRIDAY

Chapter 7

Alice - light a candle, say a prayer

Our union produced no children. I lacked the good fortune to bring a child into the world and suffered a series of miscarriages within our early years of marriage. This was not something we spoke about but my inability to carry a child to term pained me. Douglas's disappointment showed through silence. He'd previously spoken with enthusiasm of his wishes to father a boy and continue the Emery line. I feigned stoicism, hiding anguish as I'd learned to hide so many things over the years. We would try again but it seemed I was not cut out to be a mother.

Neither of us foresaw disappointment or secrecy when our courtship began. Our hearts wide open for everyone to see, our hopes ambitious for the future. When Douglas got down on bended knee I accepted his proposal before he'd had a chance to finish his question. We wanted to be married within the year, as soon as we had qualified, assuming Papa gave his consent of course. But there was no reason to have any concerns about that. Or so I thought.

We took the train from London to my parents' home in Gosport. Douglas practised asking Papa for my hand until he was word perfect. I saw the journey home through fresh eyes as we left the city and travelled south towards the coast.

I chose a cornflower blue dress for the occasion and for once a flutter of excitement accompanied my arrival home in place of the usual doom.

Professor Mason had already made his misgivings very clear when I shared the news of my imminent engagement with him.

'Think very hard about your options, Alice. There is still time to change your mind. Consider my offer too.' We both knew that my mind was already made up and that Douglas had won. The Professor's brown eyes looked even sadder than usual behind his horn-rimmed spectacles.

I expected the same resistance to my marriage from Mother, albeit for different reasons, and almost fell off the step when she greeted us at the front porch with a smile that actually reached her eyes for once.

'Do come in, both of you and welcome, Douglas. It is a pleasure to meet you.'

Not only had Mother produced her best china tea service, she also unveiled her most treasured embroidered napkins from the dresser. Every tiny detail I noted. These napkins normally only ever graced the dining room when she was intent on showing her best self. Family silver had been polished beyond gleaming point and she'd even set out cake forks with handles of ivory, sourced from Indian elephants' tusks. Not to everyone's taste. Certainly not to mine.

'I see the new housekeeper has been very busy.'

'Indeed, Alice. She is very thorough. Ah, here's your father. At last.' Papa, dressed in his best smoking jacket, looked very dapper but Mother still tutted at him. He set aside his latest copy of Wisden Cricketers' Almanack and placed his spectacles to one side with inordinate precision as though he had all the time in the world. He didn't rush to shake hands with Douglas which was quite out of character. I could only assume he'd been lost in the world of cricket and the achievements of acclaimed batsman Roger Blunt.

'How do you do, Sir.' Papa's reserve did not appear to affect Douglas's jovial mood. In fact Douglas hung onto all our words, laughed in all the right places and sprinkled compliments over every offering. I still pinched myself he'd chosen me. There was no trace of any of the cynicism I'd felt towards him when we'd first met.

'Are you a cricket man, Douglas?' asked Papa to great relief on my part as he'd stayed silent for some time. Douglas passed the cricket test with ease. The men discussed test scores and the formidable batsman Donald Bradman. With nothing to contribute to the conversation Mother ushered me into the hallway.

'You have a loose thread on your dress, Alice. Come along now. I'll fetch some scissors from my sewing basket.'

'Mother, it's just a tiny snag. There's really no need to make a fuss.'

'Nonsense, child.' I wasn't in the mood to argue, besides which our absence would allow the men an opportunity to get to know one another.

'The garden's full of colour. It looks lovely.'

'Doesn't it just. I am very proud of it. It rather makes the Thwaites garden next door look shabby by comparison.' There was a long-standing competition between my Mother and the neighbours over their garden aesthetics. We held polite conversation about her plans for the roses and what she referred to as her 'orchard', though it was really a very modest collection of apple trees. Her voice made noise rather than song and my concentration drifted, my eyes darted towards the door at regular intervals in my anxiety to return to the two people who mattered most. A wonderful celebration would surely follow. Had Douglas sought Papa's permission yet?

After what seemed like an age we returned to find both men standing and facing each other. Papa turned and opened his arms to me in blessing but his mouth was set in a firm, horizontal line. He was courteous towards Douglas but why did he appear so reticent in expressing joy that his dear and only daughter was betrothed? A distinct coolness hung in the air. When I sent furtive looks in Douglas's direction hoping for a reassuring smile he only directed his attention towards Mother. She moved to kiss him on both cheeks.

'What wonderful news! I am looking forward to getting to know you and your family, Douglas. I never thought Alice would find anyone who'd have her, let alone someone so very handsome and charming.'

Douglas shone back at her while she fluttered around pouring tea and gushing over him. Papa muttered that he'd lost his appetite. He didn't even touch the perfect slice of Madeira cake that Mother had cut for him.

This transformation in both my parents took me by surprise. Papa rendered mute while Mother, normally so crotchety and difficult showered Douglas with happy anecdotes of family life. For the first time in my life I appeared to be the subject of maternal approval. Who was this woman? Even her features became softer. I marvelled at Douglas's ability to melt the heart of the coldest person I'd ever met. It seemed blood ran through stones after all.

His spell over her lasted all afternoon and he showed no weariness of her relentless questions. If anything, he seemed happier to talk to her than look at me.

'Douglas, please tell us about your travels across the water.' Pleased as punch, he duly shared vignettes of his life that were new to me.

'Oh, Douglas. You are a good raconteur. Tell me more, do!' He obliged every time.

'Douglas, you are funny. What an interesting life you've led.'

Douglas inclined his head towards her and spoke with passion and at length about his experiences of Cape Town and Sydney. When on board he'd worked alongside the pharmacist and experienced choppy seas, stormy nights and cases of influenza. He'd swum in the surf at Bondi beach in Sydney and had evenings of entertainment that had ended in card games and all sorts. I keenly listened for clues about his life prior to the ocean voyage but he batted away any questions about earlier times. I put his deflections down to the trauma of his father's premature death.

Catching Papa's eye I smiled, but he looked away into the distance. He'd contributed nothing to the conversation and stood up to excuse himself, retreating to his study with a cup of tea. I stared hard at Mother, expecting her to call him back but she was too busy laughing at one of Douglas's yarns and basking in his attention. Papa had left. I might as well have left too.

With the pair of them giggling like teenagers I felt like the spare part. I thought about why Papa had left the room. His exit, while quiet, had been hostile. I couldn't bear the idea that he disapproved of Douglas. Maybe Papa was under the weather. Maybe he was disappointed that Douglas had not completed the full engagement cycle with a ring, though my fiancé had a perfect answer for that too.

'I didn't want to presume anything, Alice. Besides, I have a plan in mind. You'll like it.'

Unusual though it was not to have a ring I was not especially concerned to be without one. Douglas's love was enough.

'The truth is I've seen the perfect ring for you in London. I'd buy it in a flash but with all the responsibilities I face at present I lack sufficient means to purchase it.' I didn't tell Papa this, fearing it might be a mark against our union. Besides which, Douglas was adamant that one day in the not too distant future he would be in a better position to buy the ring.

'Upon which I shall place it on your finger and the whole world will see how much I love you,' he finished with a grand flourish.

'I think I'd be happy with a curtain ring. Really, I would. You don't need to prove your love with something far too expensive.'

'You are a funny creature, Alice. I suppose I should tell you that there is an old family ring that passes down the Emery line. I could give you that if you like but in all honesty I don't much care for it. It's rather ugly. Please don't tell my Ma, though. She'd be horrified to hear me dismiss a family heirloom so casually.'

'I won't breathe a word,' I promised.

'That's my girl. I'd like to break with tradition and buy you something new. Something perfect. Just as soon as I can.'

That was enough for me at the time.

Not long after that, one fine afternoon, he took me for a walk through Hatton Garden.

'Close your eyes,' he said, ignoring my protestations. Now, open them.' He pointed me towards a shop front and guided me with his finger to the most expensive ring on display.

'See, that is the ring for you, Alice,' he declared, placing a big emphasis on 'that', as though no other ring would do. No denying its beauty; clusters of little diamonds and rubies twinkled in the sunshine, inviting attention and appreciation.

'Isn't it perfect?'

'Breathtaking.'

'I shall buy it for you,' he announced before pausing, 'though not today.'

'Douglas, you're not to spend money you don't have on a ring at that price.' I almost added that it didn't look very practical for a working pharmacist and would be a ludicrous expense for a man of little means with a mother and sister still needing his support.

'I don't believe my ears. A girl, refusing a ring? Alice, you are a one-off.' The aspiring home-maker in me commended my thrift and for saving him a small fortune. The money saved could go towards our new life as a married couple.

Unlike my peers I was not fixated on large stones and it did not trouble me to wait for the single gold band that would mark our union in the eyes of God. Douglas remained insistent that one day he would buy me the ring he coveted but in the meantime he presented me with a charming gold locket as a symbol of our engagement. The locket suited me down to the ground, or so people told me. But it wasn't quite complete and Douglas had a plan.

'What that locket needs is a fine picture inside it.'

We took a bus across town and called on an artist that Douglas loosely described as 'an old friend'. We arrived in front of an enormous house in Barons Court with windows that stretched from floor to ceiling. I'd been to a similar house in the area when running an errand for Professor Mason, though had never stepped inside. I didn't tell Douglas this. He assumed I didn't know the area. There was no good reason to disclose that I'd been in these parts before, nor the reason why.

The front door burst open to reveal a short man who embraced Douglas like a long-lost cousin.

'Good to see you again, Dougie. It's been too long.' An overbearing, overfamiliar individual tried to pull me into an embrace from which I recoiled. He chuckled and winked and led us upstairs to his studio, thankfully a beautiful space filled with natural sunlight.

'This used to be two rooms but I took a sledgehammer to the wall to create this.' I hoped it hadn't been a supporting wall.

Douglas cleared his throat. 'Shall we make a start?'

'You want me to paint Alice?'

I didn't like the way he looked me up and down, more objectified than a subject for a portrait.

I forget the name of the artist though I sat for him over several weeks. However, his visual features still come to mind. Lanky hair, an inch too long under his cap, ruddy cheeks of a bon vivant, and staring eyes that narrowed with suggestion They confirmed my suspicion that he dabbled in a different kind of life drawing. I never asked Douglas how he knew this man having no wish to delve into shadier elements of his past. Instead I sat as instructed, still as a mannequin while he studied my features. His portrayal of me was far more flattering than I expected and enhanced the reflection that greeted me from my bathroom mirror. The finished product was surprisingly good.

'Alice sits like a professional. She has unusual features that I find most enjoyable to paint.' He lowered his voice and addressed his next question to Douglas. 'Perhaps you might like to pose again, together this time, maybe with a more intimate pose?'

The wink he gave my fiancé was not lost on me either. Shocked to the core I insisted we leave immediately. We weren't even married. I would have refused anything untoward anyway. In the weeks that followed I made sure we did not return to Barons Court, nor did I expect our paths to cross again.

I sourced another aspiring artist to transpose my portrait and one of Douglas into miniature copies for inserting in the locket. It was unfortunate that the young fellow lacked skill and turned us into weak caricatures of ourselves but at least he was no louche.

In fact, the miniature portraits were verging on the comical, so two or three years into our marriage we arranged for professional photographs to be taken on one of the newly manufactured Beau Brownie cameras from Eastman Kodak. I took quite a respectable picture and Douglas smiled from ear to ear at his image.

'Not bad looking at all, even if I say so myself.' Douglas had a face for the camera.

We removed the poor quality drawings from the locket and pasted our two new photographs opposite each other like bookends. The promised engagement ring stayed in the window of the Hatton Garden jewellers. Douglas still declared his intentions to save for it but by the time we had sufficient funds to buy it, other matters were more pressing.

'Perhaps when we have our first child you might buy me an eternity ring,' I suggested.

'But of course. And it will be the finest ring you have ever seen.'

If only we'd had children perhaps things might have been different.

Our wedding was a simple event. The expense and fuss young couples go to on lavish receptions, designer dresses and novelty cakes these days appals me. I read an article in The Sunday Telegraph reporting the cost of the average wedding at £20,000 or more! And my heart sinks when betrothed couples appear at Church solely for the purpose of having a traditional wedding ceremony in a lovely setting. You can spot these couples a mile off, all flushed and furtive, the fiancé casting surreptitious looks at his oversized watch, his fiancée sweeping her eyes over the Church, mentally planning her flower arrangements and colour schemes. How predictable that these same couples then disappear from the congregation for months on end until the arrival of a baby and the need for a Christening. Poor Vicar. I daresay the Lord tells him to be tolerant and he dutifully toes the line. He has aspirations to be the Bishop one day, by which time he will be numb to the hypocrisy of people.

We had a modest wedding budget, respected to the

penny with only immediate family and Professor Mason invited to the service. Unfortunately the Professor sent his apologies. I'd have liked him to have been there but understood why he didn't attend.

There was no such thing as an evening reception. This was not unusual for the time. Money was scarce and mine was a frugal generation that knew how to make do and mend. The dear Reverend Harrison conducted the service, his voice booming. He'd led our Parish Church for decades. Papa gave me away, his back straight as a rod but with hands still trembling as we reached the altar. What a poor choice of hat Mother had made, garish and attention seeking, but I let her off for once. It was my wedding day after all and I would never have to live under her roof again.

We borrowed a Triumph Super 7 and drove to Bournemouth for a two-day honeymoon. I truly believed we were happy with high hopes for our marriage. I was even able to push aside the doubt that had been bothering me in the weeks running up to the wedding. Visiting Douglas's frail Mother one Sunday I was troubled by a conversation, accidently overheard.

I'd been coming in from the garden to help prepare tea and scones in the kitchen when something compelled me to stop in the hall. Hushed, angry voices. The clatter of a plate thrust with force on a surface. Douglas, arguing with his Mother. The content of their conversation rendered me immobile.

'Why isn't Alice wearing the Emery ring?' Douglas mumbled a response I couldn't catch. His Mother raised her voice. I pictured her standing beside the larder door, gripping the handle to steady herself.

'Douglas, surely to goodness you retrieved the ring from Anne?'

'We've had no contact. I can't go and see her.'

'Why on earth not?'

I missed what was said next as the Grandmother clock chimed the half hour. I glared at the clock face with irritation. Douglas's low timbre was impossible to hear, though the gasp in response was audible. My future Mother-in-law, normally so calm and sweet in disposition, cried out in anger.

'How could you? Your poor father will be turning in his grave. You should be ashamed of yourself.'

'For God's sake, Mother! You're being ridiculous.' This time I gasped, taking in his disrespectful response. Startled by a noise behind me in the hall I spun round to face Douglas's sister Elsie. She didn't seem to realise I'd been skulking in the hallway.

'Alice, there you are. How's the tea coming along? Look, I cut this for you.'

Elsie held out a plant cutting, an abelia or some sort of tree mallow. A thoughtful girl, dear Elsie. She knew I liked her garden. Such a shame she died so young and in such tragic circumstances. I turned towards her, feeling at once a need to protect her and to allow Douglas and his mother to finish their argument in private. I would have liked to ask who Anne was but didn't dare.

The kitchen voices fell to a hush and the door opened to reveal first mother then son, both with pinched faces. Elsie didn't pick up on the black mood hanging over them, thankfully too absorbed in her horticultural offerings. I struggled to make sense of what I'd heard. Douglas was supposedly close to his mother and they were not in the habit of arguing. Or so he'd always led me to believe.

His mother's cheeks were scorched with fury, showing more colour than I'd seen in them for weeks. Her poor health normally rendered her so pallid. Perhaps an argument wasn't such a bad thing if it improved her circulation. Even so, I had concerns for her welfare and stepped forward.

'Is there anything I can help with, Mrs Emery?'

She was short of breath and it wouldn't do her heart any good to become agitated. Douglas resembled a lost boy, head downcast, ill-equipped to redress the situation. I hoped that Elsie would distract us. Thankfully she did just that, affording the rest of us an opportunity to pull ourselves together.

I expected to see pain in Douglas's face, but when he lifted his head and caught my eye he took me by surprise with a broad smile that suggested he hadn't a care in the world. For a fleeting moment I wondered if I'd misunderstood the kitchen conversation and drawn the wrong conclusions. But then I noticed his Mother's shaking hands and watery eyes.

'I think I need to lie down for a while.' She offered her apologies and disappeared upstairs. Elsie's smile faded and her arms fell to her side.

'Oh my goodness. Poor Ma. She must have overexerted herself in the garden earlier. I did tell her not to get stuck into those weeds. I'll take her up a cup of milky tea.'

Douglas did his best to lighten the atmosphere but we didn't linger in the house and an uneasy feeling enveloped me. I couldn't decide how, or even whether to broach the subject of the row. There were gaps in my knowledge that I wanted to fill. But I hesitated to pry in matters that were not my business. Did I now have the right to probe, given that I would soon be his wife?

It was no secret that there had been a string of girls following Douglas before I arrived on the scene, but apart from the tall, blonde girl I hadn't been aware of anyone significant. The name Anne meant nothing to me. Rumours had circulated around Douglas in the corridors of the College ever since I'd known him but there was more air than substance to them. The most vicious suggestion concerned a student who had left the course suddenly amidst speculation that she was pregnant. At least one of my peers volunteered Douglas as a contender but by then I had no reason to doubt him. He was popular among women but this made him a target rather than a deviant. I had no good reason to doubt him. Throughout our courtship he had behaved correctly. The suggestion of having an intimate portrait painted I put down to a temporary lapse in judgement and anyhow, I blamed the artist for instigating that disgraceful idea.

Thoughts of Anne, whoever she was, niggled away at me. I toyed with the idea of investigating her identity further, but there was enough secrecy in my own life already with Professor Mason's covert assignments.

The wisest course of action at that moment was to say nothing.

Private concerns over the missing family ring fermented in my mind for weeks rather than months. Our wedding day approached and my thoughts turned to the vows that I was about to take. Any residual concerns slipped away, just as the Emery ring had apparently slipped out of family hands.

Douglas didn't mention Anne for the next decade. Neither did I, though I can't promise I didn't delve a little deeper when the opportunity arose, just to satisfy my curiosity.

Just because Douglas didn't mention Anne didn't mean he wasn't thinking about her. He should have been thinking of me.

It wasn't the sound of the wireless that brought me back to earth with a bump. It was a double ring of my doorbell. I'm not that deaf so don't understand why people think they need to press it twice. The calendar looked clear of visitors so I presumed it must be the postman. He rings the bell with the joyful enthusiasm of a toddler learning a new skill and is most excitable when delivering interesting looking parcels.

In spite of myself I had read the 'falls prevention' leaflet left by the lady Doctor. Basic information but useful. Armed with knowledge and good sense I leaned on my trusty stick and took my time to reach the front door.

Imagine my surprise when I looked through the peephole and saw the pale, young blonde outside. Not the postman checking up on me at all but the Doctor returning for a home visit, this time unscheduled. I almost didn't answer but thought she might do something rash and call for an ambulance so I opened the catch on the door and waved her inside, perhaps with a little more impatience than merited. At least her attire had improved. The vomit-inducing green Mac she'd turned up in previously was hopefully bagged up for the weekly bin collection.

'Good morning, Mrs Emery. I happened to be passing and thought I'd pop by and see how you were getting on. You're looking much better.'

All smiles and white teeth. Too white in my book. Very distracting.

'Good morning, Doctor. That is very kind of you, my dear, but as you can see I'm managing extremely well, thank you. Don't let me keep you from attending to the sick people who really need your help.'

'Oh that's quite alright, Mrs Emery. Please may I come in?'

What a very persistent young lady she is. Although it was irksome to be fussed over I appreciated the effort she'd made to call on me. She knew I had no family and I detected in her a genuine concern for my well-being that went beyond the perfunctory interest of a GP in a patient. Feeling initially obliged to be polite and latterly compelled to be hospitable, I offered her a cup of tea and was surprised when she accepted.

'That would be lovely, thank you.'

I even put out a plate of my favourite 'round brown' biscuits, though she only took one. She nibbled at the edges and we made small talk about the erupting volcano which shows no sign of submission.

'You've barely touched your tea.'

'I'm sorry. I've been feeling a little queasy these past few days.' She was of course referring to her pregnancy. I didn't have anything more to contribute on that subject so brought the conversation back to the volcano and asked if she knew anyone affected.

'We have family abroad at the moment so we're keeping an eye on events. I wouldn't say they're in dire straits, but they are in limbo at the moment.'

I showed what sympathy I could. We agreed that the best place to be was firmly on the ground, here in England. This has always been the country I have loved most and I hope I have served it to best of my abilities.

We admire my pretty garden and I am reminded of my good fortune to be living here and independently. Aside from my weakened shoulder I am in remarkably good health.

The Doctor's initial visit had left me in bad humour. Today's visit simply left me in peace. No evil green Mackintosh and two whole chocolate biscuits which made a very tasty mid-morning snack.

One mustn't grumble and it'll be my birthday soon, so that's something of an achievement too.

Chapter 8

Kate - keep on calling

'Wake up, sleepy. Friday's arrived.' Kate is full of cheer when Struan finally answers the phone with a groan.

'Already? I slept through both my alarms. Thank God it's almost the weekend. Can I call you back once I'm dressed?'

The weekend still seems a long way off to Kate who is working her way through the list of people she needs to call. Kate is an unashamed maker of lists and always has several on the go.

'Can't you go anywhere without highlighter pens or sticky notes?' Ellie asked when they last met for lunch at Joe Allens in Covent Garden. Kate opened her mouth to protest.

'Since you're almost an hour late you're hardly in a position to criticise. You may be the supreme queen of spontaneity but some of us,' she waved her shopping list in the air, 'don't like surprises. My system works fine.'

Next on the call list is Juliet who smiles down the phone as she fills Kate in with anecdotes of her pregnancy.

'At first I thought your brother had given me food poisoning again!' Kate pulls a face.

'He made me a stir-fry when I came in from a late shift and I started being ill that same night. At the time I blamed him for reheating the rice.'

'Well, it wouldn't be the first time.' Craig hadn't meant to poison them all a few years ago with his Boxing Day attempt at turkey burgers so Kate can well believe that her brother might have unwittingly poisoned his poor, unsuspecting wife. He's blessed with cerebral agility rather than culinary skill. Even though he throws himself into the cooking process with abandon, inspired by Saturday Kitchen and countless episodes of Master Chef, his enthusiasm won't amount to a Michelin star anytime soon. He'd be lucky to make it past an invention test. As a student he survived on pot noodles and toasted sandwiches and frequented his local Chinese restaurant so often that he was invited to the chef's New Year celebrations. Why Juliet, an excellent cook lets Craig loose in her kitchen is something Kate will never understand.

'When the nausea carried on and I started nodding off at three o'clock in the afternoon the penny finally dropped. You'd have thought that two medics would have realised a bit sooner that I was pregnant. I feel a bit of an idiot, to be honest.'

'It's understandable. Maybe subconsciously you didn't want to get your hopes up?'

'Probably. I'd begun to lose faith to be honest.' Juliet's voice tails off as she recalls moments of abject disappointment. An inability to conceive over the past few years. Moments of anticipation, excitement, trepidation. And then disappointment. Hope followed by its opposite number. They tried everything they could think of. Craig even placed himself on a virility diet made up predominantly of venison, scallops, avocados and strawberries.

'Virility diets aren't cheap,' he told them. 'They actually involve eating out in some of the best restaurants in London.' Kate could only shake her head at him. Produce that had been 'air freighted for freshness' was off limits, costing necessary virility points as well as having a damaging environmental impact. Craig became an expert on locally sourced produce and enjoyed the excuse to gorge himself on soft fruits from Kent and Perthshire, comparing the fruits of England with their cousins in Scotland. According to him, both were delicious and hard to separate in quality terms, especially when consumed alongside great dollops of whipped cream. He assured everyone that dairy products were also essential for his diet. Perhaps there was some good science involved. After all, Juliet was pregnant and on her way to motherhood at last.

'The irony is that after being so unsuccessful we decided at Christmas to give ourselves a break and forget babies for a while. I nearly passed out when the test showed positive. All I have to do now is practice what I preach and lay off the alcohol. Not that I fancy it anyway. I can just about stomach a milky coffee and that's about it.'

Kate is so delighted that her brother and sister-in-law have been caught positively off guard with the pregnancy. Juliet often spoke to her about wanting to have a large family and is brilliant with her nieces and nephews.

The exact moment that Kate discovered she was expecting Isla is firmly etched in her mind. It's not the sort of thing a mother forgets. Her monthly cycle was so predictable that she'd known something significant was happening early on. An unmistakably thin blue line appeared on the pregnancy testing stick one Thursday morning. Perched on the edge of the bath Kate held the positive result in her hand and held the news in her heart for a few minutes. A momentary secret before she rushed into the kitchen to share the news with Struan. Their relationship was still in its infancy but she never doubted for a minute that he'd react with joy. He didn't disappoint. On hearing the news he lifted her off her feet and twirled her round and round the room until she became so dizzy she had to tell him to stop. Later he wrapped his arms around her as they lay on the sofa watching Love Actually and demolishing a large bar of dark chocolate made from the purest Peruvian cocoa beans.

They waited until Isla was born before getting married. It wasn't that Kate was bothered about not fitting into a dress, but she'd been afflicted by the kind of morning sickness that wasn't confined to the morning. Aside from that, neither she nor Struan was concerned about re-jigging the order of life's big events. Who was to say whether getting married before having children was the right thing to do when neither of them held firm religious beliefs? They opted for an understated humanist service at the registry office on Victoria Street with only immediate family, a handful of close friends and baby Isla in attendance.

Kate's only regret was that her parents hadn't lived long enough to see her happily married. An area of very low pressure took hold over her when her father died, a sudden heart attack cutting his life short by too many years. Bleak times prevailed with the passing of her mother the following spring. Everyone maintained she'd died of a broken heart even though her death certificate recorded pancreatic cancer as the cause. She'd either ignored or missed the symptoms. When Kate had pointed out her mother's sudden weight loss her concerns had been dismissed, her mother's diminishing frame attributed to grief. Being prone to back pain meant she hadn't recognised anything more sinister. Or had chosen not to. By the time cancer was diagnosed there were no treatment options available. Only palliative care. Many tears were shed and Craig, Ellie and Kate leant hard on each other for support.

With both parents gone and an acrimonious relationship break up all in the space of 12 months it was hardly surprising that the acute sense of loss Kate experienced left her in touching distance of a nervous breakdown. Even the kind words of the Vicar at her parents' funerals left her searching. She'd been let down by the world but felt most let down by the God she'd been told to believe in from childhood. She renounced religion.

And yet it felt like some sort of miracle when she found Struan. He was the beacon of light at the end of a very dark tunnel.

Kate wondered if her mother would have been disappointed in her. Not in her choice of husband. Everyone agreed that Struan was a great catch. But the wedding itself was understated and secular. Her mother would have urged her towards a more traditional ceremony and a more rigorous agenda. Even the photographer had turned up late. Kate, normally so organised, for once hadn't been concerned. The people who really mattered had all been there and some of them even remembered to send cards in time for their first wedding anniversary. Struan's mother had also forgiven Kate for stealing her only son from under her nose. She whispered to her husband behind her hand, just loud enough for people to hear.

'At least she's a thrifty lass, Campbell. This one won't be causing Struan any financial bother.'

The wedding marked the first time that Kate had done anything more unconventional than her sister; her non-religious ceremony a smack in the face for the Christian faith into which she'd been born. Ellie on the other hand had ended up with a conventional white wedding at St Mary's, the church they'd attended as children. Wildcat Ellie had been partially tamed by the very reliable James who'd proposed on bended knee the night of her 21st birthday. A corporate lawyer for one of London's big city firms, James was the only person who had ever achieved last word status over Ellie. She'd met her match at last, much to the amusement of everyone who had ever lost an argument with her. Her wedding comprised an altogether more lavish affair than Kate's with no expense spared. At the reception Kate had to stop her brother from scribbling down his estimates for the cost of the nuptials on the back of a napkin.

'Craig, behave yourself! That's Egyptian cotton. You can't write on that.'

Kate smiles at the memory as she doodles on the hotel's complimentary note pad, wondering why Struan hasn't called her back yet. Worried that he might have rolled over and gone back to sleep she dials home again.

'Hello?'

'Thought you were going to call me back?'

The call turns out to be short and sweet, but not very satisfying as Struan's running so late and is in the throes of getting a very belligerent Isla ready for nursery.

'Did you have a good night's sleep?'

His response is curt and uncharacteristically grumpy.

'No. After you phoned last night I stuck some washing in the machine and then stayed up past midnight to watch a documentary about murder and gang warfare in Glasgow. It was really interesting.'

Kate grimaces.

'Oh dear. It sounds like you spent the night binging on all the TV programmes I can't stand.'

'Well, I found it so good I forgot to unload the bloody washing machine before going to bed. Then, just as I dropped off to sleep Isla woke up and needed to be settled. That took a full hour.' Struan's normal good humour is several steps behind him.

'You do sound a bit harassed.' This is all the support she can offer him given the several hundred miles that separate them.

'I could murder a strong coffee! Look, everything's under control, but since you're on the phone do you know where I can find Mouse? I've only just realised there's a teddy bears' picnic at the nursery today and Isla only wants to take bloody Mouse. None of the other 55 soft toys lying on the floor of her bedroom will do. Oh, and does she have a clean pair of tights? Not Mouse, obviously. I mean Isla. I can't find any. What drawer do we keep them in?'

Kate does her level best to guide Struan in the direction of the tights but can do nothing to help identify the whereabouts of Mouse, Isla's favourite soft toy. Mouse could be anywhere from the laundry basket to the kitchen cupboard. It's impossible to even hazard a guess because her daughter has a habit of hiding toys in the most obscure places.

'Maybe we should have Mouse electronically tagged?' Struan is only half-joking as he rifles through wardrobes and drawers and swears under his breath.

Judging by the noises over the phone he's turning the flat over with the speed of an opportunist intruder but without the precision of the forensic scientist. Kate can only imagine what state her home will be in when she gets back. She wishes him luck. He barely hears her because Isla is wailing in the background.

She picks up the phone again. This time she dials the number of brand manager Daniel, or Dan as he prefers to be called. She takes a deep breath. This conversation won't be easy but she's hoping that by calling at this hour she can get the pain over early.

'Daniel, it's Kate Gilmore. I'm calling from Paris with news from the research groups. How was last night's awards ceremony?'

'Kate, thanks for calling so early. I had an amazing night. I'm only sorry I couldn't come to sit in on the focus groups.' His tone sounds anything but regretful. Kate hears the giggle of a female companion in the room. This should make her job easier. At least Dan has something positive going on at his end to take his mind off the bad news she's about to break. Even so, she doesn't want to be the one to burst his bubble.

'I hate to be the bearer of bad news, but based on last night's feedback we need to revise the concepts.' Dan gives a frustrated sigh and Kate pictures him pacing the room at the other end of the phone, his companion shooting a quizzical look in his direction.

'I don't buy that. The concepts look fine to me. I wrote some of them myself. What are the key headlines from the research? I don't have much time. Make it brief, will you?'

Dan's retorts to Kate's verbal summary become more and more challenging until he cuts across her to stop her dead in her tracks.

'I've heard enough. With all due respect, I've been to a few research groups in my time. In my opinion most consumers know nothing and French consumers know less than nothing. There wouldn't have been a Walkman if Sony had listened to consumers.'

Ever the diplomat Kate holds back and counts to 10, although she's itching to put him in his place and tell him he's an arse. She'll save her response for the full report and she won't let him get away with writing off his customers so easily. Last night's Parisian ladies were eloquent and insightful, qualities that her fresh-faced brand manager doesn't possess. She tactfully puts it to him that the audience he's referring to, whilst dismissive of his ideas, are his customers. Their loyalty will pay his bonus.

He snorts with derision. 'I'm not killing these concepts. This is my baby, Kate and they're strong ideas.'

'I'm not suggesting we 'kill the concepts', Daniel but this is an iterative process, not a fait accompli. All I'm suggesting is we listen to customer feedback, make revisions where necessary and improve on what we have.'

He might have won a shiny award for marketing excellence but they both know Dan will be judged on the failure or success of Bon Appétit! and Kate begins to wonder if he might have an intolerance to lactose. He starts to choke on something and Kate cuts in while she has the chance.

'Let's schedule a meeting as soon as I'm back.' Even though she doesn't particularly rate him Kate will do her best to help Dan shine. He'll need all the help she can give him to turn this one around.

'Agreed. I'll get my PA to call you.'

Kate breathes a big sigh of relief to have that call behind her. She can at last make her fourth and final call of the morning to check the status of her return flight at lunchtime. More bad news. A recorded voice informs her that the airline is 'experiencing an extremely high volume of calls' owing to the volcanic ash cloud and she's placed in a queue. Indefinitely. Kate turns to the internet. The airline's website initially crashes before eventually confirming flights are being cancelled left, right and centre.

With UK airspace likely to remain closed, Kate toys with the idea of staying put for one more night. A second night in Paris would have thrilled her to the core once upon a time but the pile of project work in the office and the ever-increasing ironing mountain at home are nattering her conscience, not to mention her desire to get back to Struan and Isla. She just wants to be at home enjoying a soak in the bath in the comfort of her own bathroom, playing her own music and relaxing in the warm glow of her Diptyque candles.

The internet casts up more information about the plume of ash spewing from the volcano. Kate sits in front of her computer, transfixed by the imagery of the volcano and impressed by the sheer force of nature.

A further announcement tells her the prospect of

reopening UK airspace is due at lunchtime. Kate weighs up her options. At a push she can stay another night in Paris. Furnished with all the latest technology, working remotely offers a solution of sorts. Alternatively she could chance her luck and head out to the airport in the hope that flights might resume before too long. And if planes stay grounded she could just head back to Gare du Nord and catch the Eurostar direct to London. Her confidence grows based on a belief that options for returning home are still open.

Ever the optimist Kate settles on the airport option as her first choice. She packs her bags and retrieves her jewellery from the bedside table. The locket falls open to reveal a smiling Struan on one side and Isla on the other, plastered over the top of the mystery woman. Pictures on the left hand side have changed over the years but not until Isla was born was Kate able to paste anything over the rightful owner's picture on the right hand side. She acknowledges that it's misplaced nostalgia on her part but she reveres the austere lady's image all the same.

The girls at reception try to deter Kate from heading to Charles de Gaulle, telling her it's pure madness to leave the city centre.

'Madame, why not spend another night in Paris and enjoy the opportunity to go shopping?' Kate might be tempted were it not for the fact the hotel is fully occupied for the coming night, so she has to vacate her room anyway.

'We regret you cannot stay with us, Madame, but there is a very smart hotel across the street that has a vacancy for tonight.' With folded hands and a small shake of her sleek hair, the petite receptionist is a vision of contrition. Other than suggesting the neighbouring hotel she doesn't offer to source alternative accommodation. The phones on the desk need to be dealt with but more importantly her cigarette break is 20 minutes overdue. Kate has already paid for her room and handed back the key. She's no longer a guest. The concerns of the reception staff lie elsewhere.

Kate folds her hotel bill neatly and gathers her things together. She's no desire to root around for a new hotel, quelling any remaining doubts she might have had about heading for the airport.

Finding a taxi is easy enough and this boosts Kate's confidence further. En route to Charles de Gaulle Terminal Two, she reassures herself that she's made the right decision. The taxi driver, a macho Latin type is less convinced and takes great pleasure in teasing her, imploring her to stay in Paris, if only for the purpose of pursuing an amorous liaison with him.

'You can always stay with me, Mademoiselle. You would let me take care of you, yes?' He tries to catch her eye in the rear-view mirror but Kate finds him very easy to resist.

He's not a bad sort and she takes his banter in good faith. Even so, the crumpled card he thrusts upon her with his scrawled phone number makes it no further than the first bin she finds outside the airport's terminal building.

As she steps through the sliding doors to face a seething mass of people, Kate's residual confidence about returning home is sucked clean out of her. She kicks herself for being so naïve. What on earth possessed her to believe that it was a good idea to leave behind a comfortable hotel on the Left Bank for this? She looks around in horror as she surveys the scene. The airport has descended into utter chaos. She made a mistake in coming here.

THREE

She looks back through the sliding doors but the taxi driver is long gone.

Chapter 9

Kate - take me back

The airport churns travellers and the space between them decreases by the minute. People with tickets for elsewhere are stuck in the system, desperate for reliable flight information that's not forthcoming. Everyone receives the same brush off by the airline companies. Frustration fills the air. Kate joins a line of people going nowhere. A rip current pulls the crowd towards an area where a smartly dressed member of the ground crew looks set to make an announcement. Speculative noise dips as the woman opens her mouth to speak. Kate strains to hear and understands enough from the collective sigh of disappointment and murmurings from those closest to the staff member to understand that travel news is not good. The blanket banning of flights over the UK has been extended to include most of Northern Europe. No one will be flying anywhere for several hours at least.

'We need a bleedin' magic carpet,' suggests the giant of a man to her right. His arms are weighed down by Disney merchandise acquired from a trip of a lifetime to the magical kingdom east of Paris. He looks over his shoulder and gives a thumbs down sign to his partner, a lumpy woman with two-tone hair. The pink top she is only just about wearing features the sketched face of a famously slim catwalk model. Kate wonders if the woman thinks osmosis might step in to help her shed some pounds. If so, she'll have a long wait. Her t-shirt is bursting at the seams. The woman screws up her face as she decodes her partner's signal underlining the continued delay.

'Oh, for fuck's sake.' She starts dishing out sweets to the three children who've been clambering over the luggage trolley. They immediately begin to squabble and push and in doing so nearly propel the trolley in one direction and bags in another.

'Jaxon! Liberty! Mason! For Christ's sake, stop that right now will you or you won't get no more sweets.'

As the woman bends down to catch her vanity case, her t-shirt rises up to reveal a wide expanse of flesh bound by the thin elastic of her underwear. She has the figure of a secret snacker. A rose tattoo grows more like an unruly weed from the belt of her white jeans and her jeans sit a good inch below the line of her pants. Kate can almost hear Struan muttering, 'Mmm, classy' under his breath at the sight. Embarrassed to realise that she's staring, Kate hurriedly looks away and takes a defensive step to her left as the crowd surges again. She brushes against someone, who then stands on someone else's foot and resulting apologies spring forth over luggage battered knees and trodden down toes. How long before all the people collapse on each other like dominoes?

'I don't understand why we have to wait here in this maelstrom. Charles? Are you even listening to me? Why aren't we sitting in the BA lounge? I thought you were a silver card holder.' In the next tidal push of the crowds Kate finds herself alongside a well-heeled couple in their 40s. She catches the eye of the woman who's just spoken. Her husband is intent on reading the small print of the document in his hand, the terms and conditions of his insurance policy absorbing his full concentration. Kate feels the warmth of the woman's approval when she receives a direct smile and a nod of recognition that she too is deserving of a place far away from the hoi polloi. The man called Charles grasps the opportunity to escape and slips away under the pretext of making a call. He leaves his wife as a marker just in case a miracle flight to London is called. He needn't worry. The line won't be moving anywhere anytime soon. The woman's eyes flash at his parting figure. Eager to strike up conversation she leans towards Kate so that her voice can be heard over the noise of the crowd.

'We're trying to get back to London for the start of school.' She gestures to two dark headed boys standing behind her. They've made a very good job of being inconspicuous, one with his head bent over a computer game, the other plugged into an MP3 player. Kate reckons they must be in their final year of primary school. They look like twins. She can't see much of their faces, their heads locked into their gadgets. But what she can see of them suggests they came from a single cell that divided. Both remain totally oblivious to the ambient noise and uncertainty around them. They have the nonchalant look of seasoned travellers in spite of the fact they can only be 11 or 12 at most.

Kate welcomes the distraction of conversation with the boys' mother spurred on by a sudden pang of loneliness, a longing for home and the need for a bit of female solidarity.

'London? You might be in with a chance of getting there.

I'm waiting for news about Edinburgh.'

The woman's face lights up and she coos with delight. 'Oh, Edinburgh. One of my favourite cities. We visited last year for the Festival. One of our good friends was performing in a show there, you know. Not in the Fringe. He's a professional opera singer. On the international stage. He sang in Macbeth with one of the better companies. We took a suite in The Balmoral.' She has a faraway look in her eyes. 'It's a wonderful hotel. In the most atmospheric of cities. You're lucky to live there.'

'Yes, I think so too.'

'You don't have a Scottish accent. Were you schooled in England?'

'No, I'm from the south coast originally but my husband's from Edinburgh so I moved up there after we met. I love the city too. It has so much to offer and it's a perfect place to bring up a family. I just wish it were a bit closer at the moment.'

'Yes, yes, I know exactly what you mean. We've been in Paris for a mini break. I wanted to pop over so the boys could improve their French before they take their entrance exams for big school.' She nods at the two dark heads still locked into their devices before lowering her voice.

'We assumed this whole thing with the volcano was simply a storm in a teacup, but Charles thinks it may go on for days and days. The boys are meant to be back at school next week and I've still got to have them fitted for new shoes. They've both grown so much. Our dogs are in kennels. I thought I'd be picking them up tonight, poor darlings.' She thrusts the latest smartphone under Kate's nose to show off images of two English springer spaniels.

'See, my babies! Far less trouble than children, believe me. Just look at them. Aren't they adorable?' She doesn't bother to wait for a response from Kate, affirmative or otherwise. 'I also have my hair and nails done on Saturdays. I hate having to cancel,' she finishes off with a heavy sigh. 'It's a complete nightmare.'

Kate considers whether missing a haircut or manicure is really that important, and decides that it doesn't quite meet her criteria of 'a complete nightmare'. The dogs will survive an extended stay in the kennels, roughing it alongside regular dogs even if they are pedigree with treble-barrelled names. As for the boys, well Paris is hardly bereft of shoe shops. Kate has a good handle on world events and calls to mind sinister scenarios in corrupt and conflict-ridden countries, each one of which could be credibly described as 'a complete nightmare'. All the same, she understands a mother's frustrations and the irritation that comes from breaking a commitment. Being stuck in limbo is inconvenient, and worse when you have children in tow. She makes the right kind of sympathetic noises while her mind calculates a shift in strategy. This queue is locked in place and heading towards a dead end. It doesn't look like any of them will make progress if they stay here.

'I'm going to check out options on Eurostar,' Kate declares with naïve confidence. 'It's going to be a long journey home but at least I'll be heading in the right direction.'

'I'd hurry if I were you,' says the woman as she slips her phone back into her Mulberry handbag. 'My husband's PA has been on the case all morning. She's the most tenacious woman I've ever met. But even that fierce bulldog can't get us on Eurostar to St Pancras until Monday at the very earliest and you'd think we'd be a priority, what with the boys going back to school on Tuesday. The only saving grace is that Monday's an in-service day for the teachers so the boys won't miss anything then. But they'll be back at their desks on Tuesday even if it means I have to send them via courier.' She laughs heartily at her own joke and then leans in again towards Kate with a serious look on her face. 'Do you know how much it costs to educate two boys at Carrow Court?' Kate, who has no idea shakes her head, an unnecessary gesture given the woman's obvious penchant for rhetorical questions.

'Exorbitant. That's all I can say. I could have had a yacht and moorings at Puerto Banús for the amount we've paid already. But what choice does one have?' Kate nods out of politeness but isn't really listening. It's not as if the woman has noticed that she's switched off. When Kate tunes back into the conversation the woman is still harping on about the fees.

'We pay far too much to allow the boys to miss even half a day's teaching. Imagine if they fell behind in their Latin? They have perfect attendance records, both of them. One hundred per cent. Even when they've looked a bit peaky, a spoonful of Calpol still works wonders, thank God! I'm thinking of buying shares in the company that makes it. Bloody marvellous stuff.'

'What do you think you'll do about getting home?' Kate asks as she gathers her bags together.

'I suppose we'll be forced to head back into Paris for a couple of days.' The woman shakes her chestnut highlighted hair and Kate is reminded of a horse. 'I'm not really in the mood but we'll just have to get on with it. We're English so it shouldn't be too hard to raise some Dunkirk spirit.'

Kate gives a weak smile. She's heard enough and anxious stirrings in the pit of her stomach are kicking in. Her heart beats a little faster as she fears her options for returning home are dissolving as more people continue to arrive, pressing for information.

'I'm so sorry but I'm starting to feel a bit unwell.' Kate edges away from the queue. Struan will manage well enough without her, won't he? Under normal circumstances, yes. But nothing is normal. Irrational worries press the surface of her consciousness. What if Isla falls seriously ill and has to go to hospital? What if Struan trips and breaks his ankle on the way home? Isla will be the last child left in the Tweenie room at Cheeky Tiger Cubs waiting with her coat and empty lunch box, wailing at the top of her voice and wondering why her parents have abandoned her.

'Stop these ridiculous thoughts,' Kate tells herself but claustrophobia and a lack of control feed her anxiety. She walks at speed against the flow of people in the terminal building when suddenly her vision fogs and her legs threaten to give way. She should have had breakfast and her sugar levels are probably low. Kate looks around for a place to sit down so she can retrieve the bar of chocolate from her handbag, a staple for emergencies.

She finds a seat on a hard, aluminium bench just as her phone begins to ring. It's a withheld number so she almost doesn't answer in case it's Daniel and his ego, but it might be important and she needs to silence the annoying ringtone anyway. Kate drops the bar of chocolate and answers by the third ring, holding her mobile to her right ear and pressing her hand over her left ear so that she can hear past the noise surrounding her.

'Allo âllo, Kate ma belle!'

The voice at the other end is joyous and relief washes over Kate as she recognises her sister's voice. This conversation won't require the level of concentration she'd have invested in a client call. She takes her left hand away from her ear so that she can retrieve the now tired looking bar of chocolate. Ellie won't mind if she only has half her sister's attention. She probably won't even notice that Kate's a bit side-tracked.

'How goes it in gay Paree? I hear you're stuck, just like us!'

Ellie is a far more amiable person in adulthood than she was in childhood and has dropped her spiteful ways, although she still bares sharp teeth to anyone who crosses her. Many a Chief Executive has received a letter of complaint from Ellie in response to bad customer service, poor communications or incompetency (perceived as well as actual) and she invariably emerges victorious with written apologies and wide-ranging forms of compensation. She enjoys a good fight with her opponents and always goes for a clean knockout rather than a win on points.

Ellie and family have been in Florida this past week, ostensibly to visit Disney World with the children but in truth the trip was arranged to allow James to reveal his impressive golf handicap to one of his American clients. He also wanted to showcase his ridiculously expensive new watch to the same client who has a penchant for rare timepieces.

'You don't sound too perturbed to be stranded, Ellie.

Where are you calling from? Orlando?'

'I'm delighted. Where others see hassle, I see a wonderful opportunity to do battle with the travel insurance company.'

'Good luck. There's bound to be an exclusion on acts of God and I'm guessing an erupting volcano falls into that category.'

'Bring it on! I will challenge every exclusion they can throw at me.' Kate doesn't doubt it. Ellie will launch herself at the insurance company with a might that would leave even the Almighty shaking. Acts of God have nothing on Reactions of Ellie.

'You wouldn't believe what fun we're having. We can't get a flight back to London until next week, but wait for this! We've managed to book ourselves on a flight to New York instead and James has found us the best boutique hotel in Manhattan. I can't wait to go shopping!'

'What about the children? Aren't they due back at school next week?' Kate swallows the piece of chocolate she's been trying to suck. She assumes her niece and nephew's school term must work on a similar time frame to Carrow Court as they're also educated in London at another of the more exclusive fee-paying schools. She pictures their tarnished attendance record. Ellie and James regard holidays as a human right and an essential part of the children's home education curriculum. They have no qualms about skipping the beginning, middle or end of term and despite their affluence they still like to take advantage of cheaper, term-time flights. Besides which, Ellie has a score to settle with the school secretary, a stickler for rules and cruelly nicknamed the Pedant as a result.

'Oh chill out, Kate. It won't do them any harm missing a few days of school. The Pedant will have a fit.' Ellie's childish scorn makes a brief reappearance. 'I can almost feel her fury from here. Besides, New York is an education in itself. It'll be good for the kids.'

'I'm not sure shopping in Bloomingdales is on the curriculum.'

'Whose side are you on? Anyway, remember James has funded that Scholarship for Cultural Achievement. It was my idea and I think you'll agree it was a stroke of genius. I'll take the kids to the American Museum of Natural History and the Pedant will just have to clench her teeth when she calculates the absence figures for the term.'

'I don't know whether to admire or disapprove of your audacity.'

'Approve, obviously. Watch and learn. Admire and adopt.'

Maybe it's the chocolate, maybe it's her sister's energy or perhaps it's a combination of the two but Kate has perked up with Ellie's call. Her own anxieties sink back below the surface.

'So while we're off to NYC, what are your plans? You'll have to ride out the storm in Paris, lucky thing. You couldn't have chosen a better place. Pick up some macarons from Ladurée while you're there, won't you? I'd ask you to order a dozen for me but they won't be fresh by the time we get back.' Kate is about to answer when a loud announcement overhead cuts her short. She can't make out a word of it and Ellie is speaking again.

'James was talking to Bill earlier.'

'Bill?'

'You know, one of the partners at the firm. The one who does all those ultramarathons. You met him at our New Year bash. Anyway, he's in Paris too. You should meet up with him. After all, there are no spaces left on Eurostar, are there?' Kate isn't reassured to hear this particular piece of news for the second time, but Ellie has more.

'And you can't even take the train to Calais to catch a ferry.'

'Can't I?'

'No, you can't. Because of the rail strike. See how knowledgeable I am?' Ellie finishes with a flourish. 'So sit tight, sister and enjoy yourself. That's an order!'

'Bloody Hell, Ellie. Since when were you a global travel correspondent?' Kate's flummoxed by how well informed her sister is. She's forgotten the SNCF staff grievances about working conditions. She hadn't actually thought of a channel crossing by boat but now her mind starts to compute new options.

'Ellie, I'm so glad you phoned. If I get myself to the port at Calais I might be able to get on a ferry.'

'Well, if you do you win the complete fucking madness award.' Ellie's frustration rings through clear as a bell. 'For Christ's sake Kate. Live a little, will you. It'll be good for Struan to have some daddy time with Isla and you can treat yourself to a much deserved weekend in Paris. Think about it. No bath. No bedtime routine. No screaming tantrums. Imagine, you could be sitting in a Michelin-starred restaurant with views of the Eiffel Tower enjoying a glass of wine and a sensational meal. No need to sit there on your lonesome either. I'll text you Bill's number. Be a good girl and promise to give him a call.'

'Absolutely not.' Kate protests but Ellie's insistence gathers momentum.

'He's not an ogre, Kate. Just do it. You have nothing to fear and only fun memories to gain. I'm telling you to go out for dinner, not have an affair. Hey, I have to go, they're calling our Newark flight. Don't let me down now. Ciao bella.'

Her whirlwind of a sister is gone. Kate has no intention of calling James's partner from the law firm, ogre or otherwise. Nor has she any intention of staying in Paris for the weekend. Come what may she is determined to get herself home. Train travel is out, what with the strike, but there's nothing to stop her from hiring a car to drive to Calais. Kate stands up and promptly sits down again. She hasn't brought her driving licence. She only has her passport and that won't be enough to get her hands on the keys to a car. She'll need a healthy dose of charm and good luck to persuade the staff to rent out any vehicle without the right documentation. She gets to her feet again, brushing a tiny shard of chocolate from her sleeve and makes her way towards Arrivals in search of a rental car company and an understanding member of staff.

Another massive crowd swarms around the car rental booths and Kate groans. Once again she's been too slow to act and her exit route is blocked. There's no way that supply will meet demand. Even the biggest company won't have a ready fleet of cars to accommodate the needs of every traveller. Kate's overnight bag suddenly feels as though it's been filled with rocks. She drops it with a thud.

Kate turns to the right and makes her way over to a small area in the corner where a little bar is doing a great trade in coffee and alcohol. She needs to rethink her options and makes a beeline for a small table in the corner, half of which is concealed behind a pillar. Only when she walks around the pillar can she see that the table is already occupied. There are three chairs at the table, two of which she hadn't seen. A man with greying temples, probably in his early 50s is sitting in one chair, one ear glued to a smartphone. He's gesticulating with his free hand and firing rapid instructions into the phone in an American accent. The chair to his left is piled high with luggage.

Kate makes an open, friendly gesture to the man, non-verbally asking if she might be permitted to sit in the vacant chair. A momentary look of annoyance at being interrupted sweeps over his face but he shifts from his seat, without drawing breath, to make space for her. His American accent makes her think of Ellie who by now will be pushing past people to board her plane to Newark. Kate glances at her watch. Struan will be in a meeting, drinking his second cup of black coffee of the day. Isla will be outside playing in the nursery garden with her best friend Tom, her red duffle coat vibrant in the spring sunshine. Kate misses her little girl. If only she could be home by pick-up time. From nowhere, tears threaten with a tell-tale lump in the back of her throat. She's unable to hold them back and fat drops trickle down her cheeks. She focuses hard on the surface of the table in a futile attempt to regain some composure. It's embarrassing to lose control like this, especially in a public place. Not daring to look around in case she catches anyone's eye, she bends over her bag to look for a pack of tissues.

'Excuse me, ma'am but are you alright?'

Kate freezes. She's mortified. The man is speaking to her,

loudly and slowly as though she's a child. Or worse still, some sort of idiot.

'Do. You. Speak. English?' He builds deliberate spaces in between each word, trying his hardest to be understood, assuming she's French.

Kate attempts a wobbly smile and looks up, watery-eyed. She nods, not trusting her voice to speak but aware that she needs to explain she's actually British and can understand him perfectly. More importantly she really needs a tissue. Her eyes are glassy with tears and her nose has started to run.

'I'm sorry but do you happen to have a tissue?'

An enormous hanky is thrust into her hand and Kate breathes a sigh of relief when the man's mobile phone rings. It's turning out to be a good day for the mobile phone providers and the networks seem to be holding up so far. She discreetly blows her nose and takes a few deep breaths, closing her eyes as she does so. What's happening to her? She can't remember the last time she felt so flaky.

The American finishes his call and smiles at her, revealing very white teeth.

'I'm going to fetch a coffee.' He points to the adjacent bar. 'Can I get one for you?' Kate's just about managing to compose herself and is relieved to hear that she can speak without bursting into tears.

'Thank you, I'd love one actually. An espresso, please.'

He isn't gone for long and returns with two espressos and a small glass of a golden brown liquid that looks and smells like Armagnac. He places the glass in front of Kate who has moved her chair a little way behind the pillar, as though to better shield herself from the surrounding mayhem.

'I thought you looked like you needed something stronger.' Kate hesitates. She's on the brink of declining the drink as it's a bit presumptuous of him. The man catches her hesitancy.

'For purely medicinal purposes you understand. I'm told a drop of Armagnac is very good for shock. And for relieving redness of the eyes,' he adds, his own cheeks a blush pink. Kate smiles gratefully, willing to concede. She won't be going anywhere soon by the looks of things. What's the harm in having a small drop of something to calm her nerves? It's not so different from the brandy her grandparents used to prescribe when she was in her teens and learning about life.

'Thank you. That's really very kind of you. I've just been a bit overwhelmed by all of this.' She indicates the terminal building and the stagnant pools of people that fill the floor.

'You're welcome. I'd join you in a drink but I had a heavy night last night.' His cheeks are still flushed now she looks properly at him, though she suspects the red tinge shows more than one night's overindulgence.

Ten minutes pass. Kate sips her drink alongside her espresso while explaining her predicament. Her companion has introduced himself as Brett Maslan, Vice-President of a company she's never heard of, one which is entering 'a new growth phase', according to Brett. This means making the most of business opportunities across Europe.

'Harlaw International will be a household name in Great Britain in five years, six years tops. I guarantee it. We're recession proof.'

'Well, that's great. Not every company has that confidence.'

'I can smell success, Kate and it smells good. Real good. Failure's never an option for me.'

Brett constantly checks emails on his phone while making vague attempts to listen to Kate's predicament. Judging by the number and frequency of bleeps alerting him to new messages he is much in demand. He nurses his phone in one hand as though his five-year strategy for growth depends on it.

'Well, Kate. It's very fortuitous that you happened to stop by my table. I believe I have the solution you're looking for. In actual fact, I am the solution you're looking for.' He puffs out his chest and Kate is overcome by a sudden urge to giggle. The Armagnac must be doing its job. Her heart rate's dropped and she's starting to feel more relaxed, even if she has no idea what he's about to propose.

'You're looking at the last person in Paris to have procured a rental car.' He locks his hands behind his head and leans back, showing damp patches of sweat under his arms. 'It's the smallest car I'll ever drive but a small car is better than no car. They're just cleaning it up for me. See, I need to be in London for a very important meeting on Monday. I gave the rental guys a small incentive to help. I'm driving up to Calais this afternoon.' Kate sits up in her seat as she takes in what he's saying. Could she, would she dare to ask this man for a lift? Is he about to offer her a space in the car? Would someone sensible like her even consider a car share with a man she doesn't know?

'I already offered a lift to a guy I met here. I don't mind helping out people in trouble. But I can't take a carful because of all this.' He gestures to the luggage. 'How much luggage do you have?'

'Just these bags. I travel light.'

'Good girl. You're slim. I'm sure we can squeeze you in. So, what do you say?'

Under normal circumstances Kate would have declined his offer. There is something about the lingering way he looks at her that makes her squirm. But normal circumstances have taken their leave and no one knows when they'll be back. And with the other guy acting as a proxy chaperone in the car what harm can she come to?

What's the alternative? Take the RER back into Paris and wait for a volcano to stop erupting? There's no contest.

'Thanks, Brett. Are you sure your friend won't mind?' she asks out of politeness.

Brett looks her over again and laughs.

'Hell no, why would he? Everyone wants to get to the UK, right? That must be why it's *Great* Britain!' He laughs at his own joke as though it's the funniest thing he's ever heard and then looks above Kate's head and waves with enthusiasm.

'Right on cue, look, here he comes now.'

Kate takes another small sip of her Armagnac in celebration of her improving fortune. She feels a whole lot better about everything.

She turns to acknowledge the man that Brett's waved over and promptly chokes on her drink. Surely not. Surely it can't be him?

'Jesus Christ,' she mutters, turning back in shock.

Brett shoots her a quizzical look. Kate shrinks in her seat, heart racing, wishing Brett's luggage mountain was even higher. She'd escape if she could but she can't very well dive under the table. She is as trapped as a fox boxed in at a hunt. Just when she thought everything would be OK, her luck's run out again. Of all the people in the world. Why does it have to be him?

Brett gets to his feet to greet the new arrival.

'Kate, meet Marc Loseley. Marc, this is Kate. She's my damsel in distress and she's agreed to let me rescue her.' Marc extends his hand and then quickly pulls it back as she lifts her head and their eyes lock.

Time stands still. For a split second that lasts much longer, Marc stares and Kate holds her breath. His eyes narrow and a frown deepens on his forehead. It's obvious he can't believe his eyes either. He makes a reasonable recovery and holds her gaze without blinking.

'Katie. This is an unexpected surprise. Bit early for a drink, no?' The relinquished hand of friendship is now a pointed finger jabbing accusingly in the direction of her almost empty glass of Armagnac.

Kate winces. The bastard clearly hasn't lost his touch. Her initial uncertainty gives way to sheer defiance as they glare at each other over the table. He has the benefit of height but she is grateful to be sitting down. At least her legs can't give way. She tries to fix Marc with a hard stare. It's only when Brett cuts in that she remembers the American.

'Jeez! You're not telling me that you two actually know each other? Folk told me Europe's a small place but even so! This is one hell of a coincidence.' He chuckles, seemingly oblivious to the negative charge that crackles in the air.

Kate picks up her glass and swallows the remaining liquor in one clean mouthful, her sight firmly fixed on Marc.

'Your very good health,' she says. '*Up yours!*' she thinks.

Chapter 10

Alice - return to sender

I must have fallen asleep in my armchair this afternoon for I missed the play on the wireless. No matter. I awoke to the soft tones of Eddie Mair on Radio Four's PM programme sometime after five o' clock. The ash cloud situation has worsened and British airspace remains closed and locked tight. Much of Europe is now affected and the BBC's various correspondents are reporting events from major cities around the world, interviewing stranded passengers who have nowhere to stay and no means of returning. On the whole, people seem to be getting on stoically which is a breath of fresh air amidst today's culture of rampant sensationalism. Their spirit isn't a patch on our wartime resilience but is at least a diluted version of it. Then again, these people are hardly in battle, unless their drink-fuelled trips to Lanzagrotty and Benigorm provoke argument.

Puddy the cat is curled up at my feet having returned from a couple of days hunting over the wall. He makes a very cosy mock pair of slippers. Insofar as cats belong to any human, he really belongs to the unmarried Antipodean couple downstairs but since they are so seldom home he has adopted me, which I rather like. He visits every day and I do love to see his little face as he chases through the front door. He's most partial to the pilchards that I now buy just for him. On occasions, Puddy presents me with small gifts of mice and birds that he has caught but I try to discourage the habit. He once left a dead shrew in my house slippers, the discovery of which was not at all pleasant. These days I lift each slipper with my stick to check the way is clear before I edge my arthritic feet inside.

Puddy's company brings me so much joy. By contrast (much as I regret saying this) the company provided by my poor old friend Beryl is no longer as uplifting as it once was. She called on me briefly after the Doctor left and her visit contributed to higher than normal levels of sleepiness and extended shut eye this afternoon.

Beryl's heart is in the right place but her insistence that we read passages from the Bible together is irksome. Since I've been unable to attend Church for a couple of weeks, Beryl is adamant that my soul should not suffer as a result. Ever since her adored husband passed away she has become more pious than the Vicar himself. I'd go as far to say that the Vicar provides more entertaining company than dear Beryl. For one thing he wouldn't dream of arriving on the doorstep empty-handed. My guilty pleasures include jam doughnuts from the bakery and Merrydown from the village store, and the dear Vicar brings plentiful supplies of both. He also becomes very indiscreet about his parishioners once he has consumed a few glasses of the cider himself. I didn't used to be one to gossip but when one is old and gets out so seldom it is good to have a snapshot of the goings on in the community. Some of the news is banal – who's leading the collection for the lifeboats and that sort of thing – but there is also plenty of salacious content that would make you blush from head to toe.

Beryl is from the banal side of the gossip spectrum and the Vicar has nothing but praise for her. With all the work she does around the Parish she has firmly secured direct passage to Heaven and golden wings to get her there. She is a whole generation younger than me but we hit it off straight away when we met at night school back in the 60s. She had a rare sense of humour in those days -hard to imagine that now - and became the first person in whom I confided the bitter truth about Douglas, though I drew the line at telling her about the role of Professor Mason in the war years. That's a secret that will die with me.

I remain in Beryl's debt for her unfaltering support through good times and bad. The long passages from the Bible that she insists on sharing are a small price to pay for a genuine friendship. I am mindful that it is God's words (rather than the Vicar's gossip) that should provide the optimum antidote to the pain and suffering that consumed me for decades. My faith remains steadfast but I cannot deny that I experience a greater sense of love and peace from watching Puddy in the garden then I do from trawling through endless passages and chapters from the book of Revelation. I yawn just thinking about it. I suppose I should feel blessed, not weary.

Early years of marriage were satisfactory, aside from our failure to produce a child. Douglas behaved well towards me on the whole but I did find the physical side of our marriage difficult from the start. I could barely conceal my shock at the activities he was so keen to undertake between the sheets in sole pursuit of his pleasure. I did not mean to push him away but the disappointment and pain that came with every miscarriage was too much to bear. As the months passed he stopped making carnal advances and turned instead to his books. This came as both a relief and a surprise given that he'd never really been a literary man. He took to sitting in the study for hours on end with the door closed, not inviting entry. I'd hear him grunting in a way that was reminiscent of our nocturnal couplings and it embarrassed me so much I dared not dwell upon it. I was not well-equipped to address the matter and too ashamed to discuss my concerns with anyone, including my husband. Perhaps I was wrong to keep my own counsel. My young New Zealand neighbours would find such reserve laughable. This is what happens when people dispense with surnames and become overfamiliar.

To the everyday outsider Douglas and I appeared to be perfectly normal, settled as we were in our new detached home on the south coast. A young couple making our way in life. Douglas had borrowed a sum of money to procure the lease on a tiny pharmacy in Eastbourne. It was situated at the rear of the Grand Hotel which was the only four-star hotel in the town. It was a busy location and we benefitted from both regular and passing clientele. Although I was also a qualified pharmacist by this time (indeed having received far better results than Douglas in our final examinations), he preferred to take charge of the dispensing side of the business, leaving management of the front of the shop and dressing of the window to me. I resented being pushed away from the pharmaceutical side. I wouldn't have stood for it once upon a time but for some reason I relented. I was trying to be a good wife, to prove to Douglas that I could be a good support to him. My earlier notions of independence hadn't entirely left me but I kept reminding myself to invest fully in my marriage. At least I'd married a man who did not laugh in my face when I expressed my desire to continue to work. He had never relegated me to the low ranks of simple housewife. I was fortunate in relation to other women in that regard. My husband was rather progressive and as such was receptive to middle-class women continuing with employment beyond marriage. Of course, he was also quite lazy which probably played a part too.

We existed like this for around ten years. Ten years of making our home and building a successful little pharmacy business. Ten years of muted pain but on the whole, good companionship. Ten years of great uncertainty in the world.

To mark the decade milestone in our marriage, Douglas gave me a gift. This might not sound like much but the Second World War had been declared and apprehension filled the air. Churchill had replaced Chamberlain and life looked thoroughly bleak. I was surprised that Douglas even thought to give me a present given the tension and austerity around us, even if it was a special anniversary. And what he had chosen was simply exquisite; a French tin box in the style of Chinese art decorated with a red pagoda, gold birds and orange and white blossoms. Each of the four sides featured flowers and cranes in gold, orange and white on a black background. No name to distinguish who had made the box and Douglas never revealed its source, but I loved its elegance and charm and it took pride of place on my dressing table. Each night I would remove my locket and hair slide and place them with meticulous care inside the box.

Douglas was called up for active service. My heart raced a little less when we learned he was to be given a position within the Medical Corps. This made him safer from enemy attack, or so I hoped. In his absence I took charge of the pharmacy. Times were hard but I made the most of those years dispensing what medication I had and becoming more formally respected as a professional woman. There were also the special errands for Professor Mason, essentially delivering messages that nobody in my close circle had the faintest idea about.

The war. I try not to dwell on it. All those losses.

I gave thanks to God when Douglas returned to me. His face was hollow and all remnants of youth had left but at least he was alive. So many wives and mothers were less fortunate. Too many received letters of condolence and notifications that their fathers, husbands and sons were missing in action, presumed dead. Collective, public sympathy was of little comfort to them. The only consolation was that we had won against the worst of kinds of people and our many loved ones had not died in vain.

An unintended consequence of war included wives left home alone who fell prey to the advances of visiting American soldiers. I was not among their number. Nor was I well acquainted with any loose women, although my neighbour's new baby arrived early enough to get tongues wagging as customers lined up to collect their prescriptions.

Conflict continued into the post-war period, this time familial. Married couples who'd vowed to stay together for better and for worse began to separate and later divorce. My religious conviction prevented me from condoning such behaviour and I lamented the demise of British society.

Another sorry consequence of war. I thought my marriage was secure. How mistaken I was.

Unfamiliar letters started to arrive some months after Douglas returned from active service. I didn't wish to pry but could not fail to notice the green envelopes personally addressed to him with their spidery script. These were no official letters from the Army. When more envelopes appeared on the doormat, only to be hastily removed by Douglas for private reference behind the closed door of his study, I decided the time had come to be bold and ask him for an explanation.

But how to broach such a conversation? We had all learned to tread carefully around our war-scarred husbands and I have never been one for making a fuss. I pondered over whether to ask him about the letters. Were they really my concern? They weren't addressed to me so were none of my business. I was sensitive to the needs of my husband. No man welcomes an interfering wife.

The letters in the green envelopes were not all he received. Other correspondence would arrive from the most unlikely of places around the world, often containing stamps from friends that he had acquired during service. Directly on his return from the war Douglas had decided to start a stamp collection; a peaceful and innocuous past-time that must have offered some catharsis to him. The grunts that had once emanated from his study in the pre-war years gave way to a silent perusal of his growing collection.

It was this cherished stamp collection that provided Douglas with the almost perfect decoy. It's just unfortunate for both of us that I'm not susceptible to decoys.

I'm a scientist at heart, so natural curiosity got the better of me. I needed to know what was going on behind the scenes. I broached the subject of the green letters with my husband. He took a sharp intake of breath before brushing his trousers with his hands as though smoothing out a crease. A benign smile crept across his face.

'Come, Alice. Join me. I'd like to show you something.'

'What?'

'My stamp collection, dear girl! Come and see for yourself how I'm getting on with it. It now stretches across continents and generations. I have achieved depth and breadth.' He beckoned me to join him.

I sat by his side as he talked me through pages of carefully placed stamps. He became quite animated, enthusing at length about the kindness of those who continued to send him stamps.

'I receive letters from all around the world. One correspondent in particular has been a very useful source and has put me in touch with a number of excellent collectors.'

Overall he made a valiant job of implying that the intentions of the green envelope sender were strictly stamp-related.

'Just another friend with a mutual interest.' Or so he'd have me think.

His explanation seemed plausible. However, his overall delivery undermined its credibility. I inclined my head towards the stamp collection under review, ostensibly to approve it and the story but I scrutinised him as though he were a specimen under the microscope. His focus was fixed. Even when I searched his face with mine he failed to look me in the eye. He fidgeted on his seat, touching his handkerchief to his nose as though attempting to mask the truth. His pitch was higher than usual, his cadence faster. I knew damn well he was lying.

It became impossible to let go of my preoccupation with the green letters. The itch could not be scratched. Letters continued to arrive like ants marching into my home. No strict pattern as far as I could see but relentless nonetheless. Weeks might pass without one but then two would arrive on consecutive days. Douglas's reaction was always the same. Poker-faced, he'd remove them from the doormat, never uttering a word. He'd disappear into his study. No trace of any letter nor envelope among the pile of rubbish that I searched through before the weekly uplift. I dared not search his study. Something, misplaced loyalty perhaps, held me back. Even when I cleaned his mahogany bookcase I refrained from opening the neat box files stacked on a shelf beside the writing bureau. I still respected his privacy. To a point. But the itch remained and the urge to scratch it grew until it became unbearable.

One Friday I came across a spherical glass paperweight planted on the surface of the bureau. This was a new object I'd not seen before. Lifting it up in my right hand I felt its smooth, cool surface. My fingers curled around it as I brought it closer to view in the light of the window. Within the glass was preserved the complete head of a dandelion clock. Time slowed as I cupped the paperweight in my hands and rotated it 360 degrees. Where had this loveliest of artefacts materialised from?

From then on, whenever I felt uneasy about matters and when Douglas was out I would enter the study just to hold the paperweight and feel it in my hands. And to wonder.

Weeks passed. Business at the pharmacy was brisk which pleased Douglas, driven as he was to make more money from it year on year. He had also been invited to join the secret society of the Freemasons, thus affirming his status in the small community in which we lived, although again this was not something that one discussed. He would leave the house with a small briefcase, the contents of which I never saw. He forbade me to look inside it. He needn't have worried. I was not in the least bit curious about the case so it was easy to comply on that front. I was far more interested in unlocking the mystery that lay within the study.

One July evening Douglas left to attend another of his meetings. Having baked a tea loaf and completed my chores for the night I was again drawn to the study and the energy of the glass paperweight. After holding it in my hands I was about to return it to the bureau when a noise outside startled me. The paperweight slipped out of my hands and crashed onto the hard surface below.

It was too robust to shatter but it made a substantial crack as it made contact with the bureau. I held my breath, horrified that the force of its fall had left it scarred. A new fault line stretched wide around its circumference. With clammy hands I stretched out to retrieve it. The poor article no longer felt smooth. Its vital energy had seeped away leaving a damaged shell behind.

Douglas returned in amiable mood from his meeting and I called out a greeting to him and dashed into the kitchen, a little flustered.

'Would you like a cup of tea and lemon?'

'Yes please, and a slice of cake wouldn't go amiss.'

I waited until he had a cup of tea in front of him before I confessed the consequence of my clumsiness. I anticipated some initial disappointment and criticism from him but not the onslaught that was to follow.

I'd witnessed Douglas's moods shift enough times over the years. For the most part he'd switch from troubled and pensive when he thought no one was looking, to gay and carefree when his antennae picked up the signals of an audience in waiting. But his mood changes could be darker and more threatening. On this occasion the shift was immediate and troubling, as a great chasm opened up between us. A dark shadow crossed his face as he shed the persona of the perfect husband and Freemason to become a seething ball of angry nerves. His good mood had been felled as quickly as the sorry paperweight. I should have been more careful.

'I'm sorry, Douglas. It was a mistake. I can see you're upset.'

'Upset? I'm bloody furious!' He banged his fist on the table with such a force that the tea spilled over the cups into the saucers. He berated me as though I were truly wicked. The sheer force of his response winded me. It seemed disproportionate but words failed me. I stared at him, aghast.

'For God's sake woman, can you do nothing right?' His eyes were bulging. 'You haven't the first idea of what you've done.'

'I dropped a paperweight by accident and it cracked. Is that such a terrible crime, Douglas?'

Evidently it was. He raged that I had no idea of the significance of the item I had damaged. But when I asked him to enlighten me, he swore.

His was a visceral response fuelled by attachment to a cherished item; one imbued with far more than simply monetary value.

What else could I say? I had no defence. I was astonished because my actions seldom provided a catalyst for such an outburst. It was upsetting and affronting in equal measure.

He left his cup of tea unfinished, threw his chair back and stormed out of the house. He slammed the front door so hard behind him the letterbox shook in his wake. I considered following him but dismissed the idea as foolish. It was all too clear that he needed to take some fresh air and calm down and I didn't want to invite the unwelcome attention of any of our neighbours.

I sat motionless at the bottom of the staircase then gave myself a shake and a jolly good talking to.

'Stop being so pathetic, Alice! Get up, dust yourself down, put a smile on your face. Be a better wife.'

Without knowing why, I returned to the study. The scarred paperweight had lost its allure so I pulled the heavy oak chair away from the bureau and sank into it. It was the first time I'd sat for any length of time in this room. Usually I was too busy dusting and cleaning to sit down. The curtains looked as though they could do with a jolly good wash. As I went to take them down my gaze fell on the box files to the right of the window, and although I knew this would stoke Douglas's fury further I bent down to open the first box. The time to act had arrived. It was my turn to take back a bit of control; to face up to a threat as yet undetermined and unknown.

Pandora's Box it was not. It contained Douglas's stamps.

Nothing untoward to report. It was impossible not to appreciate my husband's enthusiasm for the small rectangles that represented different countries and themes. He had gathered an impressive number, enough to qualify as an established collector. I finished my comprehensive look through the file and returned it to its correct position. Then my attention shifted to the second file.

Again I saw stamps. Lots and lots of them. However, unlike the stamps in the first file, these stamps were no more than standard, first-class, British stamps that one sees every day. They were still stuck fast to the envelopes on which they had been pasted. These were not stamps intended for an album. This box contained a sizeable collection of another kind. Letters, tied together with green garden string from our shed. Full of trepidation as to what I might find I nonetheless pressed on.

I pulled at the ends of the string in an attempt to release the letters from their hold. There were well over two dozen letters in this pile alone, all with the same postmark; Brighton. Nobody I knew lived in Brighton. My parents were still in Gosport of course. Each envelope had been slit open at the top so neatly he must have used the silver-plated letter opener I'd given him for Christmas.

Removing the first envelope from the pile, hands quivering, I pulled a folded sheet of green paper from within. It was not good quality paper, a stark contrast to the Basildon Bond paper that I favour for my own correspondence.

A fleeting doubt. A tiny, almost imperceptible voice. My moral code told me to stop and leave well alone. Too fleeting; too quiet; too weak. A stronger force, a far stronger force was driving me to trespass on Douglas's private matters. My own audacity shocked me but not enough to stop me in my tracks. I continued in my pursuit of the truth. I steeled myself as I unfolded the letter for I had a moment of foreboding, and how right I was.

'My dear Douglas,

I hope that this letter finds you in good health and that you are not suffering too greatly with hay fever this summer. I was extremely touched to receive your latest letter and to hear that my gift reached you safely at the pharmacy. I did not wish to create any difficulties for you at home by sending it to you there. It pleases me no end to hear that the paperweight will be useful. The moment I saw it I thought of you. You have been so very kind to us.

Little Robert and I are managing quite well on the whole, although once I have put him to bed in the nursery at seven o'clock I do feel rather lonely. Even the relentless household chores do not occupy me fully.

I am painfully aware that we missed our chance to be together and I remain so grateful to you for indulging me with the comfort of our correspondence. I do hope that you are happy in your marriage, as I was in mine. However, should you ever feel that there is a chance for us to rekindle what we once shared I would like you to know that my heart is open to you. I hope my candour does not frighten you, dear Douglas, and as ever I wish you my very best and fondest wishes,

Anne'

Darkness fell. I read and re-read the letter, my fingers white as I grasped the single page in my right hand. My left hand clutched my locket as though for support, nails digging into my palm. Memories of the hushed conversation in Douglas's mother's kitchen resurfaced when I had read Anne's name. The news that she had returned to his life was an unpleasant shock. It is one thing to be suspicious of one's husband. It is quite another matter to have one's suspicions confirmed.

My heart burned as I read the letter, the intentions of its writer all too unpleasant. Anne was a very forward woman. Her words left no room for misunderstanding. What would Douglas do next? He must surely have encouraged Anne to write or there would not have been more than one letter, and her letters were meaningful to him or he would not have kept them. The study grew colder as the evening wore into night but still I sat there, undecided as to whether to torture myself further by reading on or whether to close Pandora's Box having seen more than enough already.

So absorbed was I in my shock I heard neither the front door open and close nor the study door open as the man who called himself my husband returned. He stood over me, thunderous expression on his face as he registered what I was doing, what I had seen and what I now knew about Anne. I looked up towards him, aware for the first time that my face was damp with tears. A single tear fell onto the pile of letters, blurring her blue inked signature.

Douglas's face was set hard, his mouth downturned. His eyes narrowed as he strode towards me, his voice a cold whisper that froze my broken heart.

'And what in Hell's name do you think you're doing now?'

Chapter 11

Kate - sleeping satellite

Marc has aged well. Kate prickles with annoyance. Trust him not to go to seed as he approaches middle age. No sign of jowly cheeks or a potbelly. The man facing her isn't George Clooney but he'd come a very close second in an identity parade. The only obvious sign of aging is the odd silver hair around his temples and that just serves to make him more attractive. Marc's skin is clear and smooth, his cheek-bones as well-defined as his arm muscles. His slim, athletic build and tanned skin suggest a recent skiing holiday, probably in Val d'Isère. Life's been good to him. Too good by far.

Kate rises to her feet. If she remains seated she'll run the risk of being regarded as potential prey. She pulls herself to her full height but even in heels she's shorter than him. A more assertive position is called for; hips square, shoulders back, chin raised. It's bad enough that he's shaping up so well. But worse still is her instinctive need to measure up under the scrutiny of his glare. *It's not as if you have feelings for him anymore.* Christ no. That would be ridiculous. It's more that she needs him to see how well she's done for herself too. Without him. In spite of him.

The initial shock of seeing him is enough to send shivers

down Kate's spine. For a moment that lasts too long she's locked into a connection with Marc so tight she loses peripheral vision and starts to feel a little faint. An intervention from Brett breaks the coupling and opens up her awareness to her wider surroundings and watchful audience.

'Guys, this is so neat. How do you know each other already?'

Left to their own devices they'd become animals staking their ground, circling each other, poised to fight, but this spectator poses no threat. Kate backs off, recovers herself and Marc mirrors her actions. They are temporarily thrown back into the realms of relatively normal conversation. *Don't cause a scene. Not here.* She purses her lips and crosses her arms over her chest waiting for Marc to come up with a response to Brett's question. *Go on. Tell him how we know each other. I dare you!* She's still seething that he stood in judgement over her when she took a sip of the Armagnac. The cheek of the man. How dare he, of all people, claim the moral high ground.

She counts to three in her head, adamant that she will not give him the satisfaction of knowing he has rattled her cage. His tone is civil but still prickly.

'Oh, we go back a long way. Don't we, Katie?' Marc swivels neatly on his feet to face her head on. 'So what brings you to Paris? Work presumably.'

Kate's blood boils. Rhetorical questions are the only things flying in the air today. Trust him to bring up the subject of work knowing how that will make her feel. Even though he's answered his own question, she plays along.

'I prefer to call it business.'

'Semantics.'

'Or artistic labour. Work doesn't really do it justice. And you?'

'I've been helping Monique sell some of my father's things.'

Monique. Marc's mother. Kate's only ever known him address her by her Christian name. Monique stopped being Mama the day he turned 13. Not at Marc's instigation. Monique took great care to explain why she wanted her own son to address her as Monique, keen to avoid any misunderstanding. She wished to safeguard her identity as a person in her own right.

'She still loves me as a mother. I just call her Monique,' he'd explained casually as though their arrangement were the norm rather than the exception.

Monique's position was respected by all who knew her. Kate accepted her choice as unconventional and hadn't dwelled upon it at the time. However, since giving birth to Isla she has a different perspective. Kate loves her identity as a parent and sees no reason why she can't be mother, wife, lover, friend and businesswoman without renouncing the descriptor 'Mum'. She remembers Monique as a principled woman who made many a stand on matters close to her heart. All the same, Kate now suspects that Monique's request to be addressed by her Christian name had more to do with her quest for eternal youth than a statement about individuality. With her marketing hat on Kate decodes brand 'Monique' as classic: timeless, ageless, priceless and abundant in positive equity and aspirational values. 'Mother' tells a different story. Less differentiating. More universal. Motherhood is rewarding and brings associations of joy and fulfilment, but it can be characterised by dark shadows under the eyes, fine wrinkles, grey hairs and a sagging waistline. The casualty in the story of motherhood is sex appeal. Monique refused to compromise hers, even by association. It wasn't that she sought the attention of the many men who cast repeated looks in her direction as she passed. Her focus was to keep alive the chemistry she shared with Marc's father. Their relationship was enviable and they never took each other for granted.

Kate returns to the present as she absorbs what Marc's just said. His parents surely can't be separating. They were closer than any couple Kate knew. Her heart sinks at the thought.

'Where's your Dad?'

'In the cemetery.'

God, he's blunt in his responses. Kate reels with the weight of his words. Marc looks away into the distance as he recalls Christmas Day in the hospice at his father's bedside. Holding his hand. Listening to the rattle of his final breaths. Monique sobbing for hours. Darkness falling over his father for the last time.

'Cancer.'

How can one word be so evocative? Kate experiences the familiar tightening in her chest. Cancer is a weapon of a word, capable of piercing the heart in a single shot. It packs a deadly punch. One small word that renders people speechless. Kate's own losses rush over her. Compassion for Marc sweeps away her earlier fury. In an instinctive gesture of friendship she reaches out, as if to catch his grief in her hand but stops short when she sees the look on his face. There's a cold anger written all over him, barely contained.

Her words catch and freeze in the air between them.

'Not your Dad? Oh, I'm so sorry.' His eyelids drop like shutters as he wills away painful images. When he opens them again he's in a remote place she can't reach.

'Yes, well, thank you for your condolences.'

Kate is stunned by shock and sadness. She'd been so fond of Marc's parents. If things had worked out differently she'd have been their daughter-in-law. She'd have been there to say goodbye.

She gets on well enough with Struan's parents but had enjoyed a very special relationship with John and Monique. When Marc had flown her to Toulouse to meet them for the first time John had taken an instant shine to Kate. In particular they shared a love of literature, Frank Sinatra and Monty Python films. Monique had been a little guarded in the early days, protective of her only child but her initial reserve was short-lived as she was charmed by the English girl who had won her son's affections.

Kate might have stayed in touch with John and Monique had the split with Marc not been so painful, sudden or bitter. She'd sent his parents one Christmas card a few months after the break up and received a long and searching letter from them in return, but then she'd cut contact completely, compelled to remove all traces of Marc from her life. She missed them but a clean break had been a key component of her survival plan. She'd had no idea about John's ill health. How long had he been living with cancer? She doesn't dare ask now.

Brett's phone rings again, a brief reminder that life goes on even if it feels your heart has stopped. He excuses himself, palpable relief on his face that he's been handed an exit from this awkward exchange between former lovers. Kate glances at his retreating figure and lets out a deep sigh.

John would have been in his early 60s, young by today's standards. He'd have been looking forward to retirement. How will Monique be coping? Her devotion to John proved by her gestures every day. The care she took in ensuring his coffee was steaming hot, the Christmas cakes she made each October that he loved but without the marzipan that he hated. He was the love of her life.

They had first set eyes on each other on an Air France Airbus. Several thousand feet in the air John had charmed Monique from the aisle seat of the Heathrow-bound plane while she prepared a gin and tonic for him. That same evening he'd wined and dined her at the Ritz and within weeks she was sporting a sizeable rock on her engagement finger. Her career with Air France never quite took off after that. No need. She found herself projected instead to front of house management with one of John's private art galleries on the Left Bank in Paris. Maintaining an apartment in the seventh quarter of Paris and a flat in Kensington, John and Monique enjoyed a very comfortable life and Marc was brought up to appreciate style and aesthetics from a very early age. He'd experienced the most cosmopolitan of upbringings and found himself equally at home in the bookshops of Gilbert Joseph on Boulevard St Michel as he was in Foyles on Charing Cross Road. He could distinguish a Monet from a Manet by the age of five.

Now here he is again, standing over her, older and grieving but still emitting a power so magnetic that she's losing her equilibrium. She tries to ground herself, reaching out for the back of the chair she's not long vacated.

If only she could be impervious to his energy. Deeply concealed feelings which were wrapped tightly are starting to unravel and rise to the surface. She concentrates on lengthening her breath, trying to slow her heart rate and calm herself down. Thank God she's learnt how to stave off the anxiety attacks.

Marc's arrival presents a significant problem. Kate faces a dilemma. Her ticket out of France in Brett's hire car means being stuck with Marc for at least the next few hours in a very confined space. *Can I bear that?* She's not at all sure she has the mettle for it. *Endurance tests aren't really my thing.*

Alongside thousands of other people in airports all over the world, Kate curses Iceland and its erupting volcano.

She's so close to declining Brett's kind offer of a lift and prepares an explanation that she's decided to stop in Paris for a few more days after all. The prospect of sharing Marc's space for more than a few minutes is hellish enough, let alone a few hours in one of the smallest cars Renault manufactures. Then again, this is the only route home open right now and she's come this far already. In her mind's eye she can see little Isla in her 'I'm berry nice' pyjamas, ready for bed, demanding to hear what's at the top of the Faraway Tree in the next chapter of her favourite book. Kate is consumed all over again with a deep longing to be home. Saturday is fast approaching which heralds the usual walk to the farmers' market on Castle Terrace to buy a selection of produce for the week ahead. The market visit is a Saturday morning highlight, the weekend stretching out in front of them like a carpet of enjoyment. She can almost smell the hog roast and hear the sizzle of ostrich burgers. Even though she won't make it home in time to join Struan and Isla for this week's trip, there's still a chance she'll be home by Saturday night.

As long as she leaves with Brett and Marc.

You're going to have to bite the bullet and accept Brett's offer. It's the sensible and obvious thing to do, plain and simple.

Struan's voice pipes up in her head, reminding her that you can't make an omelette without cracking an egg. Impossible to argue with that. In this case the journey with Marc is a messy inconvenience but essential to getting a desirable outcome.

Marc seems to be having similar misgivings about sharing a car with Kate as he struggles to hide his feelings and hops from one foot to the other. He wears his reluctance all over his face and the look he shoots in the direction of the rental car booths gives a clear indication that like her, he's looking for an alternative way out. There is none. On cue, staff plaster signs all over the booths to notify prospective customers that there are No More Cars Available in the fleet for the time being 'owing to unprecedented demand'. Two women wearing the uniforms of one rental company make off towards the office behind their front desk. An extended coffee break that may reach until tomorrow.

Marc at least has the option of returning to Monique in her Paris apartment near the Musée d'Orsay. Kate reckons he can make it easier for both of them by just leaving now. She waits in vain for him to do the right thing. Annoyingly, he shows no sign of wanting to head back to the city or his poor widowed mother. What business does Marc have on the other side of the Channel? He's obviously in a hurry to return to something. Or someone?

Brett reappears. Attached to his mobile phone like a vice he signals to them that he's wrapping up his conversation. Like two obedient children, Kate and Marc stand and wait for him in silence. At least Brett seems blind to their open discomfort as he grins broadly and gives them a jolly thumbs up sign. Perhaps he's put their initial terse exchange down to the sad news of Marc's father's death.

'Well guys, now we're all here I'll go see if they're done with cleaning the car. I don't know about you but I want to get moving, pronto.' He clicks his fingers. 'And I also need to get this cell phone charged again.' He shakes his mobile as though it's a rattle. 'The batteries on these things are a crock of shit, if you'll pardon my language, Kate.' She brushes his apology aside with a smile. She's unperturbed by his swearing. She's heard a lot worse in her time. She's said a lot worse too. Mostly in relation to Marc.

Brett continues to explain himself.

'See, I can't afford to be without phone contact for even five minutes or there'll be total meltdown, guaranteed.'

Kate's reflex is to giggle at Brett's risk assessment. To be fair she has no idea what his job entails so perhaps it's too soon to comment but his manner, language and demeanour all smack of a man prone to exaggeration. He works in sales, at least that's what she remembers him telling her. If that's his role, five minutes of 'downtime' will hardly create a total meltdown. He isn't the President of the United States or a surgeon in the midst of a critical procedure in the operating theatre. But it won't do to make fun of the only person who's offered her a ticket home. She turns her head to ensure Brett sees nothing of her upturned lips but needn't have worried about offending him. He's already set off towards the rental car booths in hot pursuit of car keys.

Marc hasn't taken his eyes off Kate and her brief grin and supressed giggle are not lost on him. For the briefest of moments they make eye contact. Dark pupils dilate and an invisible thread starts to bind them together. But almost as soon as the connection is made it blows like a fuse and they break contact. Abruptly. Kate looks around, anywhere and at anyone but him. Marc runs his hands through his hair and paces, turning his back, searching for Brett as though he's an escaped convict that needs to be apprehended. The intimacy has unsettled the pair of them every bit as much as their earlier encounter over the glass of Armagnac.

There are so many questions Kate wants answered by Marc even though his life is no longer her concern. She hasn't the first idea of where he lives, where he works, whether he's married or not. Curiosity compels her to look to see if he's wearing a wedding band but his left ring finger is still bare. There's a small scar on his third finger that's new but no distinguishing marks to identify his marital status.

Kate blushes as he runs his fingers through his hair again in visible frustration, reminded of how these same fingers used to tug provocatively at her hair when they made love. These same hands have touched her face, her neck, her breasts. Other places too. Her blush deepens in recollection of the many ways in which his fingers once played with and teased her. They've probed her very being. Now they're drumming on the surface of an airport pillar as Marc's impatience pulses through them.

I've shared the most intimate of experiences with this man who now stands before me as a virtual stranger. A stranger who almost became my husband.

Neither of them finds peace. The uncomfortable silence grows and deepens. Embarrassed but still transfixed by the memories of base desire, Kate forces herself out of her reverie. She needs to get a foothold in safer territory so makes an attempt at a fresh conversation on more pedestrian grounds. Small talk. Everyone always says the English have a national obsession with the weather. Sticking with a geographical theme, the volcano provides the natural subject for discussion.

'This volcano erupting is crazy, isn't it? I wonder how long it will last.'

Marc casts her a scathing look. 'That's anyone's guess.' He's not making this easy for her.

'At least we should be able to get home. I feel sorry for all the people who are properly stranded. It can't be much fun, especially if you've got kids.' She immediately regrets saying this, fearing she's given away too much. Marc's eyes narrow as he tightens his focus on her, revealing a curiosity about her circumstances that is every bit as keen as her speculation about his.

'So,' he pauses but there's no chance he'll beat a retreat. His voice is soft without being gentle. 'What about you, Katie? Do you have any children?'

Shit, shit, shit. She had no intention of inviting direct questions about her personal life. Now she's exposed all over again. There's no reason to lie and yet she doesn't want to grant him access to the life she's made since she left him. Struan and Isla can't become pawns in this game and her desire to protect their existence and withhold their identity from Marc is fierce. Then again, she can't lie. She's already thrown enough of a hook to draw him in. She mirrors his expression and speaks directly with equal cool.

'Yes, I have a little girl. Do you have any children?'

He looks straight at her.

'Not to my knowledge.' A glib response. Marc's back on the offensive and they're back in a vacuum, locked in uncomfortable silence. Marc finds his tongue first and faces Kate head on. He's building up to a showdown.

'OK, Katie. Let's be honest. This situation isn't ideal for you or for me. In fact, it's bloody crap. Clearly, like everyone else around here, we want to get back to the UK. Now, I don't know about you but I need to be in Brighton by eight o'clock tomorrow night at the very latest so I need this lift from Brett. As I say, I don't know anything about your circumstances or commitments, and I'm not remotely interested either, but for both our sakes could you not just stop in Paris for a bit longer and allow me to go on ahead?' He gives a slight pause before throwing out a closing uncompromising statement. 'I don't want to travel with you.'

Kate has to keep a lid on her temper. She's fizzing on the inside. This man still has the capacity to make her furious. No one else has ever been able to break her seal of self-control so deftly. This time she doesn't even remember to count to three before coming back at him.

'Well at least we're agreed on something. You think I want to travel with you? I'd rather be locked in a dark room full of spiders and perhaps you'll remember how much I hate them. You expect me to stay in Paris and fork out for God knows how many nights in a hotel when you could perfectly well stop over with Monique? Come on, Marc. Be reasonable for once in your life. Should I relinquish a lift and stay here in Paris just to help you? No. The only thing you're right about is that you know nothing about me anymore. Nothing. Nada. Rien. Zilch. So don't you dare comment on my life, my circumstances or my commitments.' *Ha! That told him, the smug, presumptuous wanker.*

The fight is on. Marc ignores the spider comment and latches on to Kate's mention of the hotel.

'If it's the cost of a hotel that's worrying you then I'll gladly pay for you to stay here for a couple of nights, and in somewhere decent. I can afford it.' He shoots her a defiant look but all Kate sees is arrogance.

'Do me a favour, Marc! It's not the cost. I don't want anyone's money and certainly not yours. If I wanted to stay in Paris I would, and what's more I'd bloody well pay for it myself. But I need to get back just as much as you, if not more. If you hate the idea of travelling with me so much then it's really very simple. Don't come. Stay here.'

Marc laughs and shakes his head to patronise her, as though she's a mere child. He's not about to give up. Kate remembers his bullish persistence which might be a positive character trait but only when he's on your side.

'Now, Katie. Just listen to me. You'll agree that I got talking to Brett first, yes? So it follows that I should have first refusal on who gets to share the car if there has to be a third person. Regrettably I can't and won't endorse you as either a passenger or a navigator.' Kate recoils at his vile blend of childlike petulance and proprietorial air. Struan would never behave like this.

'My God, are you that desperate to avoid me? You sound

like a four-year-old child who won't share his toys.'

'Don't patronise me, Katie.'

'Actually, it's Kate. And you're the one being patronising,' she snaps back. 'Anyway, you can so much more easily get back to Brighton than I can to Edinburgh.'

That stops him in his tracks. He regards her with renewed interest.

'Edinburgh?'

Shit. She hadn't meant to give that card away. Marc lets out a low whistle.

'So that's where you ended up. I had no idea.' He shakes his head again as he surveys her but this time his look is softer. He's lost the edge to his anger. 'You never cease to amaze me, Katie.'

'And what's that supposed to mean?'

Marc is almost smiling. 'It means that after all these years you still have the capacity to surprise me. Remember, you're the girl who said that she could never settle permanently in the UK. You said it was like living in a cold, damp cupboard You're the last person I'd have down on the list for a foggy life in Auld Reekie.'

Kate glares at him. 'And you're supposed to be the culture vulture! There's more to life than sunshine and beaches you know. I'm not that shallow. Anyway, I've got used to the weather and it's not that bad. In fact, on a cool, sunny day looking down from Arthur's Seat, you feel like you're on top of the world.'

It's true that Edinburgh wasn't the city that Kate had pinned her future on, but it emerged quite spectacularly on the horizon of her life at a time when she'd needed to feel grounded, and she'd found happiness there. The very soul of the city enveloped her. The rugged hills and crags were solid and secure. It was a city that told a good story. A city that accommodated incomers, especially those of presentable appearance and cultural intelligence. She'd found herself in the city by chance, had been offered a reasonable job and stayed. She'd taken up running and pounded along cycle paths, hill trails and seafront promenades until her feet were blistered and her body ached. Edinburgh was the city in which she'd found refuge, new experiences to replace painful memories and a good husband.

She'd literally collided with Struan while running along the canal path early one Sunday morning. She'd emerged from a short tunnel under an old railway bridge. He'd been running in the opposite direction and was about to enter the tunnel when he'd tripped on a tree root and hurtled into her, knocking both of them to the ground. He escaped with a sprained ankle while she emerged with a mended heart. Struan still joked about how he'd fallen headlong in love with Kate that Sunday. For her part, Kate's introduction to Struan cemented her commitment to the city and now she couldn't imagine living anywhere else.

The jovial American reappears brandishing 'The Key'. He's sporting a wide smile and an over-whitened set of teeth.

'Kids, we're in business. Let's get this show on the road.'

With neither of them willing to relinquish their seat in Brett's car, Kate and Marc reach a silent, stubborn stalemate. Glowering at each other they collect their luggage and duly follow Brett to the waiting Renault outside. The sun might be high in the sky but a heavy cloud hangs

overhead and the outlook is uncertain.
  Two minds have the same thought.
  'Why did it have to be you?'

Chapter 12

Alice - the man child

There are some situations in which one feels completely in control. There are others in which one has little power to effect any change. I believe it is imperative to assess a situation and then do what one can to try to gain control. This is not to take advantage of others. Heavens no! Rather, it is to prevent one's enemies from being exploitative at one's expense.

With Douglas and Anne I found myself facing a scenario in which I was at best a third party, at worst voiceless and anonymous. This was not at all satisfactory. I put aside my shock to analyse what was happening in a calm manner so that I could move back into the frame and redirect proceedings before matters deteriorated further. It would not do for both of us to lose our heads.

That's not to say I wasn't hurt by his behaviour or his implication that somehow I was in the wrong for having rooted through his possessions. To say I was upset and angry is an understatement. He needed help to acknowledge his errors. I would help him see sense. If only there had been a friend or parent in whom I could confide the sorry news. Someone I could trust who might offer sound advice. But no one sprang to mind.

Other daughters might have packed an overnight bag and headed to the parental home. Not I. For one thing, I sought to protect Papa from the truth. Pride also played a part. I had to prove that I was still equipped to handle my own affairs. Mother was my final consideration. She would side with Douglas, the golden boy, who in her eyes could do no wrong. In my head I heard her admonish me for neglecting the needs of my husband and pushing him into the arms of another woman. She'd never made any secret of the fact that my plain face was a disappointment to her and reminded me at regular intervals of my good fortune in landing myself a husband so dashing and desirable.

I needed time to gather my thoughts and come to some conclusions about what I had learned, and the implications of these learnings on our marriage, but I would have to do this alone.

I retired to bed, telling Douglas in no uncertain terms that we would discuss the situation further in the morning and that in the meantime I would make up a bed for him in the spare room.

He did not come to our bed that night.

Sleep came to me in the early hours but it was fitful and not restorative. The rumble of snores from the other room nattered me. How was he able to sleep? It took all my powers not to storm into the spare room to shake my errant husband until his heart rattled.

I made sure I was up first, well attired and ready with a considered response. I lay in wait in the kitchen, listening to the clock as minutes of my life ticked past.

With the rising of the sun, Douglas's temper had subsided and when he entered the kitchen he was the picture of contrition. For my part, the anger had swelled in my belly in a way that no baby ever had. Perhaps I was not the perfect post-war wife, but my loyalty could not be questioned. As his wife he owed me an explanation and I was adamant he provide one.

I placed a cup of tea on the kitchen table as an invitation to join me. We faced each other, forensic scientist and sample under observation. My husband sat down. One didn't need a microscope to recognise what he was made of. The heat of his anger had gone to leave a round-shouldered wimp of a man. Like a lump of lead. Soft, malleable, tarnished and dull. Entirely lack lustre. The wife and woman in me wanted to reach out to him. The scientist within warned to maintain a safe distance. Lead poisoning is unpleasant and wreaks havoc on the nervous system. The pain Douglas had delivered the previous night still hurt.

Eyes downcast, he cleared his throat and then began to speak.

'I met Anne at a tea dance in 1925.' A good three years before he had come across me in the library at the Pharmaceutical College. 'It was love at first sight.' Assuming such a concept exists, I almost responded but stopped myself. He smiled as he saw himself in a memory in which I was absent. Jealousy took root in the pit of my stomach.

'We courted for over a year. They were magical months, especially as there had been so much sadness in my life with my father's death. We danced. She could have been a professional dancer.' Another clear memory as his face lit up. 'We took long walks and talked for hours and became very close.'

'What went wrong?'

His voice turned bitter. 'Her parents didn't approve of our friendship for some reason. I moved up to London for my studies but continued to return home at weekends to see her, even though this was against the wishes of her family. I could not stay away. I did not see why I should stay away.'

Anne's father, like my own, had evidently not approved of Douglas. Unlike Papa, he had refused point blank to give his blessing to their courtship. A military man, he was not one to soften easily.

'I knew that permission for Anne's hand in marriage would be denied. The old man made it very clear that I had a long way to go before he would consider me worthy of his daughter.' His face hardened and an ugly look passed across it.

'I was young. Impatient. I was desperate to declare my intentions to Anne herself so that she would wait for me while I worked on persuading her father to accept me.'

'What did you do?'

'I left a note for Anne asking her to meet me in secret in the woods. I took the Emery family ring from my mother's jewellery box and gave it to Anne in lieu of asking her father for his blessing. She said she'd wait for me and promised not to breathe a word to her father. We both felt certain her father would come round in time, especially after I'd qualified with good prospects for setting up a business.'

But the old man was not daft. He was all too aware of the clandestine meetings and had other plans for his daughter which he put into action with impunity.

'One weekend in December 1926 I returned home to learn that Anne had been stepping out with a senior officer in the Royal Air Force.' Douglas's voice broke as he recalled his frantic journey to find her.

'I ran over to Anne's house. I didn't care that I was out of breath and doubled up on her porch. The housekeeper came to the front door. I thought she liked me but I'm sure she was lying when she told me that Anne wasn't home. I raised my voice until Anne's father appeared. He told me I was no longer welcome to visit. As if I ever had been, the miserable old codger.'

For hours Douglas waited for Anne to come, taking shelter under a tree further along the street when it rained. Cold and tired, he had almost given up hope of seeing her when he heard light footsteps approaching. He fell upon Anne in a state of upset, his words clumsy and vexed, jealousy distorting his handsome features.

'It was our first argument.' It would also be their last.

In a fit of pique Douglas stormed off, abandoning both studies and Anne.

'I had to get as far away from my life as I could. I joined a cruise ship destined for South Africa and Australia. You know about that. I'd been offered a job as an assistant to the on-board pharmacist. I had no reason to stay and suffer.'

'Didn't you need qualifications? I thought you were only halfway through the course.'

'Possibly and yes, but a friend helped me with my papers. You may remember him. The artist.'

'Him? You mean he forged your paperwork?'

'I don't expect you to understand, Alice. We can't all be pure and virtuous. I'm telling you what happened. Make of it what you will.' Some might consider his actions resourceful, but to me his behaviour was impetuous and downright dishonest. Perhaps I am too harsh a critic. Too judgmental.

Months away at sea gave Douglas plenty of time and space to consider his feelings towards Anne. Absence made his feelings stronger and confirmed his commitment to her. He vowed to win her back at all costs.

'Of course, the opportunity for relationships with other ladies presented itself on numerous occasions. I succumbed to the charms of a widow in her 30s travelling to Cape Town.'

I shuddered.

'And yet you say you were committed to Anne?'

'I was a young man, with needs. It's normal, Alice. There was nothing in any of these little liaisons. Those ladies were welcome distractions. Nothing more. My heart belonged to Anne. I decided that on my return to Southampton my first action would be to seek her out, and if I could not persuade her father to accept me we would just have to elope to Gretna Green.'

He wrote her postcards, cryptic and light-hearted, saving the important words for his return. He was desperate to present himself as worldly, even more worldly than Anne's suitor from the Royal Air Force. Douglas had a vague recollection of the man and did not consider him to pose much of a threat out of uniform, diminutive in height and devoid of humour. He told himself that Anne was only trying to please her father. He set his store on a happy reconciliation.

Douglas didn't need to tell me that his dream would not be realised and I would never have entered his life had he and Anne married.

'The ship docked in Southampton and after the guests

had disembarked I made straight for Anne's home.' Douglas stopped in his tracks and looked towards the ceiling, recalling a memory that must have been painful.

'Suffice to say that my impulsiveness to leave shore cost me far more than my passage. Whilst I was at sea Anne had been married off to the warrant officer.'

Douglas had no legitimate place in her life. His pride broken, he drowned his sorrows in alcohol until his mother and sister found him and took him home. They implored him to pull himself together and return to his studies. It was the only option open to him.

He blew his nose loudly like a foghorn and the table shook as he rested his elbows on it. He cut a pathetic, ruined figure at the kitchen table. Although I was beginning to see the picture more clearly I was not yet satisfied that it was complete. If Anne had married her RAF man then why on earth had she been corresponding with my husband and behind her own husband's back? There are words to describe women of that sort, none of them complimentary.

Douglas looked up, searching my face for a response. Was he asking for my forgiveness? At first I was at a loss for words. What a sorry face he had. What was I to do with him? The blood vessels in his eyes stood out and his face was slippery with tears. I had never seen a man cry before and it made me squirm. It was such an ugly sight. Outbursts of rage were preferable to this outpouring of emotion. Open grief stretched out in front of me and I didn't know where to look. His nose had ballooned and turned a deep shade of red, swollen with the pressure of the salty wash that had risen up from some hidden cavern in his body.

I will never know what he read in my face. I was trying to process what he was saying without showing my disgust, my horror or my fear. So when I requested that he continue, he looked relieved. I barely recognised my own voice. How civil I sounded. How magnanimous.

'Douglas, I am listening. Please, carry on.'

So I was a fraud too. He sat up a little and seemed to regain some of his spirit. I understand that confessions of sin to a Priest engender a similar sense of calm. But I could not and would not be able to grant him mercy. That was up to God. But could I ever forgive him for not loving me enough?

'I was shattered, Annie. I don't mind telling you. I turned my attention back to the bright lights of London where I found fleeting comfort in the arms of pretty but vacuous girls. It was hard, for I only ever saw her face. I tried to lose myself, don't you see?'

I listened to his confession of love for another with an impassive face but behind my mask I was bristling. Two things in his short but eloquent speech troubled me greatly. He had not even been aware that he had called me by her name for one thing. What wife wouldn't be aggrieved at that? Then, the suggestion that pretty girls had thrown themselves at him, an unwilling victim, stood at odds with my memory of Douglas, the Pharmaceutical College Lothario. My eyes narrowed, judging him a better actor than I'd credited although he'd do well to learn his lines more thoroughly for his next performance. Calling me Annie, for pity's sake. Barefaced cheek of the man.

'What am I to you, Douglas?'

He raised his head and opened out his hands as though

merciful. A small attempt at a smile but I doubted his sincerity.

'It wasn't until I met you, Alice that I felt for the first time that I had a viable future with someone. I've told you before, you're so different to all those other girls and the opposite of Anne. I admired your no-nonsense approach to life and your unusual sense of humour. I felt stronger in your presence.'

Every nerve ending on my body prickled. His speech centred on him and what he could take.

'What about me, Douglas?' I heard myself crying inside. *'What of my feelings? Was I merely a convenient antidote to your broken heart?'* How convenient for a serial narcissist to find a sap like me. He had not attributed the word love to me, just fortitude to be gained from me. I had long assumed that men did not use this word owing to a discomfort in their psyche. But I now had evidence in the shape of his words and tears that he'd loved Anne deeply, as a man should love his wife. It was my sorry loss that he'd spent his full quota of love on her to leave not even a slither of a ration for me. I'd given him my whole heart. What a waste. Professor Mason had warned me about him. I hadn't listened. More fool me.

Throughout our marriage I'd been under the misapprehension that his physical approaches towards me signalled that he loved me, but it was blatantly clear that they were no more than a selfish release of his own pent up love for her. This went a long way towards explaining why I'd never felt at ease with him in our bed. I was no more than another substitute in a long line of failed understudies. His wife in name only.

In keeping with his preoccupation with self, Douglas remained oblivious to the stream of rejection that was coursing through my soul. I prayed to God to give me strength and compassion. My faith was being sorely tested.

'We had no contact for years, Alice. Please take comfort in that.' Small comfort. I emitted a whimper of a sound, somewhere between a laugh and a cry. Now we would explore when this whole sorry affair raised its head again. I had to play the grand inquisitor, objective and steely rather than the wronged wife, scornful and desperate.

'When did Anne contact you? And what possessed you to write in return? Was it all at your instigation?' This last question was weighted more heavily than the preceding two. It would be easier to accept that vanity had prompted him to respond to a letter from his first love than to accept that dissatisfaction in our own marriage had driven him to seek her out. Douglas hesitated for a long time. He took a slow, deep intake of breath that revealed the extent of his lung capacity. He produced an explanation that read like a statement, true or false.

'Anne sent me a letter while I was serving at the Army hospital. Her husband had become a squadron leader flying Lancasters over Germany during the bombing campaign. His plane was shot down in an air strike. He was missing, presumed dead, along with two of his men. Anne wrote to me because she wanted to take the opportunity to wish me well while she could, in case I also became unstuck, as it were. I hadn't the first idea at that point that she was expecting a child. I wrote back to offer my condolences, nothing more, you have my word on that but when she wrote again by return I penned a second letter. We began to correspond. It was a tough time for all servicemen, Alice. You know that.' I did. I had done my damnedest to understand what our men had been through in that terrible war.

'We needed every ounce of support that came our way. And Anne needed my support too. She was alone and pregnant, poor lamb. I couldn't abandon her a second time when she needed me more than ever. She's not strong like you, Alice.'

No one could dispute the fact that our servicemen needed and deserved our support. Douglas had played a good card with that one. I might have been foolish in love but I was no fool and it struck me hard between the eyes that the relationship they had rekindled was fuelled by a whole lot more than platonic support. Perhaps scared by my stony silence he attempted to further substantiate his actions.

'There's a child involved, Alice. A child without a father. How could I abandon a child and his mother in their hour of need?'

I surprised us both with the force of my response.

'But you're my husband! Not hers. And that baby isn't yours, Douglas.' How could he put me through this after all we'd suffered? All those miscarriages. All those lost babies. I felt sick to my stomach. But his concern was not for me. His concern had never been for me.

'The boy must be four by now.'

'Four years old?' I shrieked in his face, losing all objectivity of the high inquisitor and reverting to wronged wife. Four years hit hard.

'You mean to say that this has been going on for as long

as that? I've been a blind fool. How could you keep such secrets from me? Dear God in heaven, you'll be telling me next that you're providing for the boy.' The expression on his face brought more harsh truths to my door. Of course he'd put money Anne's way for the baby. Of course he had.

'Douglas, this boy, is he yours?' I expected a pause and a lie. There was no pause.

'Not mine, no. That's just silly. Alice, I know this is hard for you to take in. It's been hard for me too. I've always wanted a son of my own. I don't think I ever made a secret of that.'

He might as well have battered me. My body gave way and I slumped at the table, reminded of my own barren body and my rotten womb. He could have reached out to me to offer some solace but he sat immobile, a seismic distance opening up between us. I'd been steeling myself for bad news. To think that another woman had been casting a shadow over our marriage for all these years was bad enough. That she also had a ready-made son lined up for Douglas as additional bait brought hot tears to my eyes.

'Are you going to leave me, Douglas?' I had to hear it from him even though I already knew the answer. I tugged at a button on the cuff of my blouse. It came off in my hand as if everything I touched was flawed.

'No no, Alice. I'm not about to leave you. Of course not. You're my wife.' So he had remembered. It wasn't the answer I'd expected.

'So, what happens now? Where does this leave us?'

'Look here. Our situation's not conventional. I know that. But you're a sensible woman and now you know everything you will understand our predicament. It's a relief to unburden myself to you at last. This has weighed heavy on my mind I can tell you. You see, I feel honour-bound to you both.' He held his hands in the air like scales balancing weights. His renewed self-confidence was in poor taste. I couldn't share his view even if I was relieved not to be facing a separation. I wanted to scream. Of course I did no such thing. Somehow I found restraint though it took a great deal of effort to apply it.

'In truth, Douglas I find all this news difficult to comprehend. Nor is it a situation that I can accept. Surely a simple letter of condolence would have sufficed? How did you ever allow yourself to arrive at this point?'

Silence was his best defence.

'Douglas. You asked me to listen. I have listened but now I've heard enough. You expect me to understand but I do not. I am your wife, not your sister. You must recognise that your liaison with that woman has to stop. With immediate effect. I may have taken an oath before God to obey you, but you have also committed to love and to honour me, not her. It is neither appropriate nor reasonable for you to maintain contact with that woman or her son. He is, let's be crystal clear about this, Not Your Son.' I spoke at a slow pace, punctuating each word with precision. I left no room for doubt. I watched him crumble all over again. The man had no mettle.

'Please, Alice. No.' His pleas hit my ears but bounced off like pea shooter pellets hitting steel.

'Douglas, there is no other option. How many times do I have to tell you that you married me, not her? We took vows, for better for worse. I shouldn't need to remind you that she left you for another man.'

My comment hit him like a slap to the face. He looked broken and I sensed defeat. But my victory was bitter, acrid and empty. When people refer to victory as sweet I tell them they have no idea what they are talking about.

He sighed and rubbed the spiky growth on his chin. He needed a good shave to smarten himself up.

'Pull yourself together, Douglas. You've had your time to be self-indulgent.' He looked at me with an expression I found impossible to read.

'Very well, Alice,' he sighed. 'Since you leave me no choice, I will of course honour my marriage vows but at least allow me to write to Anne to explain what has happened.'

'Absolutely not. I'm not convinced you have it in you to leave well alone. If you'd had one iota of sense your first letter would have been your last. You will refrain from writing and from behaving like a benevolent uncle and allow Anne to get on with her life. She's still young. She will find another husband when the time is right.'

Horror filled his face and he dropped his head so low to hide it from me. I stared at the top of his head and noticed for the first time how thin his hair had become.

'No more secrets, Douglas,' I continued, a little more gently this time but it was more of a threat than a request.

Later, as the clock chimed three I carried clean sheets upstairs to the airing cupboard on the landing and heard a pitiful cry as though from a wounded animal. The bathroom door was locked and the wash-basin taps were running hard in an attempt to mask his sobs. I listened at the door, only for a minute, but the housework still needed to be done. Besides, he'd created his own problem. How could I comfort him?

I did not cry though I wanted to howl with the injustice of it all. As the days passed I locked away my feelings and focused on practical matters around the house, ensuring that we ate well and that the house was in good order. These were the things that I was very good at and focusing upon them allowed me to cope. I also spent more time at the chemist. Whenever I wasn't working in the shop I could be found furiously washing, drying, starching and ironing like a woman possessed.

I indicated to Douglas that I was ready to share his bed again as his wife. Since intimate relations left me feeling so vulnerable it was a big gesture on my part. But I needed to ensure he had no reason to stray, even though his occasional advances brought tears I gulped to hide. We settled into a new pattern and a semblance of normality resumed. Sometimes, when I caught Douglas out of the corner of my eye, he looked quite bereft which reflected the way I felt inside. Two lonely souls living together under a patched up roof.

Just as I had brought an end to his correspondence, so the curtain fell on his stamp collection. It was a shame for it could still have been a positive distraction for him. The albums lay in the study and would have gathered dust had I not been so energetic with a cloth.

Douglas turned his attention to a new hobby of wine making, which wasn't strictly legal at that time. Nonetheless, he managed to procure great glass bottles and endless pipes and tubes along with various essential ingredients: fruit, sugar and active agents. He migrated from the study to the garage adjoining our house in which the bottles were left to bubble and brew. There was still just about enough room to accommodate his car, a burgundy Triumph Roadster which he cherished like a child. We enjoyed occasional runs in it along the coast when the weather was good.

Douglas lost much of his spirit after the crash of the crystal paperweight and moped around saying very little. He reminded me of a cat that had been neutered. Not a very agreeable metaphor, but there you have it. I was grateful for the relative calm that filled the house and thankful that I had addressed a situation and avoided a very unsatisfactory ending.

One day everything changed again. He returned home from the chemist with a fresh spring in his step, the first sign that he'd left behind his period of self-imposed mourning. On my birthday he even took me out for a three-course meal in a smart Italian establishment on Terminus Road, after which we walked together along the promenade taking in the salty evening air. At last we were moving on. We stopped by the bandstand, looking out at the choppy waves of the Channel and he handed me an envelope.

'Go on, open it! I can't wait to see what you think.' He watched me, all the while smiling as I pulled out the paper contents and turned a letter in my hand.

'Oh my goodness. Two tickets to see The Firebird at Sadler's Wells in London? Really? What a wonderful gift. Thank you so much.'

'I'm glad you're pleased. It's been heralded as the ballet of the year. I thought you deserved a treat. Happy birthday, dear Alice.'

I squeezed his arm, touched by his gesture.

'Oh I will look forward to a trip to London.'

'That's exactly what your Mother said when I told her about the tickets.'

'Mother?'

'I thought you might enjoy spending an evening uptown together,' he explained. 'Ladies' night in London. You can buy a new frock.'

'That would be lovely but I just thought we might go up together. You and me.'

'I'd have loved that but really the ticket would be wasted on me. I don't know the first thing about ballet. But I'll be glad to hear all about it on your return.'

The first spark of excitement I'd had in months crackled within me. I could just about tolerate an evening with Mother. It felt as though Douglas and I had turned a corner in our marriage, to leave difficult times behind. Married life has its ups and downs. We were on the up again.

I didn't hear the doorbell at first. It rang several times before I realised I was back in my flat in Woodhall Lodge in 2010, not on Eastbourne seafront in the early 1950s. Nor did I notice how much my eyes had been watering until I touched my hand to my damp cheek. What a silly, sentimental old fool I have become.

It is taking me longer each day to shuffle to the door and when I open it I'm as surprised to see the young lady Doctor as I am by the feeling of pleasure at her unexpected appearance.

'Another unscheduled visit?' I have a little joke with her. 'And so late in the evening? Is the National Health Service looking to improve the survival rates of elderly fall 'victims'?' The Doctor responds with a warm smile. I think she is beginning to understand my humour, just as I am beginning to warm to her.

'Hello again, Mrs Emery. I hope you don't mind me calling on you so late, but I had to pop into the butcher's and he mentioned that you hadn't been in to collect your usual order for the weekend. I don't think he was aware that you'd had such a nasty fall. We didn't want you to go short so I offered to drop your sausages off.' She spots the concerned look on my face and reassures me that she's not been inconvenienced.

'I was passing anyway.' When she smiles she is a pretty thing.

I scrabble for my purse but she holds out her arm to stop me.

'No, please don't worry about the money.'

I would have insisted but she's assessing me carefully.

'Mrs Emery. Are you feeling quite yourself?' Calamity! She must have spotted my dewy face. I soon put her right.

'Please forgive me, my dear. I was just having a little moment. It is so thoughtful of you to pop in. The toad in the hole I was planning to make for tomorrow's lunch would have been a solitary Yorkshire pudding had you not called round. Have you time for a quick cup of tea?' She barely glances at her watch.

'Actually, I'm gasping for one.'

'Come along, then. Tea for two. My treat.'

Chapter 13

Kate - Hell Highway

On a good day the drive from Paris to Calais can be completed in under three hours, for less than 300 kilometres stand between capital city and coastal town.

Today is not one of those days. Over an hour has passed since three weary travellers packed their bags into the cramped hire car and Brett, Marc and Kate are still trying to reach the outer gates of Paris. Their silver Renault creeps towards the intimidating ring road that loops around the city. Travelling on the roads on a Friday afternoon is hard work at the best of times, but as the country finds itself in the grip of train strikes and flight cancellations every inch of tarmac is carpeted by a snarling snake of cars. At least it isn't snowing. And at least they're on the move, even if it is only at a snail's pace.

Kate sits jammed between numerous cases containing samples of products that Brett intends to showcase to prospective buyers. She volunteered to take the back seat, reckoning it would be far easier to stomach Marc's company for the journey if she only had to look at him from behind. Far preferable to feeling the heat of his breath on the nape of her neck.

Marc didn't protest when Kate readily jumped into the

back of the car, finally located in the belly of the airport's car park. He was still seething at her refusal to return to the city and clenched his teeth so hard Kate wondered if they might crack at the roots.

The seating arrangements were also influenced by a far more practical consideration. Brett's abundant haul of luggage. He brought so many bags along that only the smallest of bottoms could squeeze in beside them. All those miles pounding along the canal paths of Edinburgh have paid off and Kate squeezes in relatively easily, not that she's ever been big. She wedges herself in between two bags.

Maybe Marc could have fitted in the back. He's lean enough but he also measures just over six feet tall. Unless his disposition has changed over the years (which she doubts) he'll be a grumpy traveller, complaining about the lack of leg-room, irrespective of where he sits.

The boot barely accommodated both Kate's small overnight bag and the sizeable canvas bag that Brett almost left behind while he took yet another phone call. Marc travelled light. He settled himself into the front passenger seat, stony faced but at least able to move.

What would Struan be like in the same situation with his mostly easy-going nature? He'd probably be passing round mint imperials and loading an Eagles CD into the car stereo. Last summer they'd set off for a holiday cottage on the Isle of Skye only to be stuck in heavy traffic for several hours. A very nasty road traffic accident to the north of Fort William had caused major tailbacks and closure of the dual carriageway, which was pretty much the only credible route to the north. A diversion took them to an excuse of a road that zig-zagged across farmland and countryside. Struan had to navigate this very difficult single-track, reversing in convoy whenever they met a string of vehicles approaching from the opposite direction. The conditions made Kate jumpy and she pressed a hand to her right eye, a headache building behind its socket as daylight began to fade and headlights flashed in all directions. At one point she expected to be thrown in a ditch and stranded overnight. They'd survived the journey intact thank goodness, the only damage being a slow puncture from a loose nail in the road. Struan maintained his wide smile throughout the whole journey, declaring it a great adventure. His Cheshire cat grin wouldn't have been out of place in an audition for a part on Top Gear, or a role as presenter on a children's TV show. He could be a wee dafty at times. Kate, by nature more uptight wasn't a bundle of laughs, too tense to absorb his positive energy. Luckily Isla slept through the worst of the journey or Kate's headache would have been twice as bad.

How would Marc have coped in such circumstances? Kate casts a sneaky look in his direction. She can't see his face but guesses that he still looks like a wet weekend. Misery personified. The question of how he'd have coped on the Skye trip isn't really up for debate. He'd have been intolerable of course. He is intolerable. Insufferable in fact.

Brett is neither a natural nor a skilled driver. It doesn't help that he's only used to driving an automatic car. He isn't at all accustomed to manual controls and demonstrates this with each crunch of the gears. Marc winces with every grind of metal, the sound engineer in him distressed by the clashing discord. Kate, a smooth driver shivers. To make things worse, Brett also eyeballs pretty French women in other cars and makes weird leering faces at them. The only thing that stops him is the bleep of his phone and his desire to reach for it. It's a wonder they haven't caused an accident. Yet. There's still time for a collision. At one point Kate is propelled forwards in her seat. They stop just short of the car in front, bumper looming.

'Brett, do you think your phone might be a bit of a distraction?' Kate tentatively suggests, a little too diplomatically.

'I can't afford to be out of circulation,' he postures. 'Not even for a few minutes. Every second counts in my business.'

The traffic comes to a standstill again and Brett checks his phone for messages, batting back a short response to as many as he can, his focus fixed on the small screen. Marc lets out a final snort of despair and growls to indicate that he's seen enough.

'Bloody hell, Brett. I don't know what you have to do to pass the driving test in Michigan but over here there is some skill required. And driving with a mobile phone in your hand isn't a good idea, no matter where you are. It might not be illegal in France yet but it is in Britain. Why don't we swap over for a bit? I like driving and I know the route. Plus my licence is clean.' He says this as though no one else has a perfect licence to drive and Kate bristles at his arrogance all over again.

Brett lets out a generous laugh. Apparently he doesn't believe his driving to be deficient but he takes Marc's comments with good grace and jumps at the chance to stand down.

'Sure thing. Thanks, Marc. You know, that'd be real

great. I do need to keep touching in with the guys back home and these poxy European cars of yours are so anti-American!'

Kate's relieved to find she can breathe again. It's been a tense journey and she's been busy sending text messages of her own but is starting to feel a bit sick from looking down at her phone. So far she's been in touch with Struan, Craig and Ellie to let them know that she's faring well and making her way home 'with a couple of business people in a hire car'. She keeps her tone light and deliberates over her words, especially when crafting a text for Struan.

She presses Send on the short message she's drafted to him, a neutral text too bland to invite concern. She isn't about to disclose that she's the only female in a car with two men so she refers to them as 'people' she's met. Struan might be reassured to learn that one of them is familiar to her but would not be happy at all if he were to find out that the familiar face belongs to Marc. It doesn't matter that the two men never met. Struan's seen enough of Marc in photos of Kate's pre-Edinburgh life to recognise a credible threat. He's not a threat though, Kate reminds herself. Merely an irritation.

Struan responds within seconds, also by text, which comes as both a relief and a surprise for he generally prefers to pick up the phone for a chat, dismissing text messages as lazy. However, he's too caught up in work to speak.

'Glad you're OK. Stay in touch and stay safe. X'

She fires back a response.

'I'll call from Calais later. X' She doesn't want to embark on any intimate dialogue while still within earshot of her male travel companions.

Brett stops the car in the next available lay-by and relinquishes the driving, settling down into the passenger seat with a contented look on his face. Marc, by far the more accomplished driver has already adjusted the rear-view mirror, checked his blind spots and pulled out seamlessly between a white van and a battered old Citroen. They are back on the road.

Sitting diagonally behind him, Kate has a clear view of Marc's right profile. If she weren't so tightly lodged between bags she'd have shifted across the seat. Instead she cranes her neck and looks out of the window as though her life depends on forensic study of the passing countryside.

How did I end up here?

The traffic begins to flow at last, or perhaps the journey simply feels smoother with Marc at the wheel. He's a master in control and despite herself she's impressed by his natural ability to take charge.

Images of life as a couple flash in her mind and she can't suppress them. They'd covered many miles together, catching the ferry from Dover or Portsmouth and occasionally Plymouth to drive to different regions of France every few months to snatch days away. He'd shared her insatiable appetite for travel as well as her love of France and they'd toured the country extensively, sometimes roughing it but more often than not finding a secluded gite to stop for the night.

When Marc graduated from university his parents sold the flat in Kensington in favour of a substantial second home outside Toulouse, complete with swimming pool and vineyard. The villa nestled into a hill overlooking the vineyard below. It boasted seven bedrooms, all en suite and a kitchen so enormous it would have been a travesty not to host parties within its walls. It became the scene of many a memorable soirée. Laughter bounced off its walls and echoed around the valley below like joyful bird song. Great firework displays marked the arrival of New Year and Bastille Day. One year Monique even commissioned a troupe of actors from the Central School of Speech and Drama to fly out from London and put on a performance of Romeo and Juliet in the villa's courtyard. Open invitations to visit the villa, satirically named Chateau Mojo, were issued to family and friends. Marc took Kate as often as he could, whether his parents were in residence or not.

Before she can stop herself, Kate puts a voice to her thoughts.

'What happened to Chateau Mojo?'

Marc is in the process of overtaking a lorry. There's a discernible increase in acceleration as he presses down harder than is necessary while he absorbs the shock of her question. She should have kept her thoughts to herself. Once they're safely past the lorry he shoots her a scorched look via the rear-view mirror. It could almost have cracked under his glare. He seems to be treating her question as though it's a loaded gun, holding back his answer before firing. He changes lane and fixes his gaze stubbornly on the road in front. His jaw clenches again and his hands grip the steering wheel even more tightly.

Kate didn't intend her question to rile him and not for the first time wishes she'd stayed silent. She's lost her earlier fury and is beginning to adapt to the strange new situation in which she finds herself. Curiosity has got the better of her. She should have known better than to give in to it. It wasn't the safest question to have thrown at him. While the villa had once held happy memories for them, it would be an understatement to describe their last visit to the area as marred. It was an unmitigated disaster. Kate's enduring memory of Chateau Mojo is not of the villa itself but rather the garden of a neighbouring villa and what she witnessed there. She vows to keep a lid on her thoughts from now on. Some questions will just have to remain unanswered.

Marc speaks in a flat monotone as though referencing something as inconsequential as his weekly shopping list but Kate isn't fooled. He's trying to keep his emotion out of his answer.

'The villa's still standing but Monique wants to sell up. She'll probably buy something smaller and more manageable a little further down the hill.' He pauses and then adds, 'She still has all her friends there, after all.'

Kate feels the magma of rage rise inside her again at his latest barbed comment. Does he have to bring the Loseley's friends into the conversation? He must know how much that still hurts. Among this collective are the English family she would rather forget. And the party that extinguished any hope of a future with Marc. She turns her face away in search of happier thoughts.

Kate feels his stare bounce off the mirror to bore into her. She refuses to acknowledge him, instead focusing on a tiny speck of dust that she's spotted on the window. Is the whole journey going to be like this, punctuated by little bombs waiting to go off every time either of them open their mouths to speak? She doesn't dare utter another word and tries to occupy her mind with neutral subjects but her brain is addled from the effort of the day.

Brett's finished firing out emails and text messages to everyone in his address book. But this doesn't mean he's done for the day. Quite the opposite. Declaring that even the west coast of America must be open for business he starts prodding away at telephone numbers, asking Marc and Kate if they can hold off their conversation for a while so that he can 'touch in' with his team. Whatever that means.

Even if Kate and Marc did want to talk amongst themselves it would be impossible to compete with Brett whose voice is the kind that upstages all others, in volume and in content. He talks the most extraordinary language; a language Kate has not heard before; a cocktail of war references, mixed metaphors, sporting discourse and general bullshit. Kate recognises the most obscure marketing jargon but even she is amazed by the phrases that trip off Brett's tongue. This is verbal masturbation of the most slippery nature.

'Hey, Gabe. It's Brett here. What's the order of play for today buddy? I need you to get down into that ballpark and bat some balls about for me, OK?' Brett lacks the physique of a sports coach, so Kate wonders what on earth he's asking poor Gabe to do. What Brett's dialogue lacks in sense it more than compensates in entertainment.

'So I'm still in Europe. Yes, I know. The brakes have been pulled on all flights so I can't connect with my guys! So Gabe, listen up. I need you to get out there, line up those ducks and shoot them out the water. Hit them hard with those balls, OK? I want us to be on the same page by the time we speak later. Do you get where I'm coming from, buddy?'

Brett waves his free arm about and his cheeks turn red as he agitates over Gabe's response. For his sake Kate hopes Gabe has understood and will be on the right page after returning from 'the park'. If so, the guy deserves a medal of some sort for code-breaking. Brett's heart can't be faring too well with all this excitement.

'Buddy, I'm not sure we're reading from the same book right now, let alone reading from the same page.' No bloody wonder, thinks Kate, her sympathies lying with the poor man on the other side of the Atlantic who's probably under a table by now, whimpering and blocking his ears from the verbal diarrhoea that is Brett Maslan.

The next call is even more obtuse but confirms Brett's suspicions that Gabe's not up to the job, whatever 'the job' is.

'Stacey, it's me.' He rubs the back of his neck as he speaks leaving blotchy red marks behind. For a split second Kate wonders if Stacey is his wife before she remembers he dropped his single status into an earlier conversation. Stacey must be his PA. Or his second-in-command. Or both?

'Stace, I'm having to touch in with you because I seriously need you to reign in the latitude with Gabe, and mitigate it. He's not moving the dial in equity terms. I've given him a brief to go into the theatre of war and go viral. I can't reach out to all my guys from here.' Brett's on a roll again. Kate wonders if he always speaks like this or whether he's putting on an act for his small but captive audience in the pop-up theatre of the car. How awful if this constitutes Brett's usual discourse. It's becoming easier by the second to understand why he's a single man. Stacey must be used to his carry on. Brett's still talking absolute nonsense and leaves no gaps to allow any response from the other end of the line. If Stacey has any sense she'll have recognised an opportunity to put the kettle on while he prattles away at her.

'Gabe needs to convert these guys from enemy to ally. I want to see the trail of blood he leaves as he captures them and moves them over to our position. I need him to create more chances. Stacey, you still there?'

It becomes more and more difficult not to laugh and the more Kate tries to suppress her giggles the harder they push to the surface. Involuntarily she chokes, making a noise that she tries to pass off as a cross between a cough and a sneeze. Thank God Brett's oblivious to her mirth, and not for the first time she thanks her lucky stars that she's planted in the back seat. She can't help but notice the growing smirk on Marc's face. He's never been one for this type of verbiage. Marc commands an extensive vocabulary but never speaks gratuitously. Her giggle dies in her mouth as it occurs to her that she can't be sure if Marc's laughing at Brett or potentially mocking her.

But when Brett starts on a third call she's overwhelmed again as open laughter threatens to break the surface. Kate tries to think of serious matters but Brett is too large, too comical to allow anything else into her head. By now she's quietly giggling in the back of the car, stomach muscles tight. And Marc's shaking shoulders indicate how he too is struggling to contain himself. Waves of laughter rock them sideways. Kate forces herself not to look at him for fear she'll collapse on the back seat if she catches his eye.

Too late. Eye contact made, they are tipped over the

edge. Marc winks at Kate and as he does so they explode with laughter, much to the surprise of a very naïve and perplexed Brett. He must think they've taken complete leave of their senses. From open hostility to complicit mirth in the space of an hour.

It's been years since Kate heard the sound of Marc's laughter; deep, generous and all encompassing. When he laughs it's as though the whole world is being tickled into submission. Sound becomes music and light takes on colour. Hilarity mingles and fills the space in the car and something ineffable shifts and stirs inside her. Without warning, images of Rome, breakfast in bed and the Trevi fountain float to the surface of her consciousness, flooding her soul until she's left gasping for breath. Emotion spills over as the present is swept away by the rush of the past.

Chapter 14

Kate - stop and search

Memories from 15 years ago are as vivid as last night's dream.

Looking back. It's Friday night. Spring 1995. A young couple arrive at Rome's Fiumicino airport after dark. After disembarking the plane, they leave the airport at breakneck speed. They head straight for the taxi rank. As young people with good salaries and no dependents they haven't bothered to research public transport options. They can afford to take taxis on a whim.

Turbulence on the flight from London only added to the thrill of Kate and Marc's first weekend away together. They drank enough gin to loosen tongues but not so much to draw attention to themselves for inappropriate conduct. The previous week had been painful without each other. Every conversation on the flight a pretext for what they want to do just as soon as they are alone together.

'Had a hard week?'

'Yes, but looking forward to some relief this weekend.'

'I've a present for you but there's a condition attached. Will you help me test it out later?'

'Of course, Katie. Count me in. I'd be delighted to help you in any way you please.'

'You won't regret it.'

Kate's been working on new product prototypes for Strobe, the UK's fastest growing manufacturer of condoms and lubricants. Her bag is bursting with samples for trial. Most of her previous week was spent traipsing around the UK, checking in and out of multiple hotels and meeting groups of sexually active men and women to discuss the ins and outs of their love life. Each establishment was as anonymous as the smiling blondes and effeminate orange tanned staff that manned their respective reception desks. Over the course of a few days Kate became an expert in the sexual habits and fantasies of British people. On occasion it was hard to distinguish fact from fiction and Kate couldn't believe some of the stories people shared. In the comfort of a quiet room and warmed with a drop of the strong stuff, people revealed more about themselves to strangers than they ever would to close friends. Kate listened open-mouthed, more intent to learn than ever. The timing could not have been better with this exciting romance with Marc Loseley warming up.

She saw herself at the entrance to a maze, the centre of which she yearned to reach but not too fast or too easily. Like savouring a chocolate with a caramel centre. Making it last for as long as possible.

Meanwhile, Marc managed to pick up a valuable new contract at Studio Central, the recording studio in London coveted by every celebrated artist in the music industry. The studio corridors were adorned with impromptu photographs of bands while recording and framed platinum albums that gleam against the monochrome.

Marc is currently working as the chief sound engineer on

the début album of a young female singer, a massive achievement for someone his age.

'She's tiny but her voice is huge. And beautiful. Silky smooth like Karen Carpenter but with the power of Stevie Nicks.' A streak of jealousy stirs in the pit of Kate's stomach as she sees the admiration for someone else's talent written over Marc's face.

'Should I have heard of her?'

'Not yet, but you will. Remember this name. Gayle Force Ten.'

'Seriously?'

'I kid you not. That girl is destined for success on both sides of the Atlantic. I predict a nomination for best newcomer at the Brit Awards with odds on to win. Just thinking about her voice gives me shivers down my spine.' He's been working round the clock but shows no sign of fatigue. Marc is a mass of potential energy, alive with possibility and suggestion.

'I'll play you some of her music. I know you'll like it. And as for you young lady, no need to be jealous. I can't take my eyes off you. I wish I could get my hands on you. Every intimate part. Thank God this is a short flight.'

Barely two weeks after they met Marc had pressed a shiny pound coin into Kate's hand and made her an offer she couldn't refuse.

'Did you know that visitors who throw a coin into the Trevi fountain are destined to return? Come with me. To Rome.' He placed two Alitalia airline tickets in front of her and gently placed a hand on her thigh, locking eyes and drawing out her desire. Kate traced the details of the itinerary he'd sketched out with her index finger and whispered his name.

It still unnerves her how instinctively he knows what makes her tick. How he's woken a base desire in her that has her rapt in wanton lust and complete abandon. She's beginning to think he knows her better than she knows herself. He's brought a woman out from within that she barely recognises as herself. And these days all she can think about is Marc. Making love to Marc. Enjoying furious sex with Marc. Anywhere and everywhere.

Kate thinks back to when they first met. That house party in Clapham Junction. A belated New Year's gathering held by Vanessa, an old university friend Kate hadn't seen since graduation. One she'd promised to stay in touch with but they'd so far only managed to swap Christmas cards in the four years since lugging possessions out of student residences for the last time.

Although she hadn't been in the mood for a big night out it would have been lame not to make an effort to go. It was only a house party after all and not a million miles away from Ellie's palatial new home on Wandsworth Common. She could show her face for a few hours, catch up with some people from university and then head back to a luxury guest room with cotton sheets and a soft dressing gown. Ellie had also insisted that Kate try out the new hot tub while she and James were in Antigua with their kids. Meanwhile Kate had a report to write for work and reckoned it would be so much easier to start the first draft in Ellie's sun-drenched breakfast room than in the half-light of her own pokey basement flat.

She arrived at the party just as it was becoming interesting. There were enough familiar faces and buckets of punch doing the rounds. The usual suspects had been hard at the bottle since lunchtime by the looks of things. Most people were still at the stage where alcohol made them brighter and more confident versions of themselves.

Someone handed Kate a deceptively sweet fruit punch, its sugary ingredients masking the true nature of its alcoholic content. Over by the bay window of the living room she got chatting to a dark haired girl called Marie. Kate remembered her quite well because Craig had tried his luck one weekend when he'd visited in Kate's first year. He failed to make an impression. It turns out Marie prefers girls anyway.

'So what are you up to these days?'

'Local government. Environmental health. Spend a lot of time in kitchens of restaurants and answering complaints about noise between neighbours. It's more interesting than it sounds.'

Just as they were catching up, Kate was grabbed at the waist from behind and her glass refilled by one of the usual suspects from university. One of the extrovert lads. She remembered him. His nickname was Wardy. His spatial awareness was by now so impaired that he failed to notice the magazine rack that lay on the ground by the girls. He stumbled, sploshing a sizeable quantity of punch over the carpet and almost pulled Kate down on top of him.

'Shorry, darling. You look fucking gorgeous by the way. Oh shit...'

Wardy managed to catch the jug before it made contact with the television. That would have made for an explosive night and a visit from the fire brigade. Kate turned on her heels.

'I'll get a cloth.'

The carpet looked like becoming a predictable casualty of the party, alongside broken door handles and several glasses judging by another crunch and yelling from the stairs. Kate weaved through the throng of people in the hallway, apologising as she squeezed past. The party had gathered pace, people were shouting to make themselves heard and there were more faces but few were familiar. Kate resolved to clear up the mess and then give her excuses once she could locate any of the actual hosts. Vanessa had disappeared into her bedroom with a broad-shouldered, rugby-topped Welshman. She'd always had a thing for rugby players. And Welshmen. Kate checked her watch. Almost 10 minutes to 11. Early, really. But she'd seen enough. And if she left before the local pubs called last orders she'd still be able to find a cab.

The kitchen door hung loosely on its hinges and after she squeezed past a couple snogging Kate saw Marc. It wasn't just his good looks that set him apart. He stood head and shoulders above the dunderheads mixing lethal cocktails. He was wearing a black t-shirt that showed enough muscle to reveal a man in peak fitness. He seemed oblivious to his surroundings as he filled a thin-handled teapot with boiling water which seemed rather odd in the circumstances. He turned to Kate and casually offered her a drink as though he'd been expecting her.

'Darjeeling?'

'I guess every party needs a sober and responsible adult to watch over the children. Yes, please. No milk, thanks.' Suddenly Kate didn't care a jot about the deepening stain on the carpet and her urge to leave the party was cut short.

She cradled her hands around the teacup he handed her and felt her lips tingle as she pressed it to her mouth.

'Careful. Don't burn yourself.'

'Are you teetotal?'

He laughed.

'Most certainly not. But I'm abstaining tonight. I'm about to head off to help a friend de-rig a theatre set under the arches in deepest, darkest Vauxhall.'

'At this time of night?'

'You'd be surprised what goes on after dark. I'd love to show you. But maybe a daytime date is more appropriate. What time are you free tomorrow?'

'Presumptuous.'

'Always. OK, what are you up to tomorrow?'

'Nothing much,' Kate lied, surprising herself at the immediate emptying of her diary. She wasn't spontaneous by nature. She was a planner who liked to look ahead, to weigh up scenarios and choose before committing. But then she reasoned that Ellie's hot tub would still be in place the following weekend. All of a sudden the deadline on her report was shoved back to become a mere speck on a distant horizon, far enough away to allow for a little diversion. Kate could also hear her sister's voice in her ear telling her to 'go for it.' If ever there was a time to seize the moment, this was it. Marc was the sort of guy for whom plans are rewritten.

They met for a walk in Richmond Park, a refreshing change from the unimaginative suggestions by most British men to meet in a pub or bar. He produced a simple picnic from his bag that belied the effort he'd put into making it. Followed by two cut crystal champagne flutes that he'd magically chilled. And a bottle of Lanson.

'You've gone to so much trouble.'

'I like doing things well.'

They spread out on his tartan rug and dipped into strawberries and raspberries while sipping champagne and learning about each other. Words flew freely and laughter came easily and often.

The kiss when it came was pure Turkish Delight; sweet, mouth-watering and leaving both of them wanting more.

'You are beautiful, intelligent and mind-blowingly sexy. We hardly know each other. But I know I want you. For a long time.'

'I want you too.' They were words Kate had not uttered before. Not to anyone. She'd never desired a man so much. But everytime she whispered, 'Now,' he'd whisper, 'Later.'

His resolve didn't last long. With bodies entwined they neither knew nor cared if they had an audience but were undisturbed by man or roaming deer. And later when they slipped into Ellie's hot tub they found their perfect rhythm again.

Nothing was off limits anymore. The excitement of a new relationship was just the half of it. The education by an experienced and thoughtful lover left Kate dizzy and breathless. Only the inevitable arrival of work broke them apart when Monday morning arrived.

This trip to Rome marks their three months as a couple. Their free time spent together, mostly naked or talking for hours over the phone planning how to excite and pleasure each other the next time they meet. All of a sudden there is mutual dependency, even addiction, a need to explore the very depths of each other's bodies and souls.

Friends and family have been dropped for the time being

but Marc and Kate are too wrapped up in each other to feel guilty. Only work still benefits from their attention because they are both ambitious and keen to prove themselves. They are flying high. Kate in particular feels like she is soaring, giddy and at risk of flying too close to the sun.

There is no shortage of taxis outside the airport terminal and the young couple jump into the back of the one at the head of the queue. In perfect Italian Marc gives the driver the address of a hotel, sourced on the internet after scrupulous research. It's barely a five minute walk from the Trevi fountain and he's already given Kate a coin to throw into the water. This will secure their return to the Eternal City.

Before Kate's managed to fasten her seatbelt, the driver takes off. She soon realises she should have prepared herself better mentally for the hair-raising taxi ride. Juliet insisted on visiting Rome and Vatican City on her honeymoon with Craig and had warned her about mad driving but Kate hadn't given it much thought. Now she is scared.

The speedometer creeps higher as though unrestricted, scaring the living daylights out of her. She looks with fear at the car in front which dominates the windscreen as their taxi races towards it at breakneck speed. This goes against everything Kate's learned from the Highway Code and flies in the face of basic common sense. Safe stopping distances don't feed the egos of professional drivers in this city. Thoughts flash through her brain. Is this how they're going to die and why hasn't she made a will? Or perhaps they won't die but at these speeds, if they crash they'll end up with serious, life-changing injuries. Terrified, she digs her nails into the palms of her hands and tries desperately to stay calm.

Is the driver playing games because he can sense fresh visitor blood, or is this really normal practice? Kate looks towards Marc for signs of reassurance but he's rifling through his leather bag for something as though it's any normal car journey. Kate wills him to notice and to care enough to tell the driver to slow down. *Please, slow down.* She can't find her own voice. The driver looks completely relaxed. His left hand rests loosely on the steering wheel as though it were a Sunday afternoon amble in the countryside at 10 miles an hour.

Kate must be alone in thinking this may be the last journey any of the three of them will take.

At last Marc looks across and sees the fear in her face.

'Are you OK? You look like a rabbit stuck in headlights.'

'I'm scared, Marc.'

'Don't worry. I've got you.' He takes Kate's trembling hand in his and starts to rub his thumb over hers in a gentle, soothing rhythm. He leans in and his mouth brushes against her neck as he murmurs, 'When in Rome, Katie… When in Rome.'

There are so many firsts with this man. Kate loves the feelings that rise up in her when he calls her Katie. He started doing it when they made love in the park that Sunday, whispering that Kate was practical but Katie was passionate. There were plans he had for Katie that Kate might refuse. It made her feel alluring and wanted. Plain Kate had taken a back seat. But safe Kate is the one sitting and still fretting in the back of the taxi. As soon as they get to the sanctuary of the hotel she'll readily morph into Katie again. Assuming they make it that far.

No one ever thought or took the initiative to play with her name before Marc. They might have done so if they'd known how easily she'd capitulated when he started doing it. He is whispering her name again now, fully aware of what he has unlocked in her and the deliberate stroking of his thumb tells her he has no fear. Her whole being is in a high state of alert from being strapped rigid in the back of a car driven by a crazy Italian but she allows herself a chance to breathe and finds that by focusing on Marc her anxiety slowly comes under control. The stroke of his hands. The fullness of being. The life in him. She's willing the car to arrive at the hotel.

They almost hit another car but the driver shows off his reflexes to avoid contact, swearing wildy with dramatic effect. At last they reach their destination. Still in one piece and still alive.

The taxi driver speeds away with an unfeasibly large tip. Marc's urgency to get inside is as pressing as Kate's and he doesn't bother to wait for change from the large euro note he hands the driver, who rubs his hands together, deciding he can afford to call it a night.

The hotel is tucked away in the corner of a quiet piazza. Its butterscotch walls radiate warmth like a sandy beach and the glow emanating from the enormous doorway beckons them up a short flight of marble stairs to a small reception area.

'Like it?' As if he needs any reassurance. Marc has done it again.

'I love it.' Kate is still breathless from the journey. She lets Marc take her hand and he gives it a squeeze.

'Come on, then. Let's go inside.'

They are greeted by a brunette with hair so bouncy and glossy she could be a model for L'Oréal. She's young but may well be older than she appears. Her ruby red glasses match her lipstick and give her the air of a woman in charge who knows what is what. They hand over passports and Marc fills out a short registration form under the young woman's still but smiling gaze. She alerts the hotel porter with a nod. He sweeps them up in his care towards an extravagant winding staircase and their room, three floors up at the very top of the house. Sculptures and paintings line the hallways and fresh cut flowers stand tall and proud in half metre vases that could be test tubes from a giant's castle.

In some hotels the top floor is the luxury penthouse. In less salubrious establishments it's the low-cost excuse for sleeping quarters. They arrive to find a room with all the makings of a penthouse wrapped up in the most intimate space. Kate walks over to the window which stretches from floor to ceiling and is thrilled to find they are overlooking another piazza at the back of the hotel. The window is framed with blue, wooden shutters but she has no inclination to close them on the scene below. Little groups of people sit chatting and laughing, clinking glasses of limoncello ahead of a night of dancing in the square.

Rome breathes warmth and a self-confidence, the like of which other cities can only dream.

'I can't believe this city hasn't made it onto my trip list before. How did I manage to miss out on all this?'

'Well, you're here now. And I'd hate to think you'd been here already with anyone else.'

'Unimaginable. I'm here with the perfect companion.'

'Companion? I prefer lover. Mon amour. And remember, the best things come to those who wait.'

There's an element of truth in this, but Kate can't wait much longer for Marc to dispatch the porter who is insistent on talking him through the workings of the air-conditioning and the trouser press.

She signals to Marc and heads into the en suite bathroom to freshen up. It's another elegant space of sandstone walls and mirrors which create optical illusions with every turn. Kate is struck again that plain old Kate must still be in here somewhere, in amongst all these Katies with their eyes wide open, chins lifted, lips parted. She blows herself a kiss in the mirror. Who is this woman?

Kate kicks off her heels and stretches out her toes like a ballerina freed from pointe shoes. She rises and fall on the pads of her feet, stretching calf muscles and relishing the feel of the cool, marble floor. The shower has the most enormous watering spout she has ever seen. On returning to the bedroom Kate is just in time to hear the porter's departing words and Marc ushering him out of the room. At last.

'Breakfast is from six-thirty until nine o'clock. I wish you a very pleasant stay.' Marc shakes his head and makes a point of locking the door securely.

'Thank God he's gone. I was beginning to think this was some horrible endurance test saved for new visitors who just want to make love.'

'Poor you.' Kate grins because maybe Marc is a bit too used to getting what he wants when he wants it. It's hard to put up any resistance where he's concerned.

'Yes, poor me. What do you think of the bed?'

'Mmm. Big and firm. Just how I like it. I'm sure we'll get a good night's sleep,' Kate teases as she presses down on the springs.

'I told them we were married. I don't think they believed me for a second, especially now they have our passports in their safe.'

The bed is the focal point of the room. Impossible to ignore. Its smooth Egyptian sheets are positively virginal but they won't stay that way for long. Marc is edging towards Kate, step by step. He implores her in low tones to turn around. She does it without question, waiting for him to make his next move.

He approaches slowly with the agility and poise of a big cat about to pounce. He's just close enough that Kate can hear his breath, though the sounds from the piazza below swell up and bounce through the window whenever there is laughter. He pauses then moves an inch closer. Anyone looking up from the piazza would see a young couple moving together in slow motion, but it won't be long before the accelerator pedal is flat on the floor.

Marc lifts Kate's hair and brushes the back of her neck with a kiss. One hand slides around her waist and comes to rest like a butterfly on her stomach before sliding upwards to the curve of her breasts.

Slowly, excruciatingly slowly, he begins to unbutton her blouse.

'Five.' She squirms in a futile attempt to turn around and reciprocate but he's having none of it.

'Four,' coincides with a cheer from the piazza below. Someone's timing is spot on.

'Three.' He is over half way there now and his hands start

to venture further across her skin.

'Two.' Kate hears a low moan and realises it is hers.

'One.' He holds her attention. Her blouse flutters to the floor as she pushes her shoulders back.

He's still taking his time. Kate's not sure how long she'll be able to last. His hand glides towards the band of her skirt to unclasp and unzip it until she stands before him in nothing but her underwear, her skin covered in goose bumps. Marc lets out a soft whistle.

'Look at me,' he beckons. She does as she's told and turns to face him.

'Do you want me, Katie? Yes or no?'

She wants him as she's never wanted anyone before. They haven't even kissed yet.

'Yes.'

'Yes, you want me? Will you say it.'

'Yes, I want you.'

'Here?' He finds a path of no resistance and breaches the thin shield of silk that's as fluid as her need for him is deep.

He pulls her towards the window frame while removing his belt and trousers as though they are made of paper. His intent is alive. He leans her against the warm window pane and Kate gasps again as the skin on her back meets the smooth surface of the glass. He doesn't bother to close the shutters.

'Let the world see how beautiful you are. And how beautiful we are when we're one.'

As he enters her the whole world tips upside down.

The weekend rotates in a constant cycle of exploration and experimentation. The bed sheets give way to easy pressure. The shower proves big enough for two and its jets of water hold them under for lengthy periods, as they join together again and again in heady euphoria. The wide window continues to frame their sensual dance every evening, lights twinkling over the piazza, sounds of the city absorbing the cries of satisfaction that spill over from the top floor.

Any attempts Kate's made to play it safe are futile at best, mere pretence at worst. Shyness and prudishness carry no weight with Marc who is armed with a touch so delicate and a hold so firm that he commands access to all areas. She might as well have handed him a sexual passport to roam wherever he wants, however he chooses, whenever he sees fit.

Kate loses count of how many times they've been together at the open window. One time he ties her hands loosely to the shutters. All she wants is to be his. She calls out his name from the rooftops, her locket swinging back and forth like a hypnotic pendulum with the rhythm of their dance.

Somehow they also manage to explore Rome but much of it passes in a blur of excitement and wonder. On Saturday they studiously throw their coin into the Trevi fountain, as instructed, avowing to return.

They don't make it down to breakfast at all on Sunday, too preoccupied with what they can savour of their own love making in the room. They had every intention of making it down to the dining room on time but when they turn up, fresh from the shower, still damp and giggling like idiots the restaurant staff are already in advanced clear up mode. Not even a pastry to take away.

'Don't worry, Katie darling. I'll buy you a large bar of chocolate when we get to the airport.'

'Thanks, Marc but there's no need. I'm really not a bit hungry.'

This is true. Kate has lost her appetite for everything other than him. Even chocolate is superfluous to requirement these days.

'You don't need chocolate when you're in love,' she tells him.

'Oh, Katie. Your initiation is complete.'

Chapter 15

Kate - the long and winding road

Kate's leg starts complaining of cramp, the by-product of being jammed in between two suitcases for so long. She looks for a passing road sign to see how much further until they reach Calais. By her calculations she'll be able to stretch her legs within the next 50 minutes. She rubs the back of her neck, takes a deep breath and exhales, eyes closed, rolling her shoulders and wriggling her toes to get some oxygen circulating around her body. Fresh air taunts her through the window. The car lost its new rental aroma within an hour of leaving the airport and has taken on a musky scent that comes in waves every time Brett makes arm gestures. He is a man who speaks with his whole body.

With Marc behind the wheel the small Renault has made smoother progress on its journey north, but the roads have remained busy and patience inside the car is wearing thin. Brett continues to receive calls at an alarming rate as problems escalate among his hapless sales team. At one point Marc turns on the radio muttering something about a travel report but Kate surmises his real motive is to dilute Brett's conversation. After about 20 seconds Brett's chubby hand reaches out to turn the volume control anti-clockwise to a low buzz. Marc swats the off switch as though it's a fly.

Optimistic hitchhikers gather at the side of the road, thumbs extended, makeshift boards highlighting felt-tipped destinations. Calais, London, Dover, even Manchester. Not all the faces fit the profile of the stereotypical hitchhiker. Kate sees their determination to progress. It's not so different from her own. The clear focus on a goal that grows from having one's plans disrupted. Although she's sympathetic to their plight, she hopes there won't be hundreds more of them at the port to hold her back and keep her in France even longer. Quite selfish of her really but it's how she feels.

'How many people can the ferry take?' she wonders out loud.

'They'll have to put on additional services to accommodate the extra traffic. Supply and demand. I majored in economics. They'll put on more ferries. Right, Marc?' assures Brett.

'Not necessarily,' adds grim-faced Marc.

Every time a mobile phone rings in the car it's safe to assume someone is trying to reach Brett, so when Kate's mobile chimes she doesn't even flinch to acknowledge it.

'Aren't you going to answer that?' Marc snaps, the sound engineer in him offended by the tinny jingle.

Kate only just manages to answer Struan's call before her device switches to voicemail. She slips down her seat, lowers her voice and keeps her responses short to exclude the others from her private conversation. Kate lets Struan take the lead and for once wishes that Brett's mobile would ring, denying Marc the opportunity to eavesdrop.

'Kate? At last! I can barely hear you. Sorry I couldn't talk properly earlier. I had to negotiate a long drawn out meeting. Employment law at its most arduous. How are you getting on, sweetheart?' Kate closes her eyes to block out her immediate surroundings. Her husband's voice is soft and soothing. For a brief moment in time she is wrapped up in the fleecy blanket of his Edinburgh accent, shielding her from Marc's Arctic chill.

'Better, thanks. We're making good progress now.'

'Whereabouts are you? Do you mind if I eat a bit of my sandwich while we talk? Late lunch.'

Any other day and she'd tell him to call back. She can't abide people talking while they eat but in the current circumstances her disapproval seems churlish. Kate opens her eyes and looks out of the window, a faint smile as she sees they have less than 20 kilometres to go.

'No, I don't mind. We're nearly at Calais.'

'Are you booked onto a ferry?'

'No, not yet.' Struan is chomping on his sandwich and has the good manners to finish his mouthful before answering.

'It's mayhem everywhere but I heard they're laying on extra ferries from Calais and Le Havre so you might just be alright. I'd check for you at this end but I'm about to head into another meeting. Listen, if you can't sail today don't hang around at the port. Find somewhere decent to stop for the night in Calais.'

'OK, I will.'

'And keep in touch. These people that you're with, what are they like?'

Irritating and bad company,' Kate wants to say but she isn't about to tell Struan that. 'Fine, nothing special to report. We're all in the same boat, I guess.'

'That was quick. Thought you were still on the road.'

'Yes, very good.'

Struan chuckles. 'You can't talk, can you? You've got your telephone voice on. Look, just keep me posted. I have every faith in you but I just wish you were back home safely.'

If only he knew. What can she tell him that would be truthful and reassuring? Not that he has anything to fear from Marc. But she still can't relax in his company in a cramped car. It's like sitting on a fault line.

Kate closes her eyes again, calling to mind her husband's face and dimpled smile. Struan is one of life's Good Guys. He's the kind of son who visits his parents once a week, never turns up empty-handed and routinely checks the tyre pressures on his dad's old car. The kind of husband who buys presents for his wife when it's actually his birthday. That's the kind of loving, generous man she married.

'And you? Are you OK?'

'Me?' He sounds amused that she's asked. 'I'm sure I'll just about survive. Once I've wrapped up this meeting I'll head straight off to pick up Isla. I found Mouse by the way. Mum's invited us over for tea. Talking of which, make sure you get a hot meal inside you too. Hang on a sec.' Kate's not sure if he's talking to her as his voice is muffled but then there's a sound of metal hitting metal followed by a groan of disappointment. He'll be trying to throw his empty can of cola into the waste-paper basket. Struan can make a game of anything, even in his austere wooden panelled office.

'Luck or muck?'

'Muck. My aim's getting worse. Only three out of five

this week. I'd better go. Call me later.'

'I will.' Kate doesn't want him to go. He's her anchor. She winces when she thinks that not so long ago she was calling to mind intimate details of the better aspects of her relationship with Marc. His presence is over-powering. Toxic. *Remember, you're married to Struan. Handsome, sexy, kind and dependable Struan. That episode with Marc is finished.* Of course it is.

Kate looks around for the bottle of water she picked up from the hotel earlier but it must be in the boot of the car. Rummaging through her handbag all she finds is a tin of Moffat's Mini Mint Imperials. Without water to quench her growing thirst, the mints will have to do. She offers the tin first to Brett who empties a generous pile into his palm with a hearty 'thank you' and then to Marc who declines, muttering something about the fact that he's driving. Brett looks bemused.

'Hey fella, you sure take your driving seriously. You won't even take a sweet for the journey?'

'Oh I forgot. Mints make Marc sneeze.' *Shit,* she's done it again. Spoken out loud without thinking. Forgetting to filter what she says before speaking. But it's true that Marc was prone to bouts of sneezing if he ate mints, drank white wine or stepped into bright sunshine. On such occasions he'd sneeze three times; no more, no less. It was one of his quirks. Kate stops herself from visualising the other idiosyncrasies that made him unique in the bedroom.

'There's not much I don't remember about you, Katie.'

Blood rushes to her cheeks at his insinuating comment. *How dare you go there, you bastard.* How is she ever going to respond to that? Brett rubs his hands together with interest and speaks, his mouth full of mints.

'So when did you two last see each other?'

'A long time ago.'

'Can't really recall,' lies Kate, diving into her handbag for a distraction.

They breathe a collective sigh of relief as the car draws closer to the port. With evening beckoning it's no longer a surprise to find yet another endless queue for information that leads to disappointment.

Earlier in the journey while driving at a modest five kilometres per hour, a rough plan had been discussed and agreed to travel together as a group as far as Dover. In the UK, Brett will continue on his way in the hire car to south London after dropping Kate and Marc at a railway station, probably Ashford. However, after an hour of waiting at the port they concede that this leg of the journey will have to wait until daybreak.

'Messieurs, Madame, there is no available space on any of tonight's crossings.'

'Not even for a tiny Renault?'

'I'm afraid not.'

'Putain de merde.' Marc strides away muttering further expletives under his breath. Brett takes the news with better grace but looks over towards Kate to solve their next problem: where to stay for the night? The thought of sleeping in the car is too hideous to even contemplate. She makes a quick suggestion.

'Shall we head into the town and see if we can find somewhere to stay?' Brett's face lights up as though all his Christmases have come at once.

'Great idea! And we can amuse ourselves in Calais for the

evening. Maybe find a bar or club and make a night of it. Do you like to dance, Kate?' He wriggles his wide hips like an ageing rocker and gives her a wink. Kate wastes no time in bursting his bubble. Did he really think her idea had some sort of hidden meaning?

'You'll have to count me out of dancing. Anyway, I expect you'd like to charge your phone and I'd certainly like to talk to my husband in peace.' She places a strong emphasis on 'my husband'. Brett deflates slowly. *Aren't sales people supposed to know how to read people?* Kate wonders idly. Then again, she's met enough estate agents and car dealers to know that self-confidence gives them vision for what they want to see, not necessarily sight for what stares them in the face.

Marc strides back towards the car. He's oblivious to the appreciative looks he's attracting from a lycra-clad party of female cyclists on top of the range Specialized bikes. They lean on them as he storms past as though he's some kind of God.

'What a hotty.'

Intently focused on his phone conversation Marc carries an intense red aura of bad temper around him, adding fuel to an already heated discussion. He ends his call without saying goodbye.

'Kate and I have made an executive decision,' Brett explains to Marc's torn face, thankfully leaving out any mention of the failed proposal to party the night away in Calais. Kate lets him do the talking and squeezes herself back into the tiny space afforded to her on the back seat of the car.

They drive around for a good half hour before they see

anywhere with advertised vacancies. In the end they pay an exorbitant rate for the last two available bedrooms in a hotel in the old town, quartier Saint Pierre.

The hotel's seen better times but given the delays and dead ends of the day, Kate would be grateful for a bed in any inn or stable. She takes the only double room leaving a twin for Brett and Marc. No one questioned the sleeping arrangements but Kate can't help noticing the colour drain from Marc's face as he considers a night in shared accommodation with Brett, the walking mouthpiece.

Kate daren't ask if Brett switches off his mobile phone at night. She'd hazard a guess that he keeps it on all the time. On call, 24/7. As though he is scared to be off the grid. Kate derives guiltless pleasure from Marc's obvious discomfort.

'An uncomfortable night with Brett serves you right for all those sleepless nights you gave me,' she silently tells him.

'Guys, we really must make the most of our night in Calais,' Brett insists at the reception desk in the dimly lit lobby. 'Let's see if there's some place good round here where we can get a decent meal and a drink.' Although Kate cringes at the idea of enforced socialisation with either of the two men, neither of whom she would ever class as a 'buddy', she has little option but to acquiesce. After all this time she's hungry. *And you did promise Struan you'd get a hot meal.* A medium-rare steak and chips washed down with a carafe of red wine is a mouth-watering proposition. Besides, they don't have to stay out late.

The hotel proprietor, a hunched man with grey hair and slow, laborious movements recommends a local restaurant.

'You must absolutely go to 'Chez Philippe.' Let me assure

you that you will not find a better meal anywhere else in this town. Chez Philippe is the best restaurant and I should know.' He presses his fist to his heart. 'After all, I have lived in Calais all my life. Much has changed, not all for the better sadly, but this restaurant will not disappoint.'

'Don't think much has changed here over the decades,' whispers a voice in Kate's ear. She jumps sideways as though stung. Marc is actually smiling at her. It's definitely not a grimace this time. Unsettled by this new persona of friendliness Kate almost topples over in shock. The silent and moody Marc she can deal with; this whispering confidant should be viewed with caution and handled with care.

Kate keeps her reservations about the quality of Chez Philippe to herself, trying not to let impressions of the hotel proprietor prejudice her expectations of his shortlisted restaurant. As she sees it, the most compelling feature of the restaurant is its proximity to the hotel, a mere five-minute walk according to their host. A table for three is duly reserved for eight o' clock.

'May I say that you are extremely lucky that Philippe is my very good friend. Without this introduction you would not be so lucky to find a table at such short notice. Especially tonight. Our town is full of visitors.'

'If you'll excuse me, I'm going to freshen up.' There isn't much time before dinner and Kate isn't willing to forego a shower. Three pairs of eyes burn her back as she heads upstairs to her room, taking exceptional care not to miss a step on the threadbare carpet. Her room is at the end of a corridor and after fumbling with the key for a good minute she gains entry before closing the bedroom door behind her with a firm click. A long sigh escapes as she leans against the door and practically slides down it, grateful to be alone at last.

The bedroom is sparse and tired but at least it is clean. Kate sticks her head around the door of the en suite bathroom. Bland décor at best. Chipped tiles and a wobbly toilet seat complement the overall air of benign neglect that hangs over the entire establishment. None of this bodes well for a restorative night's sleep and Kate readies herself for a pathetic dribble of water from the shower. She's pleasantly surprised to discover plentiful hot water and good pressure. If only she could sit underwater until all the tensions of the day are gone. But time is limited and she wants to phone Struan with an update.

The moss green bathroom towels are more in keeping with Kate's low expectations: frayed and scratchy to touch. To compensate for the abrasive exfoliation she liberally applies her favourite body cream which she loves more for its fragrance than she believes in the youthful, soft and supple skin it promises. Time will tell if its age defying claims are valid but the neroli and grapefruit ingredients certainly have an uplifting effect on her mood.

Kate scrutinises the contents of her bag for something suitable to wear. There isn't much to choose from. She hadn't factored in a volcanic eruption or an evening out. Her trouser suit would be comfortable but she'll wear that tomorrow for the final leg home. And she doesn't want to step back into any of the clothes she's been travelling in all day.

This only leaves one option. The simple halter-neck dress purchased yesterday. A striking dress bought with her imminent wedding anniversary in mind. An evening in Calais with Marc and Brett is not what she'd envisaged for its first outing but Kate is getting used to having limited options. She slips it on anyway. It hugs her body in all the right places whilst leaving plenty to the imagination. Struan will love it. And why not give Marc a very clear impression of what he's lost? It's a mischievous thought but what the hell. The full-length mirror in the wardrobe concurs. She might not be the fairest of them all, as fabled by the talking mirror in Snow White, but she's well in the running for a podium finish.

She turns her attention to her hair and make-up. Since Isla's noisy entrance into the world, Kate seldom has a minute to herself. Even though she only has about 10 minutes to complete her look, it is 10 minutes of peace that normal family life denies. The face that smiles back from the mirror looks presentable. The locket is the final touch and then she'll be ready to venture out. Just as soon as she's called home.

Kate re-reads Ellie's text and shakes her head. Sent hastily from Newark it includes the phone number of James's associate in Paris. She presses delete and then attempts to call Struan, keen to speak to little Isla to wish her goodnight. Kate tries her home number first and then remembers that Struan told her he's taking Isla over to see his parents for an early tea. Maybe they're still there. She doesn't know Struan's mum and dad's phone number by heart but they top her list of contacts. Her mother-in-law, Audrey answers in a flowery voice.

'Oh Kate, dear, how nice of you to call. Struan's been telling us all about you being stranded in France. What an adventure for you.'

Struan's mother is easy to get along with as long as you agree with everything she says. Conversations with her tend towards the one-sided as Audrey prefers to talk rather than listen. She's not very chatty just now, as though she's itching to be somewhere else. With her darling son, of course.

'Now, don't you go worrying yourself daft about young Isla. She's having a wonderful time with us and hasn't even noticed that you're missing. We've had home-made lasagne because I know how much Struan likes the way I make it with the chicken liver and I've baked an apple pie. Isla's dashed outside with Grandpa Campbell to see the frogs in the pond. I'll have to go, dear. I need to call them from the garden before the egg custard's ruined.' *And you're holding us up* is the critical and not so subtle subtext. Audrey calls out to Isla to come in and wash her hands but doesn't bother to cover the mouthpiece. Kate rubs her deafened ear and swaps the phone to the other side.

'Audrey, do you think I could have a quick word with Isla? If it's not too much trouble?' she adds hastily.

'Sorry, Kate dear. I missed that? You don't really need to speak to her right now do you? Oh, the good girl. She's run to the bathroom with Daddy to wash her hands. I'd better not call her to the phone just now since we're eating. I'll tell Struan you called. Perhaps you could call him back a little later when they get home?' Kate opens her mouth to protest and promptly shuts it. No point. Audrey isn't in receiving mode. 'Campbell wants to watch his nature programme at nine o'clock so they'll be away home by then. Goodbye dear.'

Struan's mother means well. Yes, Audrey is kind to have Struan and Isla at short notice but even so, Kate feels small and lonely. She's physically aching to speak to her little girl. Surely Audrey must realise that. Kate takes comfort in the truth that Isla's having a good time and she'd never deny the grandparents time alone with Isla. But Audrey's insinuation that Kate is essentially surplus to requirement brings tears to her eyes. *For God's sake.* Kate brushes tears away, angry and frustrated with herself. Isla is fine. Struan is fine. The only problem here is insecurity. Her own insecurity. And now is a very bad time to show weakness. She still has to face Marc. She needs to be less of a worrier and think more like a warrior.

She takes a series of deep breaths, as advised by the counsellor she used to see when her anxieties were at their peak and looks up at a spot on the peeling plaster ceiling. Once calm she lifts her handbag from the bed and leaves the room.

Marc has also made use of the time to shower and change. He stands alone in the lobby as Kate glides down the stairs towards him, conscious of his gaze. He looks sharp in a pair of well-fitting Levis and a crisp blue shirt. Maybe he's been a little too generous with his aftershave but the quality of the scent allows for some extravagance. She picks out citrus fruits, verbena and warm woody notes. Not a scent she recognises on him which is a bigger relief than she cares to admit. No uncomfortable memories to make her blush. The blend is still provocative and heady. She'll find it difficult to relax in his presence and her eyes dart around the lobby area in search of Brett. Marc's crooked smile is even more unnerving. Why is he playing Mr Nice Guy all of a sudden?

'No need to fret, Katie. Brett's on his way. He's closing an important deal over the phone.'

'There's a surprise.'

'Sorry, guys. Did I hold the party up?'

Brett is the only one among them not to have changed his clothes, too busy attending to his urgent trans-Atlantic business to take a shower or even go to the trouble of swapping his shirt. He's a world apart from the fastidious, all American hero, clean to the extreme. He too has thrown aftershave about his person but if Marc's scent takes Kate on a transcendent journey towards a candlelit bedroom, Brett's prompts a gagging reflex, mentally dumping her in the pipeline of a heavy chemicals plant. The aroma hits the back of her throat causing her to cough and step back. Her defensive manoeuvre doesn't go unnoticed by Marc who shoots her another dangerous, conniving grin. Somewhere between arriving at the hotel and meeting in the foyer he's ditched the angry young man that drove them here. Kate remains suspicious and intends to keep a safe distance reckoning he can't be trusted not to turn back into a snarling wolf.

'Shall we?' he gestures to the entrance of the hotel and the promise of fresh air.

'Yes, Sir!' Brett bounces towards the door and rubs his expansive stomach. 'I don't know about you guys, but I am literally starving. I hope that provincial restaurants are more generous with their portion sizes than the ones in Paris. I spent several hundred euros taking a client out to dinner last night and sent the plates back because it looked like they'd missed off the main dish. Where I'm from the plates are twice as big and twice more full. You order steak, you get the whole damn cow. I swear I've lost two kilos since I arrived in this country and I only arrived Monday.' Appraising the tight buttons on his shirt Kate is hard pushed to tell which part of Brett has shed two kilos. *Must be his wallet.*

'I'm sure we'll get a good meal here,' Marc ventures with more feeling than Kate can muster. As promised by the hotel proprietor it's only a short walk to the restaurant. They reach the small, fatigued exterior with the words 'Chez Philippe' peeling from the sign above the door. Kate sneaks a look at Marc and credits herself for her prediction. He's wearing his crosspatch face again. For the hundredth time she wishes she were several hundred miles north with Struan and on their way to Timberyard, her favourite restaurant in Edinburgh.

Marc opens the door and stands to one side. A short, dim passage leads to a second door.

'Ladies first.' He's being polite but Kate would have preferred him to take the lead.

The impression set by the exterior of Chez Philippe is in stark contrast to the ambience inside. Kate's immediately struck by the warmth and noise as she rounds the corner into the main restaurant. Every table in the house is taken She stops still and stares in stunned relief. She'd expected the place to be saturated with the worst kind of lager drinking, chip munching British tourists all stuck in miserable transit.

'Friends of Marcel, bienvenus chez moi!'

This generous greeting comes from Philippe, the eponymous owner of the restaurant, a diminutive and jolly

Father Christmas of a man with red cheeks and bright eyes. He speaks at breakneck speed.

'Marcel phoned me to say that you were coming.' He lowers his voice as though letting them in on a great secret. 'We do not generally advertise ourselves, you see. Too many English people coming out on the booze cruises, you know? They have caused me very great trouble in the past but Marcel said you were not typical. He was impressed that you were looking for a good French meal.' He chuckles as he casts a look at Kate. 'Marcel must like you, and I can see why. You should know that he sends those he does not approve of to the poisonous pizzeria beside the hypermarket! They have an excellent record of inducing illness in tourists. Come in, my friends and be seated. You will be desiring an apéritif, I am sure.'

Philippe escorts them to a cosy table in the back corner of the restaurant.

'I bring you drinks, a little compliment, how do you say, on the house? Whisky for the men and a Kir Royale for a beautiful lady.' Kate is partial to a dram but doesn't say anything. Besides she fancies something fizzy.

Philippe's introduction sets the tone for the rest of their meal which is delicious, authentic French cuisine. Even Brett is impressed, declaring that his fillet steak is as good as any he's tasted back home. Kate raises her eyebrows that Brett has finally found something that makes his grade. He even asks Philippe about the provenance of the beef.

'A very intelligent question, my friend. We use only the finest French beef from the finest French cows, of course.' He wags his finger at Kate as though she is a naughty schoolgirl. 'None of your mad English cow in my cuisine, thank you very much.'

Brett is swift to distance himself from Britain. He announces his American status to Philippe with a puffed out chest, prompting Philippe to commence a lengthy discussion about the new Democratic party and the United States' first ever black President, Barack Obama.

'He is better than that Bush man, no?'

'Now, I'm a Republican through and through.' Brett shows strong allegiance to the previous Bush administration and a lively debate ensues about the merits of opposing parties. At long last Brett has dropped his artificial 'business' patter and in so doing becomes altogether more human and likeable. Even if Kate doesn't share his views, in particular those he upholds in relation to the constitutional right to bear arms, at least she now understands over half of what he says.

'Brett, you're learning to speak plain English. Well done!' The cosiness of the restaurant combined with good food and a very tasty Kir Royale have taken the edge off Kate's anxiety, even around Marc. The exceptional wine that seems to flow endlessly from bottomless decanters has also loosened her tongue. Philippe is as adept at pouring the wine as Marc has proved to be in ordering it.

Over coffee and a small digestif Philippe, Brett and his host continue their chat moving from politics to golf.

'Brett, I insist that you come with me. Yes, yes, immediately if you please.' Philippe pulls a red-faced Brett to his feet. 'I will take you to the very back of the restaurant, to the private room behind the kitchens. There you will see my exquisite and much guarded collection of cups, clubs and photos of golfing legends. Jack Nicklaus. Seve

Ballesteros. I have met them all.'

Brett doesn't wait to be asked twice.

'You would like to see also?' Philippe graciously extends the invitation to the whole table but Marc declines.

'Please, you go ahead. I am going to savour this delicious calvados and if my memory serves me right, Kate isn't a golfer.'

Philippe looks shocked at the revelation. 'But Mademoiselle, you have such good players. For example, your Rod Andrews, master of all golf tournaments. Although I always joke that he should be a Frenchman because then his little romantic liaisons would be applauded! The British take things so seriously at times.'

Rod Andrews was the champion of every golf tournament and widely celebrated around the world until his extramarital affairs came to light. A very public dressing down by the world media had left him humiliated and he'd recently started to lose form. Philippe is not at all perturbed by Andrews' shenanigans as he explains to Brett.

'To my mind you expect too much sometimes, you Americans. You expect perfection in all areas of a man's life. We French, we appreciate beauty and pleasure; the aesthetics of love. Our love may be transient at times but it is pure. It is a thing of beauty. Perfection is important in the kitchen and the bedroom but that is all. Every personality needs his flaws, his little imperfections, no?'

Only someone with Philippe's charisma could get away with such a statement. Kate would agree that perfection can be over-rated but she is diametrically opposed to his views on transient love. It's probably not worth debating but she has a point to make.

'Hang on a minute. Love, by which I mean true love, cuts deep and deep cuts leave an indelible mark.' The exclusive interview with Rod Andrew's wronged wife on the front cover of Britain's biggest tabloid newspaper certainly left a scar on the sportsman's reputation. He's out of contention for this year's BBC Sports Personality award.

The men all stare at Kate as though she's dropped off another planet. She sips her drink feigning indifference but under the cool surface she's bubbling. Marc nurses his calvados, his dark eyes boring into her like a laser on the scar he left behind.

'Perhaps you are right, beautiful lady.' Philippe concedes, more for show than because he is persuaded. 'Forgive me and please, excuse us.'

The two new best friends wander off to explore Philippe's cache of golf memorabilia. Kate's temporary veil of security is swept away with Philippe's exit. He hasn't just removed Brett from the table. He's also taken with him the positive spirit that kept their table joyful and light hearted. Left alone, Kate and Marc stew in silence. He hasn't taken his eyes off her. Kate plays back Philippe's words about character imperfections and finally summons up the courage to look back at him. With an incline of his domed brandy glass he gestures towards her neckline.

'Whose picture do you keep in your locket these days, Katie?' His question has a mournful air. No shred of mockery. She stays silent but should know better. Marc isn't one for letting go.

'Your husband?'

She might as well tell him what he wants to know. 'Yes. And my daughter.'

'Your daughter,' he echoes. 'What's her name?'

'Isla.'

'That's a pretty name. Very Scottish.' Kate is overcome with dread. She doesn't like the direction of his conversation and wants to change the subject but her mind is blank. Too late.

'You used to keep my picture in your locket, remember? What did you do with it? Bury it or burn it?' His brittle laugh and resurgent bitterness hits Kate like a bucket of cold water filled with jagged shards of ice. Sullen Marc has resurfaced with his accusing Loseley glare.

'I did no such thing. I'm not that callous. Anyway, what's your story, Marc? Who's so important in your life that you have to be back in Brighton by eight o' clock tomorrow night?'

'It's a 'what' actually, not a 'who'.' He looks away, drains his glass and the darkness lifts from his face. Kate is relieved to find respite from his mood but this relentless Jekyll and Hyde switch is exhausting.

'And? Am I supposed to guess what you're going back for?'

'I'll tell you. I'm opening my own recording studio.'

'Marc, that's fantastic.'

'Yeah, it's the right time. I've a big launch planned for tomorrow night. I obviously need to be there for it.'

'Of course you do and wow, that is a big deal. Well done. Really, I'm pleased for you.' Kate's encouragement is sincere and it's no real wonder that an ambitious guy like Marc would want to run a studio on his own terms.

'You've worked hard enough and you're great at what you do. You deserve to be a success.' He leans back, eyes narrowed, to study her from a distance, more objectively.

'I'm just going to let that sink in for a minute. You think I deserve success?'

'Since you ask, yes, I do. Why? Don't you?'

'I work bloody hard, so yes. But I've made mistakes as you well know. And since most of today you've been looking at me as though I'm a complete arse I'm touched by what you just said. Thanks, Katie.'

She nods in acknowledgement. This is a truce of sorts, animosity between them lifted, for now anyway. To prolong the peace she should keep the conversation trained on his work and plans for the studio. Safe territory. He's clearly bursting to tell her all about it but Kate can't stop herself from picking at old wounds and prying into his private life. False confidence from the alcohol has weakened her self-restraint. She copies Marc's earlier gesture and empties her glass of its last few drops.

'So, a big launch? A party among the good and the great in the music world? You're not telling me there won't be a special someone there to share in your celebrations?' She tries to keep an even voice but she's fishing for more information and there's a risk attached. He holds her gaze, unblinking for a full five seconds before shaking his head and exhaling. He casts a look skywards as though asking the Gods a question and drags his words out like painful splinters that need to be removed.

'There is someone in my life, yes.'

Confirmation of the inevitable. A man like Marc wouldn't have been on his own for long. A ripple of shivers runs down Kate's spine. What else had she expected and what does it matter anyway? She is happily married. Marc is entitled to have someone too.

'Well, that's nice.' She cringes at her choice of adjective. 'Good for you.' Why does she sound so brittle? So patronising? Surely her voice isn't cracking? Her relationship with Marc is history. Terminated. Transient love. She forces a smile.

'Spill the beans then! What's she like?'

'Does it matter?'

'Probably not. I'm just making small talk.'

'No you're not. Why do you want to know, Katie?'

'Oh for God's sake, Marc. I'm trying to be civil. You don't have to share anything with me you don't want to, and if you do it's no great shakes. We go our separate ways tomorrow and there's no reason why we should see each other ever again. I have my family and my life in Edinburgh and you'll be busy making sweet music in Brighton. Our paths led us in different directions in life. This, now, it's just a random blip in our timelines. In 48 hours we'll be miles apart. Again. Tell me. Don't tell me. I honestly don't care.' The force of her outburst triggers something in him.

'Look, Katie. I never meant to hurt you before and I don't want to hurt you now.'

She makes a face. 'What do you mean?'

'Exactly that.'

'How could you possibly hurt me now?'

Marc sighs. 'OK. If you really want to know I'll tell you. It's better that you hear it from me anyway.'

Kate feels the rise of goosebumps on her skin as her nerves grow more unsteady. What on earth could Marc possibly tell her about his new girlfriend that could hurt her after all these years? All the pain from their relationship is behind her. Or is it? There is a lifelong scar but it's not the open, bleeding wound he left her with.

She sits and waits with a question mark hanging over her head. Marc is still hesitant, troubled even. She hadn't realised her hands were so cold until he reaches for them across the table and covers them with his. It's the last thing she expected him to do. This must be bad. He leans in towards her. At close range his dilated pupils are enormous, dark, deep pools that she could jump into to be lost forever. Except she'd drown in them. He tries to speak but winces as though someone's sticking pins into his legs and he can't find the words to raise the alarm.

'Go on,' she urges, even though she knows he's about to tell her something she won't want to hear.

The restaurant fades away. For a split second it's just the two of them again, in sharp relief. An ephemeral moment. One she will never forget. When he drops his bombshell it thunders down from the Gods. A direct hit.

'I'm seeing Jessica, Katie.' She gasps but he's not finished yet. 'And we're getting married.'

Chapter 16

Alice - time to fly

As a general rule I am not a poor sleeper and am prone to dropping off day or night with ease, but tonight I found myself unable to get comfortable and was still tossing and turning well past 10 o'clock. Sleep refused to come. My shoulder was playing up all evening, niggling me and shooting pains down my side as punishment for overstretching myself. This is what I get for trying to prove my stamina to the Doctor, to stop her from drawing a conclusion that I'd be better off in a nursing home; a ghastly thought that makes me shudder. A frightful scenario I may have to consider unless I take better care of myself. My bony frame crumbles like a chalk cliff following a period of stormy weather.

After an hour of clock-watching and futile sheep counting, I gave in and went in search of the pink pills that purport to deliver instant pain relief. I would be well advised to keep them in my bedside cabinet in future as the walk to the kitchen brought with it a rush of stars to the head and a near blackout that would have seen me in that nursing home by next week. I stumbled into the sitting room and grabbed the back of my upright armchair in the nick of time.

I felt my way around the chair until I was at last able to collapse onto it, thankful not to break any bones in the process. The crepe skin on the back of my hands snagged on a loose upholstery nail. Damn, damn, damn the pain. The gaps between the wrinkles on my face closed as I winced. Silly old fool. Frail and decrepit. How much longer will I be able to live independently without compromising my health?

I found neither the energy nor the inclination to move. I was exhausted rather than restful but proximity to the garden allowed a natural calm to filter through. My little patch below was floodlit by the full moon and I sat still as a statue in my chair, hollow cheeks, silver hair and flaky bones but otherwise intact and still of sound mind, thank the good Lord. A small fox emerged stealthlike from behind the overgrown hebe plant, the one that needs attention before it encroaches on my marigolds and antirrhinum. Another reminder that I need help to stay on top of things.

The animal I initially took to be a small fox turned out to be Puddy on the prowl. He is a greedy puss. He'll return in the early hours of the morning sated, claiming his rights to my armchair but will be forced to settle for the bony lap of a silly, old woman who sleeps fitfully in the light of the moon.

The night of my trip to the ballet at Sadler's Wells was equally clear and cloudless with a full moon that had everyone craning their necks to gawp at it. I took the train to Victoria and then onto the underground, emerging at Angel which was the nearest tube station to our hotel, the small but perfectly adequate Victoria Park. Mother had already arrived and was waiting patiently in reception. The joy I felt to be back in London was enhanced by the extraordinary show of a smile on Mother's thin lips. She even managed to greet me with a kiss on the cheek. Quite unheard of. We were both eager to see the ballet and although I wished it were Douglas by my side I nonetheless appreciated the effort he'd made to obtain these tickets. He was trying to bridge the wide gap between a mother and her daughter. I was hard pushed to remember the last time I'd been alone in Mother's company. Perhaps this experience would enable us to find some common ground.

We went for a light meal in a nearby family restaurant on Rosebery Avenue where I forced myself to bite my tongue on several occasions at her irksome comments. Mother couldn't help herself dropping criticisms of me into every conversation while simultaneously singing the praises of Douglas.

'What a catch you have found in that fine man, Alice.' Then, 'He is such a perfect husband.' And to follow, 'How lucky you are to be married to a man like Douglas.'

With each song of praise I bristled internally. If only she knew the truth beneath superficial perfection. No man is without weakness and Douglas had the deepest fault line running through his core. But it would do no good to dwell on previous errors of judgement or cheap green writing paper so I kept quiet. The past was behind us. We are all entitled to one mistake if we learn from it and don't make the same mistake again.

Mother no longer broached the subject of grandchildren although she pointedly discussed the achievements of various offspring of her neighbours' children, none of whom had an iota of significance to me. Somehow I maintained a polite smile throughout the meal, concentrating on the fish on my plate which would have been tasty without Mother's verbal seasoning. I suffered a brief bout of indigestion as we hastened to the theatre, attributing acid reflux to Mother's conversation rather than the food.

I relished an evening of ballet almost as much as I looked forward to Mother's enforced silence once the curtain was raised. Absorbing our surroundings it was impossible not to feel a jolt of excitement. Unlike too many theatre-goers today, everyone had dressed for the occasion; ladies in full sweeping skirts with fitted waists and pearls to complete the look. Grace Kelly was alive in all of them that night. No one would have guessed that the country was still enduring a period of austerity.

We purchased a programme and made our way to fine seats in the stalls. No need to scrabble for coins for binoculars to improve our view of the stage. The orchestra made last minute preparations. Violin strings finely tuned. The final call sounded. The lights dimmed and the velvet curtain lifted. I held my breath.

Not a dry eye in the house that night. The company moved us to tears with a production that was nothing short of exquisite. No duff notes from the orchestra while the cast moved around the stage with the lightness of angels. Hypnotic viewing. Diminutive dancers soaked up the applause at the end before retiring back stage, presumably to soak their tired feet in warm water and Epsom Salts.

The departing audience remained under the spell of the performance long after the final curtain touched the ground. Even Mother was rendered temporarily speechless, unable to find her voice until we stepped onto the pavement to hail a taxi. Her tear-stained face showed vulnerability and an alien emotion close to affection came over me. The ageing process was softening Mother's features. She was starting to reach for bannisters on stairs where once she would have strode down the middle in a hands-free, territorial fashion. Tentatively I linked my arm through hers and she did not reject my gesture. It felt neither right nor wrong.

We were fortunate not to have to wait too long for a cab and were assisted by a middle-aged gentleman who'd been in the bar area during the interval enjoying a large gin and tonic. He waved his bamboo walking stick in the air to attract attention.

'Please, I insist you take this car.'

'Thank you,' Mother replied with a coy look that made me wonder if she had been making eyes at him.

'Well, wasn't that marvellous,' she said, I assumed in relation to the performance.

'Magical.'

'And how thoroughly decent of Douglas to provide us with such a treat.'

'Yes.'

'Almost too good to be true.'

What would Douglas be doing at this time? I still found I had to reassure myself that there was no need to distrust him. The green letters had ceased to arrive. He appeared more content, humming as he went about his business.

He would most likely be sitting by the fire, poring over recent correspondence from members of the amateur wine makers' circle, honing his wine-making techniques. He had no masonic commitments, leaving him free to deepen his knowledge of wine production, a rapidly growing hobby for men of his type around the country.

Mother decided against a cup of tea before bedtime, instead retiring directly to bed. I sat at the dressing table in the bedroom and in the dim light of a solitary lamp I crafted a postcard to Douglas exclaiming what a wonderful time we'd spent at the ballet. *Dear Douglas, thank you for thinking of me. Yours, Alice.* The postcard would arrive at the house a day or so after my return but this was no matter. My simple intent was to capture a happy moment and share it with my husband.

Mother snored through the night and alien sounds from the streets below woke me at intervals. Having wondered what Douglas had been doing earlier, thoughts now turned to Papa. How would he be feeling without Mother? She was hard to live with but his devotion remained steadfast. To me he was a saint.

After a good breakfast of scrambled eggs on toast, we paid our hotel bill with money that Douglas had given me to cover all our expenses and made our way back to Victoria by taxi. I for one was tempted by the bus for the sheer pleasure of travelling on a smart, red Regent III RT, but Mother's age and new frailties had to be considered, not to mention her cemented views that those who travel on the bus were N.Q.O.C..

'N.Q.O.C.?' I queried.

'Not Quite Our Class,' the fearful snob enunciated.

I insisted on seeing her safely onto her train, as much to ensure she was gone as to fulfil my duty as her daughter. We shared an awkward embrace, skin barely touching as we kissed goodbye.

On balance, I appreciated our time together in London and felt confident that she would take some fond memories home with her, even if none of them involved me. The probability of such excursions becoming a regular feature in our yearly calendar remained low, but this trip had brought about a reconciliation of sorts and it was fair to ascribe its success to Douglas and his meticulous planning.

Time to return home and resume marital life. The trip, though brief, had confirmed my commitment to Douglas and so I had closed the final chapter on the book charting our difficulties. Show me a marriage that hasn't been tested. It won't be a marriage that has come of age.

My journey home on the Pullman provided an enjoyable interlude thanks to the delightful older couple with whom I shared a compartment. They had been up to London to visit their son. They alighted at Lewes and for the remainder of the journey I had the whole compartment to myself which allowed me to enjoy views of the South Downs. I appreciated such moments of quiet contemplation and had never been one to fear solitude. One's status as an only child requires a degree of self-sufficiency. I've always been comfortable in my own company. This is fortunate since I have spent much of my life alone. Sometimes this has been my own choice but often solitude is a condition that has been imposed on me. I have simply learned to get on with it and not make a fuss.

I expected Douglas to greet me off the train. He'd made all the travel arrangements and knew the time of my arrival but there was no sign of him when I stepped onto the platform. He might have been delayed by his habitual

Sunday morning task. He was no great Church goer but he religiously checked the weekly accounts. It seldom took him more than a few hours to reconcile the figures so he'd have completed them by lunchtime. I hurried along the platform towards the station itself, eager to see him.

No Douglas by the ticket office either. I told myself he'd been held up and waited underneath the station clock, a well designated meeting place.

I waited and I waited, like a character in a Beckett play. After an hour it became clear that I was waiting for nothing more than time to pass.

Since he was nowhere to be seen and there was now an absence of porters to assist with my suitcase I made my way outside and claimed a vacant taxi, looking out for Douglas on every pavement as we journeyed towards the house. The only person I recognised was Mrs Harrison, a local widow and regular customer out walking her little terrier, Byron. Douglas called her dog 'the rat on a rope', though always smiled serenely to Mrs Harrison's face, asking how Byron was keeping.

'Arthritic knees, Mr Emery. He's not long for this world I fear.'

The streets that separated our home from the station looked like the Marie Celeste after the bustle of London's roads. Still no sign of Douglas. He must be waiting for me at home.

I turned my key in the lock. It seemed stiffer than usual.

'Hello? I'm back.'

My greeting bounced off the walls. The daffodils I had placed in a vase before the weekend caught my eye. Short of water, they had begun to wilt. I tutted and shook my head but wasn't too cross. Men tend not to notice such matters. I placed my little case on the floor and carried the vase into the kitchen where I ran the cold water tap directly into it. The tap coughed and spluttered to life. Things weren't quite right.

The house was deathly still and cold as though the stove hadn't been lit. A noise outside caught my attention. A banging door, suggesting Douglas must be somewhere in the vicinity. If not in the house then perhaps in the garage or garden? I went in search of him but found no one. The noise I'd heard was the door to the shed. It had blown open, each gust of wind causing it to knock against the fence. I closed it properly and noticed the flutter of a net curtain next door.

Still failing to find Douglas in either the garage or the garden I recognised the uneasy sensation that accompanies a rapidly beating heart, a dry mouth and clammy palms. Douglas was a creature of habit, so when I found the accounting books lying incomplete on the desk in the office I feared something terrible had happened.

I ran through the house calling his name. Still nothing.

Few homes in those days had their own telephone. They were an expensive luxury. Thankfully we were fortunate enough to have had one installed in the New Year. I lifted the receiver and dialled the number of the shop, thinking Douglas might have decided to undertake a stock audit or collect outstanding receipts from the week. No reply. I thought I must be going mad. Perhaps he'd walked down to the railway station to meet me after all? Somehow we'd missed each other. This seemed the safest, most feasible explanation for his absence and I tried to accept it as fact.

But my heart beat faster and I knew something was wrong.

Rather than chasing back to the station to search for him I decided to be sensible and distract myself by unpacking my belongings. Surely he'd be back before too long. I would impress him with a fancy spread for tea. We should still have half a fruit loaf in the larder.

Suitcase unpacked and tidied away, I made my way downstairs to the kitchen and filled a pan with water, placing it carefully on the stove. A cup of tea is a much underestimated medicine. I glanced up at the kitchen clock and prepared two cups and saucers. Still no sign of Douglas but the pot would stay warm for a while yet and I could always add a drop more boiling water when he came through the front door. The nagging feeling that something was wrong was still there.

And then I saw it.

How I failed to spot it I do not know. A single piece of paper lying on the kitchen table. I suppose I'd been preoccupied with the flowers, the shed door and latterly with tea making. My mind had been on Douglas. And where he was.

It was only when I carried the cups and saucers to the table that I saw a single sheet of paper lying like a discarded napkin. The paper was folded over once to make a perfect rectangle. My name in capitals, printed, in Douglas's neat hand. ALICE. He'd used black ink. Quink black ink, dark as coal. Black, absorber of colour, absent of light. In my case, black brought down the curtain on my marriage. A marriage I'd thought was in recovery.

Later I took a match to the crumpled ball I made from the note, but his written words cut so deep that even now, decades later, I still see them in my mind's eye. They tormented me over the years though I refuse to allow them to define me.

'This is not an easy letter for me to write.' Typical opening words from Douglas who only ever saw things through his own lens. Scant regard for other people's feelings unless they impacted upon his own. If the letter was hard to write he hadn't the first idea of the sheer agony I experienced reading it.

He was leaving me. No, I should be more precise. He'd already left me. The house was cold as death because he'd taken the tiniest flame of our marriage and pinched it hard between his finger and thumb, extinguishing it, depriving it of all oxygen without even bothering to hear if I had anything to say on the matter. His selfish words flashed before me, a sorry excuse for an explanation that should have been delivered to my face. Husband to wife.

'I'm sorry to break difficult news by letter.' The monstrous coward. I read on, incredulous that he'd gone to so much trouble to get me out of the way so he could slope off without fear of confrontation.

'While it pains me to write this, I can no longer continue with our marriage. My intentions are to give up the dispensary and the shop and move to Brighton. I plan to marry Anne and become a father to her son. This is not a decision I have taken lightly. I will not leave you destitute and will see to it that you are provided for financially. I have always said that you are a strong and capable person. You will find someone better suited to you. I hope you find the compassion to understand. Regards, Douglas.'

I have sat through many films and read many books in

which unpleasant bombshells are dropped on unsuspecting characters. Some swoon, others break into shrieks of anguish. Most have an opportunity to share their pain with others. I cried.

I read and reread his words, refusing to accept that he had found them hard to write. The letter dropped from my hand as easily as he'd dropped me and it fluttered to the ground, belying the weight of its contents. My chest tightened and my knees gave way. I lay on the floor as the day ebbed away. I had no one to hear my words or share my pain. No one to turn on the light.

Agony. I'd never experienced pain like it. Everything around me was the same but all the dimensions had altered. Distorted through sabotage. I shouldn't have bothered to replenish the vase with water. Dying flowers provided a fitting tribute to my new status as a deserted woman. When the initial shock passed, anger surged in me from the depths of my soul. I wanted to rage at Douglas, force him to face me and face up to our marriage. The vase cracked against the wall when I threw it, my shoulders heaving with every sob. I cried so hard for the rest of the day, until the day became yesterday and my head thumped from the strain.

Needless to say there was no change of heart from Douglas. Nor any direct contact. Absconded like a common criminal. I was left embarrassed, angry and hurt. I couldn't stomach food at all and ate nothing for days, while simultaneously developing a nasty kidney infection that had me doubled up in pain. I didn't just lose my appetite for food. I lost my appetite for life. I walked in a daze for miles up and down the promenade, pulling the brim of my hat low to shield my face from passers-by who might recognise me and enquire after Douglas.

'How is Mr Emery? Keeping well?'

Terrible I wanted to say. *He has a fearful disease that's rotting him from the inside out. Unfortunately it's not visible to anyone other than me. I hate him.*

I couldn't bear to venture anywhere near the shop. It's possible he was still opening up each morning. He still needed an income until the shop passed to a new owner. More so now than ever with a child to feed, an estranged wife to support and a mistress in tow. I couldn't even bear to utter her name.

I loathed the tiny part in me that wanted him to come home but I never expected his return. He stood on the threshold of his new family life, a welcome mat at a green front door. He'd left me on the brink of a breakdown in a house without colour.

I'd forgotten all about the stupid postcard mailed from London. When it dropped through the door a few days later I lost all control, screaming and scratching at the walls until my fingernails were broken.

It was a bright and joyful postcard, sent by a woman with flawless skin and a promising future ahead of her. It was loving and thankful, intended for a man she thought was hers. In the shadow of his departure it became nothing but a worthless patch of brittle paper, received by a broken woman with tear-stained face and cracked heart, her past contaminated, her loss complete.

Chapter 17

Kate - to lose, Toulouse 2002

Kate and Marc were invited to Marc's parents' villa in the south of France for a fortnight every August. This fast became Kate's favourite time of year thanks to balmy nights under the stars and hot days languishing by the swimming pool. Pure, unadulterated bliss. John and Monique took their responsibilities as hosts very seriously and all guests were guaranteed an excellent stay. A bottle of wine or Ricard on tap. Plenty of fresh, seasonal produce in the kitchen. Meal preparation was a fun event in itself and set the ambience for lively discussions on every subject from art to politics. Marc's relaxed relationship with his parents meant that Kate also looked on John and Monique as close friends, not remote out-laws.

The young couple lay in a double hammock on the terrace after dark, counting shooting stars and making wishes, some silly, some serious. The previous summer on this very terrace Marc had proposed.

'When I was in my late teens I used to look up at the stars in the sky and wonder what my future wife was doing, where she was, when I might meet her.' Fingers entwined, Marc gave Kate's a light squeeze. 'What do you imagine she's doing right now?'

Kate looked over to read his face, unsure where he wanted to take this conversation.

'Jet-skiing in Mustique?' she teased. 'Hmm, let's see. What do you think she's up to? Will she be jealous if I do this?' She leaned in with a slow kiss.

'You sexy minx. You know full well she's right here lying next to me.' Was he leading up to a proposal of marriage or a hint of things to come? Kate didn't like to assume. They'd been living together for the best part of four years so he might just as well be referring to her as his common-law wife. Then again, maybe he had bigger plans.

Marc pulled her back towards him and their lips met in a more intense kiss confirming desire and, Kate hoped, love eternal. Marc believed in marriage. His parents provided excellent role models. And yet Kate also knew him as a maverick. There were no cast iron guarantees about what their relationship meant or where it was going. Nothing lasts forever, everyone knows that.

In the beginning, ambiguity had suited Kate. Comfortable in her own skin and alive in the spring of their relationship, she'd not fixated on marriage as a destination point. However, as months passed and friends began to settle down she had begun to question whether their relationship would progress that far.

Kate tugged the bottom of his collarless shirt to reach inside, but he pulled away as though their embrace had provided impetus for something other than sex.

'Marc? Is everything OK? You're looking at me strangely.'

'The truth is I've been thinking a lot recently and I'm not really happy with the way things are.'

'You're not?'

'No.' He sighed. 'And I want things to change.' He wasn't smiling.

'Change?'

'Yes, change. Permanently. I'm sorry.' He shook his head and tugged his ear lobe which he tended to do when he was nervous. 'I didn't think it would be this bad.' Kate's mouth dropped open and despite the heat, she felt a shiver of cold.

'Are you trying to tell me you want to break up?' He shook his head.

'Quite the opposite. Katie, I want you to marry me and be my wife.'

'Get married? You want us to get married?'

'More than anything. Say you will, won't you? Choose me?' Relief flooded through her. This wasn't a game. No hesitation or deviation required.

'Yes, yes, of course I'll marry you!'

'Become the next Madame Loseley?'

'I'd love to!'

Kate's mind raced ahead to wedding dresses, bridesmaids and venue. White or red roses in her bouquet? What really mattered was a shared life to look forward to. Married life with Marc and yet somehow her energies gathered to focus on one proposition: The Wedding Day. A single day in their lives. 24 hours. 1,440 minutes.

The rest of the holiday passed in a blur of champagne bubbles and countless impromptu parties thrown in celebration of their engagement. Max and Maggie Hunter, close friends of John and Monique owned a large mansion of obscene grandeur further up the hill. Max, notorious party planner when he wasn't running multi-million pound businesses saw the engagement as the perfect excuse for fireworks set to live music. Kate found it all overwhelming.

'It's like we're royalty.'

'It is a bit,' conceded Marc, 'but Max likes nothing better than to party. Enjoy it and trust me, this is as much for him as it is for us.'

Several hours into the party, Monique and Kate sat by the side of the Hunters' pool. As they dangled their feet in the water Monique let slip that her neighbours and friends put on a good show but that their life wasn't all fun and games.

'They want nothing more than for their own daughter Jessica to settle down. They've tried everything to tame her, you see.' She looked around to make sure that no one could hear, 'including sending her to the most expensive finishing school for young ladies in Switzerland and introducing her to elite young bachelors.'

'It didn't work?'

'Quite the opposite. Jessica Hunter is a self-professed wild child. She won't toe the party line unless it's laced with cocaine.' Monique shrugged her shoulders as though this was old news but Kate's jaw dropped.

'Was she expelled?'

'Maggie's never confided in me the full story but I've been told that Jessica's premature departure from the school involved an illicit affair. A liaison with one of the young gardeners. They had sexual relations.' She sipped her Cosmopolitan. 'It was the final nail in a coffin full of screws.'

Over several strong cocktails Kate discovered more from Monique who seemed only too eager to dish the dirt on

Jessica. A generous donation from Mr Hunter to the school had been discreetly made and graciously received, a gift that just so happened to coincide with Jessica's quiet exit through the back door. The word expulsion was never uttered.

Since then none of the eligible young men selected by the Hunters to tame Jessica lasted more than a few weeks. Some managed little more than a couple of hours. Those Jessica considered 'dull' were flicked aside without so much as a backward glance.

'Honestly, she takes greater care over the ash that falls from her cigarette.' Monique explained the trouble with Jessica. 'Max spoiled her as a child and Maggie wasn't much better. They realised too late she'd been overindulged. And now they can only look on and weep at the heavy price they're paying.' Monique shook her head and tutted. 'She's not a stupid girl but she will not apply herself. She cannot keep a job. It is a wonder her parents still pay her an allowance. They are far too soft. It is not how I would do things.' Kate didn't doubt it. Marc might have grown up around money but his parents expected him to work hard and earn his own living.

'There are no guarantees,' Marc had pointed out early on in their relationship. They'd been invited for dinner with Ellie and James who wanted to meet Marc and as Ellie put it, 'give him the once over'. Ellie had ushered Marc out of the kitchen to give him the full tour of the house, wine cellar and all.

'You have a lovely home.'

'Yes I do, don't I. I'm lucky James is loaded, so I'm made for life.' Kate had wanted to apologise for her sister's glib response, noticing that Marc had raised an eyebrow. He wasn't a man who took inherited wealth for granted. Unlike Jessica it seemed.

'Of course, Jessica's first problem is her looks. Face as pretty as a picture. Many people are blinded by her appearance. Especially men.' Monique wrinkled her nose as though bothered by a bad smell. 'But what she possesses in looks she lacks in integrity. She understands etiquette but dispenses with manners. She has always had a rich boyfriend in tow, though they come and go like buses. She dispatches them as soon as she acquires them.' Monique rubbed the palms of her hands against each as though to get rid of an unwanted piece of dirt. 'All she does is party. Her poor mother's found every form of recreational drug in Jessica's bedroom, though how Maggie knows what half the substances are I would not like to say.'

'Jessica sounds like quite a character.'

'She is a natural predator who enjoys the chase. As for the kill, many foolish boys have had their hearts shattered. Nice boys too, some of them.'

'She must have some good qualities, surely? What do you like about her?' Kate watched Monique frown and tilt her head to the side.

'Let me see. I can think of three virtues for Jessica. First of all she is quick-witted which makes her an agile conversationalist. And secondly she is able to laugh at herself which is a blessing. If, or rather when, she makes a fool of herself she will always tend to laugh. At least that's what I see. Or it's the face she shows us. She's not a sulker. Think of a lioness tossing back her golden locks and sharpening her claws. She once said to me, 'I know I can be a silly bitch but at least no one can accuse me of being boring."

'She doesn't sound at all boring,' Kate agreed.

'Yes, on that point we are all united. Jessica's only predictability is that she's thoroughly unpredictable.'

'She sounds a little like my sister when we were growing up. Hard work and terribly selfish, but also a lot of fun.'

'Well, Jessica can be fun of course but she needs to grow up. Her self-confidence doesn't quite spill over into arrogance but it comes too close for my liking. What frustrates us most about her is that she possesses a natural gift that she simply doesn't appreciate.'

Monica was referring to Jessica's third virtue, her aptitude for painting which Kate knew something of already. The Hunter villa showcased canvasses that proved Jessica to be an exceptional, versatile artist. These eclectic and brilliant selections of paintings she knocked out with ease, shrugging away compliments with the same nonchalance she shrugged away her every impropriety. Either she didn't care about her gift or she cared too much to let it show.

Jessica's aptitude as an artist endeared her to John from a young age. He recognised artistic talent when he saw it and encouraged her to pursue her gift full-time. He'd also tried to persuade her parents, his good friends that Jessica would be wasted at finishing school in Switzerland.

'For God's sake, Max. Her talent is too good to waste. Honestly, she should apply to St Martin's in London or the Paris College of Art.' He'd shake his head with frustration and pour himself a large Johnnie Walker when reporting back to his wife. 'They are as stubborn as Jessica is unruly.'

'I'm far less enamoured with Jessica than John is, but his failing is that he only sees the best in people.' Monique continued. 'She may be talented but talent alone cannot compensate for her multitude of sins. I have the measure of that girl and well she knows it. She tones down her act several degrees when I'm around and takes careful steps not to cross the line with me. But I know a hidden agenda when I see one.'

Monique accurately deduced that the predatory girl had fixed her sights on Marc as potential boyfriend material.

'No mother would stand by to see her son seduced into a relationship only to have his heart trampled on as soon as his novelty value had worn off.' And Monique wanted so much more for Marc than the likes of Jessica could offer. From the very first day the Loseleys met the Hunters, Monique had mobilised all her powers to thwart any chance of a relationship blossoming between their only children. She did this covertly, not wishing to create acrimony with either her new friends or her art-obsessed husband.

'So I would single Jessica out, involve her in conversation and show an interest in her. It's not because I like the girl but I believe in the merits of keeping one's enemies closer than one's friends.' She encouraged Marc to visit his extensive network of school friends around the world if she knew Jessica was home. She'd even funded a trip for him to travel around Australia the Easter Jessica was sent home in disgrace from her Swiss finishing school. Monique would not run the risk of letting her cherished son become Jessica's transient plaything.

She needn't have worried. Like his mother, Marc had seen through Jessica from the off. While he found her entertaining in small doses he had no interest in spending serious time with her. He took great pains to explain this to Kate the day after the engagement party while they stood in the kitchen of the villa preparing a light lunch.

'Jessica's due home this weekend so you'll have to meet her.' Marc made Jessica's visit sound like a visit to the dentist's chair for root canal work.

'That's fine. I'm looking forward to it. She has something of a reputation.' Marc looked over towards her.

'That's one way of putting it. Has my mother been talking to you?'

'Maybe a little,' Kate teased, popping a long stick of cucumber in her mouth. Marc put down the terracotta bowls he'd pulled from the cupboard, his face serious.

'Now, I need to give you some advice because you are sweet and she is not. Don't be intimidated by 'Jess, de fesses.'' Kate put down the rest of the cucumber she'd been chopping.

'Marc, don't be so rude!'

'I said you were sweet. There's no need to wield a knife at me.'

'You know what I mean, referring to her as though she's some kind of slapper. You've told me things about Jessica before and never without adding some pejorative comment. It's unkind.' In Marc's descriptions Jessica became variously 'Spoilt Jessica', 'Dreadful Jessica', 'Vile Jessica' or 'That Mad Bitch Jessica'. Marc said he didn't suffer fools gladly but Kate said this was no justification for open disdain.

'Calling her horrible names just makes you sound like a sexist pig.' He opened his mouth as though about to raise the stakes but must have changed his mind.

'You'll see.' He moved to stand behind her, hands resting lightly on her hips. 'Now, will you please put that knife down for a minute and come with me. We've got half an hour to ourselves. Let's make the most of it.'

Marc's disparaging comments roused Kate's sympathies towards Jessica. Since her own sister had behaved like a total toerag for most of her formative years, Kate thought herself well placed to understand attention seeking, misunderstood individuals. So when they ventured up to the Hunters' big house for the fireworks party later that evening she couldn't wait to meet the contentious wild cat.

Kate didn't see why Jessica should pose any threat to her. Marc loved her and wanted to marry her. He'd not given any reason to doubt him and besides, he was apt to say that blondes left him cold. Kate could afford to be generous to the woman who'd tried and failed to secure him for herself. Maybe her failure to do so explained her perpetual absence. Jessica failed to materialise, just as she had stayed away from their engagement party.

The party itself was declared an unqualified success and passed without event, other than the 10 minute stream of fireworks that lit up the night sky and an embarrassing moment in the speech made by a swaying Max Hunter.

'Folks, gather round and lift your glasses for a toast. To Marc and Katie! I must say, you make a most attractive couple. Katie, you're a real catch and Marc, you're one lucky guy. We'd always hoped that you might have made an honest woman out of our Jess but I guess the girl next door was too close to home.'

Maggie laughed a little too long, Marc's smile left his eyes and Monique's body went rigid until John stepped in to second the toast and to thank their generous hosts for an unforgettable night.

On balance, Jessica's presence at the party would have been awkward in the light of Max's comment. One Cosmopolitan too many also saw Monique dispense with her usual discretion and she whispered loud enough for people to hear, 'I would rather cut off all my hair than see Marc with that girl.' Mothers of all young men within earshot inclined their heads in agreement.

Jessica was none the wiser to the comments, nor worse off for missing the party. She'd been living it up along the coast in Cannes with her latest beau, an aspiring film producer. As the party wound down and the guests dispersed, Maggie apologised to the Loseleys for her daughter's absence, telling them that she was hoping that this latest boyfriend might actually last more than a few weeks.

It seemed Maggie might have been right about her daughter's blossoming new relationship as Jessica didn't appear at the weekend. Kate found herself wondering if she'd ever meet this elusive girl.

'Shouldn't we invite her to the wedding? Your parents and the Hunters are such close friends.'

'Over my dead body.' Marc was adamant that they would not be issuing her with a wedding invitation.

By Wednesday Marc and Kate had packed and were ready to head back to London. They waved goodbye to John and Monique following warm embraces and promises to call once they had arrived home. A comfortable heat was rising and Kate breathed in the warm, jasmine scented air to commit the moment to memory.

Marc turned the silver hire car to the left and started down the hill towards Les Petits Alberes, the nearest village. Kate selected a Van Morrison CD and was about to slot it into the car stereo when without warning, a red sports car came screeching up the hill. It was on the wrong side of the road, forcing Marc to brake and causing the CD case to go flying. They missed impact with the oncoming car by a slither. Marc swore and then looked over to check that Kate wasn't hurt.

'It's OK. I'm fine. Are you alright?'

'I'm furious! That bloody woman.'

A petite but curvaceous blonde sat at the wheel of the car. She wore Jackie Onassis sunglasses and a blue cocktail dress bearing Swarovski crystals that sparkled in the sunlight. Kate couldn't decide if the girl was overdressed for the time of day or underdressed given how little fabric the dress actually comprised; up close more like strips of ribbon around a Maypole. The woman reached across to the passenger seat and grasped hold of the neck of a bottle of Chase vodka which she waved in the air in an exuberant greeting.

'Marc Loseley, my absolute darling. Fancy running into you!' She spoke with an English home-counties accent, affected with a hint of upward inflection. She tilted her head to appraise Kate.

'And this must be your little girlfriend. So cute.'

'Fiancée, actually.' Kate, rendered mute by Jessica's onslaught was full of gratitude to Marc, both for preventing a collision and for correcting Jessica about her status in his life. She'd been prepared for 'Vile Jessica' to be direct and provocative but hadn't counted on her being a striking beauty. Monique had alluded to Jessica's pretty face but had tempered it with her ugly character credentials and no one had bothered to explain that the girl was also 'stunning, drop-dead gorgeous' Jessica. There'd been no recent photos of the artist in the Hunters' home to go by; the walls were monopolized by her creations and evidently self-portraits weren't her thing.

Jessica peered through the car window, looked pointedly through her sunglasses at Kate and then rolled her shoulders back and stretched out her bronzed arms as though just waking from a deep sleep. This revealed a faint scar on the inside of her right wrist and an indistinct tattoo on the back of the same hand. Jessica waved the vodka bottle in Kate's direction as though offering her a swig. She then opened her mouth to speak but Marc looked like a man about to burst. Before Kate could stop him he'd leapt from the car in a fury, leaving his door wide open, to grab the bottle from Jessica's hand. He emptied a dribble of contents onto the ground.

'You were driving like a fucking idiot! Have you been drinking? Please don't tell me that bottle isn't just for show. What sick game are you playing at now, Jess?'

She sprang back like tight elastic.

'Oh piss off, Marc. I'm not in the mood. I've been partying non-stop for three days and I need to go to bed.' She leaned back in her seat and her lips curled in a smile, revealing perfectly white teeth.

'You're still as sexy as ever. Bad temper suits you. And your girlfriend's quite easy on the eye. I like the look of that one. Better than that awful witch you were seeing before. Maybe you could both come over later and join me for a bit of no strings fun? Six o' clock suit you?'

Marc stood poised to belt her but turned his back instead. Jessica then switched her full attention to Kate. She flashed another of her dazzling smiles.

'I'm writing a book you know. It's going to be called, 'The Men I Never Slept With'.' Marc snorted with laughter, quick to put her in her place.

'Bad grammar. You shouldn't finish a sentence with a preposition.' But Jessica wasn't one to back off easily. She looked back over at him with a pout.

'Always so precise aren't you, darling? Anyway, guess who's the protagonist in chapter one? I'll tell you. Yes, Marc. You're first up.' She winked at Kate. 'For some reason that I find incomprehensible, this man,' she jabbed a finger in Marc's direction, 'has always resisted me. So far, anyway.' She looked at her nails, checking her French polish was intact. Or sharpening her claws for the kill. 'There's still time.'

'Can't *resist* you? That's a fucking joke. I *detest* you.'

Kate might have been struck dumb but Marc fired out words like bullets.

'Go ahead and write your stupid book. The men you've never slept with? I'll be glad to feature in the shortest story ever written. I take it you haven't time to capture the details of your actual conquests, assuming you can remember even half of them.'

'Murky Marc. Are you calling me a slut?' She looked at him hopefully as he turned his back on her again.

'Your words, not mine. I'm calling it a day. Go home, Jess. Get dressed. Grow up.' Jessica rolled her eyes and mouthed, 'boring' like a teenager in opposition to parental command.

'Too bad I have to go anyway but I haven't given up on you yet, Marc. Oh no.' She blew him a kiss. 'Or you, darling.' She blew a second kiss in Kate's direction and pushed her chest out. 'You look a little uptight if you don't mind me saying. I could help to loosen you up, if you like?'

Marc, back in the driver's seat revved the engine involuntarily. Kate had never seen him look so furious.

'Jesus Christ, will you just...' he began but Jessica accelerated away with a throaty growl leaving a dusty trail in her wake.

'Ciao for now!'

Marc reached out and grabbed the steering wheel, accidently blasting the horn on the hire car. Louder than expected, they both jumped in their seats.

'That fucking woman. Do you see what I mean now? She's a liability.'

They were halfway to Toulouse before Marc rediscovered his good humour. Kate urged him to see the funny side and eventually they were able to laugh off the episode on the hill.

'It's the first time I've been propositioned by another woman, even if it was only to dispossess me of my fiancé!' She recounted the story to her sister one evening over a glass of wine some months later. Ellie looked impressed.

'Wow. She makes me look like a Saint.'

'Well, I wouldn't go that far.' Ellie shot her a withering look and topped up their glasses.

'How are the wedding plans going? You've been a bit quiet on that front lately.' Kate hesitated.

'Slowly.'

After the initial excitement of the engagement the actual planning of the wedding had turned out to be much more onerous than Kate had imagined. It didn't help that she had the heaviest workload of all her colleagues. And unfortunate timing meant she was also due to be seconded for a couple of months to the firm's new Sydney office to help train up a team of graduate researchers. Marc's life was no less full and he was working round the clock at the studio. Some nights he didn't even make it home. Kate turned the pages of her diary each week with heavy heart. They still hadn't finalised a date for the wedding.

Christmas and New Year passed in a haze of work events and parties. They'd enjoyed brief respite in their schedules in March and just managed to escape to a cottage in Cornwall for Easter, but June and July upset their equilibrium again as they were constantly catapulted in different directions. On this occasion it was Marc who took up a contract to work in Los Angeles for a few weeks to help on the soundtrack of a blockbuster movie. The offer was too good to refuse.

'I miss you,' he told her when they spoke but the frequency of their conversations and the duration of their calls fell to levels that indicated otherwise.

When Kate wasn't home alone she could be found sitting in endless research studios around Europe drinking herself awake with cups of black coffee. She bounced from city to city until she felt dizzy. She listened to women in each country extoling the virtues of different brands of washing powder but they were starting to sound the same wherever she went. Idly she'd doodle a wedding dress design on a pad of paper that was supposed to be for taking notes while wondering if a Christmas wedding mightn't be such a bad idea.

On the last Sunday in June, Marc and Kate at last found themselves together, home in London. He jet lagged and irritable, she weary and preoccupied with another impossible deadline. They'd barely chatted over breakfast let alone progressed wedding arrangements.

'We should talk about the wedding.' Kate plonked a pile of magazines on the table alongside a steaming pot of coffee and a plate of buttered toast with raspberry jam. 'There's a wedding fair on at the weekend if you fancy it?'

Marc grimaced. 'Not really, to be honest. I'd rather watch daytime TV and that's saying something. But I'll come along if you want?'

'No, it's OK. I could use the time to finish writing my report anyway.' Kate's head spun like a washing machine on its final cycle. She didn't seem to know what she wanted anymore. If reading wedding magazines was so much fun then why did she feel so nauseous whenever she flicked through their glossy pages? The potential costs involved in putting on a wedding were huge and took her breath away. She wasn't even sure she wanted to wear a giant meringue dress. She felt like a fraud. Every other girl she knew seemed to love it all. Even Ellie had gone to town with her own wedding preparations with matching colour schemes, ludicrous favours and a five-tier cake.

'What kind of wedding would you like?' Kate wanted Marc to be involved but maybe now wasn't the time to pursue wedding talk. He had his nose in his well-thumbed copy of On The Road by Jack Kerouac and didn't even bother to look up.

'One with you in it.'

In the end Kate took herself off for a walk in Battersea Park to clear her head. She thought about what was troubling her and concluded that she and Marc just needed some time and space to organise the wedding. Kate reckoned they'd stand a better chance of getting both at Chateau Mojo in August. At the very least she vowed to herself that they would not return from the trip without a date in the diary for the wedding.

'We've both been working so hard,' she told Marc that night while grating parmesan over two big bowls of pasta, 'that when we go to France this year I thought we could maybe set some boundaries, so we can really spend some quality time together.'

Marc raised his eyebrows. 'OK, what do you have in mind?'

'Well, I've made a list.'

'There's a surprise.'

'You might mock my lists but stay open-minded.'

The rules Kate had in mind were communication oriented. First off, they would leave their mobile phones and laptops in London and for the duration of the holiday any mention of work would incur a penalty.

'We each note down a list of things that the other person has to do in the event that they slip up and break a rule.'

'This is getting interesting. Any no-go areas for punishment?' Marc teased with a glint in his eye.

Kate threw herself into her list. She secretly hoped Marc might just slip up. It had been a while since he'd given her a massage and that featured top of her list. She suspected Marc's list was a little more experimental. In any event she remained hopeful that the holiday would be the perfect antidote to the stresses they'd been under in recent months. It saddened her that slowly, almost imperceptibly they'd fallen out of sync with each other. Little things revealed bigger differences. They'd started bumping into each other as they moved around the kitchen to make breakfast, where before their bodies would have danced around in perfect rhythm. Or Marc would complain that he was hungry at odd times of the day so that meals shared together became more staggered and later skipped. Kate hoped that time alone without interruption from work would put them back on the same frequency.

She awoke on the day they were due to fly and jumped out of bed, anxious to empty the bins and ensure a return to a tidy flat. They'd packed bags the night before and Marc had placed the luggage in a neat pile by the front door. Kate had pre-booked a taxi and in under an hour they would be heading for Heathrow airport.

Marc was just stepping out of the shower, hair wet, towel around his waist when Kate's mobile rang. In the early days of their relationship she'd have ignored the ring and they'd most likely have ended up back in bed. But the call sliced through the air.

'Oh no, it's the office.' She should have let the call go. She was supposed to be on holiday and everyone at work knew it. But she couldn't help herself.

'It's probably someone needing a short answer to a quick question,' she reasoned. She could help them out and then turn the mobile off for two glorious weeks. Marc shot her his darkest look.

'Hello, Kate speaking.' She waved him away.

'Kate, I'm so sorry to bother you when you're on holiday.' It was Christine, a colleague from the office sounding breathless and upset.

'It's OK,' just, thought Kate as she calculated how much time she could devote to the call without causing a major row with Marc.

'It's Carol's baby boy. He's been rushed into hospital with suspected meningitis. She was supposed to be finishing the presentation for tomorrow's debrief on Spik detergents. No one else apart from you knows the project well enough. Big Eric is throwing an absolute wobbly because the global team has flown over from Chicago and he's saying that they won't commission the corporate project unless we have a decent presentation for them.' Kate took in a long breath.

'Christine, what are you asking me to do?'

'Kate, I'm really sorry about this but is there any chance you might be able to pop in briefly today to help us finish off the document? Big Eric can probably present it to the clients but he needs your help. I'm so sorry.'

Kate felt sick to the stomach. Concern for Carol's son was now accompanied by an awful realisation that she was about to postpone the start of her holiday. It wasn't that she wanted to lend a hand to Big Eric particularly. He could be a loathsome boss but she'd put too much work into this account to see it fail. And Kate knew that she simply wouldn't be able to relax until she'd left the document in a healthy state. Or better still, present it herself. She knew the project back to front and inside out. No one else knew it as well.

'I'll be over as soon as I can.' Marc stood in the doorway of the kitchen, partially dressed and rigid with fury.

'Jesus, Katie. What have you agreed to do now? We're flying to Toulouse in a few hours, remember?'

'I know, I know. I'm sorry but what else can I do? Carol's son's in hospital. No one else can do this. You'd do the same in my position.' The conversation spiralled into an explosive exchange.

'No way. I work hard but we're supposed to be on holiday, i.e. not working. You never switch off anymore.'

'I know it's not ideal, but what else could I say?'

'It's obvious. How about, 'No.''

'No?' Say no to Big Eric and goodbye to a very large account? Leave her colleagues to pick up the pieces of a project they knew little about? Compromise her position at work? By way of apology Kate shook her head and repeated her position.

'No, Marc. I know it's not ideal but I have to do this.'

'Not ideal? That's a bloody understatement. You think you have to do this? You think you're the only person who can write a few crappy slides in PowerPoint?' Kate only just managed to stop herself from rising to his derogatory comment.

'No one knows this project like I do. I can catch a flight out after the presentation tomorrow and I'll add an extra day onto my annual leave.'

'Oh, that's fucking big of you.' He gave a hollow laugh.

'Come on, Marc. Be reasonable.'

'Reasonable?' he yelled. 'I am not the bad guy here, Katie. I'm sick to death of you putting work before us all the time.' Kate opened her mouth to speak but he blocked her with the palm of his hand. 'And I've had enough. Stay here if you want. But if you can't come with me today then don't bother coming at all.'

'Marc, please!' Kate raised her voice but he was already stomping away to get dressed. She sank into a wicker chair and placed her head in her hands, a mixed bag of emotions emptying over her. She was hurt, but also angry. She'd supported Marc in his work so couldn't understand why he couldn't reciprocate when she needed his support most. She wasn't a pushy career woman but she cared about doing a good job. Why shouldn't she aspire to doing well? Why shouldn't she help a friend and colleague when they were facing a significant family emergency? Why couldn't he understand? She was overcome by the sinking realisation that he was selfish and self-seeking, happy to make sacrifices to further his own career but clearly disinterested in hers.

A taxi pulled up outside. The front door slammed. Marc left without a word of goodbye. Kate watched from the window but his stony face didn't look back to acknowledge her. Too stunned to cry she collected her briefcase and left for work.

Kate finished off the presentation, gave the performance of her life and secured the company the biggest commission they'd ever had. Carol's son responded well to medication and was out of the danger zone, prompting a collective sigh of relief around the office. In the aftermath of her work success, Kate forgave Marc his outburst and booked herself onto the next flight for Toulouse. She tried to reach him on his mobile but he'd kept to the rules of their original pact and his phone glared like a beacon on the mantelpiece at home. She tried the landline at Chateau Mojo a few times but the same message played back to her. France Telecom couldn't connect her call at that time owing to a fierce electrical storm in the region.

Kate didn't let this stand in her way, accustomed as she was to independent travel. She'd just have to hire a car at the airport and drive to Chateau Mojo. On arrival she'd surprise Marc and make up to him. He could pick any punishment for her that he wanted from his list. Everything would work out fine.

Her plan made sense and logistically ran like clockwork. The flight departed on time and landed ahead of schedule. Kate hired an adequate white Peugeot 205 and headed away from Toulouse-Blagnac towards the villa in the hills approaching the Pyrenees. It was only when she reached Chateau Mojo after dark that she was temporarily scuppered, for the villa sat still and silent, in complete darkness. It didn't take a detective to deduce that everyone was out.

Kate walked back to the car, picking up the sound of music from the large villa up the hill as she did so. The Hunters must be throwing one of their celebrated parties. Memories of last year's engagement celebrations filled Kate's mind and her need to track Marc down intensified. There was nothing to be gained from sitting in the car waiting for him to return so she set off up the hill on foot. Before she did so she sprayed her favourite perfume on her pulse points in the knowledge that Marc found this particular scent an aphrodisiac. She reapplied her lipstick and checked her appearance, keen to get their relationship back on track as soon as possible.

Further up the hill Kate found a party in full swing. People everywhere and more than she remembered from last year. She recognised a few faces but a good 10 minutes passed before she came across Monique who clapped her hands in delight and gave Kate a hug that almost made her cry.

'Katie! It is so good to see you here, at last! Marc said you were unable to join us but did not explain why. John and I were quite concerned to be honest. I am glad you're here.' She gave Kate's arm a little squeeze.

'It's good to see you too, Monique. I'm sorry I'm so late. Something came up at work but it's sorted now.' She hesitated before asking after Marc. She wondered what, if anything, Marc had told them about their argument.

'That boy! He has been horrible company and hardly spoken a word since he arrived. How you put up with him I do not know. You must be a veritable saint. Hopefully now you're here he will rediscover his sunnier disposition. He has been wearing a face like Thor.'

'Well, I'll try my best.' Monique's reassuring words helped to put Kate at ease and she allowed herself to relax a little. Marc might still be in a fury but at least she knew he cared. Anger was infinitely preferable to indifference. She looked around to see if she could spot him in the crowd.

'Do you know where he is?'

'He's certainly around here somewhere because we banned him from clattering around the villa with his long, miserable face. You could try the swimming pool. He likes to thrash out his aggression in the water.' Kate joined Monique in laughter. She couldn't wait to see him.

'I'll see if I can find him. See you in a bit.'

Kate walked around the villa and the garden for what seemed like ages, though her trusty Mondaine watch told her she'd only been at the party 20 minutes. A combination of the number of people and the darkness of the night made it difficult to cover much ground. There was no sign of Marc anywhere. French voices mingled with English and Catalan but none among them were his.

Kate reached the end of the top garden before she noticed the small gazebo. It would be just like Marc to have taken a bottle of whisky or a cup of tea inside to consume by himself in the dark, especially if he were brooding and licking his wounds.

She approached with some care. This part of the garden was not well lit with fairy lights and her heels caught a couple of times in the knotted tree roots that poked through the path.

Kate squinted. She could just make out the torso of a man through the small window on the side of the gazebo, and although she couldn't be certain of what she saw with her naked eye, instinct told her she'd found Marc.

She almost ran straight in to greet him but something in his movements caused her to hesitate and stop in her tracks. She held her breath to observe from a discreet distance. Was it Marc or someone with a similar physique? She moved two more steps closer, an adult rendition of Grandmother's footsteps, close enough to make a positive identification without being seen.

The man in the gazebo was Marc. Kate watched him, feeling a rush of adrenaline as she did so. He stood still as a waxwork and appeared to be leaning against something, eyes closed, shutting out the world. She edged towards the window until she was close enough to hear the sound of his breathing. It came hard; heated; shallow. Kate took in the details of his face as a new feeling mounted within her.

Something was out of place. His eyes stayed shut and his face distorted with what she initially took to be pain until a horrible realisation hit. What marked his face wasn't pain, but waves of erotic pleasure.

Kate gasped and her legs gave way. She sank to her knees, immobilised, horrified but hypnotised as she heard him groan and watched him climax. A few more seconds ticked by and then he opened his eyes and leaned back against the main frame of the gazebo, a lazy smile plastered all over his face.

Jessica's head popped up from Marc's lap like the proverbial cat who'd had the cream.

'Oh, you're good, Jess,' he praised. 'Very good. Very good indeed.'

Kate had heard the voice of the man she'd thought was hers for keeps. She hadn't counted on Jessica.

'You realise what this means, don't you?' boasted Jessica. 'Carry on like this and I'll have to find a new title for my book. Chapter one is screwed!' Their collective laughter ricocheted round the garden, assaulting Kate like a slap in the face.

Barely able to breathe Kate stumbled to her feet, turned on her heels and fled.

Chapter 18

Alice - survival of the fittest

After Douglas left, nothing could compel me to stay in Eastbourne. Every room of the house grew dense with shadows so I instructed a local estate agent to place our marital home on the market. I took the decision to move to Berkshire, close enough to London but sufficiently far away from the coast and the memories that brought acute pangs of unhappiness. Swapping the seafront of Eastbourne and views of the English Channel for walks along the River Thames, I paced for miles trying to come to terms with my husband's desertion and his cowardice for not being able to speak to me directly. His behaviour haunted me, shrouding me with a chronic malaise I could not shake.

Douglas eventually made contact after six months. He had been making regular payments into my bank account, so at least in one respect he had honoured his words. I also had a small income stream from a little research work I still undertook occasionally for Professor Mason with whom I'd maintained contact.

The sale of the house necessitated communication but since I had no idea where he lived in Brighton, I turned to his frail mother, by now in very poor health. I wished her no malice and was loathe to upset her. She was embarrassed enough by his flight, poor dear. She had given life to Douglas but I could hardly blame her for his life choices. He was a grown man capable of making his own decisions, poor though they were. I asked gently if I could trouble her to forward a letter to Douglas explaining my imminent departure from Eastbourne and the house sale.

'We should meet to discuss arrangements,' I explained. 'Douglas still has a number of personal effects in the house.' I had broken a few of his possessions but most remained intact. 'Should he wish to retrieve them, please would you ask him to do so without delay.' I gave him a two week deadline. If he failed to meet it I would donate everything to the Salvation Army. Full stop.

He sent a pathetic letter by way of response. Thank the good Lord he had not written on her green paper or I would have put a match to the thing without reading it. In his inimitable style he wrote that he would 'prefer not to meet face to face'. What a surprise. Spidery script skirted around the page. A coward's script. He conceded to the sale of the house, daring to suggest that he'd been on the brink of suggesting it himself but that he'd wanted to give me time to make alternative arrangements. As if he were being chivalrous, the deluded creature! He even dared ask if I might look out his treasured stamp collection and his father's gold watch, proposing that 'a mutual friend' call by to pick them up on his behalf.

Incensed by my husband's inability to face up to the consequences of his actions, I looked out the treasured stamp collection and duly marched it over to the house of a neighbour to gift the lot to her husband, another bore of a stamp collector. I had no intention of returning a single stamp to my errant husband. If his collection meant so bloody much he should have made arrangements to take it with him when he scarpered.

For weeks I'd shied away from facing the neighbours, the shame of my position too much to bear. I summoned the courage to ring on the doorbell of the house next door, home of Mr and Mrs Dundas, a couple who also tended to keep to themselves. Mrs Dundas greeted me with an awkward smile.

'Oh hello, Mrs Emery. We haven't seen you for a while.'

'No, I have been somewhat busy of late.'

'Yes, I imagine you must be what with preparations for moving and so forth. You'll want to be settled for the New Year, I daresay.'

We skirted around the difficult truth of my abandonment. People were not so direct in those days. When I handed her Douglas's box files she thanked me and asked nothing more of me than whether I was keeping well.

'Very well indeed thank you, Mrs Dundas.' A stock reply I'd practised for hours to perfection. There is nothing to be gained from losing face.

I was sympathetic towards the gold watch that Douglas wanted me to return for it signified a bond between father and son that wasn't mine to break. I wrapped the watch in a layer of soft tissue and then in a thicker sheet of protective brown paper before venturing to the Post Office and dispatching it by recorded delivery to our mutual friend.

Almost everything else that belonged to Douglas was gathered up and given away. This included a pile of shirts, ties, socks and shoes. I kept my head above water throughout this process but shed tears over the most curious items. His battered, wooden shoe-cleaning box with its deep aroma that reminded me of autumn leaves and cosy evenings by the open fire.

I had no idea how to dismantle and dispose of his accumulated wine-making paraphernalia so left that well alone. I kept one solitary item of Douglas's; his silver-plated letter opener. It had no monetary value and negative sentimental associations but nonetheless I liked it.

The house looked well-presented and was situated on the right side of town, thus facilitating a speedy sale. I handed the keys to a newly married young couple, faces pink with naive enthusiasm. I wished them happiness and hoped they would find longer lasting joy under its rafters than I had. By a stroke of good fortune the father of the young man revealed an interest in wine and happily took all the bottles and tubes off my hands for a small fee, benefitting us both.

I left the coast without a backward glance and rented a small one bedroomed flat in Woodhall Lodge, an old country house converted into four separate dwellings. I wanted to live in a house with a name rather than a number but the garden, a share of which came with the flat, proved to be the main lure. Tending to my garden contributed to my improving mental health and the privacy offered by the grounds allowed me to grieve for Douglas in quiet contemplation. My new home afforded me much needed sanctuary. Without this place it is certain that I would have gone quite mad.

I intended to rent the flat only for a few months, but once the bulbs I'd planted burst into colour and the heat of the summer sun warmed my back as I weeded the garden I felt no compulsion to leave. Extending the lease was easy and I stayed. Decades later I am as firmly entrenched as my perennials. I might not be a home owner but this place is my home. After all this time I will not leave now. Where else would I go in any case? I refuse to spend my last days in a nursing home or hospital. When Beryl was last over for tea I attempted a joke with her.

'I shall be forcibly carried out of Woodhall Lodge in my coffin.' She peered at me over the top of her glasses, double chins pressed into her neck.

'Alice, what a thing to say.'

'My dear, sometimes I say these things to provoke a reaction from you. Be a good sport.' I mean no harm by teasing Beryl. Really, a little gentle prodding of the funny bone is good for her. She's another only child and in my experience children without siblings need to learn not to take themselves too seriously.

Douglas continued to deposit money in my savings account but I was adamant not to depend on him forever. Independence aside, a person of such weak calibre cannot be relied upon to commit to maintenance payments. Besides, I wanted a job which would also help me establish myself within my new community. Without any difficulty I found plenty of work as a locum and took great pleasure in travelling around the area as a stand in for other pharmacists. I experienced a wide range of establishments and clientele, from Basingstoke to Bracknell. Women pharmacists weren't so uncommon by this time. However, we remained a minority group. I still sparred with misogynists, or 'traditionalists' as they preferred to call themselves. They would ask in all seriousness, 'Is the "proper" pharmacist on duty today?'

Their chauvinism made my blood boil but no good comes from rising to the bait and I prided myself on my professionalism. I rose above their silly tactics and dispensed their medicines without retort.

Months passed with no contact from Douglas. But then one Thursday evening I returned home to find a letter from a firm of Brighton-based solicitors. I had been expecting some sort of letter since my move and was only surprised it had taken Douglas this long to seek professional advice.

I read the letter and laughed so hard I nearly spat out a mouthful of tea. He wanted me to agree to a divorce. I presume it was to leave him free to marry Anne. I vowed to the sun in the sky that nothing would persuade me to acquiesce. Douglas might have removed himself from my life but I would not carry the stigma of divorce over my head. Without Douglas to rail at I ranted in my head.

'Why should I sacrifice my status so that your scarlet woman can become your legitimate wife?' I agreed with myself that I should not be cowed or bullied into submission.

Before the war, divorce was practically unheard of but in peacetime its incidence rose exponentially. Men returned home from active service but much had changed and the past could not be undone. Many unsuspecting husbands would discover another man's baby growing in his wife's womb, the baby a sorry by-product of a fling with a passing American serviceman. Since I remained childless no one could have thought of me as a fallen woman but even so I refused to be tarred with the same brush. And in spite of my disgust towards Douglas, I still honoured our marriage vows. He would not return to me but he remained the only man with whom I had been intimate and I was adamant I would never let another man be as close to me in that way again. After my own father died, Professor Mason became the only man I could trust and our relationship never transitioned into anything more than professional.

I wrote a firm response to the Brighton solicitors and continued to sport my wedding ring, allowing people to assume my husband was dead, leaving them to create a persona for me of 'the brave widow'. I sought no sympathy, simply the right to be left alone to live my life. End of story.

Douglas must have been desperate to be rid of me, for within the fortnight he wrote to me in his own hand.

'Please, Alice, give your consent to a divorce. Why protest?'

His pathetic pleading merely strengthened my resolve. I wrote back by return with a very clear and unambiguous 'No'.

Letters went back and forth over a period of months but the outcome never changed. How ironic that my words were now landing on that woman's doormat but my envelope contained grief, not love. Crisp, white, watermarked paper. Clinical and on point. A far superior statement to her scrappy sheets.

My intransigence caused Douglas a great deal of irritation. To obtain a divorce at that time required full consent from both parties. Without this he was stuck with me, both in name and in law. He wanted to make Anne Smeaton his legal wife and adopt her son as his own, but I saw no reason why I should give way to his request when no judge in the land would dispute that I was the innocent party.

I started to relish our communications, finding an appetite for jousting from afar, the words I penned designed to cause him anger and frustration at his impotence to effect change.

Then stalemate. Douglas's pleading letters ceased without warning. He must have been persuaded to give up his futile quest. I was surprised when he continued to send me money. By this stage I'd accumulated a notable sum. In the early 1960s I withdrew every penny and treated myself to a sparkling new Hillman Imp in royal blue. This little car took me on many adventures around the county. I even gave her a name, Gloria.

I was comfortable financially and wanted for nothing in material terms. Never extravagant by nature I appreciated the few possessions I owned. Of course, I'd have liked the affections of an honest husband and the reward of children. And I'd have welcomed a Mother who did not blame me for someone else's failings, but I refused to dwell on the missing pieces of joy in my life.

Once I'd recovered enough self-esteem to tackle social occasions, I threw myself into a string of evening classes at the local College of Further Education. From china painting to French conversation I embarked on a continuous programme of self-improvement and rediscovered my passion for learning whilst making a new circle of friends, including Beryl who was to become my closest friend of all.

She was a vivacious woman in those days and jolly good fun to be around. Even though she was much younger than me, we shared a solid set of traditional Christian values. Better still, she possessed a sense of humour and her infectious laugh united us from the start. We met while painting china teapots, cups and saucers. She wasn't at all skilful but her enthusiasm gave her attempts a certain style.

Beryl was the first person in whom I confided the truth about Douglas. When I recounted my whole story to her in class, her mouth fell open and she clean dropped the saucer she was painting. It did not fly through the air but shattered on the ground; a great shame for she'd been in the middle of her best art to date. The sound of breaking porcelain took my mind back to memories of the vase I'd thrown the night I discovered Douglas gone. Good china shouldn't be the unwitting victim of bad news, but all too often it is in the wrong place at the wrong time.

Beryl and I shared many experiences, happy and sad. We shed copious tears of laughter and periodic tears of grief. We cried together when Winston Churchill died in 1965. We laughed till our sides split the following year after Beryl slipped on a banana skin and bruised her bottom. When she developed a crush on Howard Redall, the new clerk at the bank, we conspired to get them together. Beryl has remained loyal through the years, never neglecting our friendship even after she and Howard married in May 1967, the very same month that Elvis Presley wed Priscilla Beaulieu. And when Beryl was blessed with a daughter, Valerie, following a complicated pregnancy she and Howard asked me to be Godmother to their tiny new-born, an act of kindness that moved me to tears. The toxic compound of anger and pain in the sediment of my soul at last began to dissolve. A new love took shape in my heart and with it a revelation that pure love can outshine hate. Late one night after holding the sleeping baby, I resolved to write to

Douglas with news that I would grant him his divorce.

As I sit here in my armchair with the sky blood red in the evening sun I cannot help but smile. All I seem to do these days is reflect on the past. Nostalgia is a funny friend. Many things I'd like to have changed but control over one's affairs only goes so far.

In the event, there was no divorce. And yet, in spite of this, two Mrs Douglas Emerys came into being. A sleight of hand in the card game of life. Of the two Mrs Emerys, I celebrate the fact that I emerged as the sole survivor. Against the odds, I, Mrs Alice Emery, rise victorious as the legal wife and absolute widow of Douglas Alexander Emery.

Until death do us part.

Chapter 19

Kate - jealousy

Kate's meal threatens a fast return as bile rises in her throat. Small black hexagons fill her vision as dizziness spins through her and for once this is no fault of the wine. Waves of panic crash against her rib cage as she struggles for air. The warm atmosphere of Chez Philippe that earlier wrapped itself around her like soft cashmere is now asphyxiating, as though the scarf has been pulled tight around her neck by an unseen menace. Instinct tells her she needs to get away from Marc if she is to survive. The urge to find a safe space where she can breathe again without constraint accelerates.

Kate questions the reasons of the Gods above for pushing her back to this point. They have plucked her from the secure predictability of family life and hurled her back to the very moment when her well-constructed world lost its foundations and crashed to pieces.

Having witnessed Marc in flagrante with Jessica she'd stumbled away in flight, adrenalin forcibly injected into her blood, tears blurring her frantic orientation towards the villa and her escape route: its wide front door. One step at a time. One breath at a time. Away from the storm. Away from Marc. She tried to cut her way through the small, now established party cliques and their melodious chat, her head low, willing herself invisible until she found the exit. She didn't even want to see Monique. How could she begin to explain what she'd witnessed? That Monique's cherished son had launched himself into a bold new world dominated by a fresh set of rules? That he'd released himself from Kate and unleashed himself upon 'Vile' Jessica? Kate chased through the front door, gasping in vain for relief in the dry heat of the night.

She wasn't even aware of the red raw blisters spreading on her heels, courtesy of impractical shoes that had made perfect sense earlier, as she tripped down the hill to the Loseleys' unlit villa. There she greeted the hire car like a trusted accomplice; the perfect getaway vehicle, engine still warm, tank half-full of petrol.

She collapsed into the rented Peugeot, bruising the back of her hand on the door as it swung in on her and lurched her way down to the nearest village, checking the rear-view mirror needlessly for Marc's pursuit. Steering erratically she left the road on a tight bend and jerked forward, feeling the constraint of the seatbelt as she applied the brakes with force. Small comfort to her that the roads were quiet. The lack of traffic saved her as she skidded sideways. She took at least two right hand corners at speed, placing herself on the wrong side of the road. A head-on collision would have proved fatal for any occupants in unsuspecting vehicles on approach. Each mistake she made caused her to drop her speed by a margin but Kate clung to the steering wheel, hell-bent on covering ground. A quiet voice of reason called on her to stop but it barely registered. Instead she focused on the road stretching out ahead. For once, Kate was rebelling against the rules, well over the speed limit, driving like a woman possessed. But this rebellion brought no waving of banners, no celebration of freedom. Kate's was a joyless dissent.

That she managed to reach Toulouse without causing an accident was nothing short of a miracle. Shadows danced across her memory of the journey leaving gaping holes behind. But she still recalled the thud of the Peugeot as it left the tarmac and the fast approaching tree that came to a halt just short of the bonnet. That brush with death had scared her witless. On arrival at Blagnac airport she killed the engine, cold shock rippling through her body. Sobs exploded out of her as she banged her fists against the steering wheel in a series of convulsions. She no longer recognised herself in her actions. How could so much go so wrong and so quickly reducing her to this?

I need help. She knew that much. She had to talk to someone before complete madness set in. It was well past midnight, far too late to ring anyone apart from Craig or Ellie. Kate chose Craig but when his line rang out she dialled Ellie's mobile number through her tears. Ellie spoke with a slurred party voice, tanked up with alcohol and had to shout above high decibel background music to hear herself.

'Hey, kid. I'm at Susie's hen night, remember?'

'No, no, I forgot. Sorry.'

'I've had a skinful of tequila. The room's beginning to spin. Thank God I've got an overnight pass from James. He hates seeing me pissed. Where are you? I can't hear a bloody word!' Kate could hear Blondie's Heart of Glass playing. It didn't help her state of mind.

'Ellie, I need your help.'

'Sorry, still can't hear you. Guess who's here, Kate? Remember Claudine from school? You should see her now. She looks a gazillion dollars. She's only married to bloody Neil Walker, the lucky girl. He was so hot, do you remember? And she used to be so fucking square. Not anymore. Get this, she's a frigging triathlon champion! Even you'd look fat and woefully out of shape standing next to her. Oh, I have to go and dance. Call you tomorrow afternoon, once my hangover's subsided. Bye...'

A song from Dirty Dancing played down the phone for a few seconds, but Kate was unmoved. She was not having the time of her life and was in no mood to dance. The line went dead.

Alone in the dark Kate imploded, more isolated than ever. Neil Walker, the focus of her first crush. And Claudine? Claudine of the wet pants incident at school. Suddenly everyone else's lives appeared perfect and fulfilled. Their fresh buds of love seemed to grow while her blighted dreams shrivelled up and died.

Kate spent the night shivering in the car, arms wrapped around her knees in a protective pose. She wished herself back in time to Accra beach in Barbados. She yearned for a life free from heartache when her only concern had been how to spread sun cream evenly across her back.

When the airport reopened in the early hours of the morning Kate found her way to the rental car returns area, coming face to face with the male member of staff who'd processed the paperwork the previous evening. The air of excitement in the face of the young woman had intrigued him as he'd handed over the keys, and he'd wondered where the pretty English girl was going with such a spring in her step. Could this really be the same girl? A broken figure with heavy, bloodshot eyes was returning the keys, her petite frame folded over the desk like a crumpled piece of paper. He looked at her with concern.

'But Mademoiselle, you have booked this car for three nights. Is there something wrong with it?'

A traditional boy, well brought up, and as the youngest of four with three older sisters he'd learned how to approach a tear-stained face with sensitivity.

'No, thank you. The car is fine.'

'You do not look very well, Mademoiselle. Is there anything I can do to help?' His kindness reduced her to a heap, her sorrow spilling out all over his counter. He hadn't the heart to charge her for returning a vehicle without a full tank of petrol. He'd have taken her for coffee had he not been on his own in the kiosk, as he explained.

'But my boss would not be impressed if I wandered off again with a customer.'

'Thanks, but I'll be OK,' she lied even though she felt like screaming that her life was over.

He offered her tissues and a cigarette, both of which she accepted with a weak smile of thanks. She trailed off towards the Air France ticket desk, unaware that at least one man would think of her throughout the day with every boarding call for flights bound for Britain.

Kate flew home in a complete fog, half wondering if Marc might come after her. She had no idea that he was utterly in the dark about her surprise visit to France. He hadn't seen or heard Kate in the garden and his evening did not end in the gazebo where Jessica was only warming him up. Satisfied with the successful first stage of her seduction plan, she progressed to stage two in the knowledge that Marc wouldn't be pliable for long. She had only a small window of opportunity through which to climb. She stuck to him like glue and kept him well away from 'negative distractions', most notably Monique. Marc's mother would have been sure to effect full maternal interference and pull the emergency stop cord on their accelerating train of passion.

Kate had been naive to have underestimated Jessica, who created scenarios in her life with more care and precision than people realised. Just as she'd engineered her departure from Swiss finishing school by manipulating the hapless gardener, her strategy for catching Marc off guard had been months in the planning. She couldn't believe her good fortune when he'd turned up without his insipid girlfriend in tow.

Jessica had avoided alcohol for the night, choosing instead a thin line of cocaine to enhance her mood. With heightened clarity and the seduction of Marc in hand she led him blindfolded through the garden to the side of the villa and her waiting car.

She drove further into the hills to one of the refurbished luxury villas her father would soon rent out to British holidaymakers. Having surrendered himself to her once, Marc gave up the pretence of protest and discovered an insatiable appetite for Jessica that he'd previously denied. Consumed by lust, he just about remembered to borrow her mobile phone to leave a message on the answer machine at Chateau Mojo.

'Hi, it's Marc. Just thought I should let you know that I

bumped into an old friend at the party and we've gone to Perpignan. I'll be back in a few days. I'll be in touch. Bye.'

He spent all his pent-up physical frustrations on Jessica, compartmentalising his life until thoughts of Katie were shoved to the bottom of his mental filing cabinet and locked away. He rationalised the fling, for that's all he'd allow it to be as he thrust and groaned inside Jessica who played him like a maestro.

'This is just physical.'

'Sure, Marc. No emotional ties. I don't do relationships. You should know that by now.'

'Means nothing.'

'Nothing. Now come here and show me how you can make something so big out of nothing.'

After every release when guilt threatened, Marc told himself he hadn't invested his emotional being in Jessica. This brief liaison would have no lasting consequences. If anything, the affair, if it could even be referred to as such, was a straight tonic. He'd needed it to restore his sense of self-worth. To validate his virility.

Returning from the Hunters' party Monique, bemused by Marc's cryptic message on the answer phone assumed that the 'old friend' had to be Kate. She'd been the last person to see Kate and witness the girl's hurry to find Marc.

'Of course, our little lovebirds have been reconciled in the Hunters' garden.' Relaxing over coffee and hot croissants on the terrace in the morning sun, Monique and John agreed that the young couple were wise to have taken themselves off somewhere private to sort themselves out. They understood young love and weren't offended by the fleeting visit or precipitous departure.

'Maybe they've decided to elope,' John suggested, prompting Monique to sit up straight, open-mouthed in horror.

'Surely not!'

'It's a possibility.'

Monique shook her head. 'Kate's too family-minded to allow that.'

Days passed before Marc returned to his parents' villa, alone and blissfully ignorant to the fact that his fiancée had come in search of him.

'Where's Kate?' became the question that would come to haunt him. More questions followed for which he had no answers. He stood ashen-faced in the kitchen of Chateau Mojo, the realisation of what he'd done and what she'd seen suddenly hitting him like a tidal wave.

'Sweet Jesus. I have to find her to explain.'

'You'll need to do a damn sight better than that, you stupid boy!' yelled Monique as she launched a scathing verbal attack. 'Kate is so perfect for you and you go and do that. And with Jessica of all people. I think I'd have preferred to learn that you'd been with another man!'

'Monique.' John sounded a caution but his wife cut his words dead.

'I'm not finished, John. I did not bring him up to be a liar or a cheat, and as for you,' she addressed Marc with a glacial tone, 'I am ashamed to call you my son right now. Get out of my sight!'

Marc wished he'd not left his mobile phone back in London. Monique at least allowed him to call the flat before John drove him to the airport, but the only trace of Kate was her melodious voice on the answer machine. By this time, the extravagant velvet curtains they'd chosen from John Lewis for the living room hadn't been drawn for three days. Kate hadn't wasted any time. On automatic pilot she'd packed and moved out of their place, posting her key through the letterbox with a dull thud.

She found sanctuary in her brother's spare room where Juliet brought endless cups of sugary tea that Kate couldn't swallow. She sobbed on her brother's shoulder, asking 'why' over and over again but he had no answer to pacify her.

'I'm so sorry, sis. If I ever get my hands on him…' was about the best response he could come up with, the professional patter of a psychologist temporarily irretrievable in the maze of his mind.

'How could he possibly do that to her?' Craig whispered to Juliet as he took his turn to watch over his little sister after she'd cried herself to sleep. 'He'd better not turn up here.'

Marc unlocked the door to an eerily quiet flat, devoid of Kate's things. Almost every human trace of her had gone. She'd left some old clothes but little else. It was only when he collapsed on the bed, exhausted with the effort of the last few days that he caught sight of Kate's engagement ring. The simple band of white gold with a single stone. A timeless classic that deserved to be cherished. Like the woman who used to wear it.

The removal of the ring had been Kate's final gesture before leaving, poignantly placing it on Marc's pillow. She'd had no strength to write him a note. She'd tried to find words but tears alone flooded the page. No language captured the depths of her misery.

The vacuum she left behind sucked Marc's breath away.

The ring on the pillow told him he'd made his bed and had to lie in it. Alone. While Kate sobbed for Marc in Craig's spare room, Marc shed fat tears of regret that rolled onto the pillow on her side of the bed.

He was determined to win her back. It didn't take much guesswork to track her down to Craig's flat where Marc bombarded her with messages and calls, pleading with her to listen to his version of events.

'Please, Katie. Hear me out. Jessica means nothing to me.'

'That's not how it looked when I saw her on her knees in the gazebo. Now leave me alone!'

End of conversation. He kicked himself and tried again.

'Katie, I made a terrible mistake. Please pick up the phone.' Kate listened by the answer machine and sat on her hands to stop herself caving in. Again he persisted.

'Katie, I wasn't thinking straight. I know there's no excuse. I promise you it won't ever happen again. You're the only woman I want. Please, please can I just see you and explain?'

No mention of the word sorry, Kate noted as she pulled on a pair of skinny jeans that used to be quite snug but now hung loose over her hips. She couldn't remember when she'd last stomached a full meal.

The calls came every day until, against her better judgement she agreed to see him.

'OK, I'll meet you at Café Andaluz,' a coffee shop she'd been to once in Richmond and an easy trip to make on the bus. Kate hoped to arrive first but Marc had already found a corner table and the empty mug before him signalling he'd been there a while.

He looked terrible, grey in fact, and Kate almost said as much. She loosened her coat but didn't remove it and sat down.

'I've not slept in weeks,' he told her by way of greeting.

A girl took their orders for coffee and Kate envied her youthful sparkle as she twinkled away in her flowery Cath Kidston apron.

'I wish I knew where to start.'

'I wish you'd known when to stop.' Kate stirred her coffee too vigorously, spilling it onto the saucer.

'Katie,' Marc tried, reaching for her wrist across the table but she pulled back every time he made an approach. If only she could make light of it and put the whole sorry episode behind her, but his betrayal filled her vision and she obsessed that Jessica had an inherent magnetism that she herself did not. All Kate saw was Marc's face at his moment of abandon and all she heard was Jessica's exuberant purr of delight.

'I have to go, Marc. This isn't doing either of us any good.'

'No, Katie. Stay, I'm begging you.' His dark eyes were tinged with red.

'How can I possibly stay?' she spluttered, anger rising to the surface at last. 'What kind of future do we have after you slept with someone else?' she hissed at him. Marc screwed up his face as other customers' ears pricked up, attention piqued.

'It meant nothing. Come on, you can't throw away what we have. I made one stupid mistake. I would never have done it if you'd come with me in the first place. I felt abandoned. You chose your job over me. That's how it felt.'

Kate pushed back her chair and sprang to her feet, poised to leave. Marc tried to grab her hand again, desperate to have the last word.

'You ran to your work and now you're running away from us. I want to sort this out. You're just giving up.'

'I am not giving up. I am walking away. Big difference.' She marched through the door without a goodbye, leaving him to pick up the bill and refused to look back, scared she'd capitulate.

A light extinguished. A relationship ended. All contact ceased. A couple decoupled. Two people, separately grieving the same loss; the promise of a life shared. Friends looked on from the side lines, shocked and mute, shaking heads in disbelief as news of the split travelled.

Everywhere Kate looked she was reminded of Marc. His spirit filled all four corners of London. She suffered panic attacks, each one set off by sights and smells that seemed innocuous but signified in some small way the life that left with him. Deer in Richmond Park, the tiled walls of the Underground, a bottle of Valpolicella, home-made tiramisu. The urge to leave the city squeezed her hard as the tally of claustrophobic, airless weeks increased.

'Don't tell me that time heals all wounds,' Kate snapped at Craig one night as he tried to coax her to eat a chicken curry.

'Clinically speaking, that's not correct,' agreed Juliet in an attempt to lighten the mood. She poured three large glasses of Shiraz and handed one to Kate. 'I'm not sure that patients on trolleys in A&E would be too chuffed if we told them that.'

'I need a change of scene. I can't stay here much longer.'

'You can stay as long as you need. But maybe a holiday is a good idea.'

'No, not a holiday. Something more permanent.'

Craig and Juliet tried to persuade her not to rush any decisions, but Kate quit her job within the month and surprised everyone by heading north rather than south. She started out in Newcastle as a contract consultant for a new digital marketing agency before finding a permanent position in Edinburgh where she threw herself into a new routine, hoping that if time couldn't heal then keeping busy might. She didn't expect to cross Marc's path in the future. She'd learned to accept that she wouldn't see him again. It was what she'd requested after all.

Fate or circumstance has seen fit to change all that, Kate thinks as she stares unblinking at Marc over the table in Philippe's restaurant. Here he sits within spitting distance calmly telling her over his digéstif that Jessica, yes Vile Bloody Jessica of all people, is to become his wife. Jessica? The woman he claimed meant nothing to him. The woman he used to openly despise. The woman who'd manipulated him. The woman who'd won every part of him in the end.

You shouldn't care who he marries,' Kate reminds herself for the umpteenth time. *'But I still care too much,'* wails her inner voice. Her mouth dry, she reaches for the carafe of water only to find it empty.

'Katie, are you OK? Please breathe. I'll get more water.'

'No.' She shakes her head and grapples for her purse in search of money to pay for her share of the meal. 'I really have to go.' Marc shoots out his hand and grabs her wrist, a gesture that reminds them both of their failed meeting in the Richmond café.

'Not again. Katie, put your money away for Christ's sake.' Kate shakes him off.

'Let go of me, Marc. Look, I wish you and Jessica well, really I do.' *Liar*. 'It's all water under the bridge.' She chokes on her own insincerity and takes a hefty gulp of air before repeating with more confidence than she feels. 'Now, just let me go. Please.' Why is she pleading with him? He's not in control of her movements.

'Fine, we'll go together. You're not walking back to the hotel by yourself.' Marc waves to a waiter who materialises within seconds at the table, delighted that they are at last leaving so he can clear up and get home to his wife. Still no sign of Brett or Philippe. Marc pays the bill in cash and hurries after Kate who's already retrieved her coat and stepped outside, putting valuable space between them.

The cool night air urges Kate forward. She inhales deeply and wills herself to calm down. She pulls out her mobile phone as though it's a crutch, expecting to have a missed call from Struan but there's no sign of communication. Not even a text. Digging her hands so deep into her coat pockets that she rips the fabric, and although she's annoyed that she's created something else for her To Do list, it offers a temporary distraction as her fingers play around the edges of the tear. She'd bought the coat from a ubiquitous high street store and it was just another of life's disposable garments, not made to last and will be outdated by Christmas. She'll probably give it to charity once she's mended the lining. Kate sticks her finger through the hole, making contact with her dress beneath.

'Katie, stop! Wait for me!' Marc's in hot pursuit. He's fit and not a bit breathless despite his recent consumption of a full meal. He picks up her stride and passes her a small bottle of Evian.

'Listen, I know you don't want to hear this but I still need to say it. After you left me, my life became a void. The whole world turned rotten. I'd been a total idiot and I knew I'd lost you and I felt powerless to do a thing about it. You made it abundantly clear that you wanted nothing more to do with me.' The withering look she shoots in his direction isn't lost on him.

'As you had every right. But here's the thing.' Marc steps in front of her so her path is blocked and faces her head on, resting his hands on her shoulders, dark eyes searching hers. 'I never stopped loving you, Katie. Do you hear me? Never. And there was never any question that I'd leave you for Jessica.'

'But don't you see, Marc?' Kate rounds on him, a hollow laugh escaping her mouth. 'That's exactly what you did. You left me for Jessica the minute you dropped your trousers.' He winces but she's not finished. 'I saw you, remember? And now you're getting married. How lovely. You're obviously meant for each other. End. Of. Fucking. Story.' Marc shakes his head in vigorous protest but she holds up a flat palm.

'Don't speak. Your words are empty.'

'No, Katie. You don't understand. It isn't what it seems. You and I were meant for each other, not Jess and me. You were the star in my sky, not Jess.' Kate grits her teeth so hard they squeak.

'Not what it seems? She was eating you alive. She had you halfway down her throat. And that was just for starters. For God's sake, Marc. What is it with you? Besides which, if she means so little to you why the hell have you asked her to marry you?' She's disarmed him for the first time. He shakes his head.

'I didn't ask her. She asked me.' His voice cracks. 'I waited for you to change your mind, to forgive me, to take me back. Jessica and I were history the day I left France. She knew the score. She knew I loved you. There was no contact after I came back to London. For two years I worked my guts out. I wasn't interested in seeing anyone else. But you sent all my letters back unopened and told me to leave you alone. I wasn't going to stalk you but everywhere I looked I saw reminders of you and knowing that you didn't want me drove me demented.'

'It's not that I didn't want you. I never loved anyone the way I loved you. But you gave me no choice.'

'Katie, I was hurt and angry because I wanted to see you and you spent all your time at work. I'd go to bed and you'd say you'd be five minutes but two hours later you'd still be sending emails. I played second fiddle to your job. All the time.' He punctuates his final sentence and blood pricks Kate's cheeks.

'That was not the case.'

'Maybe so, maybe not. Maybe it's perception. Maybe it's reality. You didn't board that plane with me. All I can say is that I felt rejected, over and over again. So I made a mistake, the worst kind, I admit. And I wanted to make amends, to win you back. But you told me to go, Katie and in the end I had to do as you asked.' Kate bites her lip, remembering how she slammed every door in his face.

'I needed a fresh start so I took six months out, rode a motorbike around New Zealand and when I came back I moved to Brighton. I asked for news of you from a whole bunch of people and heard you'd moved away, but that's all I knew. I thought you'd gone abroad. No one was willing or able to tell me where you'd gone, let alone that you were married. I tried to contact you on social media but you must've blocked me.

'So when did Jessica come back on the scene?' Kate can't stop herself, the old emotion of jealousy never far away.

'She'd also moved to Brighton.' Kate makes a face. 'Coincidentally,' he adds.

'Coincidence indeed.' Sarcasm runs like a cold current through her voice and she shivers. 'Can we start walking again, please? I'm getting cold.'

'Yes, let's. Here, take my jacket. No arguments. So, Jess moved to Brighton but it wasn't planned on her part or mine. Honestly.' Kate still finds this hard to believe. She didn't have naive down as one of his characteristics. Duplicitous and intense yes, naive hardly.

'Dad set her up in a gallery and she was finally concentrating on her painting and doing really well for herself. But she'd got involved with some idiot.' Kate decides not to comment, though a whole raft of retorts springs to mind.

'In fact, he was worse than an idiot. He was a thug.'

'A thug?'

'Yes. He knocked her about.'

'Jessica? Seriously? I didn't think she was the kind of woman who'd end up being a victim.'

'No, nobody did. He wasn't her normal type. She fell hard. And he broke her. The last time he took his fists to her and she ended up in a bad way. I happened to be in

A&E myself with a dislocated shoulder after some old woman crashed into my bike.' Kate frowns with concern and he gives a wry smile.

'It's OK, it was nothing serious but I needed my shoulder strapped. And the bike was a write-off but that's another story. Anyway, I came out to the waiting room and saw Jessica sitting there.' He winces at the memory. 'Katie, her face was a bloody mess and she was shaking all over. The bastard knocked the spirit out of her. She pretended she was fine but it was obvious she needed someone to look after her. I sat with her while she was treated and then took her home with me. She stayed. She needed me. I guess we started to see each other differently. So she never left.'
Unlike you.

Jessica's had a rough time but as Kate sees it, even in her lowest ebb she got what she wanted. Kate rubs her temples, brain addled by the scenario Marc presented. She can't condone violence but Jessica remains the saboteur of their relationship. A fleeting, uncharitable thought pops into her head, that Jessica aggravated her idiot boyfriend to the point of violence. '*No*,' Kate screams inwardly, ashamed of herself. '*There's no excuse for abuse.*' Even Jessica, promiscuous and self-seeking though she is doesn't deserve that. No one deserves a violent partner. Kate wonders what Monique thinks about all this. She can only imagine her horror at the prospect of gaining Jessica for a daughter-in-law.

'I'm sorry,' Kate offers. What else is there to say? Marc closes in on himself. He doesn't seem to want to talk any longer. They walk the short distance that remains to the hotel and she hurries ahead. It's after hours and the front door is locked but Marcel has given Marc the main key so

Kate has to wait for him to gain entry. He holds the door open and she studiously avoids his gaze as she brushes past.

The lobby lies deserted. Neither of them utters a word, as though even the slightest noise will wake everyone from their dreams. Kate tip-toes up the stairs and then wishes she'd said goodnight to Marc downstairs. She feels him with every breath. At the top of the stairs before walking along the landing to reach her room she pauses and turns to face him.

'Well, goodnight then.' She can't bear that he looks as though he might cry.

'Bonne nuit, Katie.'

She moves down the corridor. Her room seems to be further away than she remembers. Is he still standing there, watching her?

She stops at the door, reaching for her key and realises she's still wearing his jacket. She wriggles out of it as he moves to retrieve it and they freeze. The jacket hangs between them, still warm from her body and when Kate extends her arm and offers it to him, he still doesn't move or take his eyes off her.

As she spins on her toes to open her bedroom door she almost drops his jacket on the floor. She should turn her back on him but is hypnotised, caught in the fullness of his gaze.

He closes in on her and she takes a sharp intake of breath. He's tentative, taking his time, aware that a misplaced word will send her fleeing backwards and see him alone in the corridor facing the hardboard door. She can barely hear his low voice, her senses focused on every approaching inch of him.

'Katie, I can see that you can't wait to get away from me but there is still something between us. I know you feel it too. After tomorrow, you won't ever have to see me again. You said so yourself earlier. You can go back to your life and family in Edinburgh. I won't stand in your way.' Kate trembles, reminded that Struan still hasn't returned her call.

'What do you want, Marc?'

'I just want…' He hesitates. 'I just want to say I'm sorry.' She leans against the door for support. I'm sorry. Words so full of meaning when finally offered without malice. Words he'd failed to find after his deceit when she'd needed to hear them. Who could say if they'd have made a difference?

'I apologise, for then and for now. I know this is hard for you. All I'm asking for is a little more time with you. Now. Tonight. One last time. To talk a while longer and explain a few more things. I don't want to rake up the past or bring you pain. But I'm not ready to call it a day. This is our last chance to talk without anyone else interfering or judging. One last night. Please, Katie?' he urges.

A tiny voice tells her to walk away from him but her body still faces his, the door supporting her back. Frantic messages from her brain to instruct her limbs to move are lost in transit.

'Can't it wait until we're on the ferry tomorrow? It's been a long day. It's late and I am so tired.' Marc's face falls and she's struck by how she feels his pain as though it is her own.

'Please, Katie. I'd really rather not. We'll have Brett in tow by then.' He manages a wry smile. 'Anyway, I won't be able to do this once we're on the ferry.' He cups her face in his hands and brushes his lips against hers for the briefest of

304

moments. Kate feels the pull of gravity as her knees give way and her back slides down the door that was her only safe support. He lifts her back up towards him.

'This is our time.' Kate touches her fingers to her lips. His eyes tell her that she won't be saying goodnight to him just yet.

'Let me come in. I promise not to take advantage and when you want me to leave, say so and I'll go. I'm just trying to share something, to help you understand and allow us both to move forward.'

Kate tries to tell herself she's moved on already. *Aren't marriage and motherhood strong enough proof?*

Sometimes the truth dawns gently, in tiny gradients. On this occasion a harsh truth hits Kate with the force of a heavy goods vehicle, knocking the air clean from her lungs as she loses grip of where her past finished and her future began. With trembling hands she places the key in the lock and opens the door to her room, allowing Marc to slip inside.

PART THREE

SATURDAY

Chapter 20

Alice - good heavens above

Unable to get back to sleep after sunrise, I got up and found things to do while the day was still young. The overflowing top drawer of the dresser in the living room needed to be addressed. Although I am meticulous in cleaning and organising my affairs, this drawer is the one area of the flat that remains a perpetual disgrace since it contains all the administration I find tiresome. Tedious paperwork. Most irritating are the begging letters from charities asking for my money. Audacious requests leave me ill-tempered. I don't mind giving some cash in their little envelopes when I see fit but I jolly well object to these incessant demands for my bank details. The price of the stamp, let alone the paper and printing costs add up to a dreadful waste and I refuse to support inefficient organisations, charitable or otherwise. Alongside these are Douglas's letters, kept for reference not posterity. On rare occasions when woolly nostalgia muffled my negative opinion of him and I yearned for his return, I forced myself to reread his letters to remind myself of the recreant he was.

His final letter arrived in 1972, the very day I swapped Gloria, my trusty Hillman Imp for a cherry red Morris Marina, a fine looking car with cream leather interior. It took me over 10 minutes to park it outside my flat, narrowly avoiding a scrape against the low wall. I stopped for a quick chat with my landlord, Mr Penry. He was overseeing repairs to the rendering of the building. We were mid-discussion when the postman arrived on his bicycle bearing bills and the letter, unmistakably from Douglas with its Brighton postmark.

Many years had passed since I'd offered my consent to a divorce. I'd established a respectable position in the local community and no longer feared being ostracised. A dark mood still descended when I thought about Douglas but I'd made a comfortable life without him and enjoyed good health. Loyal, trustworthy friends had re-introduced me to laughter and fun. I had no complaints.

The fact that my consent letter hadn't provoked a response from Douglas left me bewildered. In the context of his persistent pleas for a divorce over the previous decades, I'd awaited proceedings from his solicitor. But when the months passed without news, my mind toyed with the idea that things had not turned out so well for Douglas and his fancy woman after all.

As it turned out, my overactive imagination was playing tricks on me. Douglas stuck to Anne until the day he dropped down dead on her doorstep in the summer heat of 1976. He'd taken retirement a mere three weeks before. He'd have been looking forward to a future revolving around world travel and grandchildren. Perhaps he shouldn't have exerted himself quite so strenuously. Perhaps, had he chosen the moral path, he might have lived to enjoy annual cruises in the Mediterranean and free bus travel up and down the country.

His last letter to me featured a stamp celebrating the Silver Wedding Anniversary of the Queen and Prince Philip. Douglas and I had been married almost twice that long. I hurried upstairs to my flat to read what he'd written, keen to escape the gaze of Mr Penry.

Dear Alice, I trust you are still well after all this time. Thank you for finally giving your consent to divorce. As you know I would have preferred to have concluded matters a long time ago. Your belligerence over the matter forced me to remedy the situation via alternative means. My Anne is already Mrs Emery having changed her name via deed poll. As such she is already my wife and I see no need to progress with expensive divorce proceedings.

And so it went on. What barefaced, brazen cheek! Anne must have been desperate to go to such measures. I for one would not recognise her as his wife even if she took his name, and surely anyone who knew the truth would feel the same. Douglas was fortunate that our Lord forgives those who sin, but Anne Smeaton could never be Mrs Emery in the Church's register.

After the initial shock I laughed until tears rolled down my weary face. As usual Douglas wanted nothing but an easy life. This name change fiasco provided more confirmation of his flaky character. Having secured a credible surname for Anne, he had neither the guts nor the decency to do the right thing by the woman who was purportedly the great love of his life. I pitied her. In the rest of the letter Douglas penned his usual nonsense that he wished me no ill. He even dared to suggest, and not for the first time, that I might meet someone special of my own. I recognised his motive. He wanted me off his conscience.

But I remained committed to leaving an indelible mark upon it.

I looked out my old Chinese tin box in search of the locket that marked our engagement. I hadn't worn it since the fateful weekend in London. The box lay underneath a pile of towels at the back of a cupboard. I retrieved the locket, struck anew at its delicate beauty. It fell open in my hand to reveal a fresh-faced Alice, an innocent young thing to my older, cynical self. Age and disappointment ravage one's face as well as one's outlook. The chasm between young Alice and old Alice stretched out as wide as the distance between my husband and me.

More confounding was the absence of Douglas's picture in the opposite panel. Art had never mimicked reality so well. The photograph I'd pasted of him into the frame of the locket was nowhere to be seen. First the man had left. Now even his image had absconded.

I tried half-heartedly and only once to form a friendship with another man. Beryl's husband knew a widower whom I invited to partner me at bridge. We made a winning combination at the table but outside the game his dull company bored me rigid. He lacked passion for anything other than golf and wore his club jumpers like a second skin. I suggested that the game of golf ruins a perfectly good walk. He failed to see the joke. His diamond V-neck almost quivered with the slur. We did not make a good pair. In the end I had to ask Beryl to stick to matching Howard's odd socks rather than his friends.

'Alice, you are stubborn at times,' Beryl chided. 'If Howard's friends don't suit, isn't it about time you increased your social circle?'

'My circle is complete, dear,' I told her. Having been bitten once I preferred the company of my female friends and the various animals that came to my door. Before Puddy adopted me I rescued a sweet cat from a neighbouring animal sanctuary. Shamefully neglected by her previous owner she was at death's door when the rescue team pulled her from his filthy, rat-infested house. Kittens at the sanctuary were easy to home, adult cats less so. She shook with terror in the corner of her cage, a mere day away from being put to sleep. I had to bring her home. Paperwork concluded I took her in and named her Tabitha after the bible story in which St Peter raises a woman of the same name from the dead. My Tabitha wasn't long for this world but at least she died in a safe home with a sleek coat and a stomach full of fish.

Tabitha passed away three months before Douglas but unlike him she left peacefully in her sleep. I learned of Douglas's demise from The Telegraph. Leafing through the family announcements as usual, the words EMERY Douglas (Brighton) 1908-1976 leapt out at me. I dropped a slice of toast onto my blouse and just missed spoiling the page with a coarse-cut shred of marmalade. It took several attempts to read the piece before the words sank in.

'Suddenly, at home on 10th August, Douglas, aged 68 years, beloved husband of Anne, much loved father of Robert and Margaret and treasured grandfather to his four grandchildren. A funeral service will be held at St Mary's Church, Brighton on Wednesday 18th August at 12.45pm to which all are welcome. Family flowers only. A collection will be taken for the British Heart Foundation.'

I had known about the boy Robert, of course. But over

the years I'd tried not to think of Douglas and Anne together in an intimate way and the implications of their union. The article revealed that Douglas must have fathered a child of his own with Anne. A girl. Margaret. Named after the Queen's sister, no doubt.

So where I had failed, Anne had succeeded. Douglas was a father in his own right. In the barren blue corner: a wife in name only, with no dependents and a dead cat. In the racy red corner: the mistress, armed with two children. I hadn't even made it past round one.

The old pangs of anguish returned, along with an acute sense of self-pity that I'd been denied the experience of motherhood. It wouldn't have surprised me if Margaret had been unaware of her illegitimate status. Douglas made up his own truths. I pondered over the matter of his grandchildren and whether or not they were biologically his. Had Robert fathered four children of his own, none of them would be blood relations of Douglas. Curiosity consumed me. Here was a family to which I was connected but about which I knew so little.

I decided to attend the funeral. The newspaper entry had been explicit, issuing an open invitation of 'all welcome'. No exclusions for wives, interested observers or serial funeral attendees.

I was shocked that he had passed, but no sudden grief befell me. Douglas died for me years ago and had become an abstract concept, so my heart was cold to him. All the same, I had no idea how I might fare at the funeral in the full glare of his family love. To attend the service alone would be madness.

'Beryl, dear. How do you fancy a trip to the seaside?'

She tried her best to dissuade me.

'I can't possibly go, Alice. And you aren't seriously considering it yourself. Are you? Oh, good grief you are.'

'Please, Beryl. You're a good Christian. In spite of everything I feel honour-bound to pay my last respects.' Perhaps I took advantage, knowing her religious beliefs would compel her to support me. It's fair to call my tactics underhand but I felt justified in deploying them. I had no wish to cause a scene at the Church but Douglas hadn't given me the option of saying goodbye to him in person while he was alive. Now that he was dead, as his rightful widow, I could say goodbye as I jolly well pleased.

We took the coast train and sat in a stuffy, closed compartment, heavy funeral clothes weighing us down in the hot, airless space. England was still in the grip of the heatwave and Beryl complained of feeling faint. The temperatures that summer were enough to tip anyone into an early grave.

Arriving in Brighton ahead of time, we stopped for much needed refreshment in a café where we shared an egg and cress sandwich and a pot of tea. We hailed a taxi to take us to the funeral and sat in silent contemplation, Beryl casting anxious looks in my direction that I pretended not to see.

The Church loomed ahead of us. It was a modern looking building, ugly as sin and not at all to my taste.

'It's an eyesore,' our driver concurred. A pretty stretch of woodland reached out to me from the other side of the road and I was tempted to forego the service and take a walk through the trees instead. Outside the grey Church I counted around 60 people with more arriving at the gate. Enough for us to blend in. But we stopped short on the opposite side of the road. The lead funeral car had pulled up outside.

Anne, the grieving 'widow' stepped out of the black car. She was not the figure I'd seen in my mind's eye for all those years. I'd pictured a petite, blonde, delicate creature, pale but fair of face with freckles and a snub nose. Instead, a tall brunette with ample bosom and wide child-bearing hips stepped towards the Church, supported on the right by a younger man, her boy Robert I assumed. To her left an even younger woman, no older than 30, caught my attention. She looked far more like the person I had visualised; fair and slight. This had to be their daughter, Margaret. Even from the other side of the road I could see Douglas written all over her.

Beryl and I took seats in the back pew of the Church, the furthest corner from immediate family.

'Alice, are you coping?'

I hushed her and tried to wear a poker face but I am no actress. Some might argue that any residual feelings I had for Douglas were at best misplaced and at worst out-dated and irrelevant. I was no more connected to this man or his family than any other casual observer. Legally Douglas might have been my husband but our union was worthless here. As far as these people were concerned I was just another friend of the family paying her respects. I meant nothing to this man's life or death.

'This is a mistake,' I whispered. I couldn't bear to listen to the eulogy, to hear loving memories of a man who had cut me out so cruelly. I slipped out of the Church with Beryl hot on my heels, her eyes wide with concern for my precarious emotional state.

Beryl was a good sort and had been an invaluable support up to this point. But, not unkindly, I shook her off.

'I need a little time alone. To think.' She put up a meek protest.

'Alice, let's just go back to the station.'

'You go. I'll meet you there. I promise not to do anything rash. I'd like to take a short walk, alone. It's alright,' I reassured her. 'I won't be going back in there,' jabbing my finger at the dismal building.

We agreed to meet back at the railway station in time for our four o' clock departure for London Victoria. In spite of her misgivings Beryl waved me off. I walked briskly, the words of 'Dear Lord and Father of Mankind' ringing in my ears.

I made my way towards the trees that had beckoned earlier. Walking through the woods was cathartic, listening to bird song and feeling the heat of the air on my skin. I reached a small clearing. A trickle of water, barely a stream, ran to my left behind which were more trees and a row of houses. Smoke rose from a bonfire in one of the gardens and I wondered if the committal had taken place yet. Soon Douglas would be cremated and his body would be nothing but dusty contents in a jar on Anne Smeaton's mantelpiece.

I heard a distant sound of children laughing. I stopped near the stream, opened my black handbag and pulled out a green, leather glove which happened to contain the engagement locket.

I'd chosen this glove to transport the locket for its colour alone. It was one of the green gloves I'd worn the day my courtship with Douglas began. The Sunday when we'd walked through St James' Park. Back in the early days, happier times, the colour green had no pejorative connotations. Later, after Anne's letters penned on that awful paper, I vowed never to wear green again. I'd shoved the gloves to the back of a drawer.

On the eve of the funeral, I'd taken the locket from my jewellery box and wrapped it in a handkerchief before looking for something else in which to secrete it. The green glove seemed fitting; a hand over of sorts. I pressed the handkerchief inside, securing the locket until it was snug.

I planned to remove the locket and hurl it into the undergrowth before discarding the glove. I had no use for the glove and saw no point in reuniting it with the odd one I'd left behind. Separation for perpetuity. Symbolic of Douglas and me. An incomplete pair.

Before I had a chance to remove the glove's contents I heard the shouts of fast approaching youths. I had no desire to be interrupted, so took the glove, complete with handkerchief and locket within, and hurled the lot into the wild blackberry bushes that grew in abandon along the path.

My might was strong but the throw was poor and the glove did not travel as far into the brambles as I'd have liked. I'd wanted it to stay concealed, but any observant person could see it from the path. Nonetheless, it had left my hands and I had shared a farewell moment of sorts with Douglas. Unconventional, but I did it my way. His passing had atoned for his desertion. I spoke the words of the Lord's Prayer and turned away before the noisy youths arrived on the scene.

That was my last visit to the coast. I have not been back since, nor have I any intention of returning. When my time comes, my ashes will be scattered in the garden at Woodhall Lodge underneath the plum tree. Just pray that Mr Penry won't be greedy in years to come and sell the grounds to property developers. I should hate to see my garden converted into a giant supermarket one day. I'd prefer to lie amongst my flowers and fruit than be covered over with tarmac.

I spent over an hour tidying the dresser drawer and congratulated myself on my efforts. The satisfaction of a job well done is hard to beat. Chaos tackled, I decided it was about time for a cup of tea and a slice of toast finished off with a generous spoonful of Beryl's marmalade.

I picked up my old Bible from the drawer and in doing so something fell out of its pages and fluttered to the floor. I put down the Lord's book and bent over to pick up the tiny oval paper that had landed at my feet. What I saw shocked the life out of me.

There was Douglas, fresh-faced and photogenic, smiling back at me with a sparkle in his eye. As good as gold.

Chapter 21

Kate - the long goodbye

Kate at her most anxious experiences a recurring dream. She's standing centre stage in a packed theatre. The eyes of the audience follow her every move while hot stage lights bore into her. Beads of sweat multiply on her forehead under thick layers of make-up.

She takes the role of Dorothy in The Wizard of Oz and is about to meet the scarecrow, or perhaps it's the tin man? She can't be sure. The whole theatre lies in wait for her to speak but she has no voice. The lines she's learned evade her and the harder she tries to remember her words the fewer she recalls. Panic grows. The audience starts to heckle. She spots an old red telephone box down in the stalls. The telephone is ringing so she leaves the stage to answer it, wondering vaguely if the person at the other end of the line might be in a position to help. She should have put in more preparation before opening night. The audience is angry. Everyone will demand a refund and the critics will make mincemeat of her in their reviews.

Kate wakes with a rush to her head which pounds to the ring of a real phone. The signal has cracked open the nightmare. She lifts her head off the pillow, arms wrapped around its width. Her mobile buzzes furiously on the other side of the room, well beyond reach. The half-light suggests a time of day when night has gone but morning isn't yet established. Kate's eyes adjust to her surroundings until she remembers exactly where she is. The hotel room in Calais with its tired furniture is a world away from the Parisian luxury that preceded it.

Kate remembers who held her in his arms last night and for a whole host of reasons she's relieved that Marc has gone. A space in the universe briefly opened, sucking them into a vacuum beyond the reach of real life and laws that bind. She hadn't meant for him to stay but she had hardly insisted that he leave. She doesn't remember when she dropped off to sleep and has no idea what time he tiptoed back to his own room, but his aftershave lingers on the pillow and she inhales his presence on her skin.

Lacking her usual grace she clambers over to reach her phone before it stops ringing, stubbing her toe on the corner of the wardrobe as she does so.

'Fuck.' She only just picks up in time, flung from one life to another.

'Kate, are you OK? I was just about to hang up. Sorry, did I wake you? I couldn't sleep and thought you'd be up.'

'Oh, Struan. It's fine. I was having a horrible dream and I've just stubbed my toe. What time is it anyway?'

'Still early o'clock. I've been awake for bloody hours. Isla woke at three and came through to our bed insisting it was time for breakfast.'

'Did she?' Struan, Isla, home; her normal life shimmers in the distance, remote and abstract. Even the phone line crackles causing small breaks in reception, rendering his voice disjointed and unfamiliar. Kate sinks to the bed, wretched as her husband continues his woeful tale of sleep disruption.

'I managed to persuade her to stay in bed until ten to five, but she arranged herself in the middle of the mattress and kicked off all the covers. She took up the entire space. How is a child so small able to do that? I've hardly slept.' He yawns. 'Thank God the BBC has finally come to life. I've plonked her in front of CBeebies.'

'Oh no. Is she feeling all right?'

'Isla is as fresh as a daisy. Save your sympathy for me. I'm exhausted. Much as I adore our daughter, she saps my energy sometimes. I'll put her on in a minute, once Balabloodymory has finished.'

'I missed you last night. When I spoke to your Mum she said that you were all busy and you'd call me back.' Kate hears the hurt in her own voice and the accusatory tone levelled at her mother-in-law.

'She didn't, did she? She told me you needed a good night's rest and that I wasn't to disturb you. I guess she got her wires crossed.' Kate feels a renewed rush of irritation at Audrey and suspects a deliberate oversight.

'And after tea Dad asked me to check an electricity bill he's querying. I swear, now he's retired he has nothing better to do than write letters of complaint. That took ages because he couldn't lay his hands on the right documents and kept showing me letters that were two years out of date. Isla was half asleep when I got her into the car.'

'Sounds like you had your work cut out.'

'Yes. But that's not all. I'm afraid I have a confession.'

'Pardon? What did you say?' Kate splutters her reply, wondering if she's heard him correctly. When has Struan had time to get up to anything?

'I have a confession,' he repeats with a solemn voice. 'Are you ready? Don't be cross.'

'I won't.' As if she has a right to be cross with him after the night she's just spent.

'I didn't brush her teeth last night. I didn't even rub toothpaste over her gums. And she ate a massive piece of Mum's apple pie with an even bigger dollop of ice cream. There, that's it! Are you mad?' Kate can't believe what she's hearing. He is serious. She feels a hundred times worse than before.

'Struan, that's nothing to worry about. I understand.'

'Really? I thought you'd be horrified. You never let the teeth cleaning routine slip. Then I fell asleep on the sofa and woke up after midnight. I didn't think you'd thank me for calling you so late.' Nausea sweeps through her. She'd only have been talking to Marc at that point.

'I didn't sleep much.' What else can she say?

'I suppose you didn't want to oversleep and miss your ferry. So, what's your plan of attack today? Do you think you'll make it home? We miss you.' Hot tears well up behind Kate's eyelids.

'I hope so,' she hesitates. 'We're booked on a ferry this morning. Then once I get to Dover I'll head up to London and get myself on a train from King's Cross.' It all sounds so simple. Just head north. If only her moral compass were as well calibrated. 'It'll be late though. I can't see myself getting back much before midnight.'

'Can I make a suggestion? Why don't you break your journey and stop over at Craig and Juliet's? I'm sure Isla and I can manage one more day without you. The house is a bit of a disaster in places but we're managing.' Visions of overflowing laundry baskets and toys strewn around every room come to mind. Mess everywhere. Struan's tidy desk policy at work is unenforceable at home. As long as he has clean, ironed clothes and an orderly kitchen, Struan exists quite happily amidst household chaos. Kate has a lower tolerance for mess and has to frequently remind herself that in the great scheme of things a pile of books here or there, or a small ironing mountain in the living room doesn't really matter. And right now she's in no position to criticise trivial matters. Deceit is a far worse crime. It's petty to take issue with Struan's untidiness when he is a good, kind and trustworthy man. He values the things that really matter.

Unaware of her throbbing conscience, Struan updates Kate on the latest travel situation.

'Still no flights. It's the main headline in the news. Broadcasters are having a field day interviewing weary travellers and featuring people who can't fly to Vegas for their weddings. It's the visitors from overseas I feel sorry for, having to sleep in some of our crummy UK airports. Imagine being stuck at Terminal Three at Heathrow, poor buggers. On the other hand community spirit is flourishing. Locals are bringing food and drinks for stranded travellers by the trolley-load. British hospitality at its best.'

'I don't suppose the bars and coffee shops at the airport are too thrilled about that.'

'They think they're magnanimous whenever they have to hand out free hot chocolate vouchers. It'll be interesting to see whether the insurers will pay up.'

'They'll try their best not to. All those stuck travellers would cost them a fortune.'

'Talking of stuck, did you know your sister's stuck in the States?'

'Yes, I heard. Not that she'd rough it in an airport terminal building. They've found five-star accommodation in Manhattan and she promised us all scrumptious gifts from Dean & DeLuca. Then again she's more likely to be melting James's credit card on Fifth Avenue.'

Struan chuckles. 'I thank my lucky stars you're the low maintenance sister.' His comment carries no spite. He's fond of Ellie and has a lot of time for James. But then Struan gets on well with everyone and knows how to bring out the best in people. What he'd make of Marc and how Marc would relate to him Kate can't begin to guess. She gives herself a firm kick for daring to imagine the pair of them in the same room.

'Do you want me to call Craig and see if he'll put you up for the night?'

'Thanks, Struan, but no. I'd really rather head for home. I know I've only been away two nights but it feels so much longer.'

'Well then, why don't I get Mum and Dad to take Isla overnight so I can come and meet you at the station? I'll bring you home, run you a hot bath. You can look forward to candles, a glass of chilled white wine, the works.'

Kate wonders if 'the works' is a euphemism for sex. She and Struan have a healthy and active sex life, but all she wants from him tonight is a reassuring cuddle. Nothing more elaborate, especially after last night's tangled web and all the confusion that came with it.

A high-pitched noise pipes up in the background with the arrival of Isla. The little girl grabs the phone and on hearing her daughter's voice, Kate hits rock bottom. How could she have let Marc step across her threshold? Tears stream down her face and her voice catches in her throat.

'Bon joo, Mummy! When are you coming to see me? Are you at the airport? Daddy says you are lost. Are you walking home? Is France near my nursery?'

'No, honey.' Kate sniffs through her tears and her hands grip the phone. 'France is a bit further away than your nursery, so too far to walk in one day. I'll be home just as soon as I can, sweet pea. One more sleep, OK?' She's reassuring herself as much as she's pacifying Isla.

'But Mummy, I want you to take me to the park. Today,' Isla wails. 'Why can you not take me to the park today?' Kate lets out a muffled sob. 'You sound all funny, Mummy.'

'It's OK, honey. Daddy will take you to the park today and then tomorrow when I'm back, we can all go together.'

Kate promises a trip to the Botanic Gardens, a chocolate ice cream and three more chapters of The Magic Faraway Tree until Isla is placated. Struan comes back to the phone.

'Steady on, love. Don't make promises you might not be able to keep.'

'Oh, Struan. I'm so, so sorry.'

'Sweetheart, what's wrong?'

'You're so far away.'

Struan tries his best to reassure her. 'It's not even five hundred miles,' adding, 'I could walk it if I had to,' but his voice tails off as Isla calls for him which only serves to make Kate feel worse.

She showers and gets dressed before packing her few items and leaves her room for the last time, taking small steps. She has no appetite whatsoever but Marc and Brett wave her into a poky dining room where Brett tucks into croissants as though he's not eaten for days. Marc is leaning back towards the window with a double espresso in one hand and a large glass of iced water in the other. He nods and smiles at her as though she's the most beautiful woman he has ever seen. All traces of anger and frustration have lifted from his face. He looks years younger. *How can he look so fresh?* Then again, he never needed as much sleep as Kate. His shirt is crisply ironed. *How's he managed that on top of everything else?*

'Good morning, Kate,' roars Brett between mouthfuls. 'Did you sleep well? Marc's been telling me all about your night.'

'Has he?' Kate shoots Marc a pointed look but all he does is smile serenely. She changes the subject.

'I'm sorry we left the restaurant without saying goodnight but we didn't want to interrupt you and Philippe.'

'Ah, the great Philippe! What a charming guy. We shot the breeze until after two! I've invited him to my family's Texan ranch for a summer vacation. I'm going to kick his ass at golf!'

Brett's blend of playful enthusiasm and confidence brings a fleeting smile to Kate's face. She can't help but admire his self-belief. Brett the brand, Brett the salesman extraordinaire and Brett, supreme master of golf. He has questionable habits but he's not a bad guy.

They don't linger over breakfast, checking out by nine o'clock and driving to the ferry port. It's still jam-packed with cars and foot passengers. Kate distracts herself by trying to come up with a collective term for the rental cars that dominate the lines of waiting traffic. A pinch, perhaps? Only suitable for the smaller 'hot hatches'. Or a smash? Most rental cars wear little scars from ill-judged parking attempts. A 'smash' of cars is fitting but unlikely to be adopted by car hire companies, even in jest. She counts registration plates from France, Spain, Italy, Portugal, Switzerland, Austria, Poland and Bulgaria as well as the ridiculously big yellow plates on the back of British cars.

Marc assumes position behind the wheel, tactfully suggesting that Brett stays 'hands-free' for incoming calls. Brett laughs and concurs, content in the passenger seat, nursing a final pain au chocolat swiped from the breakfast buffet.

'Thanks, bud. Anyway, today being Saturday I'm taking a day off work, so you folks can enjoy my undivided attention for the rest of our trip.' Marc catches Kate's eye in the rear-view mirror and pulls a face.

Kate can't distract herself for long from the big thoughts that are running rampant through her mind. As Marc negotiates the ramp into the belly of the ferry she wonders if similar turmoil is bothering his head. He shows no sign of unease, elbow resting lightly on the door, one hand on the wheel. He gives the impression that he's completely at one with everything that's happened and yet the potential for destruction is greater than it's ever been. This isn't just about Marc and Kate anymore. Struan, Isla and Jessica are all implicated.

Marc made his position clear in the bedroom the night before.

'I still love you, Katie.' That's what he'd said. Kate plays their conversation back over in her mind like the chorus of a song that refuses to give way.

'I have never stopped loving you. I care about Jessica and I'm fully prepared to marry her, but…'

'But what?'

'But not if there's as much as a glimmer of a chance for you and me to try again.' Kate couldn't believe her ears.

'I'm married, Marc. I love Struan. He's my rock.'

'I can be your rock, if you'll let me. I want to be your everything.'

'We've had a daughter together. I could never leave them.'

'I'm not asking you to leave Isla. Bring her with you. Don't look so scared and yes, I am serious.'

'You'd bring up Struan's daughter?'

'She's your daughter too.'

Kate pictures Struan at home in Edinburgh making toast and cutting soldier fingers for Isla to dip into a boiled egg. By now he'll have burned at least one round of toast and set off the smoke alarm.

She's brought back to the here and now by Brett who lets out an enormous burp. His timing is horrendous.

'Sorry, guys. Too much pastry.'

Car parked in the bowels of the boat, they make their way up steep and narrow stairs to the main deck. Brett, true to his word about giving Kate and Marc his undivided attention, promptly links their arms and steers them towards the bar.

'To mark our departure from French soil and to celebrate new friendships.' Marc sidesteps Brett and leans in to whisper in Kate's ear.

'I'll drink to rekindling old friendships.'

Kate orders a mineral water and Marc a diet cola.

'Seriously, guys. Drinks are on me. I'm having a double whisky. Won't you take something stronger?'

'Remember, Brett. Katie and I will be catching trains from Dover so you'll be your own in the car. I'd stick to coffee if I were you. I'd hate to see you deported for driving under the influence.'

'Hell, Marc. You are one sound guy. You're right. That would be the end of my career. I'll have a full-fat cola in that case. Diet products make me gassy.'

They clink glasses and as the ferry leaves the port Kate is suddenly hit by a wall of fatigue. She stands up to excuse herself.

'I think I'll leave you both to your drinks, if you don't mind. I could do with some air.' Without waiting for a reply she hastens for the exit, climbs up a short series of steep, metal stairs and pushes open a heavy door onto the top deck. A chill wind whistles through her thin coat and she tastes the salty air.

At the stern a family of four huddles together as one to wave goodbye to the disappearing coast. From their neat and precise appearance Kate presumes they're French but it's impossible to determine nationality from a distance and the wind carries their words away. The mother is around Kate's age. She's wearing a bottle green velvet coat and long, auburn hair blows around her face without making her look dishevelled. Her colouring suggests Anglo-Saxon rather than Gallic descent but Kate remembers the fair colouring of people she's met in Milan. Who knows where anyone's from anymore? Displacement, migration and opportunities to travel mean people constantly move around and settle in new places. No need to align with a country just because your colouring matches you to a particular climate.

It's not always possible to make a fresh start in a new place, but access to the right kind of passport helps, likewise having good connections. Kate knows the option to leave and start somewhere new is still there for her. If she chooses to go. If she wants to start again.

Kate is mesmerised by the family but stops herself from staring. She might be disorientated but she doesn't want anyone to think she's unhinged.

The woman holds the hand of a small girl who wears a maroon, velvet coat. The mother shields the girl from the wind, reducing the risk of the little one being blown overboard. Beautiful long, brown ringlets curl down the girl's back. Kate reckons she's about six years old. Two years ahead of Isla. The woman's husband is carrying a toddler, a little boy who shares the same auburn colouring as his mother. He waves wildly at the screeching gulls overhead and his gleeful shouts of 'bye-bye birds' reveal a British accent. Kate follows his gaze towards the gulls and almost waves them off herself.

This family is happy. It could almost be a vision of her own future with Struan. Or with Marc?

So many reasons compel her to respect the status quo and the life she's built in Edinburgh. To uproot Isla and leave Struan is unthinkable, irrespective of the enduring chemistry she shares with Marc.

The family moves back into the ferry's warm interior. Kate takes up their position and edges as close to the side of the ship as she dares. The wind picks up again and its force makes her cheeks smart and her ears ache. She clutches her locket and with shaking hands unclasps the chain, driven by an urgent need to see physical evidence of Struan and to confirm him in her life. She clicks open the locket and presses it to her lips with a whisper.

'Everything's going to be alright.'

From a distance, Marc is watching. Even from the corner of her eye Kate knows he's there. She'd known he'd follow but not quite as soon. He must have given Brett the slip more easily than she'd expected. Kate closes the locket and pops it into the pocket of her coat. She has to keep her life with Struan distinct and separate from this episode with Marc. There can be no more blurring of the boundaries.

Marc walks towards her, eyes watchful and stops short when he reads her face. He's close enough to be able to speak without shouting but not so close to scare her away.

'You've made your decision.' Kate is about to disagree but realises she can't. With no good reason to delay the inevitable she nods her head, eyes searching his.

'I have.'

'You don't need to rush it, Katie. I'll wait.' She runs her fingers through her hair and scratches the back of her neck with a rough nail.

'You can't wait forever. That's not fair on you or anyone.' His face crumples and he's about to speak but she holds up her hand. 'I'm truly sorry, Marc. I'm glad we've met again, really I am. We've come so far in a few hours.'

'It seems a lot longer.' Tears gather in his eyes.

'It does, but we have to walk away now with what we have. Nothing more.'

'It hurts.'

'It's painful, but then it always has been for us, hasn't it?'

Marc smiles and moves a step closer, taking her hands in his. This time she doesn't resist.

'You're shivering. I want to wrap you up and take you home. Is there nothing I can do to change your mind? Really nothing?'

Kate's tears run down her cheeks as she hangs her head and whispers the word he didn't want to hear. Marc looks broken, his face streaked with pain.

'Maybe you're right, but I had to try. I had to. You understand?'

This time she says yes. Marc leans in towards her for the last time and their lips meet to share a kiss so tender and so sweet that Kate has to pull away before she loses herself again.

'I'm going back inside. Please don't follow me, at least not for a while.'

Marc lets Kate's hands slip through his fingers and he stands motionless, bereft on the top deck, watching her go. His shoulders sag and his head drops as the fight drips out of him like blood from a gaping wound. He should never have raised his hopes.

Something bright on the deck catches his eye and he bends down to take a closer look. At first he doesn't recognise it, his sight still blurred from tears. But as he kneels on the ground he lets out a low whistle. He reaches down and picks it up, comforted to find it's still warm from being close to her. Clutching it tight in the palm of his hand, Marc straightens up and brings his fist to his heart, Kate's gold locket safe within. He drops it into the pocket of his jeans intending to return it when they get back to the car.

Marc stands at the stern and looks across the water to the horizon, losing himself in the patterns made by the crashing waves. He wishes he'd played his hand differently. He wishes he were the man inside Kate's locket and the man she'd chosen. He curses himself out loud and slaps his hands against the cold, hard railings of the ferry. If only he'd been stronger.

One terrible decision cost him the woman who will always own his heart.

Chapter 22

Kate - take me home

Much of Kate's journey home from Dover is a blur. If she tries to reconstruct her memory of that time, only snatches of the day come to mind. There are gaps that will never be filled, as though there was an intermittent fault in her consciousness. Disconnected from the world and then reconnected, with each reconnection making small but irreparable changes. An insight gained here and there but plenty lost along the way. The sensation of arriving somewhere after a long drive but not remembering all the twists or turns. A waking dream.

Every train was full of people attempting to get somewhere else. No-one could stand still for even a minute. All keen to reach a final destination. They were no longer in limbo because at last things were moving but the end point was still beyond reach for many, like the pot of gold at the end of Dorothy's rainbow.

Kate looked around and felt utterly disconnected. Things that had seemed familiar a few days ago now took on a different shape and hue. On the trains people all around shared their travel adventures loudly and openly. It reminded Kate of people showing off new tattoos. She didn't want to show anything to anyone. Marked on the inside she held her experiences close to her heart.

Stories spilled out of individuals as ash had spilled from Eyjafjallajökull. Travel reports became strong social currency where the richest among the travelling public were those who had deployed the greatest tenacity to get this far. It was comforting to be surrounded by conversation, and sheer relief not to have to participate in any of it.

Kate only realised that she'd lost her locket when passing through the ticket barrier at London Bridge. As the gate opened she retrieved her ticket and popped it into her coat pocket where her fingers touched the gold chain which had caught in the lining.

She tugged, fingers feeling all the way along the chain towards a locket that was no longer there. The hole she'd made in the lining of her coat had been large enough for the locket to breach its defences. She checked the floor but her search proved fruitless. The locket could be anywhere; on the deck of the ferry, the stairwell down to the parking bays, the back of Brett's hire car or the station platform at Dover when she'd kissed goodbye to Marc one last time.

For three decades that locket had accompanied Kate on her journey through life and it saddened her to think she would never see it again. The warm, draughty, underground tunnel was a sorry place to reflect on what she'd lost and she stood disconsolately waiting for the tube to take her north to King's Cross. Much later, by the time the InterCity train reached Newcastle she'd adopted a more philosophical response. She remembered a tale shared by one of her aunts about an old man with a collection of antique, crystal glasses.

The man invited a friend to drink with him one night.

All went well until the friend dropped his glass and it broke. Knowing the value of the glasses the red-faced friend apologised for his clumsiness and promised to source a replacement. The host shook his head and smiled with reassurances that the loss of a glass, no matter how valuable or cherished was of no consequence.

'For years I've imagined the whole collection is broken already, in preparation for the inevitable. We only borrow what we have.'

Kate tried to apply the same logic to the locket which arguably had been lost for years and was never truly hers. In her heart of hearts she'd never really thought it was hers. Possession is distinct from real ownership. She hoped the little treasure would be discovered by someone who'd value it and look after it. In the right hands it might arouse some curiosity about the identity of the people contained within. Just as it had for her all those years ago.

Kate was still upset to have lost Isla's little photo. It wasn't that she didn't have hundreds of bigger and better pictures at home. They'd even splashed out on an expensive family photo shoot, producing an over-sized black and white picture that hung above the fireplace. It featured Struan and Kate cuddling on a sofa and Isla playing quietly like an angel and grinning like a little devil.

Kate's upset centred not on the loss of the photo in its physical form, but rather what it symbolised. She'd lost sight of her family by allowing Marc into her bedroom the previous night, a truth she'd never be able to justify to anyone, especially if she couldn't even explain it to herself. In the following weeks it was easier to attribute tearful moments to fatigue and the loss of a cherished object.

Struan did his best to raise Kate's spirits which only heightened her guilt.

'You might have lost your locket and a couple of photos but you still have the real thing. You have us.' Kate hugged him. His reassuring words had clarity and put life in perspective.

Struan wasn't a bit superstitious about material things and saw no need to charge objects with emotional meaning. He was as grounded as the rock underpinning Arthur's Seat and the only person able to pull Kate out of her parallel universe and back down to earth with a soft, safe landing.

As agreed in Calais Marc, Brett and Kate went their separate ways in Dover. It was a strange farewell. Marc and Kate stood side by side to bid goodbye to Brett who was contemplating the driving seat of the Renault and preparing for his run up to London.

'Remember, we drive on the left hand side.'

'Not like back home.'

'No, and don't use your phone while driving.'

They were like anxious parents waving goodbye to a teenage son, a newly qualified driver who thinks he is wise to the world but who's still an inexperienced youth, wet behind the ears.

Before he squeezed himself into the car Brett grabbed Kate with a big bear hug, nearly suffocating her in the process.

'Katie, it's been a real pleasure meeting you. Here, take my business card and stay connected, OK?'

'I'll be sure to send you a Christmas card.' She couldn't contemplate more regular communications without inviting awkward conversations in the future. Brett wasn't the most perspicacious man in the world but even he would have seen that she and Marc had a story that could run and run.

Clouds gathered overhead so they took shelter from the rain on the station platform. Marc was taking the coastal route to Brighton while Kate awaited a faster, direct service to London Bridge. Saying goodbye would have been horrible at the best of times. At the worst of times it felt unbearable. How to say a last goodbye without shedding tears? How to commit the face of someone to memory, knowing that memories alter and fade? There was neither a right answer nor a good one. At the end what more can you do, thought Kate than to embrace it with as much love as you can give.

She wrapped herself in the farewell. It felt like home but her journey home was only just beginning. Marc stroked her hair and his words fell like tear drops in her ear.

'If ever you need me Katie, call. And please, take this.' He pulled away and opened out the fingers of her hand, pressing something into her palm that felt like a stone wrapped in tissue paper.

'Don't open this until you're on the train. Promise?'

'Promise. And thank you, Marc.'

'For what?'

'For everything. Good and otherwise. I'm glad we met.'

'I know. You're still the guiding light in my sky. You know that now. Only you. Remember that, always.' His voice was just a whisper but his intent firm. One of them had to leave. Kate's train arrived first. Hard as it was to step away, it felt harder still to be the person left behind.

'Goodbye, Marc.' He took his fingertips to his own lips, kissed them and then pressed them to her mouth.

Kate shielded her face so that he wouldn't see her tears. To leave him alone, to abandon him again left her in bits. A piece of her stayed behind, still with him, but walking away was always the right thing to do.

For most of the train journey she gazed out of the window, zoning in and out, losing herself in the passing scenery and blurred houses that people she would never meet called home. It wasn't until she was half way up to London that she remembered Marc's gift. She felt its weight in her hand and opened out the tissue paper to find a heart-shaped piece of rose quartz, polished until smooth all over. She rubbed her thumb over its cool surface and felt a sudden surge of love.

A tiny slip of paper accompanied the heart. Marc's new mobile number and a second number, area code Brighton, which she took to be his home number. His home. Currently shared with Jessica. She folded over the paper and placed it inside her purse, but kept the stone in her hand until the train pulled into London Bridge, by which stage she was quite warm inside and out.

The rose quartz was no perfect substitute for the lost locket but brought an anomalous resolution to an impossible situation. What had passed between the pair of them seemed more and more ethereal with every mile that separated them, the quartz heart the only tangible reminder that what they'd shared was real. For a split second she wondered if he'd given Jessica the engagement ring that had once been hers, but knew he'd not be so crass. In any case, Jessica wouldn't have settled for any cast-offs. She'd have demanded a large rock of her own, unique and ostentatious.

Kate fully expected guilt to pay her a call following her

brief encounter with Marc, and of course it did. But if anything she should have felt far more culpable. She surprised herself by separating her life into component parts which helped to allay the guilt. Life with Struan was as far removed from her time with Marc as the South Pole from the North. Marc was her past. For a brief time her past life had come to visit the present. Struan was that present. And crucially, her future. He'd never given Kate any reason to leave.

She phoned Craig from London assuring him she wanted to press on to Edinburgh without breaking her journey. Whilst it would have been good to catch up in person and chat more about Juliet's pregnancy, Kate was fuelled with renewed desire to get home. Juliet was out on home visits anyway and Craig wasn't sure when she'd be back.

'One of her patients has popped her clogs so she's dealing with death just now.'

'How nice to hear you're your usual sympathetic self.'

'Even Juliet's magic touch can't bring people back from the dark side but she'll always give it a go.'

'Always the joker. Send her my love, won't you?'

'Who? The stiff?'

'Craig! You are so disrespectful.'

'Ah, you meant Juliet. Yes, I'll send her your love. She won't be home for a while though. She stepped in to help with all the paperwork as there's no family member to do it.'

'That's sad.'

'Not so sad for me. I've been watching the football in peace and I've cooked myself a sneaky bacon roll while Juliet is out doing morbid work.' He grinned over the phone. 'I'll need to open the windows or she'll give me a row later. Mind you, after sniffing round a dead body she might be glad of the smell of bacon. Perhaps the sanctions on fried food might be lifted tonight.'

'I wash my hands of you, honestly. You must be the worst psychologist in the business. Where's your empathy for your poor, pregnant wife?'

'Empathy? I'm a shrink, Kate, a clinical psychologist, not some namby-pamby, person-centred counsellor! There's no room for empathy in my toolkit. Besides, Juliet's not poor. She's got me, remember?'

'Remind me never to come to you to have my head examined.'

'You're beyond reach, sis. Anyway, I wouldn't see family in a professional capacity. You might rumble my methods. And changing the subject, I'm surprised you made it back to the UK so fast and not because of transport problems. I made a bet with Juliet that you'd be adopted by some crusty old Frenchman who'd lure you into his rusty old Citroen 2CV with a brioche and melted camembert and you wouldn't be back until the middle of next week. Your precipitous return has cost me a fiver.'

If only he knew the truth. There had been a Frenchman, or technically speaking half of one and the car had been a new Renault, not a dilapidated Citroen. Close though they were, there was no way Kate could ever tell Craig about the last 24 hours in Marc's company. Like everyone, he was a big fan of Struan. Rightly so. And like all their friends and family he was no Marc sympathiser. Craig's empty quota of empathy guaranteed he'd never be able to put himself in her shoes. Or Marc's.

When the InterCity left Kings Cross, Kate watched the densely packed rooftops of London evolve into green belt before they reached the smoking chimneys around Grantham. She fell into a deep sleep after that, missing the middle part of the journey and awakening somewhere in County Durham. At Newcastle, a fresh-faced couple joined the train and took the only vacant seats in the carriage, close by.

'We just got married yesterday!' They started chatting to another couple. 'We're supposed to be en route to Bali but the ash cloud's put paid to that so we've diverted to Edinburgh for a more rustic honeymoon.' Happiness radiated from them.

'Poor hen,' offered an older lady. 'You'll be disappointed to miss out on a honeymoon in Bali. I'm from Glasgow and believe me, Edinburgh's not what it was.'

'Oh, we've plenty of time for Bali,' announced the groom, a tall, dark-haired man with a diamond in one ear. He looped a protective arm around his new wife.

'It doesn't matter where you are in the world, as long as you're with the right person.' Kate envied their innocence. If only life were so clear-cut.

Night had fallen by the time the train drew into Waverley Station. Weary bodies pressed towards the door as everyone hurried to leave the carriage.

Kate stepped down onto the platform. She clutched her overnight bag and moved with the crowd towards stairs that would lead to a walkway and the car park where she'd arranged to meet Struan. Gripped by Edinburgh's chill wind, she shivered and pulled her thin coat across her chest.

She didn't see Struan but instinctively knew he was there.

At the top of the stairs his tall figure rose and she paused to look at him. He was about to begin his descent, a brave move against the flow of human traffic rising towards him. His eyes scanned the passengers, head darting around to take in as many faces as he could. He was looking for her but she stayed hidden in the sea of faces breaking like waves on his shoreline.

Kate watched the man she had married at the registry office on Victoria Street. A little older but every bit as attractive, loving and kind, cherishing her ever since the day she'd stumbled into him on the cobbled canal path. He'd never wavered, not even when she came close to sending him over the edge.

His face lit up as he joined the dots in the crowd and found her. Kate felt the urge to run. Never away from Struan. Always towards him. Just like school sports day, running for the finish line but this time she wouldn't drop a thing.

Struan flew down the stairs, his long legs taking two steps at a time, cutting through the crowd like scissors and risking the bruises of suitcases bashing his shins.

He lifted his wife off her feet and whirled her round and round. Just as he'd whirled her around the day she'd told him she was pregnant.

'Welcome home, Kate. It's great to see you.'

'Oh, Struan. I missed you so much.'

'I missed you too, darling but everything's good. Everything's great. My lovely wife's back and nothing's going to come between us again.'

Epilogue

Valentine's Day 2011 - three babies

It is half past five in the morning. In three separate homes around the country a baby cries, prompting a parent to stir, jump out of bed and attend to their needs.

In a townhouse in a Berkshire village, Juliet yawns and throws back the duvet. She leaves behind a snoring Craig and pads across the bedroom to check on baby Alice. Juliet has taken to motherhood like a duck to water and counts her blessings that she's produced the type of angelic baby who smiles at everyone, prompting a chorus of 'isn't she lovely?' wherever they go. Alice is almost four months old and life before her arrival is a distant memory for her parents. Juliet's reward for a pregnancy mired by nausea was a natural, uncomplicated birth and a laid-back infant who feeds and sleeps well.

Alice had started to sleep for long periods between feeds but in recent days she's picked up a cold which makes her snuffle at night and more prone to waking. Juliet lifts her tiny daughter from the cot, marvelling at how much she's grown already and rocks her gently back and forth. In minutes the baby relaxes and her eyelids close again. Juliet pops her back in the cot and sits by her side watching her tiny creation, overwhelmed with love.

Juliet came up with the name Alice, prompting Craig to cross through his spreadsheet of names in contention, a list he'd devised with the help of an enormous book purchased for 'one round pound' from the charity shop on the High Street. Juliet had liked the name Alice long before she had attended to the plucky old lady. She was on call the weekend of Alice Emery's passing and the first health professional on the scene. Juliet arrived at Woodhall Lodge to meet Mr Penry, the worried landlord who'd been unable to raise his elderly tenant when he'd called on her. They used the spare key to gain entry and found the old lady immobile in her living room chair, facing the bay window overlooking the garden with her black cat mewing at her feet. She was holding a tiny black and white photograph of a handsome, smiling man.

'Her late husband,' whispered Mr Penry.

Juliet was relieved Mrs Emery's passing had been gentle, the kind of death most patients would choose given the chance. At home, without intervention and not alone. The best way to go, Juliet agreed with Mr Penry. Juliet's only regret was that the old lady hadn't reached her century. In the snakes and ladders game of life, Alice Emery met a snake on the 99th square. Had she lived another fortnight, the postman would have placed a very special telegram in her liver-spotted hands with a congratulatory message from Her Majesty, Queen Elizabeth II. But nothing can take away the peaceful image of Mrs Emery's face and this matters more than any telegram, no matter how regal. Juliet will remember with fondness the old lady's bright spirit and sharp wit.

She bends down to kiss baby Alice on the forehead before checking that she's safely tucked in. Satisfied that all is well, Juliet tiptoes back to bed where Craig is still snoring his head off, his chest rising and falling with an even rhythm. It's still dark but Juliet is bright-eyed and wide-awake. She wonders if it's too early to send her sister-in-law a text before deciding to hold off until dawn.

Juliet creeps back underneath the duvet and snuggles in next to Craig, shaking him a couple of times in a failed attempt to stop his thunderous snores. She throws an arm around her lump of a husband and vows to wake him early so he can fry up a hearty breakfast.

***

Four hundred miles north in Edinburgh, Kate is indeed awake and would have been very happy to hear from Juliet. She's just poured herself a glass of water from a big bottle of Evian. Thoughtful as ever, Struan planted it on the coffee table earlier, along with a packet of digestive biscuits, within easy reach of the rocking chair where she feeds little Calum in the night. His dark head cradled in the crook of her arm, she strokes his soft cheek with her index finger marvelling at the intensity of a mother's love for her child. Any worries that her quota of maternal devotion had been used up on Isla were dispelled the instant she set eyes on her son.

Calum is a few weeks old and smaller than average having arrived early at Hogmanay weighing in at six pounds, nine and a half ounces. He seems to sleep all day only to feed voraciously at night and Kate is already exhausted from a lack of proper rest. It's tantamount to Chinese torture but the needs of her wee man come before everything else.

Kate and Struan hadn't actively been trying for a baby but had agreed a sibling would be good for Isla at some point. Struan could hardly contain his excitement when Kate emerged from the bathroom with a positive pregnancy test result. Within 24 hours he launched himself into the nearest hardware store to purchase tins of paint and began an enthusiastic spate of decorating. He wanted to play his part and conversion of the spare room into a nursery for the baby's arrival kept him gainfully employed for well over a week.

Kate and Juliet spent hours on the phone comparing different stages of pregnancy and varying degrees of nausea, bladder weakness and swollen ankles. Kate looks to Juliet for invaluable, emotional support, not least because her sister-in-law also happens to be the only person who knows about Marc's brief reappearance in Kate's life. There is no better confidante than broad-minded Juliet, the queen of discretion.

The arrival of a new baby has been positive for Isla, bringing out nurturing instincts that surprised everyone. So far she's shown no jealously towards her little brother and her terrible tantrums are less frequent. Isla fetches and carries wipes and nappies and laughs her head off whenever Calum burps. She laughs even harder when his tiny face turns red as he fills his nappy.

Kate traces Calum's tiny ears with her thumb, trying to commit the smallest detail to memory. There's a clear resemblance to her side of the family in his face, yet even in infancy she sees trace expressions that can surely only have been handed down from one person.

Last night, after putting Isla to bed she returned to the living room to watch Struan cuddle Calum close to his chest on the leather sofa while another random cookery programme played in the background. Her two boys. Despite her anxieties, they'd bonded beautifully and she's so thankful of the choice she made last year. Her life is settled and everyone is happy. For the time being, at least.

The Gilmores have become the perfect family of four, the symbol of completion that she envied in the tight family group on the ferry. That image had given Kate an insight into the future; a future that she could only have envisaged with Struan.

In the dim light of the nursery Kate drops a kiss on the head of her second child and wonders what Marc is doing and how he is. She'd be willing to bet that he went ahead with his marriage to Jessica. It was the right thing for him to do. Maybe one day she'll find out.

Marc might be her history but he's not confined to the past. His place in her life is more enduring than he can possibly know. He might reappear to disrupt her life in the future, perhaps with good reason, but she prays he will stay away for now. She can love him purely from a distance.

***

In Brighton, Jessica is sprawled across the bed in the deepest of sleeps having instructed Marc that he's responsible for the night shift. Again. She needs her beauty sleep. She might be taking advantage but Marc doesn't really mind because he's been bowled over by the little fellow who's just entered his life. The baby is only three weeks old but Marc cannot imagine a world without him.

Marc is an attentive and gentle Dad. He has no qualms about giving more than his fair share of baby care so that Jessica can have a break. He is fast learning how to be a good father and a supportive husband.

He enters the kitchen to prepare a couple of bottles of infant formula. In hospital the midwives tried their hardest to coerce Jessica to breastfeed but she was having none of it, declaring she'd been through enough 'down there' already, thank you very much, without having her breasts pumped 'like a lactating cow.' Even before the baby arrived she made her position on breastfeeding crystal clear, stating it was not for her and she would not be doing it. Jessica's breasts contributed to her sexual armoury and impending motherhood was making her anxious about a potential loss of sex appeal. She didn't say as much but Marc picked up a fear in her that she'd lose more than she'd gain. He didn't understand it but chose not to ask questions. Her hospital bag contained expensive lingerie and deluxe Charbonnel et Walker truffles but was light on practical pads and wet wipes. Marc had to repack it for her with the help of an understanding sales assistant in Boots.

Jessica went out with two of her girlfriends for champagne and cocktails the night her waters broke, as though she were still a carefree 18-year-old. She told Marc she'd stick to mocktails so he didn't see too much harm in a night out. Her waters broke in the toilet and when Marc picked her up to drive her to the hospital he wasn't convinced she'd stuck to orange and lemonade. On arrival they were told that Jessica wouldn't be permitted to have any pain relieving drugs for as long as any trace of alcohol remained in her system.

'No pain relief?' Jessica's roars bounced off the walls of the maternity unit and sensitive equipment around them shook. Fortunately she experienced a very quick and easy birth, if a noisy one that scared a student doctor away. Afterwards she declared to everyone on her ward that Veuve Clicquot was the best pain relief that money can buy. In the next bed, a woman wearing a bamboo nightie who'd had an organic birthing plan and a meditative water birth turned her back, a scornful look on her face.

Jessica comes across as shallow and self-centred, and Marc's only too aware that she can be both a lot of the time. But he also knows her well enough by now to recognise that much of her crass behaviour hides deeper insecurities. She's a handful and a live wire but he can handle her and in spite of her reluctance to breastfeed she's every bit as enamoured with their son as he is. It's too early to say if she'll be a good mother but he's vowed to help her all the way.

Marc relishes early mornings when the house is still and he can allow his mind to drift. He tests the temperature of the milk before giving the baby his bottle and treats himself to thoughts of Katie. He'd been fully prepared to leave Jessica after that night in Calais, but as he breathes in the scent of his infant son he finally understands the impossible situation that Katie faced. Breaking up her family would have shattered her. She would never be able to take her child from its father and leave intact. She's far too good for that.

Marc kept her locket although he ought to have returned it. Ownership means more to him than he can say. Just knowing it's in his wallet and being able to hold it from time to time gives him a tangible and comforting link to Katie. Alone he cups it in his hands and thinks of her. Even if he could send the locket back there's no way he will. To do so would raise an impossible conversation.

Monique is due from Paris in the morning ahead of the baby's Christening. Since the wedding she's put aside her antipathy for Jessica and Marc thanked his mother openly for the effort she's made. The two women will always have their differences but a baby is a great healer. And Monique was surprised and touched by Jessica's proposal to name the baby after meaningful relatives; Marc's Dad and the adored Grandfather of Jessica who died when she was a child.

Marc carries John Douglas Loseley back to his Moses basket in the bedroom and returns to the kitchen to brew a pot of Earl Grey tea. It's almost seven o'clock and the sun is rising on the horizon, marking the beginning of a cold, clear day. He looks out of the vast windows of his kitchen to see an aeroplane flying high in the sky over the English Channel. It's heading south, towards the French coast. The aircraft leaves a narrow vapour stream behind it like a long tail.

As the kettle boils, steam fills the kitchen. Then, like the vapour trail of the aeroplane, it dissipates until almost nothing is left.

Acknowledgements

There are many good souls I would like to thank for helping me get this far and for your support and love, every step of the way.

My great pal Val deserves special mention for starting us off on this writing journey back in 2010. We swapped manuscripts as gifts that Christmas and I am looking forward to doing this again with you before too long.

To dear family and friends who read various drafts in ring binders, ink still fresh on the page, or subsequent iterations on screen. Each and every one of you made a positive difference.

Nancy and Geoff, Sheila, Margaret, Uncle Ron and Arthur Moss behind the Grand Hotel. You are all there, in spirit.

Sarah and Robbie, you are the only ones who can get away with teasing me for the long decade. You always make me smile.

And to Duncan, for keeping me anchored, and for your steadfast support and confidence in me. You have helped an ideas person achieve completion and you took the perfect picture.

Thank you, one and all x

Printed in Great Britain
by Amazon

51407169R00202